The Three Loves Trilogy

Jo Martinez

Books 1 - 3

THE THREE LOVES TRILOGY
Gypsies & Gentry
Book 1

The Looters
Book 2

Lovers and Losers
Book 3

Copyright 2019 by Jo Martinez
C/- PO Box 451
Bassendean, Western AUSTRALIA 6934

ISBN 978-0-6485714-2-1

Cover:
Gypsies & Gentry by Mark Martin Digital Management
The Looters by Mark Martin Digital Management
Lovers and Losers by Mark Martin Digital Management

THE THREE LOVES TRILOGY

GYPSIES & GENTRY

JO MARTINEZ

Gypsies & Gentry

a novella

Jo Martinez

The Three Loves Trilogy

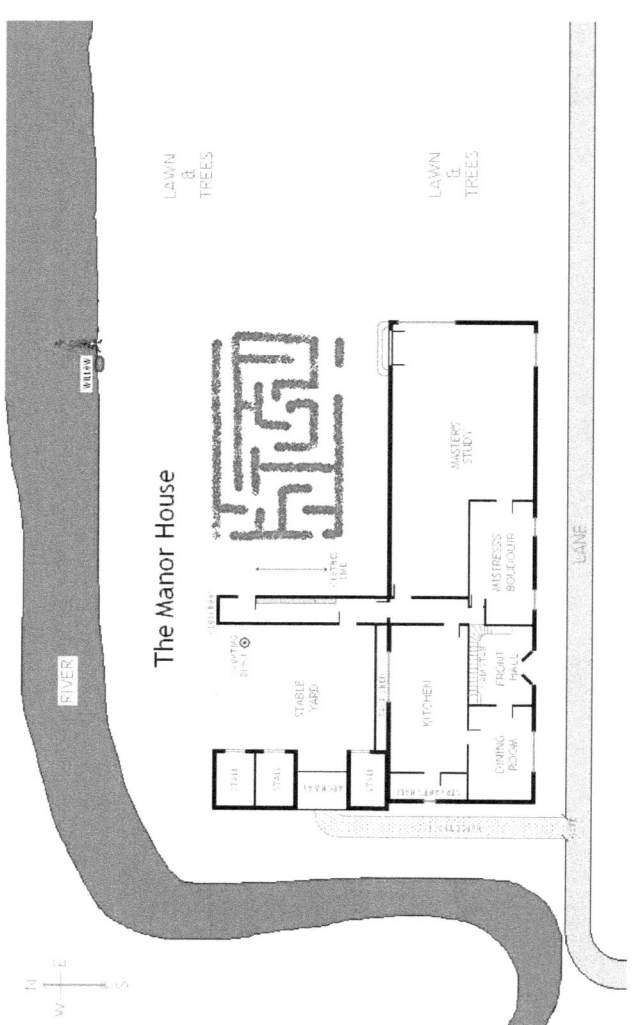

The Manor House

N · E · S · W

RIVER

WALL + W...

LAWN & TREES

LAWN & TREES

MASTER'S STUDY

MISTRESS BOUDOIR

FRONT HALL

DINING ROOM

KITCHEN

STABLE YARD

LANE

Chapter 1: Gerald

GERALD Grimshaw's lanky frame strolled round a bend in the shade of the trees. Further along the lane sharp eyes took in the elegant swing of his hips and the tilt of the soft cap on a handsome dark head before returning to gaze across the pastureland.

That summer day the heat and exotic energy of Egypt were re-ignited for a lonely man. She stood in a sunlit country lane looking across the meadows in all her dark beauty, her gypsy finery clinging sensuously to tantalising curves.

She dipped her knee as he passed. When he made bold to speak she flashed her eyes in rebuke. His suppliant hand protested 'til hers gestured a truce and they made friends. They climbed a stile to mark a path through rainbow flowered fields and rest awhile.

Later their silhouettes merged with the pencilled shadows in the lane when his touch guided her slender foot back over the stile.

They met in secret as truants, she from her tribe and he from the gentry he was born into.

One day he brought a gift, a silver claw from far away and pinned it to her shawl. So it was 'til late autumn when he set off on his travels again to study Egyptology and she moved north along the gypsies' yearlong circuit.

The following year he was summoned home by the loss of his parents within a short time of each other and set about the business of managing an estate. He intended to return to his travels and studies when a capable manager took over estate duties.

That winter Gerald Grimshaw cantered into the driveway of The Malderns after an early morning ride. A light fall of snow pastilled the trees and flecked the cap of the waiting stable boy. The Master of Malderns swung down from his mount and handing the boy the reins ran up the steps to the front porch

The servant waiting behind the door opened it just as Gerald reached the threshold and two pairs of eyes looked down at the infant lying on the doorstep, snug wrapped in a bright shawl with a silver claw clasping the warmth within its folds.

The serving woman instinctively bent to gather the bundle before her Master ushered her into the house. He unclasped the broach putting it in his pocket and opened the shawl to discover a naked baby boy barely passed suckling age looking up at him from under a dark head of hair.

Sunlit images from the past rushed into his memory. Guilt tinged feelings of past pleasures

'What'll I do with him Master?'

Sobered by a good conscience he replied, 'Take him to warm by the kitchen fire and do what must be done for one so young Martha. I will attend to the matter shortly.'

Going to his study, Gerald put the broach in with a small bag of coins. He sent for the shawl and wrapped the bag inside to make a tidy bundle which he placed in the spot where the baby had lain.

From behind a hedge eyes watched and waited until moonlight spread the shadow of the old elm across the porch. An arm branched out to curl around the shawl.

So it was that Jed joined the household of childless Gerald Grimshaw who gave him his name and adopted him as his heir.

The following winter another boy joined the household. Samuel a young didecoy came asking for work. His skill with horses and ability to repair tackle was soon noted and he became the groom and stable hand for Gerald Grimshaw.

Like the rest of the staff he kept an eye on the growing infant, taking pains to play games with him, chasing and romping in the grounds. Jed was drawn to Samuel more than any other. It was an attraction strengthened when Sam was instructed to commence riding lessons for Jed. From then on the wonders of the countryside and its natural laws opened for him. He met others than his own kind when Sam stopped briefly at a gypsy camp visiting a district where the Didecoys got on well with the true Romanies.

Such adventures were far more appealing than sitting under the tutelage of the retired village schoolmaster when Jed turned six. Growing bolder at puberty Jed played truant at will.

A disgruntled tutor aired his complaint of his pupil's wild ways when Gerald Grimshaw returned home from foreign shores. His words fell on distracted ears for Gerald had just received news of the sudden death of his sea captain friend Arthur Hervey. All of his travels were made on this one friend's vessel and the loss was heavy. Nevertheless Gerald made note of the tutor's discontent and on disembarking from his next voyage made his way into the town of Tilbury.

Chapter 2: Victoria

VICTORIA Hervey set aside the thin vegetable soup with a sigh. It was poor fare for her two daughters. She had brought them to the tiny house in Tilbury from the good care of her childless sister and brother-in-law after her husband's death. The two up and two down dwelling used to serve for brief sojourns with their daughters between voyages. The dreams and plans for a country cottage on her husband's retirement shattered, Victoria Hervey had set about making ends meet with the small savings from their life's work.

A knock at the door startled her. She opened it to see Gerald Grimshaw standing on the step.

During his voyages with her husband on the long journey home she had helped with the initial inventories of the latest artefacts, She earned his respect for her meticulous work and to the practical way she worked alongside her husband and his men on occasion.

'Please to come in Gerald Gimshaw,' she stammered, her thoughts racing to what fare she could offer her husband's old friend. Her daughters and she made do most days, with a thin gruel until evening, when a soup of vegetables, set aside in the market as mildewed, would fill their stomachs enough to entice sleep.

'How goes it with you Mistress Hervey.' I should have come sooner to see how you are settled on the land, but this last trip took longer to avoid the attention of pirates, I'm afraid.'

'I'm passing fair, Sir. Passing fair! Please to take a seat and rest awhile. If you will excuse me, I have a small errand before we have our evening meal, for which I hope you will join us.' So saying, Victoria hurried to the inn at the corner of the road.

The landlord knew her from time past when the family purchased their ale from him. Captain Hervey had joined him over a fine brandy, slipped past the customs. Of late no wares had been bought.

'Good evening to you Mistress Hervey,' then noticing the jug in her hand, 'And what may I serve you this night?' The poor woman looked embarrassed. She had lost some weight since coming back to Tilbury.

'Landlord, I come to ask a favour of you. My husband's old friend has called upon us. He has caught me unawares, Sir, and with no ale to set on the table. My purse is empty, but I will repay the kindness if you can fill this jug with your best ale for him.'

The kindly man took the jug and filled it to the brim.

'I think I owe you more than a jug of ale for all of the fine brandy your husband and I sipped Mistress,' he said escorting her, past his customers, to the door. With a grateful smile she returned home.

Gerald Grimshaw meanwhile had noted the meagre fire in the grate, and was well aware of the nature of her errand. He shared their soup that night, and was impressed with her skill of doing much with little.

Disconcerted at the poverty facing her and her daughters, and aware of his adopted son's need for the softening influence of a woman, a pact was made. Neither Gerald nor Victoria Grimshaw ever regretted their marriage of convenience.

Chapter 3: Horam

SARAH Hunt sat in the warm kitchen at The Malverns drinking hot cocoa as she listened to the cook.

Mrs Jessie Mossop was telling Jed's story, soon after Sarah's arrival at the manor.

'We all calls 'im 'is son and Jed will inherit the manor in due course, but some of us knows a thing or two.' She laid a knowing forefinger along the side of a long nose with a wart on the end of it. Mrs Mossop insisted on frequently trying the wines she used in cooking. 'Just to make sure as they aren't gorn off.' This turned her nose a permanent rosy red.

'All the old servants is gone now, but some told of Squire being a bit smitten with some gypsy queen in his younger days when 'e was 'ome from one of 'is travels. Anyways the long an the short is when the foundling was left on manor steps, Squire decides to adopt the babe even though he was still a bachelor.'

'There's some even goes as far as to say the boy has a bit of the old man about 'im. Wot do you think?' Without waiting for an answer, she bustled off to the pantry.

Sarah was Mistress Grimshaw's new personal maid. She looked round the kitchen and thought of the tied cottage she had left when her mother died. On the long table, a dish of stuffed quail lay ready for the oven. On top of the range, above the glowing hot coal box, a big saucepan simmered. The savoury smell of oxtail rose with the steam. A crown of lamb, as yet unadorned with the ruffles Sarah was making, rose from a baking tin. Heavens knows how they find room for pears cooked in red wine, thought Sarah.

Mrs Mossop returned with a basket of vegetables. Standing with an overlap of stomach resting on the table's edge, she started peeling and scraping, continuing her story as if she had never left.

'Then awhile back Master married the widow woman of 'is old friend. That's the sea captain of the ship he sailed on, all over the world, they do say. Ooh, our young fellow didn't like that, wot with two daughters 'anging on behind their Ma. Lad was jealous for his father's affections see 'cos when he was 'ome Squire spent hours teaching the boy about them orniments what he brought 'ome.'

'So that is why they seem to be at loggerheads when they are all together,' Sarah concluded, getting in a word at last.

After Jessie, the cook finished her tale, Sarah decided to try and mend the breach if she could.

To that end, she set about making friends with Jed. It was not easy, for although there was a vulnerable side to him, he could be arrogant and spiteful.

***

Sarah was thirty-five when she first met the Squire's new wife, shortly after that lady's arrival at the manor. Victoria Grimshaw enjoyed doing good works, and soon set about visiting the village, to fulfil her need to be of service.

Sarah opened the door to Mistress Grimshaw standing five foot tall, her short waisted build adding width to a body that was otherwise trim. Despite the mundane nature of her visit, she was fashionably dressed in a soft green velvet jacket and darker green skirt as she stepped un-invited over the threshold with a basket of comforts for the invalid. Sarah followed the Squire's wife into her invalid mother's room. Curious eyes surveyed Sarah from beneath a wide brimmed hat. Dark hair strayed from below its confines, framing a face that was kind, yet strong and determined.

Victoria Grimshaw continued her visits frequently for she enjoyed Sarah Hunt's quiet efficiency, and the soft tones she used to soothe her mother.

'What will you do when you are left on your own Sarah?' she asked one day. The well-tended cottage was a tied property, going with her dead father's hire to work for its owner who benevolently extended the tenancy until her mother's demise,

'I have distant family Madam, but I cannot lay claim to lodgement with them. I may seek a position near them, in time,' Sarah responded.

When the time came, it was natural for Sarah to accept the offer to go to the manor and care for Victoria. Moving to the manor gave her security, companionship, and a trusted position among the friendly household staff. The younger ones turned to her older experience for advice at times.

Bent on bringing peace into the household Sarah made a suggestion to her Mistress when she was brushing Victoria Grimshaw's handsome head of hair a few days after having cocoa with the cook.

'I believe the Bennets set much store on a woman having a 'good seat' on her mount. Their son rides to hounds regularly, 'tis said,' she observed.

'Is that so Hunt?' Victoria Grimshaw was well aware of the Bennet family. They had a place in her plans for her daughters as Sarah well knew through Jessie Mossop.

'Sam, the groom, could teach Miss Effie to ride. If they keep to the lanes hereabouts it might reign in Jed's wanderings,' Sarah continued.

'That young man needs to spend more time at his studies,' agreed Victoria. 'That will do nicely, thank you Hunt.'

The ploy worked. Jed and Effie soon became friends, and even Victoria made efforts to reach out to Jed when she rode out with him on the horse she shared with her daughter, but he remained cool and wary. Nonetheless, the atmosphere when the family were together improved until the day of the Mistress's accident.

They were gathered in the study where a white-faced stable lad stammered his account of it to his Master. In the middle of the room stood Jed a handsome boy of sixteen years or more He was seething with a dark fury that accentuated the gypsy traits in his face. His long lashed eyes were black with anger, and his thin lips were compressed in an obstinate line.

Victoria lay upon a chaise lounge, attended by her young daughters. Sarah applied a compress to her brow. Tall French windows, opened on to grassy parkland. The room with its high ornate ceilings and elegant furnishings of the early nineteenth century looked out on to gardens where men were working on a small country estate. In the background fields and copses of oak and elm climbed in gentle slopes to distant hills.

Gerald Grimshaw sat with a clenched fist on the handsome inlaid desk in front of him. The walls around him were lined with cabinets full of artefacts.

'Master Jed was leading 'is mount out when the Mistress suddenly decides to ride 'im instead of Miss Elfreda's. '

'He's a big 'orse at eighteen 'ands, Sir,' the stable boy continued, 'Well 'e took 'im to the mounting block for 'er then as m' lady settles back in the saddle, 'orse shies up on 'is 'ind legs. He were ready to bolt, and fer no reason as I could see 'cos he was no bother coming into yard, Sir. It seems Master Jed lost control of the bridle rein and let it go. Your good lady sailed into the air afore she was thrown to the ground, and Oscar bolted out of the yard. That's all I knows, Sir.'

'You may go back to work,' he was told then Gerald turned to his son 'Why didn't you keep hold of the reins? You are strong enough to control Oscar. Your stepmother was in your care and it seems you were not man enough to look after her.' Jed remained silent and defiant. He had no answer.

'Get out of my sight,' fell in cold quiet tones from Gerald's lips.

Condemned by harsh words from his father Jed was banished from their company. From then on, he spent all of his time out of doors. He only joined the family for some meals and the twice-weekly music lessons he loved.

Apart from sharing their music lessons, Effie, the eldest daughter, was instructed to end her companionship with him. A high-spirited girl, she rebelled at the imposition and stole away to meet him when her mother took her afternoon rest. This caused unrest among the servants who were expected to see nothing and say nothing.

Their disquiet increased shortly after their mistress returned from a convalescent visit to her friend's home in a nearby village allowing Sarah two days off to visit her family. On Sarah's return she was summoned before Gerald Grimshaw.

'You appear to have mislaid the lapis lazuli amulet,' her Master sternly accused her. He did not say she had stolen it, but his eyes were full of suspicion.

Service with the Grimshaws was a sought after position down in the village, for both man and wife were considerate employers. It had taken some time to earn his approbation of the meticulous way she replaced each object after dusting. She could tell at a glance if something had been picked up and replaced the wrong way.

Sarah found his mistrust was harder to bear than the unjust accusation and stood up to the Master's reproach.

'I swear on the Holy Book Master, the amulet lay in its rest when I left to visit family after the Mistress returned,' she declared. Victoria came to her defence,

'That is so husband. I do remember showing the clasp to my old friend the day after she returned here with me. Sarah was away during those two days.'

When questioned, Mary Ann the under maid, told the Master, she was only in the room briefly, to fetch a scarf left by the visitor and had set the amulet aright on its rest.

The matter of the missing artefact was unresolved and later that day was forgotten in the tragedy which overtook the household.

It was after noon when Sarah stood in Effie's bedroom looking out over the small grassed area between the maze and the wall of the storerooms adjoining the kitchen.

The sisters had adjoining bedrooms built over the study and the sitting room. She had finished tidying Effie's closet but she waited as if looking for something down below her. 'Yes, there she is, her skirt butterflying out in the light breeze,' she said to herself as Effie passed a gap in the maze, on her way towards the riverbank.

Although not strictly responsible for the girls, Sarah regarded them as her charges. She had almost come to love them as daughters. She knew Effie met Jed by the riverbank to console him whilst her mother rested.

Effie ever wilful, knew her action was forbidden whilst he was in disfavour with his father. She enjoyed the risk of her errant ways, going to the river bank in roundabout ways to avoid discovery. Sarah saw the kind intent behind the disobedience and kept a still tongue.

She went through to Shelley the younger daughter's closet and began a leisurely tidying before closing her curtains against the afternoon sun.

'Nearly a quarter past the hour,' she murmured to herself. There may be time for a cup of tea, before one of us takes in the afternoon tea tray to waken milady. I'll check if Mary Anne has drawn the study curtains.'

Clicking her tongue as she entered the study, she made her way to close out the bright beams dancing over precious artefacts. Her arm and head upraised, she sought and found the small curtain pole hanging nearby. As she lowered her eyes, she saw Effie running madly up the lawn on the west side of the maze taking the steps to the window in a bound.

Dropping the pole, Sarah opened the glass doors, leaving them un-curtained, and drew the girl inside

'They are fighting. Sam and Jed are fighting down on the bank,' she panted and set-up a wail which disturbed her mother. Victoria entered the scene to hear the story.

'Take Miss Effie to lie down Hunt. There are smelling salts on my sitting room table. I will go and see what is amiss,' Victoria Grimshaw instructed after taking in her daughter's state. She set off for the riverbank, going down the west side of the maze. Sarah took the still sobbing girl up to her room

'Now, now child, a little rest is what is called for.' Safely inside the quiet of the room, Sarah also took stock of the girl. The buttons of her bodice were unevenly holed, her skirt was set awry and her shoes were scuffed as if scraped along the ground.

'Let me help you remove your dress Miss Effie, and wrap a light robe around you. Whilst you lie down, I shall go and make a soothing drink for...' The girl reached out.

'Please don't leave me Sarah. Water from the carafe will do.'

'There, there' soothed Sarah as she lifted the unbuttoned dress over Effie's head before going to fetch the robe from the blanket chest. Turning back her eyes were drawn to bright spots of scarlet flecking the back of the girl's chemise.

Her young charge was at the mean of the female cycle. Surely, no anger among men should disrupt that rhythm, but one never knew.

'Miss Effie, my dear I'm afraid you will need to change more than your dress, for...' began Sarah, when the maiden turned to her with a face mantled in high colour. Her eyes mirrored the innocence of a trusting Eve, overshadowed by the age-old knowledge of a Sheba's Queen. Suppliant hands crossed the small rounds of budding breasts, catching at Sarah Hunt's heartstrings.

'Effie did Jed...?' The drooping head muffled a low 'Yes Sarah.' The maid caught the maiden to her in compassionate embrace as she questioned what hideous creature lurked in the gypsy foundling's form.

Remembering Victoria Grimshaw she quickly gathered the discarded garments together and turned to the door.

'There may be no harm done child. 'Tis best not to bother your good mother yet awhile. As for your clothes, I will attend to them. Meantime I will fetch warm water for you to sponge yourself and some soothing balm. Hasten and get into this robe then lie down. I will tell your Mama you are sleeping.' So saying she hurried off with dark anger gathering in her heart.

Leaving the garments to soak in one of the steeping buckets in the laundry at the end of the passage, Sarah left by the garden door. Further along the riverbank, near the race which fell into the Devils Falls, she could see Victoria kneeling over the edge.

'What ails her? I'd better go and see.' She ran down to join her Mistress. The sight that met her eyes made her blood run cold

'God in Heaven Madam, what are you doing,' she entreated in a low voice, glancing round to see they were alone.

Victoria jerked back onto her heels, her hands dripping wet, her eyes wild with some inner torment. Sarah put her arms around her to stop the shivering. She willed her to return her look until Victoria's eyes returned to sanity

'Leave this to me Mistress, I beg you,' whispered Sarah, 'You must return now. Go slowly and take time to compose yourself before you enter the house. I will meet you there.'

From within the maze, eyes watched as the two women stood up. The watcher waited whilst Sarah also knelt over the bank to reach down into the water before straightening with her hands clapped to her mouth.

She hurried back to the passage door and made her way to the study. As the passage door closed behind her the figure in the maze sped across to the spot then raced towards a willow tree shading the falls. Lying prone upon the bank its arms reached down into the depths. Suddenly, the figure sprang upright with arms flung wide in the air as if in exaltation or despair, before flying across the grass and disappearing through the passage door.

It was nearly a quarter to three before Sarah returned to the study, as Mary Ann stood at the door with the afternoon tea tray. Mistress Grimshaw had not returned. Going to the window Sarah scanned the garden for sign of her and was relieved to see her emerge from the South opening of the maze facing the study.

Victoria Grimshaw walked at a leisured pace towards the house until, seeing Sarah; she hastened her footsteps and caught up with her two servants.

'I'm afraid Miss Effie has made a lot of to do about nothing Hunt. There is no sign of anybody by the river. They must have made their peace, and each has gone their way.' A look passed between Sarah and her mistress.

'Is Miss Effie more composed now?' On hearing that she slept, she passed into her sitting room.

'I'm pleased to hear it. Now if you will fetch my tea in here Mary Ann. Oh, and Hunt, when she awakens, tell her I shall see her at four o'clock, when she joins Master Jed for their lessons with the music master.'

Before going up to Effie, Sarah hurried to the kitchen, only to find the oven firebox nearly out.

'Drat it,' she grumbled, taking some tinder to liven the flames, 'Cook will be after Mary Anne's skin for this.' She made Effie's drink and took it up to her room with a jug of warm water.

Effie turned as Sarah entered. She was sitting by the window dressed in her favourite blue gown and looking down to the river. Her cheeks were flushed and her eyes were feverishly bright.

'What are you doing by the window Effie? I told you to rest. Come sip this warm milk, then settle down before your music lesson later on.'

'I have only just got up Sarah. Is Mama back?' There was a subtle change in Effie's voice. All the hysteria had gone. Effie voice was calm and her manner detached.

'Did you not see her from the window Missy?' said Sarah.

'No I saw nothing. The maze makes a clear view difficult. Mama will bring us news no doubt.' She put down her cup and stood up.

'I shall go down and wait for the music master. Jed should join us then don't you think?'

'I would advise you to stay put until four Miss Effie. Your mother is resting and so should you.' She slipped her hand through Effie's arm but the girl quickly pushed the hand aside and went to her bed.

Satisfied that she had a little time in which to restore order to affairs, Sarah attended to Effie's garments. She then went into the garden to watch for the arrival of the music master, who came twice a week from the village. She waited as Ernest Scales came into sight and joined her as she escorted him to the music room.

'I must warn you Mr Scales that your work will be cut out today for your pupils have other things on their minds and may be inattentive.'

'Thank you Ma'am. Once we begin they will settle down for sure,' he replied bowing in Sarah's direction

A few years older than Jed and considering himself a bit of a fop, Ernest Scales was impressed with the range and mellowness of Jed's voice and did much to improve its performance. Until Effie joined the singing lessons to partner Jed in duets both young men got on tolerably well.

Once Effie arrived upon the scene, a mild rivalry developed. For her part Effie was much impressed by their tutor's sartorial style and his elegant manners, much to Jed's annoyance.

As the clock in the bedroom chimed four Sarah watched a composed Effie leave the room for her lesson, leaving the maid to tidy any trace of earlier events. At ten past four Mary Ann came up to tell Sarah she was wanted in the music room, whence she hurried fearing more trouble.

Effie and her mother sat on a chaise lounge with Earnest Scales setting up a music stand a respectful distance away.

'Hunt, will you go and find Master Jed? He is keeping us all waiting.'

'May I go Mother?' Effie pleaded. No doubt, thought Sarah dryly, she wishes to tell him that her mother has not been informed of his rape of her daughter.

'No, remain here Missy.' Effie clenched her hand over the birthmark staining her palm.

'Begin the lesson, if your Mama agrees. I will try the garden and then the stables.'

'Thank you Hunt,' said the Mistress.' Tell him to hasten please.'

Sarah made a point of first calling into the kitchen, where it was not unknown for Jed to sit and chat over a cup of tea. She enquired, but none had seen him. Next, she went down the passage past the cloak rack and opened the door to the yard to ask if Jed were there.

The new boy was bringing the trap in. Higgins and Samuel were stabling the horses. They turned and shook their heads when asked.

Satisfied she took a path directly down to the river at its steepest curve. Reaching a high point in the bank she looked each way for signs of Jed.

Turning to retrace her steps, she spied a small white piece of flotsam bobbing under the river bank downstream to the west below the falls. Taking hold of a willow trunk for support, Sarah leaned out over the river to see what it might be. Perhaps one of Miss Effie's cambric handkerchiefs had blown away in the breeze. She walked past the speeding race of the river to below the fall of white water to get a closer look.

Rigid with shock she stared into Jed's sightless eyes beneath the water. His outflung arm was entangled in reeds, a white hand ebbing to and fro. Had Victoria's madness ended like this? No, he was still moving then. I should have helped him out but my disgust repelled the thought. Merciful God help me. Did I... .Her mind reeled with giddiness and fear until a cold resolve settled over it

'One of us is guilty of murder. Now I must do all in my power to protect her. The family need her. The house needs her. Why in God's name did she act so? Did she know what he did to Effie?'

She started running back to the house, passing outside the east of the maze, screaming to the stablemen as she passed the corner of the yard

'Run to the river. Jed's drowned.'

In the music room Gerald Grimshaw stood chatting with Ernest Scales about his pupils' progress as Victoria sat, tight lipped, with Effie.

As if in a dream Sarah walked across the floor to her Master. She dipped her head as she caught at his arm, seeing the affront on their faces at her impudence.

'Master, your son has met with a terrible accident. I'm feared, Sir, that he is dead,' she whispered. His face sagged in disbelief and horror. The music master caught her low words. Both men turned towards the ladies. After a brief word with Ernest Scales, Gerald Grimshaw went to Effie.

'Effie, continue with your lesson. Your mother and I have to go. We shall be back soon. Sarah, accompany your Mistress please,' leading them from the music room.

They ran towards the river where the men were lifting something on to the bank. Dulled witless of mind the men stood, waiting for authority to restore order.

Innocent in death, Jed's body lay at their feet.

Victoria Grimshaw clung to her husband unable to look upon the scene and mindless of who saw her so defenceless.

'Sarah, take my wife back to the house and take care of her. It was thoughtless of me, I'm sorry dear wife.' Victoria, crying uncontrollably, was taken to her bedroom. There she kept calling for Effie to come to her until, to soothe her Mistress, Sarah went down to the music room to fetch her.

Fearing news of Jed's death, would unhinge the control Effie had mastered over her emotions, Sarah's look dared the music master to dispute her words.

'Elfreda, my dear child, there has been a slight accident. Your mother needs you. Will you go and comfort her? You must be brave so sit by your good mother but do not let her talk will you? Wait until your father comes and explains everything,' she counselled, leading her to the foot of the stairway before returning to the music room.

There, Ernest Scales stood waiting to take his leave of what he knew would soon be a house of mourning.

'Thank you for shielding your young pupil from such terrible news Mr Scales. I'm sure you are as distressed as we are. If you care to come to the kitchen with me, perhaps a cup of tea might....'

The young man had lost much of his artificial demeanour, and was still visibly atremble as he raised his hand to assure her he would not trouble the house any further that day.

'It is a tragedy Miss Sarah, a competent fiddler and a beautiful voice. He loved his singing lessons.' He bowed his way out, leaving her to reflect on the day's events.

When Sarah entered service in the Squire's house, Jed was a young man of fifteen. She'd had cause to hold her tongue on more than one occasion over his exploits during that time. On the day Jed died, all Sara Hunt's exasperation with him and his tiresome ways changed to deep remorse.

At day's end after the funeral she sat with Mary Anne in the attic bedroom they shared.

'Jed was as happy as Larry until they came,' confided Mary Ann, 'Me and two extra stable lads were taken on here some weeks before Squire Grimshaw came back with a new wife and her two daughters.'

'Master Jed was always off riding the countryside with Samuel the groom, and playing truant from his lessons with the schoolmaster from the village. He got away with it 'cos some of the staff pandered to 'is ways. That's not to say we all liked 'im Miss Sarah but they'd taken a hand in bringing him up when the Master was away.'

'Well after the Mistress came she tried to rein him in and he bucked at it.' Mary Ann sat silent then burst out. 'My! Miss Sarah what must you have felt, finding him drowned?'

"There, there Mary Ann, leave the past to rest,' said Sarah her mind still alive with memories.

A month later, Sarah Hunt worked quietly at the study shelves as Gerald

Grimshaw sat with his hand resting upon a small pile of papers in his lap. They were the listings of all the antiques and artefacts he had collected over many years of travelling abroad.

It was a spacious room, with walls rising to a high lavishly ornamented ceiling. Only she and Mary Ann were allowed here to dust the shelves full of exhibits with the finest of feather dusters. She checked a sneeze. Dust as she might there was no getting rid of the spicy scent of ancient times since Master Grimshaw insisted on the tall richly curtained windows being closed at certain times and adjusted to reduce the sunlight.

She felt proud to be given the care of this room along with her other duties. She loved looking at the old clasps, still brightly enamelled, from some Egyptian tomb or ruin. The few skulls set on glass shelves in the corner cabinet no longer scared her for the Master himself took care of them. Polishing the carved rosewood chairs and tables set around the room was a sensuous delight.

She looked with concern at her employer giving a shiver at remembering he'd nearly sent her to work in the kitchen for mislaying the amulet artefact

He has taken the loss of his son sorely. The Mistress is shadow of herself, and Miss Effie will hardly come out of her room now, she reflected. That morning, carrying out her duties, she had overheard Gerald Grimshaw and his wife as they stood by the window, looking towards the nearby river.

She and her kind were not counted of any import. They were just a part of the furnishings who gave loyal service in return for some impartial responsibility for their general wellbeing. Their anonymity gave access to knowledge others did not know.

'My guilt lies heavily upon me Madam. It is more than I can bear to know he took his life whilst there was ill will between us. My concern for your dear self fired my temper the day I sent him from my sight,' said Gerald Grimshaw, taking his wife's hand in his. Victoria Grimshaw looked into his eyes with deep sadness.

'Knowing you were recovered from your fall I intended to make amends with the boy on the very day, the very day he…'

Victoria Grimshaw wrestled with her thoughts of that day. She watched the flight of a wood pigeon for a few seconds before replying.

'Come and sit down husband. Let me pour you a little wine to cheer your spirits.' Victoria guided her husband to a comfortable chair and settled a cushion behind him.

'I also feel blame for I should have managed my mount better then none of the incident with Oscar would have happened.' She went to the side table furnished with a tray of glasses and a decanter.

'It is still not certain, how Jed came to be in the river. It could have been an accident. Yes, it was an accident. Remember the river ran high and fast flowing that month. Is it not possible, he could have fallen and lost consciousness?' She poured a glass of wine and came to him.

'Thank you my dear lady. You remind me. We discussed the state of the river that very morning when I sent word for Jed to assist me with some catalogues. Surely, he would not have…'

'It is greatly to be deplored the coroner recorded a verdict of suicide my dear husband. We must try to think otherwise and imagine he intended to come back to be reconciled with you. It will help your son to rest in peace my dear, will it not?' She handed her husband the glass of wine.

He sat in the same chair as Sarah finished dusting the shelves. A beam of sunlight etched the lines on his face telling their story of the sadness working into the very bones of this good man. If only she could change what occurred that day and lay his misery to rest. For now, she could tend to his needs only.

Gerald was lost in memories of his youth and his enchanted interlude with a gypsy princess. He asked himself, as he had countless times, was the boy of his gypsy princess's line. He had such a resemblance to her.

Sarah made her way back to her Mistress's bedroom, where she had earlier been replacing ribbons and fastenings on some garments. Putting them back in the closet, she sat to ply her needle anew.

Well at least I'm content she thought, stitching away busily, which is more than I can say for Mary Ann, mooning over Samuel.

One night two weeks after Jed's funeral she had come upon a wretched Mary Ann in the attic bedroom they shared. On questioning, the sobbing housemaid confessed to a deep friendship with the groom. Had they been discovered it would have cost them both their place on the staff. No liaisons were allowed there or any other well managed establishment.

'Samuel up and left the day after Master Jed died Miss Sarah and I've no news of 'im since' she wailed.

'The stable lads told me he was beside 'imself, and couldn't stand to be near the place. Another told me as he'd gone back to his didicoy father. T'was 'is father as placed him in service to Squire Grimshaw. You see Miss Sarah Samuel kept in touch with his father whenever they pitched tents on to the roadside patch of grass in the village used by the travellers. Likewise if true Romany folk came for a fair he visited and took Jed sometimes. They rode the countryside together going to other villages when the gypsy and the didecoys met for trading.'

Sensing some mystery, Sarah ever curious, and anxious to see Mary Ann more composed, suggested a solution.

'The Romany tribe are in the village. Perhaps we might find a way to go together, and seek information about Sam.'

'We could ask Mother Meg who lives with a few stragglers at Maid's Mounts. He thought a great deal of her, Miss Sarah. When he was little she stayed with the didecoys to nurse his mother until she died. She told him tales of faraway places then one summer morn she left them and never went back. Sam says they all missed her warmth and strength for a long while. Then one day she returned with a stray group who made ends meet on the road. They kept their distance from the rest but Sam said she visited come fair time. Sam always visits when she is in the village. If he took Jed along, Mother Meg never made him welcome yet for all that, Sam said whenever the boy was there, she never took her eyes off him.'

'We shall seek out Mother Meg, Mary Anne.'

'We had best go soon, before the caravan moves off on its yearlong circling Sarah,' said the maid her tears drying up.

The following afternoon, taking advantage of their weekly commission to distribute the smaller items of Mistress Grimshaws largesse to the poor and needy, Sarah and Mary Ann set off appropriately caped and bonneted for their errand.

'Before we return, I think we shall have a need for some more wooden pegs Mary Ann,' said Sarah with a knowing twinkle in her eye. 'Now where should we go for three bundles? Three will be plenty don't you think?'

'Oh more than enough Miss Sarah and I think I know where we can get handmade ones of quality.'

Quickly disbursing the gifts, the two made their way down an unmade lane at the end of the village. It went nowhere for it petered out at the foot the Maid's Mounts, two rounded hills that the fey folk swore were the signs of a sleeping goddess. In the lea of the hills, three caravans nestled unobtrusively. Six or seven horses grazed the lower hill slopes.

A man and a boy sat on two shafts, sunlight glinting off the knife blades they wielded as they whittled ash wood peg legs for the women to bind. As Mary Ann stepped forward the man glanced up warily. A smile started in his eyes, but at a small sign from Mary Ann, halted before it reached his mouth.

'Have you any ready for sale?' she asked. He went on whittling the pegs, cocking his head in the direction of the middle caravan. At the sound of her voice the upper door of the middle van was flung back. A handsome woman stood framed in the opening. A shawl lay open across her outstretched arm, resting against the door.

Sarah Hunt gazed into eyes fathoms deep where all signs of feeling submerged in the depths of their liquid blackness. The eyes moved to Mary Ann. The finest tilt of dark brows were her sole hint of expression. She drew back pulling her shawl across her breast to cover a silver claw clasped at her throat.

'Good day to thee Mother Meg,' said Mary Ann 'Miss Sarah and me have come to buy some pegs. Three bundles will do.'

Signalling the young lad to her vardo's steps the gypsy woman gave him some directions then sent him off to one of the other vardos.

In an uneasy silence of waiting Mary Ann's question hung unanswered when she asked after Samuel's whereabouts. Only after the bargain had been struck over a price for the pegs and the two maids had turned away to retrace their steps back home, did Mother Meg reply.

'Sam's gone along with his father a week since. They moved to next village. Mayhap they are still there. 'Sam thought you would have made a good didecoy wife one day. Good day to you missies.' So saying she closed the half door in dismissal leaving Sarah with more questions.

Before meeting the bustle of the village Sarah stopped and turned Mary Ann to her to speak her thoughts.

'I don't know that you have told me all there is to be told Mary Ann. Has Sam suggested you go away with him? You know the consequences of what you would be doing. How can you be so foolish?'

'With Sam and Master Jed gone there's only you as knows how foolish I've been,' the girl replied

Sarah Hunt studied the lovely face looking up at her. Probably some Irish ancestry, she thought, that blue black head of curls and the cream skin with cheeks rose blushed, a shade lighter than the dusk of her lips.

Vivid blue eyes framed with long black lashes looked innocently into hers with such trust.

She has a face like an angel's, thought Sarah whose own body would never boast such a proud bosom or trim waist as Mary Anne. Her thoughts ran on. That childlike mind, as compliant as her body, will be small match to resist the desire she will arouse in a man. It will be better for her to have the protection of a husband.

'How did you meet Samuel, Mary Ann? House servants don't usually go down to the stables unless they accompany one of the family.'

On the journey back to the manor, Mary Anne continued her story.

'As you know Miss Sarah, the stable lads and me started a few weeks before the Mistress came with her two daughters. Jed were all 'Master Grimshaw had as family 'til then. They say as Jed grew up piecemeal after the nursemaid left when he was around five or six. When Squire was about he tagged along with him and of course Sam was always fond of teasing the young'un and romping with him and he set him up on his first pony.

'A lonely life the young fellow had to be sure. Sam taught him to ride, and took an interest in showing him the countryside so to speak, There was no other to befriend the lad 'cept for the old schoolmaster. They've rode far and wide most days 'cept Sundays o' course. Cook would put up some fare for Sam to collect so's they weren't hungry being out all day. That's how I came to meet Sam, on his way past the study to the kitchen. I was dusting the study furniture as was my duty and I looked up and saw Sam. He was looking in right at me. He didn't say nothing, just went on to the kitchen. Then one day I was taking a tray back to the kitchen and he was coming out with the victuals for their ride and we sort of smiled at each other. That's how we became friends, for we are friends Miss Sarah, and no more I promise. I love him, and I believe he thinks fair of me, 'cause he was so mad at Master Jed a pestering me.'

'H'm? How so, pestering you Mary Ann?' asked Sarah, recalling other tales from the laundry maid.

'Well it would be some time ago Miss Sarah, I don't keep good account of time, and I blush to think on it, though it weren't my doing. We cleans the grates early mornings and we all take a hand, there being so many to make ready for the day.Master Jed would creep up and catch me bending with a heavy bucket of ashes in one hand and brushes and dusters in the other. I would just be wearing the old slip I keep for the dirty work before washing and changing into a dress and apron to serve breakfasts. My, Miss Sarah, his hands would be all over the place before I could drop the bucket and run. It got so I was afraid to go down to tend the study fire on my own.

'Well I told Samuel, thinking him being older than Master Jed and kind of in charge of him when they were out riding. Sam said nought but I believe he must have told 'im as he should stick to his own class since he'd moved up in the world. He told him better to mend his ways for it would be 'ladged' to his mother that her child was mochadi.' He never pestered me again to the day he died. Now this terrible thing's 'appened when all of us was 'appy and the workload easy. None of us got the brunt of the family being at odds, so to speak. Why, one day....'

'Do stop Mary Anne. What's this about Jed's mother? Who is she? Where does she live?' interrupted Sarah Hunt, only to be told that when Mary Anne had asked the same question,

'Sam shut up tight as a clam Miss Sarah.' The telling of Mary Anne's tale brought them to the gates of the manor.

Before going in Sarah cautioned her companion. 'Keep even your thoughts to yourself from now on. I shall try and see if I can find Sam's whereabouts soon.'She intended to find the man for her own reasons, for she sensed a mystery. Being of a curious nature, mysteries for Sarah were meant to have a solution.

Chapter 4: The Manor

SARAH Hunt was packing her bag for a visit to an old friend in the next village on the two days a month she was free to do as she pleased. Now she pleased to find out more about Sam, the missing groom.

If she hurried, she would catch the early train that puffed along the valley between villages on a local sideline. What a boon it was though some were always mistrustful of new inventions, especially machinery. For them the pony and trap or the draughty horse bus were safe and proper ways for folk to move around the countryside.

Sitting in the carriage with the wheels clacking over the track beneath and puffs of smoke, from the coal-fired engine, drifting past the window, Sarah decided to start her search as soon as she could. She intended to enlist the help of her friend after catching up with recent events in her life.

When she explained the reason for her visit Maud, a local farrier's wife, told Sarah there was a group of travellers still on the outskirts of the village. Later that morning, Sarah made her way towards the assortment of tented dwellings scattered along a wide verge to the road. The itinerant nature of this group found tents easier to move about with, on their annual journeying.

A lean bodied cur sniffed her skirts with a low-throated growl as she came near to the first of the tents. Men and women were moving purposefully about on the site, their clothing quieter hued than the rich colours beloved of the Romany. Their skin glowed with health. A tent flap, raised as she approached, revealed a neatly stacked interior. A boy came out his eyes questioning her right to be there. His skin was a shade lighter than the swarthy complexions of his companions.

The didicoys, as some named them, were not true Romany though they lived a similar way of life. They sometimes married a village girl, bringing her into the tribe and diffusing the bloodline. It never weakened their hardworking efforts to remain independent from the Gorgios living in their dark musty brick sties only fit for pigs.

'Hallo to you. Is Samuel from Master Grimshaw's household here' asked Sarah? The boy scuffed his toe making no reply. She tried again.

'Sam's a friend of mine I've come to give some news to….'

The boy looked towards the tent interior where a hidden nod prompted him. 'Mayhap he's down in village forge.' Sarah made her way back to the corner of a lane where the main forge stood, its walls open to whichever wind prevailed.

Heat rushed to meet her from the big central fire, fanned to white heat by a young boy pulling on the rope which worked the large bellows. Around the yard unfinished railings lay waiting their turn under the hammer. A church bell stood dull and silent until polished when its burnished curves would respond to the urgent knocking of a clapper. Old horseshoes made an uneven floor beneath her feet as she turned towards three men working with hammers and anvils.

Samuel worked a little apart from the other two. His honest face showed surprise as he recognised Sarah. He paused in his work to glance towards an older man who had come from the shadows as Sarah approached. A brief nod accorded Samuel time to take her aside from the heat.

Sam stood silent waiting for Sarah to open up. She did so with no more ado, stating her case baldly.

'I've come to see what you are going to do about Mary Ann. Poor child's that distressed I trust you've done her no harm Sam?'

'No Miss Sarah, Mary Anne was always safe with me, you may depend, and my intentions are honourable towards her. I had to leave that blighted place to come to my senses again. When the year's turn brings me round to your village if the lass will join me as a traveller, I will take good care of her. I could come back to the smithy and settle down. He has offered me work and a rented cottage but I will not set foot on manor ground again.'

'I don't understand Sam. If you are willing to stay here why did you leave a good position with the family?' Sarah reasoned. Sam face tightened, his eyes reflecting a flicker of fear in the light from the fire.

'What about Jed's real mother,' pursued Sarah? 'Does she know of his death? If not, and you know of her whereabouts Sam…' He turned, taking up tongs and a fresh piece of iron to feed to the fire. Hammer in hand; he stood at the anvil watching the flying sparks as he spoke.

'The reason my father sent me to seek work at the manor was to see how the boy was faring. 'Tis possible he may have been Jed's father. There be about ten year between us.' Fascinated with this news Sarah still pressed the question of Jed's mother.

'She was a true Romany who nursed my sick mother and took care of us when we were camped near Malden Manor. After my mother passed Meg would sometimes be away whole days. She always returned by nightfall to comfort the keening of my dad. In the autumn she went away without telling anyone she was with child. Mother Meg has lived on her own and unwedded all these years.' Sarah felt she had known when she first met Meg.

'How can you be sure it's Meg and that she was with child Sam?'

'We gypsies are a secret people of secrets. There's nought we know nought about.'

'Did Jed know all this?'

'I am not sure Miss Sarah. Rightly or wrongly I took Jed to the encampment at Maids Mount when he was about ten years old and he was greatly drawn to

Mother Meg. She was a mite sour towards the boy and shut the doors of her vardo tight against him.'

His muscled arm, sheened with the sweat of his labour, withdrew the white hot metal from the fire, and began to hammer it upon the anvil. Sarah drew back from the flying sparks. She knew there was more to the story but the forge master was looking annoyed and Sarah felt it time to leave.

'Sam I have to go back tomorrow but I must speak with you again before I leave. I will go now for fear of causing you trouble with your master.' His arm rose and fell as the hammer sang on metal.

'We may meet in the garden of the inn before sundown. 'Tis a decent hostelry though not fit for the likes of such as you to be seen in. I'll be waiting at the gate Miss. Good day to you.' He laid his work aside as he picked up a fresh piece of iron.

Sarah prevailed upon her friend to accompany her to the meeting. Both women, discreetly attired in dove grey cloaks and matching bonnets, walked to the inn in the early hours that summer evening. Sam awaited them, washed and clean shirted above a tidy pair of trousers. He led them to an alcove in the garden.

Honeysuckle and wild rose entwined an arbour where he seated them at a low bench behind a deal table. After they declined to his offer to fetch them some fare Sam went to buy ale for himself, returning with a brimming tankard to set down on the table.

Standing akimbo with his back against one of the arbour supports he waited, amber eyes narrowed now with a hint of the foxiness that fed into the half smile shadowing his mouth. Straight tawny hair rose from a low forehead beneath the cap tilted to the back of his head. His nose was sharp as his eyes.

How different he looks from the well turned out groom at the manor, and the honest smithy at the forge this morning thought Sarah. We all play so many parts in life. Oh to know the true from the false.

'Samuel I will tell Mary Ann of your intentions towards her. It is well that she wait a year to be sure of her own mind.' Sarah caught and held Sam's attention. 'If there is anything that you know which will ease Master Grimshaw's mind, for he feels solely to blame for Jed's death, speak up now.'

'I'll tell thee as much as I can Mistress.' Sam lifted the tankard and drank deeply before setting it back down on the table.

'From the time I went to the manor to take care of the horses for Squire, young Jed and me were the best of friends. We roamed the countryside, me teaching him country lore. He could set a snare as well as me any day and he was generous with the spoils, leaving a rabbit on an old crone's doorstep and fowl in the priest's porch.

'He loved to get free of the new Mistress's clutches. She meant well but he'd run wild until the widow and her girls came a year ago. They tried to make him act like the fancy gentry, bowing and scraping to the ladies. It brought out the worst in him at a time when he was beginning to notice the fillies, you might say. It didn't help when the girls mocked his efforts. Then he started to hang around the laundry and tease the maids.

'Trouble began between him and me about the time the cherry blossom began to fade come June. Some evenings Mary Ann and I met further along the river's course for a stroll. We had an understanding, nothing said, mind.'

'Yes I know about that Sam and how Jed pestered her, so there is no need…'

'Mary Ann needed taking care of Miss Sarah. Poor girl was born an orphan since her mother died in giving her life. There being no father she was sent to the orphanage and from there to the manor. That don't mean she's of no account to be handled like trash by those as should know better. I promise as the man as cares for her if she comes to me, she'll know freedom to come and go as she pleases.'

'Yes, yes,' soothed Sarah anxious to keep him telling Jed's story. Maud moved off into the garden with her ears were well laid back. Feeling easier without her presence Sam continued.

'Before the accident I'd had words with Jed. I can't tell you why Miss Sarah but I fair laid into the young devil. In the end me tongue ran away from me and I said 'twas a pity to see a Rom behave to shame his mother. That set 'im back and he rode silent for a space before telling me to speak the truth of the matter or he'd tell the Master about me and Mary Ann. I'd no choice Miss. Mary Ann is everything to me. Master's been less than honest in the matter if Mrs Mossop tells true but I believe we were half-brothers by my father and I told him so. He wanted knowledge of his mother, and that I wouldn't give him. He settled for meeting my father at the yearly race meet at Epsom a day or so on. He would be trading horses along with the others in our tribe.

'We took the horse on wheels. It's a wonder isn't it Miss Sarah, how that train gallops along passing stragglers who've lost a wheel from their vardo. We got to the field when the fair was in full swing. Have you ever been to one of the big meets Miss? All the tribes are there. So many of your own kind, you really feel proud and special, as you greet old friends. The Romany vans stand in a half circle at the edge of the course with tents belonging to us travellers dotted here and there. There's the good smell of horseflesh, leather and our own sweat as we work to set up stalls, tents, and trenches. The cooking pots send mouth-watering savours on the steam curling up your nostrils as you pass by. So much colour swirling round the women folk's legs, if you'll pardon me Miss. You can't miss seeing an ankle or two when the young'uns fly around lifting and laying out the work they do in the winter months.

'Then there are the saddles. Their beauty brings tears to your eyes as they cover the backs of the Cobs and smaller framed Arabs waiting to stretch their long legs on the course. Every family paints their vans for that meet. The patterns all in tradition y'know and bright as fresh paint can make 'em....'

Sarah lifted her hand to check Sam's racing tongue. The crafty look had left his eyes, now shining with bright memories in an almost childlike face. He heeded her gesture with a sheepish smile, and resumed.

'Our business there left little time to look around. We made our way to some tents standing between two vardos, stopping here and there for me to greet a friend and bring Jed into the tribe's way of things. He looked at ease from the time we stepped into the fields. He had found his own and didn't feel an outsider. He surely found much in common with my old man when they came face to face.

'The old fellow had just done a good deal with one of his horses and turned in good humour when I hailed him. Of course he had seen Jed growing up over the years so his face showed nought. His eyes quizzed the eyes of a gypsy staring urgently into his own. Suddenly the old man looked weary and lonely. Their faces said it all to we as read faces like an open book.'

'So you are my father? Is that so' Jed said a tremble in his voice? 'What of my mother who gave me away?'

In a voice roughened by smoking the old clay pipe resting in the palm of his hand, me father answered him.

'Hold your horses lad. I don't know the answer. She did what was best for you. Don't judge what you don't understand. Let the past rest and make your way fearless into the future'

'Who is she? My mother, who is she,' he asked, white to the lips?

'I tell you Miss Sarah I thought there might be blows between 'em but of a sudden I felt her standing behind us. Mother Meg I mean. She stared defiantly straight into the old man's eyes, daring him to speak. Jed spun round as she turned to go to her van but he recognised her. He looked dazed and sad all at once. The day fell flat after that. On the way home he said he felt a murderous hate shaft his guts for those who rejected him. He needed to know who had seduced and betrayed Meg who then left him in gentry's hands.

'The next day and every day after he rode down to the Maid's Mount encampment and other sites to find her. Best ask her about that Miss Sarah.'

'Oh I will Samuel, I will,' she replied. 'Is there anything else?'

'Well thee knows about trouble with the Mistress and Oscar. She weren't meant to ride Jude's horse any road. She'd decided Tamar was unsettled with Miss Effie sharing him with her and said she would ride Oscar if he would take Tamar and school him back to better ways.

'Even though he had a firm hold on his bridle the horse fair bolted once she settled on him. As you know it put him in dispute with the Master who sent him off with more than a flea in his ear. That coming so soon after the 'old man' did pretty much the same thing, Jed was low in spirits, and at odds with the world at large. He spent hours walking by the river or riding on his own.'

'Ah the river Sam,' Sarah interrupted. 'What happened between you and Jed at the river?'

She watched Sam' face intently, as he moved from table to arbour support between episodes of his story. The shadows of the sun dappled leaves around the trellising flickered across his face as swiftly as the chameleon expressions which told their own story. Envy and resentment fled before fear in the telling, but overall there was a sad remorse for Jed's passing.

'Thee knows all there is to know Miss Sarah, since you were there,' he hedged.

'But I was not there when you had the fight over Miss Effie,' she responded quietly.

Sam stood awhile deep in thought, then gestured permission to take the seat vacated by Sarah's friend. He sat, elbows on table, head resting in his hands. He began to speak again, slowly and clearly, as if he was trying to reconstruct that afternoon for himself.

'As you know Sarah,' dropping the 'Miss' in his reverie, 'the stables are built between the river and the servants' quarters of the manor. Only the Master's study looks out through the French windows towards the river. The main rooms face the view of the Downs. Mistress Grimshaw has her sitting room leading off Master's study in the corner from where servant quarters branch off into their wing. All we shared of that wing were the cloakroom for hanging outdoor capes to dry. We entered from yard and them from the corridor running past the kitchen and pantry and such.

'The back wall of the wing forms one stable yard wall, to which we hitch the horses for hosing down. Stables themselves is on the far side of the yard, and in between lies a low barn for hay and storing stable needs, and 'twas where we ate our fare. The view of the riverbank depended on where you were because of the walls.

'That afternoon I was sitting with Higgins our stable lad, teaching him how to replace a stirrup strap strong and sure. Jed had taken him out for the early morning ride and noticed the worn strap. The boy was slow to learn, and kept glancing to where we could see Jed sitting on the tall stump of the dead elm tree. One of the willows growing along the bank shaded him. In fact, since the business with the amulet, which I know more about than I'm letting on, and then Mistress's fall from Oscar, he could be seen walking the banks or sitting there all the time, only going to his bed at nightfall.

'We had fed and I was filling in time before watering the horses in the river around three. I'd just sent the boy to sweep the yard to liven him up, when I noticed Miss Effie come out of the maze from the eastern opening and make for the river. That's the stable side of it ye ken for river runs to north of manor. Maze was there before Squire's time. It was to hide that wing from the gentry's gaze and now it gives us a bit of space to sit awhile betimes, since the Master's took over.

'Missy had taken to sitting with Jed soon after she began her riding lessons with us. I reckon she slipped out when her mother was a-resting for we all knew milady was only trimming off the lassie's puppy fat and getting her primed for a good union with one of the families further up the valley.

'Knowing Jed was at a lusting time and angry unsettled me. I thought to water the mare early and finished the stirrup before setting off towards the mare's stable where I got a clearer view of the bank. Bejesus the sight of her on her back and Jed astride the filly sent me shooting off like a ferret to separate 'em.'

Sarah noticed the beads of perspiration spotting Sam's forehead, as he recalled the scene in his mind's eye.

'Well I hauled 'im off her and told her to get back to her room as quick as she could. She stood like a rabbit caught in a lantern's beam until we started to fight then she turned and ran for the house.

'At the first cuff all the bad blood between us rushed to our heads. We fought in deadly earnest, ending up in the river to our waists. He landed some good blows but I was the stronger and he soon looked winded. I gave him a final cuff to the head which toppled him back into the water, threshing and gasping, but alive I swear Miss Sarah. Then I heard footsteps running down the domestic's side of the maze, and I dived in the opening on the west side to hide. As soon as they passed I ran across to the east opening and made my way back to the stables to fetch the mare.'

Sam's face was wretched with anxiety and remorse as he continued his tale.

. 'You see Sarah I can't be sure and yet I know in my bones I'm not to blame for his going. He was threshing so strongly. I'm sure I heard voices, him and another, but I was running and bending low and I can't be certain.' His head fell forward on to his folded arms and sobs broke the stillness in the garden.

'Did you see anybody at all Sam, anyone'? Sarah's voice was urgent, her hand griping his shoulder brought him to his feet with a muttered,

'I must be gone, and tis best you and your friend make for home now evening is upon us.' Seeing them to the gate and on to their dwelling, he remained silent and withdrawn, pausing only to touch his cap to them, before he departed.

The farrier's wife kept a discreet silence giving Sarah a spell to think over Sam's story. The household at the manor had not doubted that some suicidal mood of darkness had driven Jed to take his life.

Sarah felt Jed was strong enough to cope with rejection? Does Sam still have a tale to tell, she wondered. I won't be content until I find the truth of this matter and find out how Jed met his death.

The following morning, after a restless night's sleep, Maud accompanied Sarah on the walk to the station. Knowing they would pass a shop selling bric a brac, Sarah intended to stop and buy a small gift for her friend.

Stepping under the low lintel of the door, the sweet aroma of lavender, soft tanned leather and polished wood assailed their senses. In a corner of the shop, a bald head shone beneath a lamp on the small desk where its owner bent over a ledger of figures .He stood to greet his customers courteously.

'Good Morning ladies,' he bowed revealing a tiny rotund figure, neatly attired in black suit with a chequered waistcoat. Small graceful hands lifted to remove the gold-rimmed spectacles set on a button nose nestled between bright rosy cheeks. Satisfied that they did not need his services, he sat to his ledger again. Sarah stepped carefully around his treasures, ending by the walnut and glass case, which served as a counter.

There she found what she wanted, a basket of lace pieces. Her gift would be some tatted lace edgings for hemming onto the fine cambric handkerchiefs her friend stitched as Yuletide gifts, to celebrate the Saviour's birth. Delving in among doilies and collars of fine lace to find the edgings, her hand struck a hard, smooth, round object.

Drawing it out, she discovered in her palm a lapis lazuli amulet. Excited with her find which was very much like one in the Master's study, she enquired its provenance. As he took the amulet from her, the little shop owner's face was full of surprise.

'Madam, this is the first time I've set eyes on it.' He peered intently through his glasses, harrumphing nervously as he slid it into his waistcoat pocket. His eyes beamed over the rims of his spectacles, now perched precariously on the end of his snub nose.

'I must make enquiries Madam. It is not for sale I fear, for it may, just may have come with the lace pieces in the basket. They are an excellent bargain Madam. All handmade from a known source.'

'Ah so you know the source of the lace?' asked Sarah.

'Well as to names, no Madam, but this lot was purchased after Epsom Meet in June. The gypsies try to sell off what does not go at the fair. This is a regular calling place.'

'Can you recall what the vendor looked like please? I may know her, and need more of this edging. It is a particularly pretty pattern is it not?' Sarah pressed.

'The lace is made by one of the older women who I deal with regularly. I trust her bargaining and I'm afraid I just let her tip her wares into the basket. A true gypsy for sure, but the fellow that came with her was of the other breed. He had small iron trivets for sale and these leather mats,' showing Sarah a round circle of leather, pierced and bound with fine leather around the circumference, and a small flower design burnt on the surface.

'I will purchase what lace you have in this pattern and one of your leather mats,' said Sarah. Duly packing and receiving payment for his wares, the shop-keeper escorted the women to his door, bowing his thanks for their patronage. One foot on the high step up to street level, Sarah turned,

'The young fellow, would he be from these parts I wonder?'

'The forge workers use leftover metal to make trivets, but leather is most often gypsy workmanship Madam. The master of the forge allows the men to make a penny with the useless iron. I really could not say. Good Day and thank you for your custom.' Sarah felt she knew the answer, and would pursue it at another time.

Their visit to the shop had taken more time than expected. They hastened their steps in the direction of the railway, where the smoke from the train's chimney heralded its approach. Arriving flustered and out of breath, fond farewells and promises to send more news were made, before Sarah sank into her seat.

With so much on her mind, the walk up the hill to the manor was easy going. Later, she sat down in the kitchen to eat some food the cook had kept back and share tit bits of her visit. She barely had time to open her mouth, before news of more missing artefacts was told in hushed tones.

'Master and Mistress 'ave been doing the six monthly inventories Sarah and what do you think 'Mrs Mossop whispered, eyes wide and lips pursed above her ample aproned bosom? 'Four ivory figurines is missing. They's a matching set wot cost a penny, for Master's in high dudgeon about it.'

Sarah rose and murmured her thanks for the meal.

'I must go back to the village. I forgot ribbons for the Mistress.'

Retying her bonnet, she set off briskly for Maids Mount, for she had a good idea where the figurines might be. This time she would be a match for the wily gypsy woman if indeed her van were still encamped there.

The lane seemed endless as Sarah toiled up towards the two hills. She was rewarded by the sight of Mother Meg coming out of the rift between them, carrying a small bundle of kindling. Hastening to intercept Meg before she spotted her and barricaded herself behind her vardo door, Sarah ran the last few steps to meet Meg at the foot of the three-step ladder to the entrance.

'Good day to you Mother Meg. I'm just returned from visiting my friend in Houghton and talking with Samuel. I thought you might like news of him.' Meg barred the entrance to her castle, her face hostile as she replied

'Thank you Miss but it's of no account. Word such as I need reaches me. I was half expecting to see you ere long, but not so soon.'

'There is some urgency which brings me here today. We need to talk privately if you will let me come in for a talk Mother Meg.'

A moment's further hesitation then, turning to mount the steps, Meg threw open the door to her home and stood aside for Sarah to enter the fragrant interior. Sarah was surprised at how the high curve of the roof allowed her to stand upright and move with ease to sit, at Meg's invitation, on the long bench running the van's length. Meg sat on a low three-legged stool. Taking from her apron pocket a tatting shuttle and some unfinished lace she plied the flying shuttle as she waited for Sarah to speak.

'We are all so very sad that Jed is, is no longer with us, and with Sam gone, there is such a big hole in our lives. I believe that emptiness may be touching you and felt…' Sarah foundered looking for the right thing to say.

The shuttle stopped its flight; the hands lay quietly in the fold of the apron, as the two women communed silently. Sarah gently reached out a tentative pink hand to touch the brown one which suddenly curled like a child's around her own, drawing down the strength and compassion it needed to let its owner speak.

'Sam sent news of your visit this morning Miss Sarah. I thank you for the goodness of heart which prompts you to seek the manner of my son's passing. For that, I will tell you what you wish to know, for it would ease the weight on my heart, should you prove his death to be an accident. Yes, we knew one another as mother and son in the end.'

Meg's face had softened and for all her forty or so years she looked younger as melancholy gave way to a shared hope.

'I returned here to the camp at Maids Mount after Epsom Fair. The next day and the day after, Jed came and knocked for entry, but I refused him. I owed it to the man who helped me in my need sixteen years ago for it is truth when I tell you Squire Grmshaw took my infant son into his care sixteen years ago and saved me from expulsion from the tribe.

'The third day Jed came, my door was open. He came in eager as a child restrained from his wants. For me it was as if this handsome youth were reborn my son. He came into my open arms. Our hearts beat as one, our minds opened into silent union. There was no place for word or rebuke. He never asked the reason why. Our trust was complete and both knew he must return to the manor and play his destined part in life.

'After the passion of our reunion and acceptance of our future roles, he sat shy and quiet, where you sit now Miss. He took from his pocket two gifts, and laid them upon this stool. They sit in the glassed-in shelf above you, a piece of old flint, found on a downland ride and a smooth round pebble such as comes from a riverbed. It was as if he was making up for the childhood we had missed together.'

Sarah stood to look on the shelf. It was a moment before she found the flint tool and the pebble. Four ivory figurines caught her gaze first as Mother Meg knew they would. Their eyes met.

'The flint and the pebble are most precious to you Meg but these will only cause trouble. I think Master Grimshaw will be pleased to see them.'

'Ah the Squire would like such as I have? He be welcome, if you will be so good as to take them' Meg's eyes smiled knowingly.

'How did you come by them?' Sarah smiled back.

'Now you'd be asking a riddle for the young ones are always leaving little things for me to find. Mary Ann now knows me as the mother she never had, and Sam as one who shared sorrow and comforted his father as we tended a dying woman. To Jed I was his true Romany mother of who he was proud. Why he even talked of years to come when he would be Master and our clan would have rights to part of his lands'

Meg took Sarah by the shoulders, standing taller by a head as she entreated,

'He did not take his life so newly enriched. Find the truth of it for me Ma'am and a gypsy's blessing on you.' She placed the figurines in Sarah's hands.

'They are of no account against what I gave to Squire Grimshaw, a handsome son. Just clear my son's memory Sarah Hunt is all I ask of you.' They parted, one who had never known a child of her own and the other who had never known her own child.

Sarah made her way home wondering who had stolen the ivories and the amulet. She suspected Jed of giving the amulet to Meg. Sam had access to the study on his way to the kitchen. Mary Ann shared the dusting duties with herself. There was a mystery to solve.

For the moment her first task was to replace the ivory figures in some obscure cupboard, where they could have been overlooked, before meeting her master and mistress again. The shop at Houghton must be paid another visit to claim the amulet.

It was all becoming too involved she decided as she entered a side gate behind the stable barn and made her way round to the small lawn outside the servants entrance. As she closed the door the bright gleam of the river below reminded her that the riddle of Jed's death was also far from resolved. Well tomorrow was another day and maybe she would find time.

Chapter 5: Secrets

SARAH Hunt crossed the stable yard towards one of the horse stalls where young Higgins was grooming the trap pony. He talked to the horse as he worked, in the manner of those who love animals. The sweet smell of fresh hay filled the barn. She peered over the half door and he looked up from cleaning out one of the hooves.

'Morning Miss Sarah, if ye'll excuse me from not rising but with Sam not back and the new lad not knowing his way yet…'Sarah smiled.

'That's fine Higgins but perhaps we could talk whilst you get on,' she suggested. 'Going back to the day of the accident, can think of any reason for Oscar to rear and throw the Mistress?'

Higgins freckled face flushed with pleasure, his carroty hair standing up like a halo, as he rose to the challenge.

'Well 'tis well known among us as Sam and Young Master had a fallin' out some time before it 'appened Miss. I'd left me curry brush in the stall and came to fetch it, though neither of 'em knew I was just t'other side of the door where they stood. Seems Sam was accusing Master Jed of taking some orniments down to some 'un, and getting some of us in bad favour.

For 'is part, Master Jed was threatening to tell Squire, Sam was meeting Mary Ann betimes. That shut Sam up sharp and he backed down with Young Master going off clock-a-hoop.

For rest of that day he fair 'ad us boys running 'til nightfall.' Harry Higgins lifted the next hoof and bent to his task with much attention.

'So how did things finish with them Higgins,' Sarah was moved to ask. 'A falling out between folks has little to do with their animals.'

'I dunno 'bout that Miss, best ask Oscar. Crafty old devil knows a thing or two 'bout the goings on 'ere.' He stood up to move to the far side of the pony away from Sarah's probing eyes and settled to clean out the third hoof.

'I'd rather ask you Higgins, so if there is anything left unsaid, you'll much oblige me by telling it,' Sarah snapped sharply. 'How were matters on the morning of the accident?'

Harry Higgins shuffled his feet and muttered something into the pony's flank.

'Well Higgins?' Sarah pressed him.

'I can't rightly be sure, but I know's it were never meant to be Mistress Grimshaw.'

Sarah moved her vantage point to find Harry had dropped the pony's hoof and sat dejectedly on the ground, elbows resting on his knees as he stared sightless, at the images going through his mind. She waited. .

'Both 'orses were saddled up when I noticed a teasel In Oscar's fetlock so I told Sam.

"Young Master's been through the teasel bushes with Oscar again Mr Sam. 'Is fetlock hairs was matted wiv 'em. Six I've taken out this morning." Groom takes the teasel to throw in the waste bin then family comes into the yard, Jed and the Mistress. She was to ride Tamar the smaller mount for Jed always rode Oscar.

Master Jed came over and led Tamar to the mounting block where Mistress asked him sommat he wasn't 'appy about. I saw Mr Sam walking Oscar out of his stall and running 'is 'and under the saddle like 'e was checking the under blanket was smooth. Harry told his tale as if he were seeing events in front of his eyes..

'Jed, sorry Miss, Master Jed. Well he comes across and takes the bridle from Mr Sam and goes back to the mounting block. I 'eard Sam mutter about teaching someone a lesson and sommat about pride going before a fall, then he flung away into stables.

Next thing I sees is Mistress Grimshaw on the block and swinging into Oscar's saddle. She never rode side saddle. Jed was steadying the 'orse and holding the bridle to her as she settled down. Then all 'ell breaks loose. That critter shoots for'ard like 'e's been blasted from a musket then rears up on his hind legs like he's a 'dancing. The lady is flying into the air, Jed is hauling at the reins alongside, and then they are all of an 'eap on the ground. She were screaming with fright, he were shouting at the 'orse, then everything went quiet.

Mr Sam came running with me to where they lay. All the wind were knocked out of Sam's sails. He looked like he'd met death 'imself.'

Harry looked up at Sarah, his freckles bright against the pallor of his face.

'Ye see Miss I don't know for rights for Mr Sam unsaddled Oscar, leaving me to stall Tamar. Ye knows the rest. It seems Mistress had asked Master Jed to change 'orses because Miss Effie had got hers into bad habits and 'e needed schooling. Against Jed's wishes the Mistress insisted she ride Oscar that morning.'

'Can you tell me about the afternoon when Master Jed met his death Higgins' whispered Sarah. 'Did you see him and Sam fight by the river?' Harry's face brightened, finding safer ground to open up.

'No Miss Sarah that I never did. I was sweeping out as Mr Sam 'ad told me to, so I never saw anyfing'

'Sam tells me you were fidgety that afternoon and not working well on the stirrup strap. Why was that?' pressed Sarah. Higgins stood gentling the pony, getting comfort as he stroked the creamy mane, then with a big sigh his confession breathed out.

'Dunno bout that Miss but the groom were terrible to work for after the accident. I did nothin' right and I was glad to ride with Master Jed next morning. He, poor fellow, was right down in the dumps. I never seen him so down. In the end to cheer 'im up, I suggested sommat might 'ave got under the saddle and no blame to 'im.

Well Miss he never let it rest until I told him wot I just told you about the teasels. Ye see I didn't want to cause trouble, only cheer 'im up, but 'is face told me I'd done wrong. Mr Sam's a good boss and I didn't say anyfing wrong did I,' he appealed to Sarah, picking up the last hoof and clasping it tight to his chest?

'You did no wrong Higgins. The truth is all you can tell and that you have done. Have no fear I will keep your story to myself. Can you can remember anything else about that afternoon?' Harry pushed his cap back, scratching his head in an effort to enliven his memory.

'Well, Mary Ann called from the cloakroom door asking for Mr Samuel urgent like. I was sweeping out, and called across me shoulder to 'er that I thought 'ed run down to the river. She belted out of stable and headed into the northeast corner of maze 'cos I watched 'er go. I never saw 'er come back. I thought I see'd Miss Effie walking along the riverbank a mite earlier but I knows she woz rushing back to the 'ouse before Mary Anne took off. Went a fair gallop up the west side she did 'cos she weren't supposed to be down there anyways.

'When Mr Sam came back, I told 'im Mary Ann went looking for 'im, he said 'ed come back from south opening and 'adn't seen anyone. Then we got 'orses ready for watering. Mr Sam used the archway between the end of the barn and the stables to take the 'orses by the lane at the front of the 'ouse. 'E reckoned to use the curve of river further upstream that afternoon.'

Sarah left the stables trying to piece together the scraps of information she had gleaned.

She knew Mistress Grimshaw had hurried down the west side of the maze to stop the fight, after Effie arrived with news of the tussle by the riverbank. She had returned through the maze around three and told those waiting in the house all was quiet and it was much ado about nothing. Samuel thought he may have dealt Jed a lethal blow to the head but said he had heard voices afterwards by the river, and Higgins story told of other persons nearby.

Her head spun with fear for her Mistress's part in the drama being discovered. It was two days since her return from Horam and today had begun badly.

Master Grimshaw had sent for her and Mary Ann to stand, hands clasped over their aprons, in front of his rosewood desk. Sarah's heart went out to this mild mannered man who had opened his home and his heart to those in straightened circumstances.

Of medium height and build, he carried a still handsome head upon straight shoulders. As he looked out of the window his profile was fine of line with a high forehead from which a wing of dark hair brushed back over the grey. He turned to them with keen regard. Full lips and compassionate eyes took the sting from his words.

'I fear your sense of responsibility carried little heed for the importance of your task. The antiquities housed here are not mine alone. They belong to many nations and shed light on times from whence they came. How can you answer for not missing the ivory figurines? Mary Ann was that shelf your duty to dust?'

The girl blushed, lowered her lids and started hesitantly, her hands knotting the apron beneath them.

'Yes Master 'tis my duty to dust the figurine shelf.'

'When did you last dust them?'

'After Master Jed returned from Epsom. He came in to the study next morning and took the pieces from me and said they were very beautiful. That is all Master.'

'Well Sarah, what have you to offer over their disappearance. You are placed in overall charge of Mary Anne?' Sarah was well prepared.

'Master Grimshaw we are truly sorry to have caused you anxiety over the figurines, but may I beg to suggest they are just displaced. With your leave may we search again most thoroughly for them. If we were dilatory in our duties, I fear it is because sadness at recent events has overcome our pleasure in their care, if you will forgive me for mentioning,'

Squire Grimshaw smiled acquiescence at the woman who went so quietly about her work and served him unobtrusively in many small ways.

'You travelled to London, Sir, when the Mistress went to stay with her friend after her fall, if I may be so bold as to remind you.' He nodded assent.

'Often on such visits in the past, you have taken some of your collection to show others. Mary Ann may have thought that was the case. It was most remiss that she did not speak to me about it but our minds were occupied you understand I hope, Sir. It is even possible Master Jed returned to admire them again, and replaced them on the wrong shelf. It is easily done, Sir. That is all I have to offer, with your leave.'

'Very well Sarah.' Gerald Grimshaw took out his watch, sighed at the time.

'Mary Ann, the study will be free this afternoon, as usual. You will search then and report to me before dinner.'

Every afternoon at precisely two o'clock he took the trap to attend to business affairs returning at four o'clock. Curtsying, the maids left their master to greet a visitor arriving at the study as they left.

At two o'clock, leaving the damp odour of drying capes in the cloakroom, Sarah hurried along the passage to the study where Mary Ann waited impatiently.

'Miss Sarah there's precious little time for a lost cause. Cook is ill tempered, for there's none to lay up the dining room table,' she announced with a finality Sarah took to be a sign Mary Ann knew the figurines were at Maids Mount.

'It will not hurt to look again so be sharp and start in the corner cupboard. I will work towards you from the door,' Silently they worked from the top shelves down to the lower rows.

Sarah opened the amulets cupboard hoping for a small miracle to return the missing one from Horam and drew a sharp intake of breath.

From where she knelt in her corner, Mary Ann waited for her fellow conspirator's discovery.

'I went to see Mother Meg yesterday and I knows all Miss Sarah. She told me of your visit and gave me the amulet.' Sarah smiled with a good grace.

'Well Mary Ann perhaps you will bring the four figurines on the shelf in front of you and we shall place all on the Master's desk.'

When the antiques were arranged on a tray Sarah stopped Mary Anne in her tracks to the kitchen.

'You owe me a little time I think. Tell me about the threats made by Master Jed over you and Sam, and what Sam knew about these,' pointing to the tray. 'This past week I have learned much to ease the Master's anguish but I believe you may still have something to tell me. Master Jed was low in spirits when he returned from his early morning ride with Higgins. He left his food untouched and retired to his room until luncheon with Miss Effie and Mistress Grimshaw.? You served that lunch Mary Ann. Was he more composed by then?'

Mary Ann backed into a corner of the study before beginning her tale.

'After lunch the Mistress went to see about the evening meal, for the vicar was invited to share dinner that night. Miss Effie and Master Jed were alone and they took little notice of me as I was passing back and forth to the kitchen with dishes but I overheard some of what was said Miss Sarah.

'Jed's was angry as he walked up and down the room then I heard him plainly as he fair stormed. "Effie I'm not to blame for your mother's fall. I mean to prove it. Higgins told me something this morning which I'm going to sort out with Sam." He said he meant to have his name cleared of not managing to hold down Oscar and if Sam didn't own up he would tell the Master about it and about Sam and me. He said he would wait for Sam to take the horses to water to tell him he knew about Oscar's saddle being meddled with .Oh Miss Sarah, Sam would never do such a wicked thing. He's the kindest of men.

'That was between half past twelve and one o'clock and, as I remember it, half hour past one by the time Miss Effie had settled her mother to rest and Master Jed was sitting by the river as usual and waiting for Sam. After two o'clock I ran through the passage to warn Sam. I called to Higgins from the yard doorway but he said Sam was gone so I started toward the bank when I saw Mistress Grimshaw come past west side of the maze. I hid in the north end until her back was turned then I ran into the cloakroom through the servants' door and back to the kitchen to my duties.'

Sarah Hunt wondered how Mary Ann could be so sure of times, when she was usually very vague on details. She needed to be certain of where everyone was that afternoon.

'Who was in the kitchen when you got back,' she persisted?

'Why nobody Miss Sarah, we all knows cook has her rest before preparing the evening meal or I never could've slipped down to stables.'

'Is there nobody that can vouch for how long you were gone then?'

A sullen 'No' came back from the girl moving towards the door. 'We all 'as our secrets Miss Sarah. Now I must go and set the table. We have a guest tonight,' and off she stalked.

Elfrida Grimshaw had left a blue velvet dress in her mother's sitting room for Sarah to stitch on a lace collar. She would work whilst she waited for Gerald Grimshaw. Crossing the floor, Sarah tapped upon the door from habit and waited to hear a voice bid her enter.

Victoria Grimshaw sat by the window overlooking the distant downs. Her thoughts disturbed by Sarah's tap, her look showed her annoyance, she sharply addressed the maid.

'Yes Hunt, what is it? You know I rest in the afternoon.'

Her face was drawn and tired. Shadows filled wells beneath the sharp eyes, and her gown fell loosely about her body where it had lost weight.

What else ails her past her grief, wondered Sarah? Heaven forbid that the vibrant woman who visited my mother and offered me security, should give the Master cause for more despair. 'I beg your pardon Mistress but it is getting late in the day and I thought you might have gone to your room. I came to fetch Miss Elfie's dress to stitch whilst I wait upon the Master with some good news. I intended to tell you when I came up to help you change for dinner. The artefacts have been found.' Her words were met with an abstracted sigh.

'Ah yes, the figurines; he will be much pleased to hear your news. Sit here and do your sewing Hunt, until he comes.' So saying Victoria turned again to the window with another deep sigh, her head drooped to rest upon her stubby hand.

Sarah sat behind her mistress to ply her needle. She watched Victoria's free hand clench and unclench on the padded arm of the chair but knew better than to disturb her fiery employer who was known to use strong language on occasion. No doubt a legacy from her travels with her former husband, the sea captain. Despite the ease of her present lifestyle that hand still expressed the solid capability of a woman used to fending for herself amidst the loneliness of moody oceans

Restless, Victoria rose and moved to the window to look at the gathering clouds then giving a little moan pressed her forehead against the pane to seek relief from the cool glass. Sarah laid aside her sewing and went to stand beside her mistress.

'May I fetch some lavender vinegar for your head milady?'

'No thank you Hunt but a little light massage of my forehead might help.' She sat for Sarah's deft fingers to smooth the tension from between her brows and ease the older woman's shoulders to relax.

Hands at rest in her lap Victoria watched the cloudscape beyond the window build up into a picture. She saw a grey sea where a towering fortress and a gold edged stencil of domes traced the skyline of land on the horizon. A small vessel foamed to one of its ports, a merchant ship plying trade between Tilbury and Egypt.

She heard voices talk of bollard and halyard, of topsail and mainsail falling easily upon her ears. In days gone by she shared the mystery and excitement of the voyage. Sometimes they sailed to St Lazaire to take on barrels of wine before battling the tumultuous gut wrenching Bay of Biscay, then through the Straits of Gibraltar before moving up the Spanish coast to Marseilles. Great ripe cheeses replaced the wine in the hold at Naples before entering the Straits of Messina to cross the Mediterranean and reach Alexandria.

What a free and peaceful mind dwelt in her body then. A sturdy body, fit from its share of keeping her husband's vessel in trim and on course. Then death came into her life .He was taken gravely ill with a fever carried on a miasma drifting around the narrow souks in Cairo, and was buried in Egypt.

Her mind returned to the present and the desire festering in her breast. Fierce protection of her daughters' futures fanned a passion to see them well wed and financially safe. She had made calls on the Cranston family, further down the valley. Their son of twenty years was studying at law, and to Victoria's knowledge, unattached.

However, the shadow of Jed's death had fallen far and wide and her visits were yet to be returned by the wealthy farmer and his spouse. No callers came to The Malderns, and invitations were begged off for one reason after another.

For now she waited upon the vicar's company at her table, for news of the neighbourhood. She had become a social outcast, with her planning baulked and the freedom to visit at will restricted within the confining limits of The Malderns.

As she revived under the ministrations of Sarah's hands, her mind quickened anew with her predicament. She must find a way. She rose impatiently, walking to and fro before sweeping out of the room.

'I shall not require you this evening Hunt. You may wait here on the Master if you wish.'

Sarah picked up the sewing and waited with the door ajar.

The sewing completed, Sarah folded the dress to take to Miss Effie's closet. She had worn the same dress on the day of Jed's drowning.

As Sarah's mind wandered back to that afternoon she jolted upright in her chair with knowledge she must carry to her grave. Jed could not have taken his life.

Gerald's measured footsteps sounded in the passage. He would give her a fair hearing over the artefacts. If he was aware of the social change in the family's life it had not changed the equanimity which ruled his every decision.

Chapter 6: Truth

LIFE at The Malderns ebbed to a stagnant pool of isolation. The rejoicing over the marriage of Effie's sister soon gave way to the habitual concern for her mother's health.

This day a hush fell over the household as the Squire sat slumped in his chair in the study, sleeping deeply.

Muted sounds came from the kitchen as if pots were being laid down quietly. The kitchen door opened and cook came out importantly carrying a small tray of refreshments. She wheezed up the stairway and tapped softly on Mistress Grimshaw's bedroom door.

An older Effie opened the door, hair braided and soberly dressed. She took the tray with a smile.

'How is my father Mrs Mossop? Has he taken refreshment today for he was up all the night long?

'Squire's sleeping Miss Effie but we will take care of him. Now take a little warmed wine for yourself and try not to worry Miss Effie.'

Spinster Elfreda Grimshaw closed the door and turned to face Sarah Hunt sitting by her mother's bedside.

The older woman had an air of authority which Elfreda deferred to out of habit. Victoria had long since handed over her responsibilities to Sarah as she sank into a steady decline after Jed's death. She used to stand hour after hour by the window looking across to the downs, taking less and less interest in her duties as Squire's wife.

Now, from her high wide bed, she spoke into the quiet of the room, riveting the attention of her attendants.

'Pray I will be forgiven as I have beseeched my Maker these past years. Your pleas may still reach His ear when I am gone. There was murder in my heart that terrible day Hunt and but for your coming I would have faced trial for his killing. We have spoken not one word since then and I have feared to ask you if I killed Jed? I cannot die without knowing. I found him floating face down, motionless. I dropped to my knees. Suddenly his fingers came over a clump of reeds and clutched the scream in my throat. His head lifted and terrified, I was looking into his triumphant face and eyes. He laughed as he flung the water from his hair.

"I've news for thee, lady. This day I have made Effie mine, body and soul. We needs must wed. The inheritance shall be safe in our hands, in my name as the male heir. Now be so good as to help me up lady, for I am weak from my exertions and the bank evades me."

'I leant over until our fingertips touched then I knocked his aside, and that smiling face was pushed below the green surface with all the strength of a mother's vengeance in my hands. I watched the frantic bubbles float to the surface and his smile fly with his spirit. Then there was only the race of the river towards the weir and the willow weeping. Hands pulled me back and you know the rest Sarah. '

Her hands plucked the sheet at the bidding of an unquiet mind as her eyes closed against the answer she feared.

'No Mama,' began Elfreda but Sarah forestalled her.

'Be at peace Ma'am for I saw Jed move after you left. You sinned in thought not deed. It is I who carry guilt for shunning his outreached hand and returning here. I was sure he could get up the bank unaided. I also tortured myself with doubt and spent much time trying to solve the manner of his death.' She laid a hand on the restless fingers of her mistress.

'I believe at least one other visited the river bank that day and I have waited all this time for them to clear their conscience. I kept silent to protect you Mistress and our dear Master from further grief.'

'Light some candles. It grows dark,' whispered Victoria.

Elfreda rose to do her mother's bidding, setting a candlestick near the bedhead. She remained standing there as she gently stroked her mother's hair. She looked very different from the headstrong girl Sarah remembered. Candlelight lit her face and the tremor of her lips as she spoke.

'Oh had I known you were so beset I would have spoken long ago,' she murmured. 'It was I who saw him last. After you left me Sarah, I dressed and rushed to the river bank. I wanted to tell Jed I loved him body and soul and would stand by him whatever the consequences.

'I couldn't see him at first and thought he had gone, until I saw him floating by the bank where the river foams into the race. I ran to him and knelt to touch his hand for his face was turned from me. Somehow I lost my balance and pushed against him instead. His grip in the weeds loosened and he floated out to the middle of the river where the race was strong. He struggled so, as he was borne downstream, then he lifted his head and saw me.' Elfreda buried her face in her hands

'I shall never forget his look of betrayal,' she sobbed. 'Had I stopped our passion earlier he would still live, but I wanted him and he knew it. I have made a vow never to satisfy my desires again as a penance.'

'Hush Elfreda, hush,' warned Sarah, 'your dear mother can hear you.'

'Give me your hand child,' whispered Victoria. 'We are all to blame and we are all innocent. How did you know this Hunt?'

'I remembered, sometime later Madam, that the right sleeve of Effie's blue dress was wet through when I led her from the window seat to rest before the music master's arrival. Her old gown was in the laundry by then.'

'You came upon me but a moment after I reached my room Sarah. There was no time to change again. You made no mention of my sleeve and I remained silent for which I pray forgiveness from Mama and you.'

'So near to Eternity I feel an endless ocean of warmth and forgiveness, breathed Victoria. 'I go home to wider seas than I ever sailed. Embark on your voyage with destiny again Effie. Steer a straight course and let every ripple you make, flow with compassion into the current of life's tides.'

Her breath became laboured with her effort. Sarah rose quickly to fetch the Squire.

Victoria's hold slackened. Elfrida felt the coldness of death slip through the hand above hers lying on the counterpane.

Gerald Grimshaw hurried through the door moving quickly towards his wife. Effie, her heart beating fast with the guilt of her deceit, backed into a corner, eyes downcast.

The candle flame cast Gerald Grimhaw's shadow across the room. It followed her into the corner and swallowed her.

The ending.

THE THREE LOVES TRILOGY

THE LOOTERS

JO MARTINEZ

The Looters

a novel

Jo Martinez

The Three Loves Trilogy

Dear Reader

Those who have read this far may recognize some of the characters in this book. Their individualities have resurfaced from two hundred years ago to continue the storyline of reincarnation, karma and the healing power of unconditional love. Like a bracelet in a jewel box, each charm reveals its tale within humanity's epic. Legend leads to the mystery of creation and creator. We are the tale, the legend the saga. We live the mystery. Some of your story is mine and you experienced, my experience. The creative energy of life is chaotic, unpredictable and has no timeline, but if we go with the flow, we make harbour. I invite you to share the passion, greed, ambition, success and failure of Jed the gypsy and his companions, reincarnated in the new age of post-World War Two.

Notices

Death notices
The County Gazette 1809

Jed Grimshaw son of Squire Grimshaw

With deep sorrow laid to rest after a tragic accident on the family property.

1923

The soul of Jed Grimshaw the gypsy slid out of Edith Rook's body. The unmarried mother christened her baby Jude on account of her lover's betrayal.

Registry of births

Boy - mother Emma Rook- father unknown

Prologue

Jude

HIS foot beat a restless tattoo, his ears closed against the gossip from flavour sated tongues around him. Blind to the frescoes on the restaurant walls, he gazed broodingly towards blank wall. It blurred through years rolling backwards as he slipped through to a scene from the past, a small boy standing in a country lane.

Yesterday's snow, grey iced the sideways. A finger of sun brushed through grey cloud veiled sky, painting a patch of rose light around him. He gazed at the ground then raised his foot and crunched it into the fresh snowfall. He slowly withdrew it, to look at the impression.

"That's me" he murmured, "that's Jude Rook."

The warning squeak of an unoiled bicycle roused him from his reverie. He looked up to see a large shapeless bottom, slopping from side to side of the saddle snuggled between fat laden thighs. How he hated his thick necked, beady eyed tormentor.

That morning he had choked on her half-eaten sausage roll, she patronizingly called him out to finish, in front of the whole class. Hunger had struggled with humiliation and fear of her authority, as he forced her leftover food down before thirty pairs of mocking eyes.

Later, he had scampered out with all the others for dinner break. then ran down a narrow alley towards the market place. The Square was crowded with stalls, animals and people. There were crates of clucking chickens, big flat scoops of fluffy yellow chicks, and mountains of eggs, fruit and market produce. The weekly bargaining between townsman and countryman was in full swing.

In a small space, encircled by his audience, the escapologist finished his performance. Chains flailing round his body; mouth grimacing in his rolling head, and body convulsed, his eyes remained cool and intent, as the last chain rattled to the ground. Then he started round, cap in hand for a few coins to reward his efforts, as two gypsies took his place.

A lithe dark-skinned man flourished and cracked a whip above his head. The woman, pert and raven haired with arched back and firm calves, tensed her body for the whip's caress. The crowd watched, finger to mouth, waiting. Her eyes defied him as his arm drew back and the lash rippled out towards her bare shoulders.

Time stood still as all eyes followed its path. In rhythm with the whip Jude's hand snaked out to the nearest nest where it curled around two eggs and smuggled them to his pocket. Then he was up and away through the market, as a fresh burst of tongues struck new bargains.

Earlier that day, he had chopped the wood and lit the kitchen stove; then stood on tiptoe to feel along the high shelf of the dresser, his fingers searching for a depleted stock of coins. Put there each week, the housekeeping money would be replenished in two days' time. The seeking fingers found a coin, a farthing. He slipped it into his pocket.

On the way to school, he stopped by the bakery for a farthing's worth of yesterday's lardy cakes. Clutching the greasy bag, he hurried past stall holders setting out their goods, coming to a halt in a narrow, walled twittern leading out of the square. Sheltering against a wall he opened the bag, slowly savouring the spicy scent within. He drew one out. It weighed heavily in his hand as he licked the sugar icing, coating the top, then he ate two dripping rich lardy cakes in short order before moving on to school.

Now, making his way across the square, towards the high street, his small hands lifted a little of this and that into his pockets. They were comfortably full by the time he broke out of the square and crossed the road to enter a dark narrow alley.

Spread Eagle Terrace, where the sparrows jostled for space, was a row of four tiny hovels, sheltering big families. He hesitated as he approached the last dwelling where he could hear the clamour of his half brothers and sisters, already seated around the kitchen table. The smell of food quickened his steps. He put his hand to the door. Soon the warmth of the kitchen fire would run in waves over his face and hands. He would wait for his pilfering to be praised as he warmed his feet by the deep red glow in the hearth.

The door sucked inwards then blew back. A large red hand poked from the slit like a pointing tongue. It dropped a ticket down to the step then slid back into the warmth behind the door as the latch clicked shut.

In slow motion, the boy bent down and laid the gleanings of his pilfering on the cold step. Disappointment, like a heavy mantle, clothed his face and frame as he drooped there, then he was up with a spurt, a sharp turn and running, running out of the alley back through the market place.

He passed from the abundance of the market to a stop down a narrow lane, pulling up short at the exit before a drab brick building. Below a large black board proclaiming it the Salvation Army Soup Kitchen, a line of men, close hugged the wall for shelter from the cold.

The boy joined the indigent group shuffling towards its open door, at the end of the line. He stood behind a tall thin bag of bones man whose sparse flesh lay hidden deep within a welter of old overcoats and torn jerseys. A mottled grey and white face peered above a long white beard, sparkling with jewels of frosted moisture. A bright red toe inched out between the sole and the upper of a worn boot, swathed in sacking. Red, blue veined hands clutched the corner tail of his topcoat to enfold their chilblained misery.

The two, man and boy, entered the thick steamy warmth of a bare hall, lined with trestle tables and wooden forms. Behind a table at the top corner of the hall, a thickset man wielded a large ladle over a big steaming cauldron of soup. He rapidly dispensed the brew with one hand and handed out a piece of stale grey bread with the other.

In contrast to the rest, he was well attired in sober black worsted suiting, his trouser bottoms tucked into waterproof boots. On his head he wore a large astrakhan hat, rising high above a sour looking face. Employed by the local council to give succour to those without it, his small black eyes were devoid of charity as they darted around the crowded benches. His job was carried out stolidly, marking out for future reckoning, those who tried for a second helping and those who dropped a crumb on the dingy wooden floor boards.

The boy handed in the ticket for his soup, took his bowl and hurried to the table where the old man sat. Even so short an acquaintance as their queuing together had forged sufficient bond to share their fare. They spoke no words as they focused on the steaming hot liquid sliding down into their stomachs and the coursing warmth easing the pain of dereliction.

Dipping the bread into his soup, Jude watched the thin trickle of moisture, dripping from the old man's nose, join the glistening droplets melting on his beard. The old tramp glanced up.

"Orlright then sonny? Sticks t' ye ribs eh?" A nod and a wink passed between them as the boy downed the last drop of soup and then pulled his coat collar tight to hoard some warmth against the cold.

Outside the snow was thickening. Everywhere, blinding whiteness sucked at his ankles.......

At the Hungry Monk Jude, felt the pressure of a foot against his ankle, and returned from his past to see the woman, sitting across from him, pouring coffee. He drank his cup in haste then stood to help her with her coat.

"Are you ready?" Outside the inn, they walked to where her car was parked.

"I'll see you tomorrow then. Don't be late because there is a lot to get through."

Linnet

THE waitress set down the silver tray. The silver coffee service reflected delicate porcelain cups in its candle lit curves. Lyn looked across to where Jude sat deep in thought and decided not to disturb him.

She layered cream over her spoon and watched the dark fragrant liquid eddy with pale creamy whirls as she stirred the cup. Her hand was small and slender and used with a dancer's grace. Her eyes followed the glinting tip of the spoon. The circle of silver bound her mind in a spiral of time back to the nineteen thirties. The fingers changed, became knotted and veined with age, the bone structure twisted with arthritis.

She watched them feed some chopped onions with a golden blob of melting butter, until the herb softened and turned translucent. Bay leaf, thyme and peppercorns released their fragrances. Slowly the flour was blended in and then the cream until a velvet lake filled the saucepan. The sauce was a sensuous and creative part of preparing the meal. The hands moved slowly and painfully, lifting the pan of creamy, parsley flecked liquid to one side of the kitchen table where a large cooked cod's head lay cooling and ready for the white flesh to be lifted from its bones.

Three stood around the table, Linnet, her mother, and her grandmother. The two women bent to their task as if to a ritual, whilst the golden-haired granddaughter stood by to watch and learn. There was much to learn at seventeen. Snow-white hair touched the dark brown wing sweeping back from her mother's head. The soft voice of her grandmother spoke.

"He'll not know the difference from stewed eels. Plenty of mashed potato Mercy and it's a meal fit for a king." The heads nodded, then the white head made to depart to a house across the way where, in a tiny garden, an old cherry tree blossomed above a carpenter's shed. The dark head tidied away, and laid the table for the family meal, in readiness for father coming home. As she left the room, the girl heard her grandmother predict: "She will find a decent husband in the bank. This war has given the bright ones a start."

"No, she will be stopping at home to take care of me." her mother replied decidedly. The household was expectant and content. Another wage would be coming in and the first child path set on her path.

Linnet went to her room to touch and hold, once more, against her petite figure, the new clothes bought the week before. Tomorrow she would wear them, when she reported for her first job in the head office of one of the big London banks. As times edged toward the forties, a change for the better had emerged. Hunger and poverty, the spectres of the Depression, had ruled the past decade of the thirties, until the unassuaged hunger marchers from the North rebelled to seek justice in the South. Frugal housekeeping measures, supplemented by scholarships, allowed a better education for brighter children. Jobs were easier to come by. Lyn studied long hours for the certificates that earned her that first post.

The family home stood in Queen's Road, a quiet street, where her grandparents lived across from them. They welcomed her at weekends to encourage her studies.

The houses were in a large square grid. Two sides of the square were quiet enough for the child, Lyn, and her friends to play in, between school and bedtime. Two broad roads, busy with traffic, completed the square, meeting at a point opposite the new underground tube station. In summer the Tube opened up the countryside for picnics, gathering blackberries, and in the winter the exciting discoveries of London town's museums and historic buildings

From Queen's Road, smaller roads led to a path which bordered the railway line. The Path began in a rich district and finished in a poor one. It was long and narrow and imbued with the curious smells of human traffic and dog droppings. Over all, hung the rich smoky smell of the trains thundering into the little station, before puffing off under The Bridge which everyone walked across, to do the weekly shopping. From the tips of the topmost branches of the tall tree in her grandparent's garden, Linnet watched the comings and goings of the shoppers.

It was always quiet in the garden. A wooden fence bordered it on one side, and the back wall of the church warden's house ran across the bottom. It lay somnambulant beneath a high summer sun, part of a patchwork quilt of colour, nestling in the square, inside the slate roofed, red brick houses.

To the child sitting high in the boughs of the cherry tree, the gardens seemed big and exciting. Pots of flowers hung from Nana's fence, and filled a wooden stand next to the mangle, outside the scullery door. A pot pourri of dried laburnum and cherry blossom lay around the base of two trees and dotted the tiny patch of lawn beneath. The heady fragrance of lilac drifted up through the branches, blending with the sweet taste of the black cherry juice staining her mouth.

The tree spread its branches over the low roof of a shed. Through the open door fresh curled shavings of wood tumbled away from a soft swishing plane, sliding to the slow rhythm of her grandfather's hands.

Later she would slide down the tree and gather the pungent spicy smelling wood shavings into a basket, for lighting the copper in the scullery, where the weekly wash was boiled clean. When the plane fell silent, she could hear the rushing sound of the burner under the pot of glue. It had a strange sweet smell which beguiled her grandfather's wrinkled nose.

Her world was full of scents, colours and touch. Granddad's clothes carried the essence of the carpenter's shed, mingling with the aroma of the Boar's Head tobacco he carried in a leather pouch, in his right-hand pocket. There was another scent which was just granddad when she kissed him and smelled the shaving soap he had scraped off with the long-handled razor. He shaved standing in front of the kitchen mirror above the mantel piece where her Nana's ornaments stood in a row.

Linnet lowered the basket hanging from a long rope, slung high in the tree.

Scrambling down, she pushed a swing into a lazy sway on its strong lateral bough, then ran into the shed and stood by a tall thin framed old man at his workbench. They were close friends. He was the only grown up who had understood why she had given the gypsy woman some of her best dresses. The tinker had asked for clothes for her children.

The workbench was a huge block of heavy grey wood, scored with many calculations amidst the smooth whorls and knots she loved to trace with her fingers. She trailed her feet in the bed of shavings in companionable silence. Talk was reserved for such times as when she sat by his side in the tiny sitting room, laboriously practicing the long flowing copper plate he wrote with such ease. He would sit doing his daily crossword puzzle, dictionary by his side, occasionally asking her if she knew the meaning of a word.

Her grandmother sometimes sat with them, knitting endless supplies of baby clothes, between visits to the kitchen. Wherever she was, the tranquillity of her love for the family floated through the little home and filled it with comfort. Linnet loved them, and listened intently to their wisdom, when she visited.

Leaving the shed, the child sat swinging to and fro, waiting for Nana to come down the path carrying a wrapped bundle, which she placed in the basket with some school books, before gathering the little girl to her.

"Be off with you to your tree top, and don't forget to learn the poem I have marked for you" Linnet imprinted a grateful kiss in the warmth of her grandmother's neck, moistly awakening the clean scent of the Wright's Coal Tar soap she always used.

Her grandmother's hands held a secret store of mysterious aromas. Sometimes it was the sharp whiff of iodine applied gently to bruised and scratched knees. At other times, they smelled of the fresh lavender she sprinkled among knitted baby shawls and bonnets. On Fridays when the furniture was polished, her hands told of their toil with the aromatic scent of cedar.

Leaving her grandparents to their meal beneath the tree, she climbed up well-worn footholds. As she disappeared into the thick leaved branches, a little scattering of dark black cherries fell below. She rested where two thick arms met in a sturdy join and opened the white linen bundle of food. From where she sat dreaming in communion with the two below, she could see the long line of freshly washed sheets and towels on the clothesline next door.

Jackie washed the household linen for most of the street. She stood taking in the dry linen for ironing, her arms well-muscled from hours of mangling heavy wet clothes through huge wooden rollers. She was rosy cheeked and always laughing over the size of the wash, for it brought in money.

The distant sound of an approaching steam engine jogged the child to put the last crumb of food in her mouth and scramble higher into the tree, to watch the gap in the far corner of the square of houses. On eye level now with the rooftops, the gardens spread out below her, like so many coloured handkerchiefs.

The track echoed the noise swelling above as the train flickered past like scenes in a moving picture book and wheezed to a halt at the station nearby. As she waited for the warning sound of the hoot, heralding its departure, her eyes wandered among the chimney tops.

There was Mrs Monk's chimney. She made the large round custard pies for everybody. Linnet went to fetch the family treat on Saturday, before going to dancing class.

There was her godmother's chimney, she who helped make the dresses for the dancing class concert. When she visited Aunt Daisy and her husband, they heaped her with gooseberries and fresh vegetables, grown in the rambling garden behind their house.

The train hooted, hissed and started up again. She listened to the rhythm of the engine fade away into the distance, and then settled back into the crook of the tree. The three of them dreamed again, the old of what they had meant to do, the child of all she hoped to do.

The peace of English gardens was soon to be shattered with the whine of bombs and the menacing drone of planes in 1939 when Britain declared war with Germany. Memories of those quiet gardens gave hope to many an enlisted man in the years to come.

During the "phoney war" period, Linnet evacuated with the bank to the north, returning home to be with her family during the blitz. Later, she joined the British forces as a nurse and was posted to Europe soon after D-Day. "Specialling" a burned or crippled man, she would slip back into a garden where childhood memories blocked out the shock of war's horrors.

Back in the Hungry Monk, the coffee had cooled. Linnet collected herself and looked at the man she who had shortened her name to Lyn. From habit she gently nudged his ankle until he roused and drained his cup. She finished her coffee and stood for him to help her on with her coat.

Chapter 1: 1947 - the Midlands

LINNET Young walked into the bustle of King's Cross station dragging a small black tin trunk by its side handle. All around her signs of the recent war lingered, from the black painted windows in the waiting rooms, to a lack of porters. A current of excitement hummed through the travellers waiting for the Flying Scot to arrive for its journey to the North,

Finding a trolley, she lugged on her trunk, dodged round empty, penny a bar, chocolate machines and loaded carts, coming to a halt next to a woman who smiled her sympathy as Linnet trundled up.

"The luggage compartment should stop about here. I'll help you in with your trunk if you like," she offered. "How far are you going? I get out at Hatfield."

"Thank you, I'm going to Newcastle-upon-Tyne for a refresher on nursing. I should have brought a suitcase, but I'm used to this old relic." The depletion Britain's work force seeded an eruption of training courses to fill technical and professional jobs. Linnet had turned down a teaching course.

"What service were you in, I was in the Wrens?" her companion asked, eying Linnet's attire speculatively.

"My mother had a bee in her bonnet about them. She was an evacuee children's mother and W.V.S. worker in the south of England after the Blitz. She saw too many girls arrive in the boat from the naval base "expecting" as she euphemistically termed "pregnant.""

"Yes, I'm afraid more than a few got "up the spout," Mavis Lake said ruefully.

Dressed in neat tweeds, she made a smart contrast with Linnet, who wore her old army trousers, renovated with a maroon dye bag, and a topcoat, transformed from her old army blanket, by a local tailor's magic.

The eleven fifteen, glorious in green and gold livery, emerged hissing and steaming from its lair in the shunting yards. The baggage truck stopped within yards and the trunk was soon stowed away. Linnet had lived out of it during the year in France and Germany, shortly after D-Day. White starched aprons were always packed flat on the base, then the blue grey nurse's dresses under the red lined navy cape. Last the grey mess dress and gabardine skirt and jacket worn with a white shirt. Navy blue knickers with elastic in the legs were usually stuffed down the side, along with black cotton stockings and the long liberty bodice with dangling suspenders. They moved around bases in battle dress which seldom got packed.

The two women moved through the third-class carriages until they found one free from torn upholstery and message marked walls. Money for repairs was still needed for the times when troops filled the carriages and corridors with bulging kit bags

"Hard to imagine that before the war, Britain had some of the smartest and fastest trains in Europe," observed Linnet.

"Now our rolling stock is run down, and tracks still harbour undiscovered bombs," replied Mavis. Settling for the two corner window seats each unpacked a paper carrier bag. "What have you got?'

"Fish paste today. I felt guilty asking for my ration book when Mum gave me these. The more books in a family the better the food goes around doesn't it?" Mavis Lake smiled.

"Look, I've got egg sandwiches, real ones not the powdered sort. Would you like to share? We get a few perks, living in the country."

With a sparkle in her eye, Linnet accepted the offer and they munched in friendly silence for a spell. As they neared her destination, Mavis went to the toilets, whilst Linnet waited in the corridor to keep an eye on their compartment. She watched Mavis walk back with a pronounced limp.

"I didn't notice you had hurt your leg. I wouldn't have let you help me hoist my trunk up," she apologised going to collect her companion's baggage as the train started its entry to the station.

"Oh! I'm used to it now. I was a prisoner of war after the fall of Singapore. I was in Intelligence but stupid enough to catch polio. Had to wait for somebody to clear some chickens out of an iron lung the Japs located, before I could move into it. I was lucky as you see." She held out her hand. It was firm and warm when Linnet shook it, before helping her down on to the platform. Earlier that day, she had kissed her parents goodbye, just as she had in 1939 at the start of hostilities and the phoney war. Then it had been to go North with one of the five major banks she worked for.

During the Blitz and its grim reality, she returned to the family, and a job where working days ended walking to transport home, through a thick blanket of choking yellow smog. Inside a blacked-out bus, eerie blue lights flickered over the faces of the ghostly figures who had felt their way, like her, along fence and wall to the bus stop.

The family meal was eaten in haste around Morrison's shelter; a large steel table almost filling the tiny kitchen. Not trusting it to sleep under, her mother insisted on using Anderson's shelter, dug into the bowels of the earth, in the garden. The shelter smelt strongly of the soil floor under the curved tin roof.

"'There are spiders in here Dad," the young ones protested.

"Bertie! Please come in here with us," her mother implored.

"Soon luv, soon, I'll see the next wave over. The bastards have already set fire south of us. I'll wait for Linnet to come home."

Linnet was on volunteer duty at the nearby Underground station where platforms were crowded with men, women and children. Many parents settled down to sleep on the hard surface once their children's eyes were closed. A group of foreign nationals clustered in the corner of the concourse at the foot of the deep escalators. Knitting stashed away, thermos flasks empty and cigarette ends carefully stowed for first light they also settled for the night. The slender Persian mother taught her how to use a circular knitting needle and the old Frenchman laughed at her schoolgirl French. Into their troubled sleep, a bomb whistled its way, hurling refugee friends down a bomb blasted pit of death.

Her father asked her to take the rest of the family to safety. She went, leaving her friends for ever.

The family travelled by a night train, beetling slowly to the South of England. Climbing down steep steps into sidings, somewhere in Cornwall, they waited for somebody, anybody, to discover them. A night linesman saw the little group and found them lodgings, where Mercy Young settled like a hen with chicks.

Linnet joined the local Red Cross where the capable Commandant drafted her into a Voluntary Aid Detachment, and she was the first of the family to join up in the services.

What a long time ago it seems thought Linnet as Hatfield station slid out of sight and she settled down for the long journey north. During the war she spent a short time at Hatfield on a posting, where military shared the grounds of a large mental hospital. She learnt good nursing skills and that Rose Cottage was not a convalescent retreat but, a Venereal Disease ward, for a confused Q.M.S found walking stark naked in the grounds.

Through the carriage window, snapshot views of people and places shot past to lull her senses into a dream state.

She was in another train. Stretchers and bodies covered a stale smelling corridor floor. Sick and wounded men, coming back from the front under morphine sedation, were being moved, with their broken bones and blackened skins, to waiting ambulances.

"Ere we go lad", said an orderly. "You'll be orlright now, won't "e nurse? Barft, powdered and fed in a blooming big orspital wiv the likes of this young lady to care for yer." Patter, patter, patter the voice went on, seeing his charges into another corridor filled with men waiting to return to Blighty.

"I've turned out of me feather bed for yer mate. Keep an eye out fer the ginger 'aired Sister. She's a terror for tidiness, but a saint when it comes to doing a dressing. Where did yer cop it? Left yer fancy bits intact eh?" A small movement of the hand acknowledged the banter of a comrade going home.

Linnet's dream state switched to a darkened hospital ward in the lonely hours between three and four o'clock. She sat at a small table, lit by a shaded light. Around her, shadows hovered over the sounds of men breathing and sobbing in their sleep. She yawned then stiffened to attention. Soft footed, Night Sister stood behind her, waiting for the report.

"Don't rest your head on your hand nurse. Sit up or you may fall asleep. How is the parachutist? Have you kept the temperature of the saline bath up? Is the young boy with Addison's still with us?" The tiny little Sister's head was only a few inches above Linnet's as she scanned the partially written report on the desk.

Used to her approach, Linnet forced her lids wider apart as she stood to greet her superior, and inform her that the young corporal, with the seeds of cancer in him before he left home shores, was no longer with them.

"He died at two this morning Sister."

They walked the ward from bed to bed, ending with one nearest the desk. It had a strange contraption slung between the side rails. A rubber and canvas hammock with sealed ends hung motionless with the weight of water in it. Hot water bottles lined the cot sides and a thermometer registered the water temperature. Inside floated the inert body of a man. Shallow breathing whispered from a nose and mouth barely surfacing the saline fluid. Long ribbons of flesh floated languidly from his body. The paratrooper had been torched by high arcs of flame as he made his drop over unknown territory.

"Has he regained consciousness at all?" the Sister asked.

"No and we have no identification because his clothes and identity disc were burnt black to his skin. He won't survive, will he?"

"No. Good night nurse," and she left shortly before dawn brought the ward to life with militant precision. The endless rows of beds were made with bed ends in strict alignment and all castors facing inwards at right angles. Any deviation risked the contempt of the Night Supervisor, to whom war was no excuse.

She came back to the present, as the carriage gently nudged its coupling, when the train stopped at East Grinstead station. She stretched and swallowed the dryness in her mouth. Memories of war-time France and markets full of summer fruit surfaced in the sudden desire for a juicy peach.

Arriving at Chester-Le-Street station in the north, she made running repairs to her face and hands in time to alight at Newcastle-upon-Tyne. Through the glass-domed station roof, the sky loured down a cold welcome. She was surrounded by strange smells and sounds. She felt the difference, the toughness here. Folk pushed by her trolley, making comments in broad vowed tones, as they glanced at her tin trunk.

She walked out from under the handsome station portico into a square. Her nostrils flinched from the acrid assault of coal dust and smoke ballooning from tall furnaces.

A drunken man staggered towards her from a nearby pub. He hurled an oath at a moth-eaten cur as he kicked it from under his feet and made his way past Linnet. The stench of his drink sodden breath and soiled clothes choked her. A paper bag woman fluttered behind him, her succour, the bottle she clutched to her breast, her home, the bundle trailing her feet. At his snarled summons, she ran like a much-whipped whelp.

"Well, well, shades of London Town," murmured Linnet, signalling a taxi and clambering in as the quickest way to move out of harm's way. Through the window, she saw back-to-back hovels behind the railway yard. They were covered in sooty grime from the coal mines, the life support of the men working them.

"I reckon there must be a lot of tuberculises around here, not to mention cancer," she said to the driver. "Whew! There'll be plenty to do."

Crossing the River Tyne where small ships lay, ready loaded for Italy, Germany and the South, the taxi climbed clear of the town. The driver turned in through two large metal gates, at the end of a lane of clean brick houses, bordered by a verge of sparse green grass.

"Here you are Miss. Where shall I drop you?" Where indeed, the site was filled with Nissan huts? As she stood pondering where to deposit her trunk, a tall young woman came out of one and waved them forward. She waited for Linnet to pay her fare then motioned her to follow.

"We women are in those two," pointing to two long huts side by side, "The men are at the other end of camp. They came to help set up the beds two days ago. Here is ours." She spoke with the same crisp tones as Linnet, following her like a duckling, as they entered the hut.

Around her were eight beds each side, partitioned off by narrow wooden screens. With a locker apiece, this was now home in a freezing cold metal hut in some bleak forsaken place on a hill. The taxi driver had predicted snow at any minute.

Before going to France, she had spent three days in Aldershot barracks, learning to march and dubbin her boots. The battle dress trousers she wore now were issued there, along with tin hat, army boots and ground sheet. The three-day indoctrination ended each night in a little cubicle of her own. What a luxury that was.

"You are the last to arrive," said Dorothy Swan, "Young, isn't it?" At Lyn's nod, she ticked the list in her hand

"Hurry up, they are briefing us shortly. Do you want to change?" A decidedly negative shake of Linnet's head invited a knowing, "It's going to get worse. Come and eat, it will warm you up. I think there is some sort of social do, to get to know each other, after the evening meal

Behind the windows in the men's hut, Jude Rook stood with a mixed group of ex-servicemen.

Leaving home, the day before, Jude was a hero to siblings who told their friends, "Our Jude was sailor, he's going to be a nurse."

At the outbreak of war, the day he enlisted began in the usual way. He had lit the stove, fed the chickens then waited for the family to come downstairs. Each heavy tread of his father's footsteps strengthened his resolve.

"Why aren't you gone to work? Got the sack eh", growled Jo Pratt entering the kitchen with his wife behind him.

"No. I haven't been sacked but I'm leaving. I told Tom, I'm enlisting. He's given me an hour off. Can I have my birth certificate please?"

His mother drew a sharp breath.

"Do you really need it now Jude", she asked anxiously?

"Yes Mum. They need proof I am who I say I am, Jude Pratt."

She turned and made a slow-footed journey to her bedroom, before coming to stand, head lowered, in front of Jude. She handed him a tight rolled up certificate. Jo's face was expressionless except for strange gleam in his pale blue eyes.

"Take it and get out. Be off with you", he ordered, a smirk smeared across his face.

Thrusting the roll into his pocket, Jude headed for the enlistment office passing a smiling girl, newly joined up. Inside the sparsely furnished room a man sat at a table piled with forms. A brief smile greeted his arrival and after the preliminaries were finished, he asked for Jude's birth certificate

"Here it is Sir," handing over the rolled paperwork for scrutiny. The man studied it for a moment then levelled his gaze at Jude.

"Jude Pratt. Is that right?"

"Yes sir."

"Then why does this say you are Jude Rook," handing back the certificate?

"I don't know Sir, but I'll be back." He cycled furiously back to the estate, his thoughts a jumble of doubt and suspicion He remembered beatings with the buckle end of his father's belt and that regular church goer's pious hand handing him soup kitchen tickets. Edie Pratt was alone when he entered the house and put his arm round her shoulders.

"What's up Mum, what's this about?"

Her eyes were full of pleading and past pain when she looked up at him.

"I worked for two sisters running a boarding house up North. He was a good man who said he would marry me and so…. Then you came along. Well son he was already married. The sisters stopped me from taking my life and helped me through until I could come back home with you. Jo offered to marry me. Your father sent money when he could. It was the money we sent you to collect from the office in town." She fell silent, such a tiny creature with so much heart and endurance. Jude cradled her and said softly,

"Mum I'm proud to have your name and never to use his again. I'll be back."

He enlisted as Jude Rook and was posted to Devonport

On his return after demob she welcomed him back happy, he was under her roof again albeit with the grudging acceptance of his stepfather.

Jude turned to the group in the northern Nissan hut as they watched the Lyn and Dorothy Swan walk across the square to the main building.

"Two more bits of skirt going across to the briefing, I reckon they must be the last. Let's go," he said. Feeling safe in numbers, the entire male section moved to join the ladies in the lecture room.

Thirty students assembled in front of a round butterball of Irish authority, and her assistant tutor, a spare fresh-faced woman of quieter demeanour. Both wore long grey dresses and white frilly muslin caps, with long ribbons tied below the chin.

At the end of a long list of instructions, trainee Young piped up with a question, turning all eyes upon her.

"Sister, may we wear trousers to the lectures? I'm not yet used to the cold up here." The white bow fluttered indignantly between Sister's many chins. Her brogue thickened tartly.

"No nurse, you will wear uniform at all times. Late attendance to lectures will be noted in assessments and there is to be no visiting between the men and the women's huts. Now, we have arranged to partner you for the evening meal by playing the game of pairing names. Afterwards, there will be a dance until ten o'clock when you return to your quarters." She sailed off with her colleague in tow, and the passing shot, "Lights out at ten thirty."

Later that evening, Linnet drew Mouse in the pairing game. Her table partner was an airman, struggling to make conversation.

"I'm perished, I'm just going to get a woolly," she excused herself. "I won't be a tic."

When she returned, a new partner sat in the airman's seat.

"Oh! Sorry, I must have the wrong table," she murmured to the dark-haired man smiling at her. Replete with a hearty stew of mutton and dumplings, Jude reckoned he had fallen in clover. There were women a-plenty and three meals a day.

"No, you are at the right table, I exchanged cards with him to sit with you," Jude said, standing to pull out her chair. "See, I'm the Cat?" She gave him a second look; should she know him, his face seemed familiar? So many faces fluttered in the kaleidoscope of the war years. Sitting down with one more, ended in them chatting like old friends, against a background of popular music.

"Shall we dance," he invited, standing up? She was surprised to see he was only slightly taller than herself as drew her into a close embrace. His broad shoulders had misled her. Although light footed, she stumbled through some intricate steps in the small space cleared for dancing.

"Let me show you, Lyn isn't it," he offered. "I have a silver medal for ballroom dancing." By evening's end, they made a natural pair and his shortened version of her name became hers from then on.

Drifting off to sleep that night, Jude's handsome face hovered in her mind's eye. She blushed as she recaptured the close familiarity of his body. 'I hope there's another dance soon,' she thought. 'Yes, he reminds me of the boy who haunts my dreams since I decided to take this refresher course.'

The boy came to her again that night. A handsome boy of sixteen years or more seething with a dark fury that accentuated the gypsy traits in his face. Long-lashed eyes smouldered, dark with anger, above thin lips set in an obstinate line.

Behind him, in a room partially darkened from bright sunlight by rich curtaining, a middle-aged woman lay upon a chaise lounge, attended by two young girls. A servant applied a compress to her brow. The walls were lined with cabinets full of artefacts. The elegant furnishings were of the early nineteenth century, and the size of the room, with its high ornate ceilings, betokened that it was set in a large mansion where tall French windows, opened on to grassy parkland. An elderly man sat with clenched fists, at a handsome inlaid desk in front of them

The view from the windows looked on to cultivated gardens where men were working. In the background, climbing in gentle slopes to distant hills, ploughed fields and copses of oak and elm, bordered a small country estate.

The dream scene changed. By a river bank, a knot of men stood a few paces away from a body lying on its edge. The man and woman from the mansion were bent over the lifeless form. The dream always ended there.

The following day, work began in earnest with their allocation to hospitals in the area. Working together, for practical experience, on a Specials ward, Jude and Lyn's friendship ripened. Special wards in hospitals around Britain gave refuge to those with shattered, burn-mutilated faces. Agonizing months of bone and skin grafting were needed to bring hope to young men, defying the future.

Jude sat with her during the intense study course back at camp and his questions showed that he knew his subject well. Discussing some points of a recent lecture, he gave a dispirited shrug.

"I won't pass this course. My grammar isn't good enough for the written exams. You have the advantage of better schooling, Lyn." She sat, looking at him from the corner of an unyielding army issue settee. Slate grey eyes looked steadily into hers.

A neatly knotted tie lay against the blue shirt beneath his demob suit. Winter had brought out a pallor in his skin.

"I'll help you if you keep teaching me to dance," she offered. His lips parted in a wide smile. Soft green tints warmed his eyes then, his chin jutted forward, and its disarming dimple disappeared.

"Would you do that? Getting this certification means a lot to me. I'll work my damnedest to get it." Soon they were inseparable, he claiming all of her free time as they walked the campus or surrounding countryside, quizzing one another. They celebrated successes and comforted failures as they moved towards the first examination.

Tea dances in the nearby town brought light relief from the pressure at the weekends. They made a fine couple though he often left her to partner a better dancer, leaving Lyn to play wallflower. On the journey home they listened to hopes and aspirations as they shared their humble backgrounds.

When the Preliminary results came through. Jude sat surveying the gentle mêlée in front of the notice board, where Lyn clustered round it with a group of nurses, searching for their names. He watched some sigh with relief and some steal dejectedly to a quiet corner.

His thoughts were moody and tense with fears he would be among those packing their bags to leave at the weekend,

'Well the old man will have the last laugh when he watches the butcher's boy cycle off to his old job. He reckons me a bastard by name, bastard by nature and a ne'er do well to boot. I'm going to miss all of this, and her,' looking towards Lyn, edging her way nearer to the front of the group.

'Pity she's so tight arsed, her body feels good against mine when we dance.' Lyn always followed his steps gracefully, but that's as far as she went. 'Ah well! If I pass muster here, I'll soon be back with those who know all about pleasing me. life will be good. I'll show those bastards back home who I am,' he vowed silently.

One family had made him very welcome during a long posting to a South coast naval base. He returned their kindness with his cigarette ration and some smuggled rations. They trusted him to be alone with their only daughter, for, in times when men were in short supply, there was a tacit expectation of marriage. The same was expected by a girl in his hometown, and a lovely little Welsh girl at another base.

As Lyn came back with the results she was smiling.

"Congratulations Jude, you've done well," she beamed, sinking down beside him. She watched uncertainty mingle with his relief.

"You sure Lyn?" he asked going across to check his name among the passes, where she joined him.

"Now it's just hard work until the finals in three months' time." A fresh fear surfaced.

"Yes, the finals. Writing reports and simple arithmetic to change medications are going to be a nightmare for me," he prevaricated.

"We can work on that," she encouraged, smiling. For a moment he imagined the full red curves of those smiling lips enclosing him.

"Yes! We'll work together. Come hell or high water, I must get a pass. Come on, we need some fresh air. Let's walk a bit." He eased her out of the crowd into the country lane.

Holding hands, they walked in silence along the high ground above the city lights, each wrapped in their own thoughts.

'I had better start cooling things off, but she's so naïve and she's fallen for me like all the others,' decided Jude.

Memories of her mother's words 'Lyn will stay with me' echoed in her mind. She wanted a future with this handsome man she'd come to know and like. Their time was coming to an end. Soon she would never feel his arms around her, accept his kisses and brief caresses on the way home from a dance. Desire filled her soul to look into his eyes and listen to the soft warm voice for ever. 'Perhaps we won't marry but it feels good to be on his arm and who knows.' She was in new and exciting territory≥

"In three months' time, I shall never see you again, so, what will you do when you qualify Lyn?" The words were quietly spoken, with just the touch of regret that fitted Jude's intention of inching out of their relationship.

Jolted from her daydreaming, her feelings overruled, and a practical Lyn surfaced quickly.

"Oh, but we can see each other if you want. We could get married, get good jobs and save for a home of our own." A startled blush suffused her face, as she registered the audacious proposal fired by her dreaming. Eyes downcast, she waited for him to reply.

Caught off guard for once, Jude was out of his depth. From habit, he had notched one last lure on his line, to play the catch anew before casting it back into the flow He hadn't meant to hurt her, only fill in time until he returned to the South. Other girls had shrugged their shoulders and turned to fresh conquests with a, "Well it was good fun eh?" 'I didn't reckon on this, but things could happen with a working wife,' he calculated. 'Most girls were home birds expecting to settle down and start a family.'

"Did you mean what you just said Lyn?" he asked guardedly, after a silence which only served to increase Lyn's shame at her impulsive approach. She bobbed her head as he put an arm round her shoulders.

"Maybe we could then," a gentle squeeze, "I'd better write to Bluey and the girls."

Concerned, for pre-empting his right to propose Lyn looked up.

"Are you sure? I shouldn't have…"

"No. You are right," he cut in, "We will make a good team. I do Lyn,"

"Do what?" she queried.

"I do love you," he laughed.

"Oh, I do too," said a happy Lyn, thinking of the letter she would write to her mother.

That's how things happen after a war, when the hand of providence is behind many a union. Jude came to marry Lyn on his list of girls, a slip of the tongue so to speak.

To mark the occasion of that odd proposal, he gave her an opal and diamond ring and a china lamb. The lamb was symbolic, for despite his philandering ways, he had never known the fullness of a woman, promising himself to wait until his wedding. night to enter into full carnal knowledge. He was innocent of the act.

They had a picture wedding. The church by the river was old and its vicar welcomed them, duly posting the banns the following three weeks. She wore a borrowed wedding dress of pre-war elegance. Three bridesmaids wore gowns in peach. Jude turned her hand and kissed the palm with the port wine stain before he slipped the ring on her finger.

At the reception, the warm wishes of friends made up for startled family members, unable to afford or make the journey. The rotund, apple cheeked Irish tutor raised her eyebrows knowingly, whilst her grey haired elder shook her head in worried wonder, at the pace of young lives. No less confused was Jude, who had not meant his life to take this turn at all, at all.

Their wedding night, in a modest hotel in a Hampshire forest, confirmed Lyn's virginity, and Jude's fears for his creature comforts. Aroused by the shapely legs rising to a small neat bottom, he pulled her into bed before her nightdress slid over breasts more suited to a gymslip. Like a traditional Victorian, she lay as stiff as a board with fright, dismayed by the demands he made of her body. Jude's inexperience did little to help his clumsy act of force.

"I will do better next time" Lyn whispered, ashamed of her ignorance.

"I will teach you to dance with me in bed ducks. You'll soon learn," he soothed her thinking, 'Well if that's what it's all about I know better ways.'

Before returning north Jude took her to meet his folks. They were a large close-knit family of four step sisters and two step brothers. Grouped about the coal fire stove in the kitchen, they took good stock of Lyn before eyeing their tiny mother.

"Jude's never had a girl like this before. Reckon she don't know him yet, poor soul."

His stepfather said nothing, but his eyes spoke volumes.

Jude had stayed with Lyn's family during a half term break to allow them to continue studies together. Her mother had not been impressed.

"We can see my family again when we are working in one of the teaching hospitals London. There will be more opportunity for promotion there."

"Hey, not so fast Ducks. I hate London, any city for that matter. Let's start off here shall we," Jude answered.

She gave in easily, with her own proposal, for she was already in love with the beauty of the Cotswolds.

"If we come here, we must find somewhere to live. We can't live with your family, there's no room. Look, why don't we buy a caravan until new private building is allowed? Rebuilding the war damage will take ages."

"Good idea, there is a firm in the town. Let's see what they can offer us."

The manager arranged for a caravan on hire purchase, conditional upon qualifying and securing posts. Outside the office, and abubble with plans, Lyn tucked her arm in Jude's.

"Look, if you want to stay here, why don't we apply now for jobs to come to. I think I might try for midwifery training if I can do it here. What hospitals are there?"

"Easy Lyn let's wait and see if I pass first," he prevaricated.

"You will," she promised. "Now, we must find somewhere to put our caravan."

"Well we could try old Harding, he's got a place just outside town," Jude recalled. They cycled to Harding's farm where the taciturn owner agreed to let

The Looters

them park their van for a pound a week in advance

"You're free to use bottom field, there's no electric and water comes from farm tap up here. There's no extra charge for that and you'll share field with a sow and a few calves."

Next day, they returned north to solve the problem of separate sleeping quarters by finding a bed-sit in the nearby village. After Sister butterball gave them permission to sleep out, they earnt the good-humoured envy of friends. They held hands in public, and his smile was proprietary when he watched her sail down their ward, oblivious to her new name, on the first day back on duty.

The finals drew close and fear pounced to mock his ability. He woke, choking in terror, from dark dreams of failure blocking his way forward. During the last week blinding migraines laid him low in camp sick bay. Sister Quail looked in there, to find Lyn reading notes to him.

"With only two days to go you won't improve matters with any more revision, he knows all he needs, to get a pass," she observed dryly.

"He still cannot see properly Sister. Isn't there anything we can do," pleaded Lyn?

"It's just a severe attack of nerves. Take him for a walk in the fresh air and encourage him to tackle his fears, my dear." Over the next two days, between the two of them, they got him on his feet and fit to take the Finals. When results were published, Lyn joined those back-patting Jude on his success.

Returning to Cheltenham, she began part one midwifery training as a resident. Jude got a post at the old Infirmary whilst, much as it galled him, he lived with his family waiting for their caravan home to arrive.

On an icy cold afternoon in late November, cycling home from his shift at the old workhouse, Jude spied a new caravan being towed through the town. Putting on a spurt, he caught up with the driver when he slowed at the crossroads.

"Where are you heading," he asked? "This looks like the van I'm waiting for."

"Harding's farm, do you know it?" the man replied.

"Sure, I'll show you," he beamed and hopped up beside him, after stowing his cycle in the van.

Under the watchful eyes of Old Harding, on what turned out to be one of the coldest days for many a year, the caravan was settled beneath a large tree,

Jude lit the small, slow burning stove with wood from the farm before, glowing with pride of ownership, he rushed home to wake Lyn who was catching up sleep, after night duty, before some days off,

"Wake up ducks, our caravan's come. We'll sleep in our own home tonight, up at the farm." Sleep fled before the excitement of packing their few possessions and setting off on loaded bikes, to battle winter's early onslaught. Cycle wheels slithered up the steep hill to the farm gate.

"Will we be warm enough," Lyn puffed, her teeth chattering with cold? As they opened the caravan door warmth poured out, engulfing her fears.

"We won't 'starve to death' tonight because we'll have a cuddle," he grinned, closing the door and wrapping his arms round her. It was a turning point in their lives. They had a home which, with few outgoings, they would own within the year. What more could they want?

The days were spent setting things to rights. Lyn filled the many cupboards and lockers, then dusted and polished until the inside shone warm and cosy in the firelight. A small tent went up for bikes, buckets and bins. No electricity meant having their larder outside. Wary of the pigs, he dug a large hole inside the tent to bury a biscuit tin for the milk and butter supply. Pushing the lid firmly on their supplies, he finally slung a washing line between two trees. Satisfied, they returned to work.

With Lyn away, on resident call at the hospital, the lonely times at the farm irked him. He brooded over snide comments at work about his change of name. On one such evening, he cycled the last few yards to the farm gate to meet old Harding by the water pump.

"Looks like you've got a bit a trouble yonder," the farmer observed in a matter of fact way, as he swilled a full bucket of water over the yard and departed.

Jude arrived at the caravan to find the growing calves had taken a bullish stand to Lyn's newly laundered sheets. They bunched, butter and mud spattered, on the grass. The pigs had ambushed the tent, opened the biscuit tin and left glutinous traces of egg everywhere. Fuming, he got stuck into the mess, moodily wishing Lyn was around to help. She wasn't, meaning another lonely night.

"I've got to get the hell out of here" he muttered, stuffing the soiled sheets in a bucket of water. He took pains with shaving, put on a clean shirt, and cycled back to town and the Grand Pavilion. Along the promenade corridor leading to the Pavilion bar, old-fashioned drapes framed graceful arched exits. Jude stood in one looking for a partner and there was no shortage of beautiful women to follow his sure-footed turns around the chandelier lit ballroom.

A sexy brunette with flirtatious eyes, invited him during the erotic steps of a slow foxtrot. Dancing sparked the sensual in him. Later, on the way home, he noticed her cycling ahead of him and caught up with her.

"A pretty girl like you should not be cycling home alone, mind if I ride with you?" She was not averse to some teasing talk and, at the farm gate, his offer to stop off for coffee.

The following morning Lyn broke rules to come home and sleep. As she cycled up the hill, she exchanged smiles with a pretty dark-haired girl singing, as she cycled downhill. She ran across the dew spangled grass to surprise Jude and delight in his male warmth.

Through the open door she saw him, sitting at the table polishing an antique brass lamp they had bought in the market. He had seen her but kept his head down, industriously polishing some Verdigris off the lamp base. It had been so easy to bait his lure once more and satisfy his urge.

The Looters

"Jude, it looks lovely, how long have you been polishing it," she said, tracing a finger along the wings of the large eagle curved about the glass shade? "Have you had breakfast?"

"No, didn't get much sleep last night Ducks, so I got up early," he replied, inspecting his work.

"Were you missing me then," she kissed his ear.

"Ah! That would be telling," he winked at her. "Put the kettle on. We can have breakfast and then go up to Devil's Point. I'm on late shift today." Closing the door before lighting the gas, Lyn caught the scent of a flowery perfume in the confined space. She looked around, expecting a pot plant on one of the shelves.

"What have you been up to?" she teased, sniffing the air. Startled, he wriggled round the answer with a laugh.

"Private men's business ducks, meant for grass widowers," he countered.

"What perfume is that I can smell?"

"Ah! It must be the after-shave one of the patients spilt on my shirt." He stood up, rolling the polishing rags into a ball." How about buying some oil, so we can try this lamp and where's that cuppa then?"

"It won't be long. I need one after last night. I made a fool of myself during my first visit to the delivery room. We were all a bit awed and excited, standing quietly waiting. Then this eight-pound baby came out so quickly, bellowing his head off. You should have seen Sister's face when I said that I thought they came out and then blew up to size. I spent the next couple of hours in a cockroach infested kitchen, cooking the midnight meal." The eldest of seven, Jude shook his head in disbelief.

"Come on, make the tea Ducks. We need some fresh air."

The climb to Devil's Point was steep. Reaching the top, they rested arms around the other's waist, letting a playful breeze refresh them. Standing spellbound in the silent heights, they drew in the panorama below, A doll's house cathedral, model villages and miniature churches were set around the glistening twists and turns in the ribbon of the Avon River. They felt like gods looking down upon Earth's toys.

"How wonderful the world is," she breathed. "How lucky we are to have all this and each other."

"Mm. Look! There's the church where I was a choir boy. See that bend in the river? There are good blackberry bushes there. We used to go picnicking for a whole day and after the baskets were full, we swam in the river."

The morning passed all too soon, before Jude set off for the hospital, leaving Lyn curled up in bed. She drifted off to sleep with the scent of hyacinths, or was it lilies of the valley, hovering in the air.

Leaving the nursing home, and its beetle ridden kitchen, for part two district midwifery training caused no heartache for Lyn. The forbidding regime meted out by the staunch Plymouth Brethren Matron did leave one sweet memory. On Tuesday nights, she served cold pork with tantalizing spiced pickled pears.

Work on the district was a revelation. Sharing the children's pride in helping Mum, whilst Dad was getting their dinner, convinced Lyn a baby should be born in the bed where it was conceived. When a husband tentatively asked to see his offspring born, she agreed with the controversial and innovative idea, feeling his presence would comfort and help his wife.

The look of joy wonder and love on his face when she turned to congratulate him, after settling the new baby with mother, was shared wisdom. It strengthened her choice to be a midwife.

Surrounded by the musky, unveiled scents of nature in the quiet of night, these women shared a miracle with a woman in labour. The busy waiting wards and blinding lights over the delivery tables in hospitals, blinded sight to the mystery.

Six months, and two broken jug and bowl sets later, Lyn qualified to practice on her own, more careful now of old family treasures brought out for home confinements. On parting, her russet haired tutor gave her good advice.

"Get on your own district. You can plan your day to manage your work list and care for your family. Apart from headquarters' inspections, you are your own boss. I should think about it if I were you." Working from home, she would be around for Jude, and so her path was set.

Jude was far from happy about his future and wondered if he wouldn't have fared better staying on with his old boss, the butcher. Towards the end of winter, he cycled home, fed up with the way things had turned out. Closing the farm gate, it felt good to see Lyn running across to greet him. He had never fathomed his response to Lyn's marriage proposal. It was as if another mind made the decision. For now, he had a loyal mate. She saw he was in the dumps.

"I've made a special treat for us tonight. How was your day?"

"Lousy! I've had it up to here with those sarcastic bitches bossing me about. I feel like throwing nursing in," Jude muttered, flinging himself down on the long window seat. "That smells good. What is it?"

"Haslet, are you hungry? I loved it as a kid, It's liver, bacon, and onions, mushrooms, potato, the lot. Come on let's eat and talk things over."

They tucked in to the meal and afterwards, Jude, satisfied and more content, washed the dishes, made coffee then joined Lyn, perched on the caravan step. Looking across the fields, she made room for him to watch the sky darken and the stars form their eternal order.

"Jude, you know I want to be a district nurse," she broke the silence. "The work may not be as dramatic as hospital episodes, but I don't look at nursing in that light now.

I see it more as part of a family tending someone with care. Their love is a vital part of healing the sick, especially where soul-mates weave strands of hope to support life. I like the idea of living in a house in your district and becoming part of the community." Jude perked up.

"A house, are you sure of that, seems too good to be true to me. How do we get that kind of job, tell me more about this District Nursing?" Lyn handed him the Nursing Times where he soon spotted a training vacancy for two in Devon, which she had already seen.

"What do you think ducks, would they accept a man? I was posted to Plymouth before going over to France, I'd like to get back there. See here, there is a job going for a male nurse in Dorset, so they must train men."

Lyn wrote enquiring if the two of them could apply for training as district nursing sisters on the Queen's Roll. They were accepted as the first resident married couple for training.

For Jude new horizons opened. He took her dancing again, his arms encircling her, his cheek brushing hers as his thigh pressed close. They looked so happy, people came up to compliment them.

Before moving south, Lyn invited her mother to meet Jude's folk. Tiny, dark-haired Edie soon set Mercy at ease as she recounted the story of the marauding pigs, her dark eyes with a hint of a cast in them, dancing with mischief. Gentle ribbing and smiles invited Lyn to join their laughter. Her mother's deep blue eyes met hers with forgiveness for an impulsive marriage

Chapter 2: Devon

THEY left Harding's farm, bound for Plymouth, on a bright sunny day. Tucked into the back seat of a hired chauffeur driven car, surrounded with last minute baggage, they held hands like two excited children on an outing. Sea Mist, the caravan, swayed along behind as they headed for an old gun emplacement, perched on the cliffs above Plymouth Sound in Devon.

Jude roused, near the end of a long journey, as the car rolled through the outskirts of Plymouth. Memories surfaced as he watched the lights of the city recede, and the car roll into the oncoming dark along with his thoughts.

He was standing at the foot of some stairs, looking up into the homely face of a girl, smiling a welcome to the family home, the second floor flat in a terraced house.

'Her family showed me more love than my lot ever gave, and I betrayed her hopes and their trust. They took me into their hearts, it will hurt if they turn me away. What will they make of Lyn? Ah well, time will tell. The hell of it is, I've still got a soft spot for Bluey.' He squared his shoulders and sat up as soft Devon rain misted the window.

His move woke Lyn, nestled against his shoulder. She looked out on a steep road winding ahead, to where the outline of a fort towered above them. A fine mist drifted across grassy headlands on either side. Reaching the fort, the car turned into a narrow road running down the side of a high wall. Some low roofed buildings stood below. Two figures, backlit in soft yellow gaslight, stood in the first doorway. One stepped forward, twilight veiling his features, as his shadow flickered across the path towards them. A brown weather-beaten face peered in the car window.

"I'm George Trump. Ye'll be the Rooks. You've just made it in time to settle y'sels. Ye cun bide anywheres over there." He pointed to a large patch of grassland sloping towards the edge of the cliff. Glad to stretch cramped limbs, Jude clambered out of the car and hurried down the slope, followed by George and Lyn, to decide where to settle Sea mist.

At the foot of the slope, Jude pulled up sharply, warning Lyn to stay back. The roar of surf, surging against rocks, echoed all around them. Beneath his feet high cliffs fell sheer into the darkening waters of the majestic Sound, the bay between Jennycliffe and Plymouth Hoe. To his left, a long breakwater, curved in, from the end of the cliff, to take the might of the ocean beyond. Lyn ran to him to share the splendour.

"Jude its glorious; so much water, so much sky, so much emptiness, so much fullness. It's like being on the edge of the world. I can't wait for daylight to see everything. I'm so happy."

"It's good to be back," he agreed with a contented sigh, putting his arm round her shoulders to guide her back to Sea Mist. The men made short work of man-handling the caravan as near to the cliff edge as safety would allow before letting down the props.

"I'll be across on the morrow. Goodnight to ye," said George Trump leaving Jude and Lyn to settle in.

"Thanks," they called to retreating backs making for home Climbing over bundles and parcels, the fort's two new tenants fell into their bed's welcome warmth and slept until daybreak.

Stepping outside, where their cycles and wet weather clothing still laid in a forlorn heap. A stiff breeze blowing across the cliff top, rocked the van and made the setting up of a tent out of question. Lyn knelt to peer below the van for storage.

"There's plenty of space here," she called, turning to see Jude suddenly dis-appear over the cliff. Heart in mouth, she raced across to the edge. He was edging along a narrow path, winding down to a strip of sand, edged by loose rocks. She watched him grapple his way back up, clutching two fair sized rocks to his chest.

"I think there are enough of them to hedge in the wheels against the high winds," he panted.

"I'll take one shall I," she offered. Jude passed it to her and chuckled as she sank down under the weight, then went back again and again until he had made two sturdy bulwarks to stabilize Sea Mist. Lyn prepared a sketchy breakfast on a neatly laid table. When he stepped up into the van, she praised him, giving him a warm hug and a kiss.

"I don't, for the life of me, know how you kept going. I'm really proud of you." He ruffled her hair, disengaging from her to suggest,

"We'll be fine here ducks. We've got a couple of days before reporting to the training crew. Let's use the time to find our way around on the bikes. Maybe meet some of my old friends."

George and Margaret Trump came by to take stock of the young ones and liked what they saw. Bronzed and healthy from living on the cliff, they lived a simple life.

"You'd better can take your showers in the old ablutions block and store your bikes there. There is plenty of room for them," George made the generous offer.

"And do a bit of washing," added Margaret. "The boiler heats the water in our house and the block. Watch out for the hot tap my luv, 'tis boiling hot."

"Wonderful, I only wish we could live here straight away but we shall come on our days off," thanked Lyn. "When do you want the rent paid Margaret?"

"Weekly please. You can buy your milk and butter from us as well and there's always fresh eggs from the hens, out back. You know about the ferry to the Hoe, do you? It will save you a long journey round the bay."

Leaving a full line of washing blowing in the breeze, they cycled down to the landing stage to catch a boat just leaving the old war time outpost for Plymouth Hoe. After piling their cycles on the ferry, they stood looking up at the fort. One of many facades, built to mislead enemy sources of information regarding Britain's defence capabilities, it was impressive

After the fifteen-minute trip, rosy faces misted from the fresh breeze and sea spray, they stepped ashore into the haunt of fisher folk and ghosts from the past. The old cobbled lanes and cottages of the Barbican bordered the shoreline. leading up over the Hoe,

"We'll cycle over the Hoe to Three Towns and see what sort of place we are going to work from," decided Jude. "This whole district is pretty hilly so the sooner you get used to it the better. People over this side of the bay live in small cottages and wealthy folk live at the other end of the city This will be our patch I expect."

They cycled past Nelson's monument, tales of old naval battles echoing in their ears. When they came to the Navy's quarters in Barrack Street, they both felt a mateship with the men and women serving behind the old, grey stoned walls. Opposite the barracks the Nurses' Home was also old and grey stoned. Standing in their deep shadow, Lyn felt small and daunted by the prospect of living there for the next year.

"I suppose we could call and say we are here," she began as a tall, neatly groomed woman, leading a Manx cat on a silk leash, stepped out of the entrance door. Her glance questioned them, prompting Lyn to step with a smile.

"Do you think we might see inside these premises? We begin training here soon." The woman looked with fresh interest at the two standing in the middle of the road.

"Hello! You must be the Rooks, I'm the Assistant Matron. Yes, you can see your quarters, and you can move in whenever you wish." Leading them inside, she left them in charge of an elderly colleague, a little slip of faded womanhood with a gentle smile, who took them up to a large room, overlooking the barracks.

"You may change them around if you wish," she suggested demurely, nodding towards the twin beds set on separate walls.

"You are most welcome and much needed for our male patients Mr Rook. I shall be your practical domiciliary trainer. You will be the only man in our community," she advised. She proved to be a strict tutor, whose wisdom they made much profit from in future years. "I hope you enjoy your stay here," she finished hesitantly when she bade them farewell. Outside again, Jude winked his approval, the next step in their lives looked promising. Lyn winked back as they cycled further on along the road which ended at a small beach. Trailing her hand in the ripples, Lyn pictured ahead.

"We can swim here."

In the town, they purchased provisions for the next two days at the fort. Jude stopped by a tackle shop to buy some simple fishing supplies, strong lines and a few hooks and sinkers.

"These should pull some fish in, if we can set them off the rocks below the cliffs."

"You will have to teach me how to fish." Life was so full of new experiences and excitement.

"Come on. I'll take you for a Tiddy Oggy at St Andrews. Used to be a church, now it's a restaurant famous for its Cornish pasties."

The mention of food set their juices flowing and prodded their feet to peddle to another grey stone building of huge proportions, where a busy stream of people flocked through a massive wide-open doorway at the top of a steep flight of steps. The inviting aroma of fresh oven baking, meat and the warm smell of onions invited them in.

Whilst Jude went off to order food, Lyn sat, relaxed, at a plain deal table, amidst a happy buzz of conversation. He returned with a short, thickset woman carrying two plates. A wisp of dark hair feathered her upper lip. A head of strong black hair, tinged with grey, grew from a broad forehead.

She placed the plates on the table, after treating Lyn to some curious scrutiny.

"So, you're Lyn? Well you won't find better pasties than these, m'dear."

"I'm sure …" Lyn started, when Jude broke in.

"This is my second mum Ducks; she and Pa were good to me during the war. Gilly works here."

Eyebrows, above dark eyes in a round rosy face, treated Jude to a quizzical lift. Her expression said, 'so, this is what you were up to.' He looked back, a sheepish smile chasing away a worried little frown. The moment passed, then she smiled.

"I must get back to the counter. Why don't you come to Sunday dinner? Pa will be pleased to see you, but I don't know if Hazel will be there?" With their ready acceptance ringing in her ears, she went her way.

"How about going to dinner and staying over that side," suggested Jude. "We can sleep at the Home and be ready for our first day on Monday."

When they gathered for Sunday lunch with the Gilds, Hazel, their only daughter, was with them. A plain, homely girl with a mop of curly hair and very round blue eyes, whose thick pouting lips curved into a ready smile whenever she spoke. Now she sat quietly listening to the others talk.

Whilst the two of them washed the dishes, after a beautiful meal, Lyn tried to make friends with her subdued companion until Gillie came into the kitchen to give them both a hug.

"All right Hazel?" Her daughter smiled back "Fine Mum."

Seeing them off later Pa Gild, his arm around his daughter, faced Jude.

"You are both welcome anytime," Jude heard forgiveness in the warm invitation from a father who had fostered hopes for the daughter he had entrusted to a young sailor during wartime. That night they slept in the Barrack Street Home.

On Monday morning Jude and Lyn shyly made their way through the nursing home's long dining room. Among this group of spinsters at table, their married status was an unspoken thought in the eyes watching their efforts to find their place in the hierarchy. It prefaced their instruction to sit at the lower end of the table.

With a good breakfast inside them, they began their first day of six months training to discover their nursing status reversed. Institutional authority over the patient as a guest of the hospital, gave way to a friendly offer of help, graciously accepted, as the nurse was welcomed in the patient's home.

By the end of the morning their heads were full of the extra duties they had taken for granted on the wards Lyn stood in the last patient's bedroom listening to Cynthia Cheam, her instructor.

"Good quality newspaper is a boon. You are lucky if you get *The Times* or *Telegraph*. The ink doesn't come off on everything," Cynthia said, showing Lyn how to fold the newspaper into neat bags for used swabs, as she prepared to dress a man's deep leg ulcer.

Earlier, his wife had welcomed them with a smile, beckoning them into the kitchen, where a large saucepan of water simmered on the stove. Sister Cheam plumped her nursing bag on the newspapers covering the kitchen table. Outer coats were removed and placed on newspaper covered chairs. Aprons were untucked and unrolled from their waist belts to cover long nursing dresses, before washing hands under running water at the kitchen sink.

The instruments required, along with a kidney dish unrolled from linen cases to boil in the saucepan, which was carried to the patient's side table again covered with newspaper.

"Spread some newspaper on the floor near the patient then unfasten the bandage and drop it on the newspaper whilst I scrub up," said Cynthia, pouring water into a large china bowl on the washstand. She then attended to her towelled off patient with strict non-touch technique, using an assortment of boiled bowls and jars for lotions and swabs. Finally, a fresh bandage was applied, and the paper bags came into their own, wrapped and folded into a neat pile, inside the newspaper on the floor for disposal.

Whilst the instruments were sterilized for packing away the two girls sat chatting to the patient and his wife, until Cynthia beckoned Lyn to follow her to the kitchen and take down a large brown envelope from the dresser.

"Will you write up the report whilst I pack the bag. Did you notice that Bill said he slept like a log and yet his wife said he was awake half the night with pain? The old chap always puts on a brave show, he will say the same thing to the doctor, so just mention it in your report. Come on let's get home. It's for lunch."

Jude was waiting in their room when Lyn returned. His smile said it all.

"How did your morning go Ducks? This is the first time I've done any real nursing since demob. Most of my old chaps had the Daily Mirror hidden under their pillow to save "Just Jane" in the centre page from the newspaper setup and the dustbin." Both now felt sure they wanted to nurse on a district of their own, after they repaid their training with a year on reduced salary.

All free time off was spent at the fort, scrambling down the cliffs to check their lines, whooping for joy when they found a catch hooked. At dawn they gathered huge mushrooms, birthed on the green turf of the headland, and bought illicit jars of thick Devonshire cream.

Lyn learnt the old art of pleasing her man, and life was sweet. It came as no surprise to the worldly-wise matron, a few days before the end of the training period, to find a sheepish Lyn standing before her desk. A tiny dame, with heart shaped face framed in high piled jet-black hair bespeaking her Cornish ancestry, her knowing dark eyes observed Lyn stammering an apology for being with child.

"It is a natural event nurse. You will be best under the care of the Home doctor, I think. Now go along and report to Sister Brook to find out if you have any new patients today. You should be able to fulfil your contract for a while."

Lyn joined the group of working women, with a secret hidden beneath her crisp white apron. One she kept from Jude who had become withdrawn and moody for reasons he wouldn't discuss.

Chapter 3: Old habits

OUTSIDE a coffee house on the Hoe, Hazel looked across the street as Jude parked his bike and came to where she waited. Since a chance meeting, they trysted often at this old haunt. They sat at their old table, overlooking The Sound.

He had been forgiven his betrayal in Bluey's soft creamy voice, whose rounded vowels were music to his ears. In the weeks to come his warm Gloucestershire tones melded with hers over the café table. Soon after their first meeting, Jude brought Lyn into his confidence.

"I'd like to invite Hazel for a meal if that's alright with you ducks. We were old friends. I will show her round beforehand then fix some food and we'll meet you at the ferry later."

Old lovers walked the headland, holding hands, as he regretted the ambition which drove him into the wrong arms. He watched the breeze lift the curls at the nape of her neck and tightened his clasp. Each crash of the breaking surf echoed deep within them until their steps turned back to Sea Mist to cradle their passion and house his despair. By the time Lyn stepped off the ferry Hazel had gone leaving him to make an excuse.

Sitting in the café, Bluey handed him his cup. Both knew their fulfilment was delayed until Jude was free.

"I love you Bluey and always have. I should have married you. What a mess I've made of things." He looked into the homely warmth of her face.

"Lyn is bent on a career. I go to bed to find one of her women in early labour between us, she never switches off. God knows, any ardour I had, has cooled since seeing you again."

Lyn was centred on the new life within her and the minor discomforts of the first few months. Unhappy with her secret and fretful with guilt, she was difficult to understand. Unaware of her pregnancy, Jude smouldered.

"She's more like a child than a full-blown woman, I've just got to find the guts to tell her the truth and see how she takes it. I've decided to talk things over with Pa. I think he'll help me explain things to Lyn and sort this mess out," he finished. kissing her upturned face.

The next Sunday, lunch at the Gilds passed with the usual banter before Jude settled down for a talk with Pa Gild. Lyn, feeling as much part of the family as Jude, decided to ask Hazel's advice. Carrying the dishes to the kitchen with her she whispered,

"I have something special to tell you."

"Have you passed your driving test at last," Hazel replied, turning on the tap?

"I wish I had, because I'm having a baby and I won't be able to cycle much longer." Water scalded over Hazel's hands as the words burned into her mind.

"We didn't plan to have a baby yet. We hoped to get our own house in a district somewhere. Things will work out I know they will." Hazel turned to hug her and hide the pain filling her eyes.

"What does Jude say," she asked?

"He doesn't know yet. It might be easier to tell him with you and Mum around. He doesn't seem all that keen on children." They returned to where the others sat, content after one of Gillis's roasts. Hazel looked across at Jude who gave her a lazy wink.

"Lyn's has some news to share haven't you Lyn."

"You'll be having the baby here m'dear," interposed her mother, coming to put her arms round them both. "Ah! I saw it in your face last time you came and wondered when you and Jude were going to tell us." The homely woman felt a tinge of regret that the baby might have been her grandchild.

"Well lad, you've got trouble aplenty now," Pa Gild said quietly. Jude's eyes were unreadable as he looked towards Lyn, smiling nervously in the kitchen door-way.

"What's one more bit of trouble Pa? The navy's here." He softly whistled a few bars of the song Pack up your troubles, in your old kit bag and smile, smile, smile. He met Bluey's eyes. He was trapped.

District work pushed future events out of focus, until Lyn was on her rounds, in The Barbican, on a hot summer morning.

A toothless smile split Annie's face from ear to ear and her broad beam spread from end to end of the settee. Leaning forward on massive arms, she lifted her skirts above elephantine thighs. Lyn loved her and the adoring family who looked after Ma. They covered the remaining seats in the tiny hovel, making a close circle. The rank odour of sweat steamed off their collective bodies. She loaded a syringe.

"Where's it goin' t'be this time? Proper pin cushion I am," said diabetic Annie, on three injections a day to cope with her dietary indiscretions.

"I'll find somewhere don't you fear, Annie Malone. You'll not get out of it that way," Lyn parried, bending to swab and inject swiftly. A strong mix of ammonia on thighs, and fish odour on the fisher woman's hands caught Lyn's throat. Perspiration beaded her brow as she held back from retching at the close contact.

"All done again then," asked Annie? "You are a good nurse, I never feel the needle with you."

"You're a tough woman Annie. I don't think I could smile with three jabs a day for ever." Feeling dizzy, she fumbled for the catch of her nursing bag. "See you this evening then. Bye all."

Out in the fresh air, Lyn leant against a wall, eyes closed and head spinning.

The Looters

When she opened them, her sight had all but gone. Fighting for control, she groped for her cycle and shuffled along, as patches of cobblestone swam beneath her feet.

Sister Mary Bunce watched Lyn's erratic progress from her patient's window, across the lane. Making a quick exit, she hurried across to Lyn.

"What on earth's the matter, have you been like this all morning," she asked? "My God look at your ankles. How long have they been swollen? You should know better."

"I hadn't noticed Mary, and this giddy turn isn't the first, but it is the worst. I went partially blind for a while back there, but look, I'm better now, you won't tell anybody, will you."

"No, I won't Lyn, but you're going to, as soon as you report back. Promise me."

Diagnosed with early toxaemia, Jude and Lyn moved to the fort for Lyn to start her maternity leave a few weeks early and have time to think of a future where babies were realities. Jude had his own thoughts.

"How are we going to manage things if you keep working?"

"Everything will be all right. We can find somebody to care for the baby during the day." On his return from Barrack Street each evening, he found her placid and confident, until late one autumn night as they were about to settle for to sleep.

"Jude my waters have broken," she exclaimed in dismay. "It's too soon." He raced across to the Trumps.

"George, she's started labour. We must get into Plymouth. Can you…?" Good neighbour that he was, George got out his old truck to drive into the city. As high winds swept the sky empty of rain, Lyn's waters drained away.

Many hours later, she nodded an exhausted, "Please," to Mary Bunce holding the episiotomy scissors ready. The cut was small price to escape the hellish pain sawing into her spine.

"Aaah!" The blades sliced through the thin barrier and a beleaguered little head birthed. Christopher Rock arrived.

With quiet and order restored after the midwives left, Gilly picked up the bathed and swaddled infant. She cradled him with a love so strong, he could have been her grandson, yet her eyes were anxious.

"Here we are m'dear, here's your son," laying him in a sleepy mother's arms.

Lyn looked down with wonder at the soft bundle in the crook of her arm. This baby was hers. He was real and so beautiful. She clasped him to the breast he would soon seek. The small hand, curled around her finger, would lay next her heart when she succoured him. The first honeyed flow stirred behind the burgeoning buds of her nipples. The erection excited her.

"Shall I try him Gilly?" she asked shyly, unsure as any new mother turning to experience.

"Let him rest a bit longer. The midwife thinks 'tis best so. She'll be coming back soon m'dear, let me take him" As Lyn lifted her precious baby, a wave of colour flooded his face. On a swift intake of breath, she questioned.

"Has this happened before Gilly." Looking at the child, now lying limp in its mother's arms, compassionate eyes met hers, as the older woman nodded.

Desperately, Lyn turned her baby over, sickened at the sharp blow she must deal to his back. Mercifully, the deep navy-blue hue faded from Christopher's tiny face as normal colour returned.

"My darling is a 'blue baby' Gilly," she wailed. "Put the cradle near me please, I'll watch over him." Wide awake, she lay propped on her elbow, willing reality to change course and not steal away, all that now mattered.

"Does Jude know?"

"Not yet lass, he hurried off to get his round done and get back to you."

Before he returned, her blood pressure reading became critical as toxins again overtook Lyn and she was placed under sedation. Before oblivion came, she watched them draw the curtains to darken the room and sensed a veil closing behind Christopher. Nearby, a nurse monitored his flickering life, on its return to the mystery he had come from.

The pain in her body became one with the pain in her heart. In delirium, she fought the bindings about her breasts, crying they were crushing her son. She spat back the Stilboestrol they gave to stem her milk flow; demanding Christopher be put to her breast.

Three days later pain drifted away, leaving vague memories of her mother and Jude standing over her bed They told her she had been very ill, and Christopher's heart had given up the fight with a faulty valve. Pa Gild made an arrangement with his employer, an undertaker, for their son to share a coffin cradled in the arms an old man.

Jude took a shadow of a woman back to the fort. Guilt and frustration bit deep as he went his way, tight lipped and of small comfort to her. Ashamed at feeling relief, once the baby was buried, Jude made amends to a surrogate, one of his patients.

Steve Harper, an ex-naval man dying of tuberculosis, had a large collection of cage birds. As the god of war increased his toll, Steve became too frail to clean the cages. Jude took on the task, taking each little ball of fluff to sit upon his hand. When the dying man's strength allowed a drive to the seashore, they talked of war and women and the moods of the sea. Steve's dry humour and acceptance of death made their mark. When he died, Jude let go his bitterness.

'I have to stand by her now. I've made my bed. Bluey will find another.' Cold Charity smiled approval, and love became a duty as Lyn grew strong enough to return to the district. One morning he woke her early.

"Come on sleepy. Let's go and set the lines, before we catch the ferry." Paddling in the water he queried, "Where shall we go when we are free to apply for a district after Christmas?"

"Wherever we can get a job," decided Lyn, already ahead of him in searching for possible posts. "The Nursing Times has an ad that might suit us. They are asking for a male nurse and an extra midwife in Essex."

"It's a pity to leave Devon we like it here," Jude ventured, loath to leave the South.

"Yes, we do, but Essex County are offering a house on a new housing estate for the midwife. It won't be ready until April, but just think, it will be our first house," Lyn. It wasn't long before the thoughts of discovering fresh fields excited his desire to join Lyn in applying for a joint post. While they waited for the fates to decide their future, they made the most of the present.

They made friends at local village functions such as the weekly dance. He enjoyed dressing up to go dancing. Looking in the mirror after brushing and combing his hair to a crested wave, the lucid hazel green eyes, under dark well shaped eyebrows, saw a handsome man and he knew it. When winter's high seas prevented the ferry from running, they met at a road junction to the cliff site, come wind or rain, to cycle along the coast together, to the caravan's warmth.

"We should finish early today," he said one morning, "let's go to village hall for the weekly dance. I'll meet you at the junction". After a fruitless wait, Lyn eventually reached home wondering how she had missed him. Setting out a blue dress which set off her fair skin and enhanced the deep blue of her eyes, she experimented with some light make-up.

Before picking up the mail. she decided he must still be at the junction and set off to cycle back whilst it was still light.

Earlier, in Plymouth, Hazel ran towards Jude as he racked up his motorcycle near their café. Looking at Bluey, the laughter bubbling up behind the generous round of her lips, Jude knew he still loved her.

"I can't bear to think you may be leaving soon, and our table empty," she half sobbed as she embraced him.

"I know love. It's funny Bluey, but when she came up with the idea, it didn't seem to be me saying I'd marry her. We became friends when she helped me through those damned exams, you know how it is. I don't think she'd ever had a boyfriend. There are times now when the same feeling catches me, and I find myself saying words I hadn't thought of. It's weird." Bluey couldn't shake off her low spirits. Miserable at the hurt he was giving, he forgot his promise to Lyn.

"Come on Bluey. Let's get out of here. There is a comedy showing at the Ritz. Want to go and see it?"

Sitting in the semi darkness, he put a comforting arm around her as she nestled her curls into his neck. They kissed and lightly caressed searching for the unfulfilled promise in each other's eyes. Time warped until the house lights pulled them back to the present and their commitments. Holding hands, they joined the throng filing out into a recent downpour and dark rain drizzled streets. He took her home pillion.

"See you tomorrow then." Sitting astride the bike he suddenly remembered the village dance and gunned the engine into gear to catch the ferry.

Heavy rain was still falling when Lyn pedalled up the last slope of the seven-mile return journey, frightened that something had happened to Jude. A yellow light streamed from the caravan windows as she reached the top. 'He's home, it's all right, or did I leave the lights on,' she wondered. Drenched to the skin, terror turned to a sobbing breathlessness as she stumbled across the wet grass. The door was flung open before she reached it, Jude silhouetted in the doorway.

"You fool" he blazed, his anxiety for her safety mixed with guilt. Emotions flared in the angry darkness of the night. His ire brooked her questions 'What…Where?' until, barely aware of how she got there, she was curled up tight beneath the bedclothes. Goodnights withered into a sulking silence, the first of many he sank into in the years ahead. Next morning, she placed a letter stamped with the Essex County postmark in his hand.

"I'm sorry about last night. Shall we read this together before we go down to the ferry?"

He ignored the olive branch but opened the letter. They read it together where it lay on the table offering them a joint post in three months' time. They had seven days to respond. If they accepted, they would live in a new council house in the centre of the three housing estates that were part of their district.

"That's it then Ducks. We'll go," Jude decided finally, using the familiar name to pick up the olive branch. They steamed across The Sound full of plans for their move to a new hometown.

"The house is sure to be furnished, don't you think. Nurses move around."

"I hope so, we can't afford to buy furniture. What did your tutor say about that," he questioned?

"Oh, she definitely said furnished accommodation." Satisfied with the prospect of a secure future, last night was forgiven as Jude reflected, 'You see, you did choose the right woman.'

Before leaving Devon, they invited their mothers for a holiday by the sea. Emma and Mercy fell in love with its beauty as they took to a gypsy lifestyle in a rented caravan. Time flew by on the headland towards the last day of their holiday. Three mothers strolled over the Hoe, in the warm sunshine, easy banter bouncing between them. Jude, Hazel and Lyn walked ahead until Lyn dropped back to ask about a childhood incident.

"Come on, I'll race you to the end of the path," Jude challenged Hazel. As they raced off, Emma's deep smoker's voice cut across a quiet moment.

"They look like couple of kids. Wonder when she'll find someone else? Did Bluey take it bad when Jude broke with her so sudden?" Words echoed from a walk high above a northern town. 'I'd better write to Bluey.'." The gap between her and Jude filled with revelation.

"Come back," Lyn called to the running pair, "we can't keep up with you."

Ashamed of the deceit, she found no opening to ask him how he could treat such a lovely family so badly. The question slid into a closed recess of her mind until the evening before leaving the old gun site.

With the horizon narrowing to close the day, light still played on the water, when he came to where she stood near the edge of the cliff. His hand resting lightly on her shoulder, turned her to face him.

"There is something I have to discuss with you Louie. I couldn't bring myself to do so before, but this is the right time, I think. You are strong enough to cope and it's something we must do together."

Her heart lurched and thoughts sharpened her features. 'Is it Bluey, does he want to leave me to go North on my own?'

"What must we do, can't it wait until we get to Essex," she questioned?

"Come back to the van with me" he said, taking her hand. "There is something I must share with you."

He set her down by the table, went to open his locker then sat across from her, placing a small cardboard casket between them.

"What is it Jude, Am I to open it?" She reached for the box only to feel his restraining hand.

"We never talked things through, did we Ducks?" He sought to release words trapped in a throat, baulking the misery of the past's departure.

"I'm sorry about the baby. Truly I am. You weren't in a fit state to decide. In the end we thought it best … Look, these are some of the ashes from Christopher's burial…"

"I so wanted to ask, but I thought you didn't want to talk." Her hands closed tight about the casket, her eyes filled with heart ache. He shook his head in quiet despair at their inability to reach each other knowing that blame had no place to settle.

"So, we thought perhaps to wait until you could let him go privately, before we leave Ducks." Concerned grey green eyes looked across the table.

She came to him sitting with joined hands cosseting the cold ashes. His arm warmed her shivers to be still before he spoke again.

"Would you like to leave Christopher here? He won't be alone; George and Margaret are here for him." He barely heard her sighed assent.

"I know what I should like if you will come with me," she whispered.

They walked back to the cliff edge, she clasping the casket, he with his arm around her shoulders. Overhead, twilight's clouds ran, scattering distilled vapours in fine mist. On the horizon, golden shafts of light escaped the pearly hem of the grey scalloped curtains of night.

At the cliff's edge, he waited for her to gather herself.

"Is this what you want Ducks?"

"Yes, I do."

He took the lid from its rest then guided her hands to bestow the contents on down spiralling currents of air. Slow was the journey to the ocean's breast. Droplets of mist carried sunlit flakes to the wide flowing sea before darkness gathered. He took her into his arms and kissed her brow, she rested her head on his shoulder. Night closed soft about them as each prayed a silent blessing for their son.

George and Margaret Trump watched from their doorway. George switched on the light as they came up the slope in acknowledgement of the simple ceremony. Lyn looked across to them.

"That's how we first saw them, standing in the gaslight. I shall miss them Jude."

Rain threatened, on the day of departure, when they waved good bye to George and Margaret. They settled back to watch the headland recede into the mist, and the road ahead unwind towards their future.

"Let's hope the tropical fish and the canary survive the journey," said Jude hopefully.

Chapter 4: Essex

UNRELENTING flatness lulled them into a fitful doze as field after field of cabbages, paraded endlessly past the car windows. They drove through villages, where taught, sharp faced men and women turned from hurrying across the village square, to question them passing through their domain.

The gap between them and the round creamy body of Devon lengthened as the afternoon inched along a timeline, they had lost touch with. Lyn raised heavy lids to see suburban dwellings and nudged Jude awake.

"Ask where we are Jude. Surely we must be nearly there." He leant forward.

"I reckon you've had enough driving for the day. Are we getting close?"

"Just ahead, we turn left and that should be it," the driver replied.

Jude opened a window to get a scent of the place. An icy blast, from the prevailing Easterly wind, blew them wide awake. It was their first encounter with the daily battle they later waged with it on swaying bikes.

Their estate, set in a large grid of neat, flower filled gardens fronting toy town houses, rolled into view. Faces peered at them from behind twitching net curtains as they stopped outside a house at the far corner of the square. Lyn eyed the rooftops of the surrounding houses boxing them in under a small patch of sky.

Jude checked the number before the weary driver helped them to settle the van on a grassy space by the side of the house. Then she saw the field.

"Look!" she called, her eyes alight with pleasure, "There are ploughed fields at the back of our house. We'll have a view, we can make a home here."

Well satisfied with his well earned, carefully saved fare, plus a tip, the driver offered to drop them downtown to get the house key. A brief farewell and he was off, leaving them standing outside a door in the High Street of Dovercourt. A raw-boned woman in her early forties opened it to their knock. A relieved smile flickered across Clara Cobb's long horsy face, as eyed them across the doorstep.

"Good you've got here then. I'm starting my holiday now youv'e arrived, so you will be staying here. The records are next the phone on the shelf behind the door, and the nursing bags are below it. Please feed the cat." She came out of the house handing Jude a bunch of keys. Fearful she might be off immediately, Lyn swallowed her jaw shut to make a timid request.

"Could you help us to fetch a few things from our van, to see us over until you return?"

"I wondered where your bags were. I suppose we can, I was just about to get your supper, so." The words dropped over her shoulder as she strode down the small path to a little Austin car, her badge of senior status, not that they needed much reminding.

Back on the estate, she raised her eyes at the canary, dismissed the tropical fish and instructed Jude.

"You had better follow us with your bikes.". Feeling dashed with their abrupt reception Lyn walked towards a nearby window to gather herself.

No curtains she thought. Her curiosity whetted she stood on tiptoe to peer through the front window. Craning her neck, she saw a single black object on the floor, the telephone, its cord trailing towards a connection by the front door. The house was bone empty. They had no furniture and no money.

"There isn't any furniture," she cried in shocked astonishment. She spoke to empty air for Jude had started back with the bikes. Lyn hurriedly gathered sufficient clothing and closed the van door.

"Are you ready," called a petulant Sister Cob? Lyn scrambled into a car filled with Clara's baggage plus the canary's cage.Whilst her senior waited on the doorstep Lyn unloaded their few possessions,

"Don't forget the cat. See you in two weeks then," Clara rattled, thrusting a newspaper parcel into Lyn's arms. Fish and chips never smelt so good. Jude arrived before she opened the wrapping.

"Jude there's no furniture in our house. What are we going to do?" wailed Lyn before he could get off his bike.

"We'll talk about it when we get inside I'm starving," he muttered.

Once inside the musty interior they were greeted by the baleful glare of a cat, arched in the corner of the living room. Undeterred, Jude and Lyn set the table and enjoyed their meal. Jude saw to the canary's needs, putting the cage safely on top of a bookcase, before they went on a tour of the house. One bedroom was unlocked. Theirs, they decided, looking longingly at the comfortable double bed, soft pillows and pleasant furnishings.

The cat and the canary had taken a David and Goliath stance and the cat had won, swiping the cage to the floor, where he prowled and pounced around a defeated scrap of yellow feathers. Jude soothed and quietened the frightened bird whilst they checked the next day's workload.

It was late when Lyn finished sorting the due dates of the many babies expected. She prayed her skills would not be tested until she had a lay of the land she was now responsible for.

Finally, Jude pumped their bike tyres up hard, ready for the morning. They trailed up the stairs, with the canary, and fell asleep before their heads hit the pillow. Two hours later the shrilling of a telephone rang through the house.

"Must be for you," said a drowsy Jude.

Feeling her way downstairs, on legs atremble under the burden of sole responsibility, Lyn answered the phone to her first summons in a strange county. Her patient, a lively Italian mother of five, took charge of the situation, after Lyn's nervous, "Hello, I'm your midwife."

The Looters

Son number six safely delivered, Lyn cycled home, light headed with a happy outcome. The bike wobbled along under its load of nursing bags and heavy gas and air machine, but she felt an old hand on that first night in Essex.

They soon mapped out their districts. Jude now responsible for all the male patients, worked the whole area. Wives gave condescending entrance to their homes, grudgingly finding old saucepans to sterilize his instruments. Watchful eyes guarded their husbands and their bed linen. They expected both to last a good few years longer, which they reckoned they did better in a woman's hands.

The quiet purposeful manner in which Jude set about caring for his patients, reassured the women hovering below stairs. They listened to his deep voice making friendly contact with their men, who liked the slow easy timing of his moves, and the strong arms, which lifted them from cramped positions where need be. He was a natural healer.

Lyn's patients gave her the same wary appraisal. Looking at the young face beneath the wide brimmed hat, one went so far as to ask,

"Are you from the guides?"

Small though she was, Lyn had her own way of lifting patients who voiced their grateful approval for feeling clean and comfortable at the end of her visit.

A furniture shop allowed them hire purchase, and Jude found a caravan site for the van. Slipping away most afternoons, they tracked back and forth with cycles loaded like mules, until their move was completed.

The day before Sarah Cobb's return Lyn made up their bed, stocked the kitchen cabinet with provisions and tweaked the new net curtains with a satisfied smile. They hid a room bare of furniture until they cleared their debt. At month's end Jude bent to pick up the letters scattered inside the front door.

"Looks like our first pay cheques have arrived Lyn," he called and gave a soft whistle as she ran down the stairs to find him looking at the cheque in his hand.

"This is more like it Ducks. A few years at this rate and who knows? Open yours and see if we get the same." He stood with his arm round her waist, waiting.

"Yes, we get the same rate Jude," she agreed, tucking the cheque in her pocket.

"Give it to me. I'll open a joint account this morning when I go down town" he said.

"I'd rather use my own account Jude. We'll be sharing expenses as usual."

"So, what's wrong with sharing an account?" he replied, nettled. The tidy sum written on the cheques brooked further dissent over her decision.

Poverty pared down the lean women of Essex, dependent on their men for every personal need. Old before their time, ill-nourished women laboured in tired lassitude. One husband snored heedless beside his wife. Faced with a truculent bully, Lyn took persuasive measures to move him to his duties elsewhere. The threat of a full chamber pot won the day before Lyn joined her struggle to bring another child into the world then reviving the exhausted woman with all the art she knew.

Her decision to ensure her back was covered with a bit of cash in her own account, promised a good life lay ahead for her.

As time went by the small Essex society made them welcome. Erstwhile matrons, who pulled wires and pillaged their husband's pockets to keep the social life alive, invited them to lesser social functions.

"We are sending our girls to Roedene next term, where were you educated Sister," said smiling lips of a forceful dame, tipping her porcelain teacup, fingers crooked?

"Trinity," beamed Lyn to Condescension, not bothering to add Grammar School.

"Oh, and I suppose your husband…?"

"Cheltenham, he is a Cheltenham man," was her airy retort.

White shirted and tie'd under a double-breasted suit, Jude listened to Lyn parry their inquisitorial lances as spoons tinkled in the cups, and gossip passed with the petit fours.

"We'll be giving them something else to talk about soon," Lyn whispered.

"What's that? Oh God, no. You can't be." She flushed with guilt under his angry glare.

"We are just getting on our feet. I thought you were taking care. How have you managed …?". Money and status were the ambition of the bastard errand boy, now well respected by all. Much in demand by doctors who handed over many procedures they formerly carried out, he was coming into his own, and that was the rub.

"You'd better do something about it Ducks. The authorities won't be too pleased if you stop work so soon. We're doing fine, why put a spanner in the works for heaven's sake" he urged? "

"It's nothing to do with them. I'll only be off work a short while," she defended her dream of motherhood and then stayed obstinately silent.

During the next few days she buckled to his persuasion when she took a slender rubber tube, bent to her task and corrupted knowledge one day.

Later that day, Jude stood in the doorway, looking across to the bed where Lyn lay bleeding from a botched attempt. 'How the hell has this happened,' he wondered. 'She stifles my desire before I raise her shift.'

"Will you be all right Ducks, I promised to help with a driving lesson, but I'll call in at Ginger's and ask her to come across?" Sister Ginger was out when he called. He left a note and drove off.

Alone, Lyn waited. The bed and a chair were still the only furnishings in the upstairs room. Frightened by the increasing flow of life from her body, she prayed for forgiveness. Time hung still. She soured towards Jude. When Betty Ginger clumped up the stairs Lyn was shivering and losing hold.

"Let's see what's amiss lass," said the older woman laying aside the bed-clothes. "My God, you're haemorrhaging, must get you to hospital," she gasped rushing down to the phone.

Before Lyn returned home, Jude worked hard in their vegetable garden, planting herbs she had long wanted. As they walked back to the house, she broke an awkward silence.

"Thank you, Jude, it's a beautiful herb garden.".

"There's something else, a surprise for you." Awkward as a child making amends for destroying something precious, he led her to the kitchen. There, in a basket, a spaniel puppy rolled on its back.

"Ah. He's adorable. I love him. Thank you dear."

Nursing the warm bundle to her breast, she swallowed her remorse and resentment and resolved to bear a new life as soon as God willed. She returned to working full time and the routine of keeping a comfortable home as the tempo of the world around them quickened.

At the start of the fifty's life was starting over again. Along Britain's coastlines Sappers had cleared rows of land mines guarded behind encircling rolls of barbed wire fencing to be dismantled by valiant men. Some died in peacetime, and like an unsuspecting child at play in years to come, blown away by an undetected mine.

Deck chairs now encircled the bandstands on the esplanades, inviting the milling crowd to pause for a moment to listen to the lilt of Viennese waltzes. Extravert amateurs vied for stardom at the Follies. Revived amateur drama groups offered discrete ego buffing. Then there was sport. When the local team in neighbouring Ipswich made it to the English football finals, surrounding councils declared a public holiday.

"Never known anything like it. Waste of time and money," said an old work-horse, ordering another beer as he sat in a pub to hear the match on the wireless. When the team won, little towns on his side of the Orwell River benefited from the backwash of the spending boom hitting Ipswich. Town dwellers flocked to the coast in droves.

"Well, can't be all bad, this madness for kicking a ball," the shopkeepers said, as they counted the takings from the day trippers.

Local business employed weekend help from a workforce of women, who came out of their kitchens once more, to work for peace not war. They used their wages to supplement the Dole paid out to their wounded and sick men. Cheers for the hero had long died away Old soldiers waited long hours in surgery and dispensary.

"Ave yer tried doc's mixture? Couple of swallows and you're in fairyland." they said of the codeine-based elixir, easing their cough. They talked hopefully of the new National Health Service.

"It won't get this bloody pain orf me back but 'twill settle me dues. At least me kids will 'ave a better chance."

Babies filled the maternity wards as war's waste tipped into the graveyard's maw. Lyn waved to a mother watching her three young children from an upstairs window. They played outside their house, most days, in all weathers.

The six-year-old twins and a wise eight-year-old hung over the garden fence chatting with her and throwing pebbles for the spaniel.

"We've got to get the fresh air nurse, now Mum's dying with the TB."

"It makes me mad Jude," stormed Lyn, coming in from the garden, "Susan's husband infected her with Koch's Bacillus before the navy discovered his condition and treated him. That damned disease hid dormant in her body, until it's too late to save her? It's rampaging through her lungs without check. Can you imagine?" She brushed angry tears away, "That innocent woman will pay a toll for war that we cannot change. Life ebbs and flows like the tides of this bleak coast."

She kept the new life in herself secret until she felt its first stirrings curled behind the tidy round of her belly. Jude. He had just bargained for a second caravan to rent out to holiday makers was unexpectedly gracious when she told him.

"You'll need some help when the baby comes," offered a mellow Jude, hand in hand with Lyn, as they walked back from the weekly visit to the cinema. "We're making big strides now and everything's going to be fine. I can feel it in my water," he quipped. "I can't believe our luck sometimes."

Thanks to thrift and the sum of one hundred pounds, Lyn had become a property owner when rented homes were offered to long standing tenants for generously low prices. A new tax had turned landlords into philanthropists, of sorts. Jude was well pleased with their prospering as Lyn's parents became rent-free tenants.

In the summer of nineteen fifty-two Jude took Lyn to the maternity hospital in Colchester. There she breech birthed a girl child, strangling by the umbilical cord she hung from. In a brief eternity of meeting, tiny feet kicked and trailed the moistness of Lyn's thigh. Then she was gone in golden haired perfection. Another dream was folded away with the bootees and bonnets until it was dragged back through a veil drawn over past memories.

Several weeks later an officious telephone call requested them to collect the tiny body. Jude returned from the long journey by bus with an inconspicuous cardboard box lying across his knees. Death's chill seeped through to his flesh. Sickened, he decided Lyn need not know further misery. There was another way.

He stepped off the bus at the next stop at the end of a narrow lane, aflame with summer glory. The remaining passengers felt a brief sympathy for the short, broad shouldered man standing there, tight lipped and uncertain.

He walked between the high hedgerows until he turned through a small gate set between two fir trees. Grave-stones, ancient and new, formed a guard as he passed by them with his tiny burden. The ghosts of the dead waited to welcome her.

On the far side of the consecrated ground, a house stood across from the main entrance to the cemetery. Tom, the vicar, and his new wife lived there.

Waiting on the porch, Jude could hear the crying of their new baby within. The boy was Lyn's first delivery on returning to duty, and the couple's first child.

Tom Merritt opened the door. When he saw Jude standing there, knowing of his loss, he pulled the door to in an effort to deaden the sounds of his own son's liveliness.

"Let's step into the garden Jude. Noisy little beggars, aren't they? "

They stopped beside a lilac covered bower whilst Tom searched for the right words to express his sympathy. before enquiring the reason for Jude's visit.

"I was wondering if you could arrange for a burial site."

"I'm most awfully sorry Jude, but there is no provision for the stillborn," the young vicar apologised. It seemed the church had no room for such.

"Look Tom, I cannot take her home. She isn't even in a coffin, man. You must help me out," pleaded Jude.

"Good heavens! Is that box…? I didn't know Jude. How could they send you home like that?" Words flew under the scent of lilac, cloying the back of Jude's throat. He stood up for air, wanting to get away with his burden. The new father in Tom spoke.

"Leave her with me Jude, I will find a place for her." Baby Bridget had found rest.

Lyn was waiting at the gate when he reached home. She looked askance at his empty hands. He took her into the garden behind sun dried fields and held her close.

"Our baby is taken care of Ducks. She will be inside the cemetery boundary in un- consecrated ground. We can go and lay some flowers on her grave, but we must be careful because Tom is out of line with church rules."

The niceties of the church were no surprise to Lyn. Recently she had run up some stairs on her district, hearing the expulsive gasp of the final push by an un-booked mother in advanced labour.

A woman, pale as death, lay on an open bed. Between her thighs, lay a golden skinned babe. The Rhesus baby and her mother were alone in the house.

"Is this your first?" Lyn asked, finding a faint pulse in the umbilical cord, as the placental life support slid next to a body, inert of its first indignant cry. A cold fear urged to ask again.

"Is this your first?" Knowing eyes looked into hers.

"No Sister. Will this one die too," came a whisper?

"I'll do my best, but I need help. I must leave you with a neighbour for a few minutes". Pressed for time Lyn opened a window looking on to the street.

"I need help," she shouted. Heads popped out of nearby windows, as she knew they would. Choosing a calm elderly woman to stay with her patients, she gave instructions.

"Can you make a warm drink for the mother please? Oh, yes and fill a warm bottle to put near the baby, but don't touch her, will you," before she pedalled furiously to the nearby hospital.

"I need an oxygen cylinder and infant mask on loan for a Rhesus negative baby, and can you page a doctor urgently," she gulped to the matron.

Minutes later, cylinder clutched in one arm, she ran back to the neighbour standing at the open door.

"Babe's gone Sister. I'll call the priest," and she went on her way.

Beset with fears that she should have stayed, Lyn ran up to the cradled infant, now overlaid with the pallor of death.

The mother lay silent, her head turned to the wall, gazing into a fathomless world of her own. Dark eyes, dark hair, pale creamy skin, her body newly slim beneath the quilt, the quiet words fell toneless.

"She'll be the third to go. The Church won't let me take precautions, you see nurse."

A bustle of feet on the stairs heralded the arrival of the doctor on the heels of a priest. One went to help his patient, the other turned to Lyn.

"Of course, you baptized the baby," the priest challenged?

"Why? No!" She faltered under his searching gaze.

"It was your duty to save this soul Sister, and you failed." With this cold judgement he turned, blessed the mother, and left the house. She was out of line, alongside Tom Merritt. Lyn shook the memory aside to reassure Jude, eyes heavy with unshed tears.

"I understand. We'll play it their way dear. I can wait awhile." Routine smothered their pain, but not her sense of failure and loss.

One day, Jude came into the kitchen where Lyn was rolling pastry for an apple pie.

"There are a couple of chaps starting an amateur drama group. They are casting for a new play Ducks." She looked up, a question in her eyes as he continued.

"They seem a friendly lot, one's the son of my patient. Roy acts and Clive produces. How about you trying for a part? It's a play about Nell Gwyn".

"I don't really think I want to Jude," she demurred.

"You've got to stop mooning over things Ducks. Come on, it's tonight. I'll come with you," he persuaded.

He had come to accept her inability to share Nell's earthy joy of sex and he had lost the tomboy, who climbed, cycled, and swam with him. She was a good partner in a working marriage and he liked her in that role. Her innocence set her apart from his other romps. Lyn soon became immersed in the familiar routine of rehearsals, identifying with parts of her own character, as she created a role.

Clive and Roy enchanted Lyn, with their blond good looks and gallant manners, on shared beach picnics and country walks. She blossomed, and when Jude set up a small business with a local pet shop, using their spare bedroom for breeding tropical fish, Clive joined in his venture. Jude warily negotiated the quicksands of a relationship with gay friends.

One evening Lyn was preparing a salad for supper.

"Clive's coming about seven. We are going to clean out some tanks for the new stock. Can you make that salad into sandwiches Ducks? I'll come down for them before we've finished."

"I'll bring them up. We can eat together, and watch the fish settle in," she replied.

"No! Don't come upstairs, we shall be busy. Do you understand," Jude snapped peremptorily?

"No, I like to see Clive." Struggling with a growing infatuation for Clive's easy charm, she looked for acceptance.

A subliminal crack opened on a child shut out in the cold of a narrow alley. Shards of fear splintered Jude's maleness. He'd invested in Lyn for comfort and gain. Clive satisfied his hunger for warmth. He stared her down.

"What do you mean by like," was his cold retort.

She clapped a hand to her mouth, her eyes startled and anxious with self-discovery.

"I mean Clive makes me feel I'm me and not the district nurse, she stuttered, but I don't want friendship to come between us Jude."

"Well" he compromised, "I'll tell Clive to pay his respects before he leaves." The crack closed. He was up and running again. Chastened she retired early.

Later, Jude strolled down to the gate with Clive to see his rival off, then he prowled back to the house his reins hot with jealousy. He stalked to their bed and covered his woman. In July, a healthy son was born.

They became a family with Lyn anticipating her coming role of working mother.

"I shall be expected to return to work soon Jude and I feel I must until we get our own home." To that end, Jude was ready with the services of a woman, recently widowed. He sold his fish tanks and turned the little front bedroom into a pied a Terre for widow Broom.

Lyn surfaced from baby feeding, walking with the perambulator patrol, and tuning her ear to a demanding cry, to fearfully try out Jude's offer of another' woman's care of Nicholas. When she met Mrs B and heard her rich gravelly voice, a mutual liking swept away her fear, and they soon got each other's measure.

"Hello! I'm Mrs B. I'll be 'appy to 'ave somethin' worthwhile to do now me 'ubby's gone. You've been sorely missed on the district," she told Lyn.

By the time Lyn returned to the district she and Nicholas greeted Mrs "B" with welcome smiles when she bundled her short stocky frame through the side door.

Clive had backed away from family affairs now the fish were gone, and Lyn spent all her time with the baby. Jude felt unwanted and unsettled as he found himself in the role of father. Soon, Nicholas wormed his way into his heart, and to capture the wonder of his growing son. he bought one of the new recording machines.

Working in the garden one Spring afternoon, he heard footsteps behind him on the path.

"How's it going?" a friendly voice asked.

"Clay and more of the same," he grinned resting his spade.

It was a neighbour, a wiry man of around Jude's age, wearing the overalls common to the men working on the nearby quays and docks.

"The wife, Di, says you have a son same age as ours. She sent me over to see if you and the wife would like to bring the little chap across for a bite of tea. It's just about ready. I'm Dave by the way."

"Tea sounds good, after all this digging. I'll go and tell Lyn, five minutes OK?" Jude accepted the smiled invite, collecting spade and hoe.

Their hostess, proud of her table set with the best tablecloth and new baked scones, poured tea and handed Lyn a cup.

"You are lucky to have a baby and keep your job. I used to be a secretary in London, and I do miss my freedom, but I wouldn't be without tiddler here." She beamed at the toddlers rolling around their feet,

"Well freedom comes at a price. I get quite a lot of jealousy and criticism directed at me because I'm the odd one out, but I don't feel I'm in the wrong," Lyn said pensively.

Jude noticed an expensive watch on Dave's wrist.

"That's a lovely thing. Does it keep good time?"

"Yes, I got it from friends. Let's go and look at my garden and I'll tell you about them." When they returned, Jude had a fresh glint to his eye and new plans in his mind.

Through her friends, Lyn found a second-hand car within their means. The little black Ruby looked a sad sight. They climbed over it and under it and tried the few simple switches on the dash board before reckoning they had a bargain.

"Needs a good polish" said Jude. At the end of two days shiny dark green paintwork replaced its black coat of grime. Their first car looked as good as new. On a test run to discover new villages and some of the inland waterways, Jude turned to tweak Nick's toes and check he was safely holstered into his seat. As he drew back, Lyn noticed an expensive watch strapped to his wrist.

"When did you buy that Jude, it must have cost," she questioned apprehensively?

"Don't worry Ducks, Dave got it for me. Lovely isn't it."

Very early that morning, Jude had cycled down to the port gates where he found a sleepy porter, nearing the end of his night shift. Asked his business. a willing pawn for Dave answered confidently.

"I'm calling on the First Aid Post. New regulations to check the drug cupboard." Hoisting his nursing bag aloft with a grin, he waited tensely for the go-ahead.

"Right mate," said the porter, swinging a small side gate open. Jude made for the hut with a red cross on the roof and knocked on the door. A seaman was waiting with others for minor first aid. Jude took him aside to look at his bruised hand, whilst taking a small package from the smuggler's coat pocket.

Port shifts had changed, and a new face bade him good morning, as he walked past the gate with the night workers to meet Dave, out of sight of the gates.

"How did it go?" Dave asked tersely.

"It was a piece of cake. Just like old times, hopping the shore leave boat with extra rations stuffed up me jumper," boasted Jude. He opened his nursing bag to take out a sealed oilskin packet and hand it over. Dave took out an expensive Swiss watch and handed it to Jude.

"You're in then," He cycled off.

Standing on the lonely stretch of road, Jude strapped the smuggled watch to his wrist. He caressed the warm gold. Spending comforted him but making money satisfied a deeper longing. The ugliness and brutality of his childhood lay behind a closed door. Now he was fired afresh to make money and realize his dreams.

"One day I'll have everything I want," he vowed as he cycled back for the family outing in the country.

Chapter 5: Family visits

THE summer of fifty-four was a time for family visiting. Nana Turner came.

Faded blue eyes quietly read the young faces greeting her at the coach station. Age declined the offer to go further than a comfortable chair to rest her short ample body. With her great grandson snuggled in her arms, she watched their comings and goings. Her intuitive Welsh heritage saw storm clouds ahead.

Nana was followed by Lyn's invalid father, a quiet man whose placid silences Lyn was well accustomed to. He was content to see her settled comfortably and when they saw him off home, the sea air had returned a little colour to his cheeks.

Jude's family came to stay the following spring. The house was turned upside down and the caravans refurbished for the overflow of the boisterous country mob. They were all out, exploring the coastline and inland waterways with Jude, when Mercy Young arrived, unannounced, late one afternoon. Lyn answered the door to her knock.

"Mum" she gasped in surprise, "How did you get here, come in, oh come in dear. Why didn't you tell us you were coming?" She guided a strangely quiet Mercy to a chair.

"Something's wrong, isn't it?" Her mother nodded, her eyes full of tears as she reached for Lyn's hand.

"Rest a bit Mum, I'll make a cup of tea."

"It's Dad, Lyn, he is very ill. I came all of a sudden by the coach, because I had to talk to somebody. Yes, put the kettle on, will you." Noting she had no baggage, Lyn kissed the familiar face, now worn with grief. What a good mother she was. The war years and her sudden marriage had left a rent in their history. Its tapestry lacked scenes of warmth and laughter. Preparing a tea tray, she returned to Mercy with her thoughts atumble.

Mercy took the proffered cup with a grateful smile and joined her daughter's pondering until a bustle in the hall preceded the Pratt family trouping in.

Emma Pratt flopped down in a chair. Emma, a very tiny woman, had a humped shoulder, a sharp pointed nose, and a generous heart. She spoke with deep Gloucestershire warmth from around the cigarette tucked in the corner of her mouth.

"Why goodness me, it's Lyn's Mum." Amidst the family chatter Mercy told of her husband's sudden dive from invalid to dying man. Her hands pressed back the flow of tears sliding down smooth pink cheeks.

"They tell me he will soon be out of pain. The doctors don't give him too long." An uncomfortable silence was broken by Jude's entrance.

"Ducks let's have supper early. Tonight's the last night of The Dam Busters and we're all going. You're coming with us."

The words were out before he saw Mercy. Lyn signalled him to follow her into the kitchen.

"What's your mother doing here," Jude confronted her, chin jutted, "if she's staying, she will have to make do with a chair?" Jude's unyielding heart denied space to any but his mother.

"My father is dying," Lyn sparked. "She needs loving for heaven's sake. She's tired out, so your mother can share her bed and let her sleep in comfort tonight." He gave a grudging agreement with a condition.

"You're coming to the cinema with us then. She is not spoiling our evening," he demanded, dark faced, brows beetled over slate grey eyes.

Lyn backed away from his challenge.

"I can't Jude, she needs me more."

"Right, the rest of us are going."

She hastened to start the meal. Kneeling to adjust the oven shelves, before lighting the gas, she rested her head against the open door to collect her thoughts. 'He's jealous of Mum.'

Jude came into the kitchen and mistook the scene for her hysteric reaction. He jerked her roughly to her feet with a stinging slap to the face.

"Silly cow, we'll buy our supper on the way back," was his parting shot. Smarting with shame and pain, she returned to the sitting room, where Emma and Mercy sat talking, heads together.

"They are going to bring some fish and chips home so, shall we have our supper together," she suggested?

Mercy and Emma looked up; the love in their faces quenched her self-pity.

"Your Mum and me have been planning dear. How about I keep an eye on young Nick tomorrow, whilst you go back with her to see your Dad?"

"Oh, would you? I so want to see Dad, and perhaps sort things out for Mum," she hugged Emma in response before turning to Mercy.

"I knew you'd understand me coming. Dad wants to see you and I need you," said Mercy. Although self-reliant and determined in many ways, Mercy delegated decisions to Lyn, whose younger head and shoulders took the weight, as her invalid father withdrew from family affairs in earlier years.

Kissing her mother 'good night', Lyn knew better then to embarrass her with a hug, for Mercy's affection was reserved towards her children.

After seeing the mothers settled comfortably in bed, Lyn set the table for breakfast. Anxious to make amends, she prepared hot cocoa for Jude and the. others when they returned, but the atmosphere remained cool. Jude's moody sulk carried over to the next morning, leaving Lyn and her mother to set off for London with just a quiet farewell from Emma.

Bright sunshine danced on the bonnet of the little Ford Ruby as they passed vegetable fields patched with yellow, green, and purple. Mercy drank in the freshness of the country air and leant on Lyn's advice as she talked over recent events over once again.

The grey bricks of North London loomed over them as they drove along the busy road to the hospital. An ugly grey building, its square shape and façade unrelieved by ornamentation, it served many of the poor in a widespread area.

Inside, a maze of drab green walls wound to wards, where the parsimony of the Hospital Board, grudgingly supplied poor quality furnishings and thin bed coverings.

Generosity marked the nurses' cheerful service. Gentle hands and stout hearts tended the ill-nourished. Their rough and ready voices quipped and roused the sufferers to fight back. Coming from their shared background, the sick responded with ready wit.

Lyn and her mother made their way to the bed where her father rested. In a tender voice Mercy beckoned Bertie's seeking hand to hers.

"We're here love, give me your hand."

He lay behind bars protecting him from the dangers of bouts of delirium. Intubation catheters snaked between the restricting bed barricades to various receptacles below.

Shocked, Lyn looked at his pale clear skin stretched paper thin upon the fine bone work of his face. A tonsure of still dark auburn hair wreathed a skull, faintly pulsing with life. Long elegant hands plucked the sheet covering his emaciated body.

She looked at her mother. Lyn had never seen such love on her face before. It lit with a smile as Bertie opened his eyes to lock with Mercy's.

During the next lucid moments, lying with hands clasped, he sang snatches of old love songs in a surprisingly strong voice, to both of them.

Lyn stepped to one side from this private meeting of old lovers, steeped in her own thoughts.

'When we were kids, during the hungry thirties, his self-denial supported Mum's efforts. On slender means, they found the money for dancing classes, elocution lessons and music tuition for us, and kept us at school for a full education whilst our peers were working. What lovely parents they are.'

She turned to them, but he had slipped back into his hell of pain and delirium. Her love for this quiet, collected man, cried out at the indignity of his dying. She longed for him to be given a final opiate.

A young doctor entered the long, many-bedded ward. She walked across to request a few moments of his time. He listened with a kind smile of understanding when she pleaded for her father's suffering to end but promised nothing. Her mother signalled that she was ready to go home. They kissed Bertie goodbye.

The small room in Queen's road was full of memories from schooldays to war days. They sat at the kitchen table sipping tea and delving into Mercy's future as they made provision for the next few weeks. Lyn's sisters lived in the district and came frequently with their support. It eased Lyn's feelings of guilt, when she left in the dark hours.

She returned home to Jude's unbroken silence. Running up to Nicholas, standing in his cot looking lost, she lifted him for cuddles, kissing's, and whispered reassurances. Such a smile lit his face as she tucked him up to sleep.

A hot cooked breakfast was ready for those finishing their packing, before returning to Gloucestershire. Murmurs of appreciation and smiles of approval greeted well-laden plates. 'Thank heavens for that,' Lyn thought, hoping their lighter mood included an absent Jude.

Mrs B arrived early to take over from Lyn.

"What an 'ouseful you've 'ad m'dear," she boomed, pushing up her sleeves to tackle the dishes piled by the sink. She rolled her eyes towards the living room. "I'll 'ave this mess sorted before you come back 'ome t'dinner. What is it t'day? C'mon Nikki, come and give old Broomie a kiss then," as he toddled over to bury his head in her skirt.

The hoot of a car horn drove everyone out to greet the carload from the caravans. Emma Pratt and her daughters piled their luggage in the hired car, parked behind them and clambered into the passenger seats, calling back thanks and farewells, as Jude came out. He slipped into the driver's seat and switched on the ignition.

"I'm going back with them," he told a shocked Lyn, then drove off.

Running into the house she went to tell Mrs B, sorting out the washing.

"He won't be away long, we'll manage m'dear," she smiled encouragement, then questioned her pinched face.

"Why, didn't you know he was going back with his Ma?"

"No! His diabetic injections, whose doing them? Oh, Mrs B, I can't think clearly," bemoaned Lyn.

"My, it's like that is it? It'll all blow over once he's taken his mum 'ome, and 'ad a bit of an 'oliday. Asked me yesterday, he did. Bit of short notice it was, I must say, but I can stay overnight if you like or what about Mrs Thompson's girl next door, sleeping in? I'll ask her while you're out this morning.

If you ask me, it seems like he's making up for lost time, so to speak. He couldn't do enough for 'em, and he didn't want 'em to go back." She handed Lyn a list from the pocket of her apron.

"You'd better get orf luv. You're late, and you've got 'is patients to do. He made out that list for me to give you. Will dinner for one o'clock be all right?"

The rhythm of life altered very little. Esme, Mrs Thompson's girl, was always on hand at night. Patients missed the little chats, Jude's visits usually finished with, after Lyn's brisker routine than usual. Nicholas still dabbled in the pools along the beach in the afternoon and night calls were few. Eventually Jude rang to see how she was managing.

"I've taken a fortnight's leave," Relieved and happy to hear some concern from him, she replied.

"We are fine here," then hearing music in the background, "Where are you?"

"I'm in the Rotunda Ballroom and I'm just going back to find a partner." The phone went dead and her longing for his forgiveness resurfaced.

Jude returned to the dance floor, justifying his need to quench the hunger of unsatisfied loins. Her Victorian response to his advances had given way to submissively fulfilling but them but was no fire of desire when she opened to him. He knew she loved him deeply and found her satisfaction in pleasing him, but it was not enough.

'It's her fault and she'll never understand why. Then she's always a step ahead of me in other ways and knows it all. I feel inferior, I've got to get some time away from her.'

He recognized his fault in marrying her. 'Later, I'll see whether…Let the boy grow up first, he will need a father's guidance into his teens and then.'

For the time being he placed her on a pedestal, an ornament to show off for her assets as a capable manager of their lifestyle.

Although he swelled with pride as he basked in the family's respect for his success, he felt empty. The thought niggled him, 'I'll always be Mum's mistake, never one of them.' His eyes ranged over the girls waiting for a partner.

'I'll try my luck with this Judy. If you don't use it, you lose it, in the navy I topped the lot for cocks.'

"Shall we try this slow foxtrot, what did you say your name was?" Taking the Judy in his arms and pressing a determined thigh against hers, Jude set about making the most of his evening.

He returned to Essex late one night. She was expecting him and lay in bed, reading a book when she heard the car drive in and the front door open. His tread was soft on the stairs. She stayed quiet, waiting. Nick's door squeaked, 'must oil that hinge.' He walked in, smiling, to sit on the side of the bed.

"Everything all right then." Another sulk was over, but this time she wouldn't come running.

"Did you have a good holiday?"

"It's good to be back," said Jude, his hand stroking her hair and the nape of her neck, "How about a cuddle." She laughed, falling back against the pillows, letting tension ease out. 'The bloody audacity of the bastard! Why do I continue to love this schizophrenic character?' The light oath was a comfort patch. Come what may, she had a son to rear and a marriage to keep afloat.

"Better hop in then" she invited, opening the bedcovers. Life fell into place again.

Her father had died the day following her visit. Her absence from his funeral was judged unfeeling by family members, ignorant of her circumstances. She let things ride until her next day off, when she went to make silent amends at her father's graveside and peace with her mother.

On her return, Jude met her at the gate with Nicholas perched on his shoulder. Putting Nick down, with a pat and promise of a story time soon, he turned to Lyn, taking her hands in his.

"We've missed you," he said. "I do, you know."

"I do too," said Lyn.

One late autumn day she sat playing with Nicholas, building brick pictures of farm animals on the floor, when Jude came into the nursery. He sat in the old rocker, watching them. His eye traced the curve of her neck, bent over Nick, as she helped him to place a brick in place, giggling when the picture amused them.

She looked lovely and, for a moment, he hungered for her but stalled, knowing her passion was all in the mind, and he had other things to attend to. Customs had got wind of the smuggling and police were sniffing around. He must run for cover and needed her to co-operate.

His silence prompted her to look up into a face looking pale and drawn. She started up.

"Are you all right, you don't look well. Shall I go and…" He waved her back.

"It is bitingly cold ducks, it's this East coast. It doesn't really suit me," he began rocking gently back and forth, "and we've got Nick to consider when it's time for school. It's all carrots and cabbages down here. What say we move to Sussex? They are asking for a married couple in today's Nursing Times."

"Jude, you've never complained before and we're fine here. We've made friends and a good reputation. Let's build up our credentials a bit longer to get a good reference. School is a way off yet," Lyn suggested.

Clinging to the safety of the known for her family, she picked Nick up. Hugging him to the panic in her breast, she went to the window and turned to him, waiting until he joined her. Looking out over the field he began his reluctant confession.

"There might be a bit of trouble over some watches Dave and I smuggled in from Holland. It could mean prison so we must move away Ducks," was his bleak news. "Sussex might be our way out." Her world spun.

"No, they couldn't, prison is for criminals Jude."

"We won't be far off if we're found out."

Weak from shock she let Nick slide to her feet, to wrap her hand around the fears invading her throat. Now she was included in his duplicity, she let words pass.

"Then we must go," she agreed tensely.

"Don't worry, it will be all right. You'll love Sussex with the lovely old villages and antique shops. I took Mum there to poke around one day and I took a shine to this. Would you like it?" He reached in his pocket.

She shivered as she looked at an ancient silver claw sitting on the port wine stain in her palm.

"No. You keep it Jude."

Over supper, she composed an application for the post, then sat with Jude poring over maps of the area. For Jude, a black cloud was lifting on a future where new beginnings beckoned. She went to bed with the old feeling of excitement and adventure to share with Nick and fell asleep thinking of the silver claw.

She dreamed of frantically running to reach a riverbank, with a silver claw dancing in front of her eyes. Glinting, it fell into the river. Panting with effort to reach the bank, she fell to her knees searching for the broach. Jude's face looked up palely green through the ripples. She threw hands high, river bright droplets sliding down from a bright red stain in the palm of one hand. A nearby willow tree wept tears of blood.

Wide awake next morning, she told Jude of her dream.

"Ha! I've no time for such rubbish. It's strange though, I felt as though the claw belonged to me."

Chapter 6: Sussex

WITH glowing references, they got through their Sussex interviews successfully. Within six weeks Jude and Lyn arrived outside their new quarters, a ground floor flat in a former music academy. The removal team made short work of their job. The small collection of Essex furnishings looked lost in the spacious rooms they walked around in the encroaching evening gloom. Standing at the windows, that faced the busy coast road, Lyn's eye travelled up their expanse to ceiling height.

"Curtains will have to be our first buy, even if we use some of our savings. Every thing's big isn't it, but there will be afternoon sunshine I expect if we make this the living room. This must have been the kitchen for yester year's 'downstairs' staff, see, it joins the passage leading to the scullery and the tiny rooms between must have been store rooms."

"We'll go shopping tomorrow," agreed Jude, joining her at the window with Nicholas in his arms. "Look Nick, see those cows in the field across the road and the lambs in the corner? Maybe that path goes down to the sea, I'll take you to find out tomorrow. It's early to bed for you now young man."

The bedroom furniture had ended up in a garden room on the 'upstairs' side of the house. French doors lead to a circular courtyard where three steps rose to the darkening garden.

"We can share our bedroom with Nick whilst we make one of the store rooms into a nursery. We'll leave the rest of the furnishing until money allows."

Come morning, Jude and Nick returned from exploring the field, to the appetizing smell of cooked bacon and Lyn tripping into the living room with a freshly brewed pot of tea and news of her discoveries.

"There's a good-sized lawn for Nick to play on, fruit bushes galore, a couple of apple trees, and a vegetable patch which just needs turning over."

The curtains were the first of many improvements which saw them living comfortably. Another Broomie, the mother of one of Lyn's antenatal patients, offered daily help. She cleaned the flat, before preparing a lunch for them five mornings a week. Nicholas started attending a private nursery school a few houses up the hill. After the bleak winds and eternal cold of the East coast, life became luxuriously warm.

At first, they both missed the down to earth mateship of families working with them, to restore their sick to health. Now they were counted as a service in the sleepy south-east coast town. Home to retired gentlefolk, it was locked into times of old-fashioned simplicity where they were respected for their role.

In town, discretely dressed stores beckoned discretely dressed shoppers. Day-trippers passed the town by in favour of the cockles and mussels and candyfloss jollity of Hastings on one side, or the brass band and flower gardened grandeur of Eastbourne on the other. Far from the bustle of London streets the sea front boasted the old Grand Hotel, a holiday resort for wealthy patrons,

On the outskirts, where town met country, the council built large new housing estates for the poorer. Ensuring none was homeless, they kept a subtle divide between countryman, working class and retired gentry. Jude and Lyn cared for the rich and poor alike since their districts cut a swath across the whole area.

At day's end, each hoped there would be no night calls to disturb the budding warmth between them. Jude's routine lovemaking stifled soft words after Lyn had learnt the right steps in bed, but never the final whirl. They curled around a dream of success and embraced on the dance floor.

A black kitten joined the family and grew sleeker and larger as the family fortunes increased, though they continued to live by the frugal standards of pre-war thirties. Back then hunger marched with the homeless men, women and children from the North, walking to London to make protest. They trudged twenty miles each day, filling the Spikes along the way, to refuel from a huge cauldron of vegetable soup for twopence and two hours work next morning, after a night's sleep.

Poverty's shadow stretched across Europe with men crossing the sea to escape its reach. The French Onion men came wheeling bikes loaded with braided onions. They knocked at the doors of rich and poor alike after shooing away the gypsy, laden with child, who offered wooden pegs with a smiling plea for any old clothes.

Lyn gave such a gypsy two of her best dresses from the chest in mother's bedroom. She was not rebuked though the clothes were hard won from meagre wages. Of the working class themselves, her parents sympathised with needs of others.

Now the world had rolled into the fifties where imposing emporiums mushroomed in the towns. Once a month, Jude and Lyn sallied forth to visit one, diligently checking prices as they sought that month's addition to one of their wardrobes or a kitchen utensil made in the new coloured Bakelite.

Jude was on good terms with his world and brimming with confidence in a future cocooned by a regular wage and time to explore the downlands and hamlets nestled in the never-ending green border of the coast.

"Things are looking up Ducks, my feet have never felt so comfortable," he beamed, inspecting his new shoes.

"Come on, we'll have tea and cream cakes, before we go home."

Jude's easy going way with his patients soon increased their number. Overlapping working hours put Nick at risk, calling for an urgent solution at a time when the day of the family servant was over. Under the keen wind of change sweeping the workplace, post war women had moved to new pastures where employers unctuously welcomed them for a lower rate of pay. Bewildered men stopped giving up seats to the women who stole their jobs, unsure where it would all lead to.

Lyn's fruitless search through employment agencies ended when she discovered a pool of young women needing work and a home. By her next day off another store room was furnished and the home generally smartened up, to meet with their prospective employee's approval. The front door bell summoned a nervous Lyn.

A tall slimly built woman of country stock faced her. Wide-placed hazel eyes below well-defined eyebrows stared calmly into hers. Lyn was not sure who would be doing the interviewing.

"I've come about the job Mrs Rook." The soft voice was assured.

"Please come in, Dora isn't it." Over a cup of coffee Lyn relaxed, knowing that Nicholas would be in caring hands if this self-possessed young woman came to live with them.

"I can't offer a big wage Dora, it is the most we can afford." Agonized Dora would reject her offer, Lyn sat on the edge of her chair, waiting hopefully.

"As long as I can have two hours off every afternoon, I could come to you," said Dora.

"Oh yes, we can manage that. I'm so glad you can come, and I hope you will be happy with us. When do you think, you could start?"

"Tomorrow," sounded a miracle to Lyn. By the end of the week a quiet, capable Dora, had taken over many of Lyn's household tasks.

One afternoon, towards the end of lunch, a call came in from a young farmer's wife, in the early stages of labour with her first baby.

"Dora can you give me half an hour to reassure her," Lyn asked hesitantly. Jude looked up sharply at Dora's decisive refusal but stopped commenting at a glance from Lyn.

"I'll be here won't I Nick," he reassured.

In a house at the end of a country track, on the outskirts of town, Lyn made the usual preparations for a delivery she expected in the night hours. Chatting to her patient as they walked to the gate, she stopped to enjoy a brood of new hatched chicks, swimming in the nearby pond.

"How will your husband manage without you?"

"We have a labourer and his wife in the old tied cottage down the lane. They are fostering a child. The mother visits regularly, see there she is, coming down the path with him."

Turning, Lyn caught a flicker of movement at the labourer's cottage. A woman and a small boy were walking towards the gate. Lyn continued chatting whilst she watched intently. She needed to be sure.

"I shall only be a phone call away, but I will be back later," she promised getting into her car, her mind on the scene just witnessed

'That was Dora restricted to playing with her son for two hours a day. I can play with Nicholas any time I wish but I choose to leave him in another woman's care. It feels unjust, and I must do something about it.'

Making a few general visits to leave the evening clear, she returned home to where Dora was building a jigsaw with Nick. Joining in to help, Lyn murmured,

"There are so many pieces to fit together aren't there and we don't always get the picture we expect. A bit like life, I suppose, what do you think Dora?" The hazel eyes met hers.

"How do you mean" she replied?

"Well I think we're all riddles, you, me, everyone. I've puzzled where you go every afternoon until I solved it today Dora. Would you like to talk to me about it?"

The old story was retold, unvarnished with excuses. Dora had fallen in love with a young farm hand, giving herself willingly. He was not so keen when, at their evening tryst, she told him she was carrying his child.

Her family, fearing the censure of the small village where they lived, sent her away until the child was born, to be adopted.

"I love David Mrs Rook. I will never give him up to please the family, Never." Dora told her story quietly, sharing her secret, now a bond between two mothers.

"Would you like David to come and live here with us, could you manage?" A flicker of hope lit Dora's eyes quickly replaced by a wary look.

"What will I have to do" she asked?

"No more than you do now, except care for David, which will cost you nothing," replied Lyn. "We shall have to find out how to do things officially."

"Oh, I can care for us all, I'm used to family ways," Dora promised gratefully. Lyn placed the last piece in one puzzle with a contented sigh of relief. Jude agreed wholeheartedly, winning a smile from Dora. The little family was growing, and it felt good.

The children accepted each other without question. Watching them play together, squabbling at times over loved toys, Lyn foresaw Nick's loneliness when Dora and her son moved on.

Returning from an ante natal clinic session one afternoon, she pulled up behind Jude retrieving his bags from the boot of his car.

"Well, how are all your Mums this afternoon" he quipped,

"Happy and expecting! They started me wishing," she answered wistfully. "I want another baby. Nick's given us such happiness and I think he'll miss David when Dora leaves us, and she will sometime." By agreement she and Jude had conceived no more children.

"Let's wait until that time comes before you start worrying about it Ducks," he hedged, walking off.

"No, he deserves a brother or sister," she pressed him, slipping round him to bring him to a halt. He was non-committal except for a shrug.

"Well, if that's what you want." That night the seed of a new soul sped through the strait between his loins.

Baby Andrew made a dramatic entry in April. After a fight for survival in her womb he needed major surgery in London. Their visits to see him in an incubator stretched from weeks to months, prompting the county to request her return to work. Finally, the doctors told them they could do no more, and they should take him home. The bonding brought a miracle as she fed and cradled the wee scrap in her arms whenever he summoned. Andrew began to put on weight and win his fight. The county reduced her hours to allow her plenty of time to nurse him and call in, during her reduced round, to check Dora was managing. It never occurred to her, to stop working. She still sought to perfect and add to her skills. Knowledge was power.

Jude found extra ways of supplementing the fall in their income. A patient, an ailing partner in a small memorial card business, discovered Jude's interest in printing. They came to an arrangement to suit both.

A small printing press was set up in an empty room where he shut himself night after night, sorting tiny bocks of metal letters, and laying them in reverse order in the print trays. He took a pride in work which took its toll. Sore eyes and an aching back the price for the small change that the shrewd brothers paid him.

There were days when he rushed home, to change into sombre black, pulling a tall black hat low down over his face. He carried the boxed remains of a corpse, he had nursed and laid, out shoulder high after recommending a local undertaker for an agreed fee. The firm paid good money for every soul they escorted on its last journey with the smooth deference of maestros conducting a requiem.

To be sure a grieving widow sometimes gave a puzzled look at the bearer whose face, shielded by a gloved hand, looked somewhat familiar. As the big black hearse passed through the town he sheltered among the wreaths. Such blatant moonlighting put him at risk of losing his job and their home.

Whilst one sought the power of knowledge, the other sought the power of gold and both thought they were on the same quest, success. Their combined energies engulfed all that threatened their path. Lyn eventually was forced to resign under pressure from anti working mothers lobby and found it hard to make ends meet. She turned to the Nursing Times.

"Jude how do you feel about me working morning shifts as a hospital midwife," she said one evening at supper?

"There's a part time morning vacancy at the maternity hospital, which means you can stop moonlighting. I can care for Nick and Andrew and I can still do what I love."

"That's just it, I like making money Lyn," he responded. "Go back to midwifery by all means if you want." Lyn felt his approval was motivated, for all cash was grist to his mill. Their plans went smoothly, even allowing Lyn to return to full time as the children thrived in the love from three contented parents.

Three years on around Christmas time, Dora received an invite to visit her family. It was no surprise when, the following Spring, Dora came to them with news.

"I shall be going back to live with my family as soon as it's convenient to you. They know of a man who wishes to marry me. It will be better so." She was to marry an elderly farmer with no heirs. She would do well for herself and David.

The happy ending to Dora's story left Lyn with no option. She must to return to work, part time, whilst Andrew was at Nick's old nursery school where Jude usually picked him up, on his way in to lunch

Jude sat astride his bike, waiting for Andrew to run out to him as he weighed up his chance of trying his luck at his new patient's hotel for retired gentlefolk. He decided to make time as Andrew ran down the path. He scooped him up.

"Been a good boy then, let's go home." An excited Lyn waited for them, a light lunch ready on the table

"Oh Jude, I've been given a chance to scrub up for a Caesarean. I've always wanted to try theatre, so I promised to go straight back for a couple of hours. Will that be all right? I shall be back for Andrew and me to meet Nicholas from school."

"I've got one more to do but I'll be back soon." Her protest hit his retreating back.

Earlier his patient's landlady had bemoaned the number of beds to make. , He intended to make good his offer to help, which she accepted with a smile, her hand brushing his, as she took his empty coffee cup.

A year or so older than Jude, she breathed the warm ease of the hotelier. Blond coiffed hair and artfully applied makeup enhanced her attraction. She laughed and giggled as she recounted saucy stories about her guests, her eyes enticing, her mouth inviting.

Now in the last room to be tidied, as she bent over to straighten the sheets, his eyes invaded the long cleft between her full breasts, deepening as their roundness filled her neckline, milk white breasts falling...

His mind's eye saw the fall of his mother's breast as she let down its bounty to the suckling on her lap, in the warm darkness of an afternoon cinema romance. The sensual pull of the flickering screen and the urgently sucking lips denying his childish demand for attention, with a brusque, "Be quiet."

The sound of swishing of curtains called him back from those memories to a room bathed in a soft pink light. The woman came to him, cupping his face between cool palms.

"You looked so lost and sad, I thought…" Sometime later they straightened the rumpled sheets. She had taken him gently and he had plundered another man's treasure.

He returned to an angry Lyn. Her thin shell of self-containment had cracked under the disgrace facing her at work. She phoned the hospital to apologise and hand in her resignation.

"I've let people down," she stormed to a pan faced Jude, on his way for an afternoon nap She tidied up tight lipped and resentful at losing her chance to improve her qualifications until she gathered Andrew up, warm and content from sleep. She let his face snuggle into her neck. His trust that she was there meant more than the conditional approval of the workplace. Later, walking in the park with her sons, their laughter enticed her out of her pet.

The night hours drew her back to question her future, her mind darkened under a cloud of despair. In the morning Jude quit the house leaving behind a sullen chill and the threat of one of his long sulking silences. Whilst the boys fretted to leave and be on their way to school, she sat unheeding in a fireside chair.

By mid-morning, when Jude looked in, she was still sitting there. The breakfast table was un-cleared, and the boys stood by the window in worried silence.

"What's going on?" Moving across the room towards her, he stopped short at her toneless 'Fuck', whispered over and over.

Turning on his heel, he went to the hall and made a brief telephone call, then gathered the boys and took them to school and nursery. He returned to wait on the front porch for the family doctor. The tall Scot, a kindly physician who loved poetry and sipped on a sonnet during the wait for new life, had attended quite a few home deliveries with Lyn. He arrived with a colleague and the three went in to talk with her. A few gentle questions elicited little response from Lyn except to say,

"I don't know why, but I keep saying fuck, and I don't want to do anything."

Jude went to some lengths to furnish proof for her to be sectioned because the children were at risk. They explained that unless she decided to go voluntarily for a rest, she would be detained under section 3 of the Mental Health Act.

She offered no resistance, thinking her cooperation would appease Jude, since he was talking to her again. When he left her outside the door to Loxton institution, he promised to send for her mother to care for the children then drove away.

Lyn took one step inside Loxton and left the stage of life a hazy blur on the far side of a grey veil. She followed an orderly through doors connecting endless corridors of garish green tiled walls, studded with mute closed doors. The music of human activity, sunlight, and nature's bounteous colours receded ever further away. A moan ruptured the silence, crawling ghostlike around the high walls. A shriek of distress arched to grey ceilings, then fell, fell into nowhere. No reference points came from the few people she passed.

The staff wore mufti in an experiment to cross the barrier between them and their patients. Their choice of dress was unappealing, thwarting their intent to fall into step with the meandering, shambling gait, of the bewitched and bewildered. The idioms used, were at odds with the chords of compassion they sought to strike. Sympathy plucked the nurses heartstrings, but there was no melody, no sonata, or few notes of hope, to catch the ears of the strangers in their midst. All danced to their own tune.

Lyn lay huddled in a curl, to shut out the shock of this new world, beneath the gentle darkness of the bedclothes. Peeking out, she looked through cot bars and met the impact of an endless row of beds. Engulfed in the loneliness of not belonging, her features contorted her into the crying face of a child. A troop of nurses strode towards her with laden syringes, then she knew no more.

Some days later, drifting up from a deep induced sleep, it was as if her very spirit shot clean and newborn from a pool of quiet waters. Free of the secrets the narcotics had released to a silent listener, she was told her there was no sickness in her. She had struggled with too many do's and don'ts and sacrificed deep needs to the external pressure of love, honour and obey. They invited her to stay awhile to find herself again.

During the weeks before her discharge, she read an advertisement for a Midwifery Night Sister. When she applied, her honesty about her plight, secured her the post. It opened a way back to integrity, where there would be no more shame for the path she walked, and the children would have all of her love and care.

"I found an answer to our problem Jude" she said on their way home. "If you agree, I can work three nights a week. It is fourteen miles away, so I may not be in until the boys start breakfast. Will you do that for me until we find new help? I'll get plenty of sleep whilst they are at school."

"We'll give it a try." Jude gave her a brief kiss of approbation. Lyn guessed he would miss his freedom in the evenings, more than her company, so help must be found. Lyn search for help with her family's needs ended, when she followed a new trail to meet Katie.

At the turn of the fifties innocent bastards were socially accepted. Adoption societies grew rich on a much sought for commodity, babies, with no legal right to know their true origins. Teenage mothers, like spoiled children, unrepentantly erred again. Fruits of the promiscuity from the recent war seeded, and bastard begot bastard.

Katie was a slender twenty-two, showing no sign of two previous pregnancies. Long blond hair framed an alert, piquant face where wide lips formed a ready smile as she fielded the questions Lyn asked.

She was an adopted baby who had run away from a good home after the death of her mother. She kept in touch with her withdrawn and over strict father in Cambridge, where he was headmaster of a small private school. Lyn quietly asked how she felt about helping with young children since her own baby was adopted. A vivid smile framed the practiced reply.

"Oh, I love children. It's just that… Well it was better that way for me you see." A little note of urgency tinged her words.

"I can do all the duties you've asked of me. I really do want to get away from the hostel, please." Still uncertain Lyn met the long green eyes searching hers with another question.

"You're well educated and still in touch with your father. Wouldn't you be better going back and…"?

"No thanks" Katie cut in, well-marked brows frowned down from their arched appeal, thickly lashed lids lowered, ending the discussion.

Jude had been listening from his desk, where he was setting up some print. He turned to join the conversation.

"Let the young lady have a trial, Katie, is it?" Her smiling mouth drew a smile in response.

Katie came to them the next day. Returning from that night's duty, the happy atmosphere and well-ordered start to the day reassured Lyn and by the end of a pleasant breakfast, Christian names were being used. Now free of the demands of district nursing and day shifts, Lyn was soon enjoying the beach and downlands with the boys and their friends. Jude's taciturn moods stopped, and he slackened off his printing to explore new activities.

He chose the local judo club, one of the town's sports clubs to put on exhibitions for the summer festival parade. and was soon proficient enough to teach. He took the boys to his children's classes in preparation for the festival. Lyn was roped in to chaperone a group of excited juniors, hopping up and down, as they waited to get down from their float when their lorry lurched to a stop. Jude in charge of the seniors, put a protective arm round a dark-haired young man as he helped him climb over the tailboard, before marshalling his troupe to a roped off exhibition area.

When Katie arrived to join Lyn, they wandered over to watch the youngsters tumbling and posturing with all the fierceness of puppies. The experienced members gave a skilled performance in the art of self-defence, ending with a little melodrama as Jude attacked the young man, grabbing the long black pigtail swinging down his back. In the struggle, the victim's robe fell aside to reveal a brief glimpse of a very feminine breast.

"Who is that," asked Katie, her eyes raking the girl from top to toe?

"Dunno," murmured Lyn thoughtfully. "Come on Katie. Let's go around the stalls until Jude comes." The sun was low in the sky by the time the festival ended. Going in line through the exit gates, the family shuffled in front of Jude's assailant.

"Your victim was a surprise, perhaps I should enrol for classes." Lyn teased.

"She's a new member," Jude countered. "The man she's with is her uncle." Their shadows moved ahead of them. One, with a swinging pigtail, cast a long shadow across Lyn's.

Summer drifted into autumn. Beaches were forsaken for the enchantment of nearby Brighton, swinging along the Esplanade, dawdling the old Smuggler's Lanes and visiting the town centre's grand shops before tea in the Creamery.

Neighbours visited for small cheese and wine soirees in the large room across the hall, where new furniture replaced Jude's printing press. The boys brought their friends home.

One midwinter's evening, when the large windowpanes darkened early under cold cascades of rain, Jude sat watching a popular television show with Lyn and Katie. The fire sent lively waves of warmth into the big high-ceilinged room, as Katie drew the curtains against the bleakness outside. With a resigned tut, Lyn rose from her chair and went for her night bag, dropping it on the floor as she shrugged on her coat

"I must go, thank goodness tomorrow I start my nights off. Tell me the end in the morning," she said, opening the door to the old conservatory A grapevine from distant days crept over its glass roof. Now a small car stood behind the wooden doors. Driving a few yards along the road she remembered she had left her night bag inside, at the top of the garage steps. She ran back.

Sitting in his high-backed chair near the door, Jude listened for the sound of the car departing, then nodded to Katie to close the doors of the slow burner. She curled up at his feet laying an arm across his knees. His hand reached to stroke the back of her neck as the conservatory door opened and Lyn popped her head over the top of the steps.

"Left my night bag behind," she announced to the back of Jude's chair then seeing Katie scramble up from the floor, "What are you doing...?"

"Just closing the fire doors," Jude answered smoothly. Katie's reply was un-intelligible as she ran from the room. On their evenings together, Jude liked Lyn to sit by his feet whilst he stroked her neck. A cold pebble of mistrust rolled around Lyn's mind.as she drove towards the dank marshes.

The half an hour drive to work, gave time to disengage from family affairs as the beauty of the landscape took over.

The low evening sun turned pools and rivulets of water into pink and red shapes of living light in the darkening marshland. Icy shapes reflected an opalescent calm as the land slept. Little villages of low thatched roofs measured her journey. Behind curtains shrugged across lattice windows, souls pulled close to warm firesides and mulled cowslip wine. On the soft lit windows of old inns flickering shadow men lifted tankards of ale to laughing lips.

In the grounds shared with a new hospital, were the sombre grey walls of an old workhouse, now the maternity unit. Behind heavy doors, the wards throbbed with life and hope, and work aplenty.

It was what she was good at, helping other women manage the pain, and achieve the victory of birth. The shared effort of crowning a head, whilst the mother controlled its final emergence, was high ritual art ushering in the eternal paradox of creativity and destruction, from the instant of the first gasped breath.

Next morning, the children's chatter shuttled her fears into the past with other un-answered questions. Jude offered to take the boys to school, leaving her to take refuge in the unnatural sleep of day.

Katie became quiet and pensive as Christmas drew near. Lyn thought the girl looked peaky and wondered if a break would do her good.

"How about spending Christmas with your father to try and mend broken fences," she suggested? Katie's alacrity in accepting the offer surprised her. On Christmas Eve, they saw her off on the Green line bus to Cambridge. Her face, pressed against the window, looked so sad.

"Oh, I do hope she has a good welcome." Lyn tucked her arm into Jude's. "She will be back to celebrate New Year's Eve together."

Katie didn't come back.

The day after Boxing Day, Jude returned, grim faced, from her phone call.

"Katie's not coming back. I'll finish early so have the boys ready and we'll drive over and see what's up. it'll bring her back."

"You cannot make her do what she doesn't want to do. Did she say why, is she all right?"

"That's what we're going to find out," he muttered. It was uncharacteristic of Jude, who usually left others to stew in their own juice unless the pot boiled over on him. To save arguing, Lyn took the easy way, followed Jude's wishes, and prepared for their late return.

Hours later they sat, cramped and cold outside Mr Skinner's house, listening to the rain pour down the car windows. Threatening grey clouds slid into an ebon winter's evening,

In even tones, Katie's father told them where they might find his daughter then bade them a quiet goodnight and closed the door.

They drove to a twittern of small cottages, huddled in a despairing row, under the tall sidewalls of a large house. Inside one dark, musty interior they found Katie and three burly young men. The men sat silently watching and listening as Jude persuaded.

"At least come back until we find a replacement. We'll miss you Katie." A white-faced Katie clung to the chair she huddled in, and steadfastly refused all pleas.

Lyn, seeing the strain she was under, moved to her to be warded off by a slender arm. Katie looked up, her eyes misted with tears, her hand reaching out to clasp Lyn's.

"I'm sorry" she whispered, drawing further back.

Jude began again but was silenced as threat filled the air from the three men seated at the plain deal table.

"Better leave it mate," said one and stood to shepherd them to the door.

Tight lipped with frustrated efforts, struggling with dark forces within him, an angry Jude drove home regardless of Lyn's attempts to placate. The boys fell into an uneasy sleep, broken by bursts of thunder in the slating rain.

Life settled into an uneventful certainty that they would eventually get somewhere. It was like a partnership in a small enterprise, where occasional highlights cemented their deal and kept it afloat.

Katie did return the following November. She stood in a shaft of late autumn sun light, when a sleepy-eyed Lyn wandered in to the living room. Hearing her step, Jude spun round.

"It's Katie and her husband, they are just going."

Katie smiled across at Lyn. In her arms she held a healthy baby of a few months or so. As the baby's face turned towards her, recognition struck home. Murmured 'Hallos, sorry to go' and 'Goodbyes' floated 0ast Lyn's ears, then they were gone leaving her in an empty room, full of new knowledge. Jude returned.

"I'll go and make some tea." Waiting for the kettle, he took stock of the last hour. He had been sitting at his desk, with a clear view of the road, when he saw Katie, accompanied by a man holding an infant, stop by the gate. He watched their approach to the front door, recognizing the man as one of the three men he had met in Cambridge.

As he waited for them to ring the doorbell, he recalled the intimacy of those evenings when Lyn was at the hospital. It had all been so convenient. Katie had knowingly aroused the manhood Lyn suppressed in her headlong rush to get heaven knows where.

The bell pealed for him to move to the door and let them in. 'Better see what this is all about. Katie's past news anyway,' he thought.

Katie's smile was brief as she moved ahead of the man with the sleeping infant's face snuggled into his shoulder. Jude signalled for them to be quiet as they passed the bedroom where Lyn was sleeping, before closing off that side of the flat. He went back to the living room to enquire why they had come.

"My husband thought…" began Katie, when the man eased the still sleeping child onto his knee, turning its face towards Jude.

"Leave this to me love," he said. "We are here on unfinished business you might say. I married Katie to make up for what I did to her some two year ago. I left her with child. Mine that I'll not set eye upon, since the boy was adopted from birth.

I shall be father to your child though, and we aim to bring him up right. That'll take a bit of money won't it son?" He tickled the sleep from eyes that stared straight into Jude's. They were his eyes and features from the nose up, above a wide smiling mouth.

"He is why I couldn't come back. I couldn't hurt Lyn. I couldn't face what I'd done. Frank here, has seen me through it, and this way nobody need be hurt," Katie's voice babbled on.

"How much do you want," asked Jude? He moved to his desk, where he sat with his back to them.

"A thousand …'

"Haven't got it"

"Seven…"

"Five hundred is all I can manage just now. I will send more when I can, but you must not come here again. Do you understand?" The young man looked him squarely in the face.

"Agreed," he said. Handing the infant to Katie, he came across to Jude who handed him a cheque which wiped out his savings. A flashback of a small boy collecting money from the welfare officer, bled into scene. But the boot was on another foot.

"Come Kate, it's time to go, we'll keep in touch." As Jude stood up, Lyn had come in.

The kettle whistled. He made tea and took the tray back to where she sat, her hand resting on his chequebook. He handed her a cup sliding the chequebook out from under her hand to lock it away. They sipped the hot soothing liquid in silence, his foot beating a protest in empty air.

"I'm glad Katie is settled with a husband and family. Who do you think the baby looks like?" Lyn eyed Jude then continued smoothly, "It would have been heart breaking to give up another child. Yes, the children. Not all those innocents fare well. She moved to the fireside chair.

"I'm still tired Jude, would you mind fetching Andrew and Nick please?" Nodding assent, he moved off as she rested her head back. Her eyelids draped a curtain over a scene of a mother, her baby and a father, until she fell asleep.

Chapter 7: Striking Out

JUDE and the boys roused her, wellington boots in hands.

"Come for a walk on to the beach with us for before tea."

"What a lovely idea. Come on then, where's Brutus?"

On the beach a fresh wind carried the scent of wet seaweed, glistening in the silver puddles of water left by the tide. Brutus raced ahead with the boys. Jude linked his hand into hers as they walked. How conventional it all was, best to keep it so, 'least said, soonest mended' and there were more pressing things on hand. Mercy Young had written to say she had arranged to move at the end of the week, to be close to them, and could they find her a flat.

A frantic hunt found the right place, just off the sea front, but it needed much time and effort to make it welcome. Her mother arrived to find three hundred new pounds notes, for extras, sitting on the mantelpiece above a freshly lit fire. Later, sitting down to reflect on the success of the day, Lyn received a call from Mercy.

"Lyn there's two pounds short." She had used a couple of notes to tip the removal man. So, Mum, always the giver, was now a counter of coinage.

Money, money, money it beckoned one and all, the key to a quick fix for peace and happiness. Housewives took the carrot of hire purchase for brighter homes, to be caught in a web of unpaid debt and future poverty. To be sure work was there for all in the sixties. The unlettered gave their muscle and cheerful service, dreaming of bright futures for children as blind as their parents to false values. The untrained laboured on, believing their children would be educated and protected under free government services.

They were ignorant of the Bretton Woods agreement, insisted on by previously war shy allies. With invading forces, a hair's breadth away, a nation with its back to the wall, signed an agreement, before might would stand shoulder to shoulder with them. Its terms for free trade across the globe would see some nations grow rich and others fall into deep debt and impoverishment.

By provident planning, the Rooks realized their dream of a home when a house came on the market, for a reasonable price, further along their road. A small mortgage, backed by monies from the London house sale and Lyn's savings, bought the property

One of a row of five, it stood on a low bank opposite their view of farmland, sea and great arcing sky scapes. At the turn of the century these good solid monuments housed the merchant class of the small seaside resort. They had long wide gardens where old walnut trees, tall oaks and elms stood amidst alien firs, vying with bushy hedges of holly and rhododendron. Underneath, old paved paths traced with moss filled cracks, lead to a big area of wasteland, the Wedge.

A 'Dig for Victory' pact, at the start of the first World War, gave permanent rights to the land a man dug in a day, on the jointly owned tennis courts. They called it the Wedge where they gathered good crops until the lean post war years of the fifties, gave place to times of increase. Kitchen gardens were neglected to watch legends of valour and fantasy on television. Weeds grew high, choking rich soil and now it was dotted with abandoned garden plots.

Three stories high, their purchase was perfect for their plan to open a small guest house for a new and fast-growing group of citizens. The waifs of Age Concern. the elderly were also part of post war society.

It was not lack of heart which left the elderly stranded on islands of loneliness. The growing prosperity offered many young couples a chance to buy their first home so long as they paid the dues. A mortgage fed on two wage packets and a child coming home from school to an empty house. The young had a choice. A rented house where mother was around, or, an affordable doll's house where there was no room for her. Finally, the old ones were left out of the equation. They trailed from cherished homes to bed-sits or family hotels where prices soared in the high season.

Their refuge became one of the small guest houses where costs were moderated to suit their few needs. Retirement homes became a new industry for such whose families could not find them space to live out their lives.

Lyn gave up her job to run their new venture with the daily help of old Nan McCallum. Nan's pregnant daughter needed Mum for her confinement but not under her feet until that time.

Auction rooms were scoured for floor coverings and furniture, whilst she spent hours sewing curtains with bedspreads to match until five rooms were ready for those no longer able to manage on their own.

On the day of the move to the Rook's guest house, the boys came back from school to a large airy attic under the front eves, its dormer windows overlooking a glimpse of sea. Jude and Lyn moved their possessions into an adjoining attic, to reassure them all was well. By nightfall the house was in fair order as they all gathered in the high-ceilinged kitchen where the family sat round the kitchen table for a late supper.

"Can I use the tiny attic Mum?" Nicholas was already making plans to use a tiny windowless space under the corner eves for his new friends at grammar school. Where better than a dark torch lit attic to hatch their plots?

All Andrew wanted was a shelf near his bed, to house his books. At school he struggled with a problem. He was seriously deaf and had been since birth. His life was a nightmare isolation as the victim of school bullies, and the backward fool of teachers. Their soundless flow of words baffled his quick intelligence.

He masked his disablement with good reading ability. Neither of his parents noticed his disability, in their rush ahead of the pack, until a private tutor informed Jude and Lyn that their son was deaf.

"We shall have a week or so before we start. It will give us time to get used to this place and put up your bookshelf Andrew," said Lyn.

"Not so fast Ducks, I've arranged for two residents to occupy the bottom room tomorrow. I'll give you a hand getting it set up before we go to bed," Jude upset the applecart.

Two of his patients came next day for respite from family bickering. A strict father overruled a quarrelsome daughter and a meek son. Outright rebellion threatened the hundred-year-old schoolmaster.

On their first day, Nan McCallum slowly inched along on her shortened leg with its crippled foot in a thick-soled boot. Suddenly, the tray she carried was whisked away.

"This is how to do it," Lyn said tartly, rushing out of the kitchen at such a pace, one of the plates shot off the tray. Red faced, she saved what she could, before sailing on to serve her guests who thought it was a splendid meal.

After a jump start and the humbling incident, their venture never looked back. Self-sufficient guests soon occupied the remaining rooms. The house took on a family atmosphere, albeit the boys were expected to know where to draw the line between its members. They took it on board like other intrusions in their lives, sharing the unequivocal outlook of friends, whose parents were also staking footholds in the future.

Teenagers retreated into foxholes of soft drugs, as consumerism and the mighty dollar gobbled up family values, spitting out stunted lives from emotionally impoverished backgrounds.

Nan McCallum moved on, to be replaced in an unexpected fashion. Answering the entrance bell, Lyn glimpsed a tiny figure through the coloured glass of the porch door. Pat Wellbright was dwarf high, a pitiful bundle of cast offs with a touch of the Mongol in her smiling face.

"I'm looking for a job Madam and I heard you were set up here. Doctor Box is where I'm working now, but it's getting too much for me on my own. I wondered…?"

Long service to the respected Doctor Box ended after she flung a half-set jelly at her mistress and for good measure threw in her notice to quit.

The doctor and his wife deemed the respect she gained working for him balanced the pittance they paid. Mistress had long turned a blind eye to her rotting and foul-smelling teeth but was quick to reprimand if the maid's cap which covered her bald patches was a trifle askew when she waited on guests. Small wonder that it stayed on at all when what hair she had was grease slippered from the sweat of a dawn start. She alone, cleaned a large house and kitchen, before cooking the mid-day meal.

Pat was a godsend, but where to sleep her called on Jude's initiative. Next day, with much head shaking, the local builder inspected Nick's tiny windowless attic beneath the corner eaves.

"Yes, I can put a dormer window in but not for a week or so Madam."

Jude whitewashed the walls squaring tightly around a narrow bed, a chair and a dressing table. The edge of the low sloping roof met the foot of the bed. They did the best they could for its new occupant, who arrived with one suitcase and a birdcage.

That evening, as Lyn climbed the stairs to make sure Pat had settled in, she heard an animated conversation behind her door.

"Come in," a voice called then rattled on.

Under a naked light bulb, Pat radiated happiness as she sat up in bed talking to an attentive budgerigar. Cracks in the board and plaster walls let in a draught, blowing sparsely veiled curlers abob. She was settled and happy.

Their guests were almost as colourful. There was Mr Pugh, still elegantly tall and fresh complexioned beneath his thistle down white hair. From his room next their sitting room, his soft voice and old-fashioned manners earned the family's affection.

In the ground floor front, was aristocratic Mrs Jardin and her cabinet full of exquisite old porcelain figurines. She soon added Jude to her possessions, gently insisting that he sit and talk with her into the late hours, because she could not sleep.

Ground floor back was still occupied by father and son from Old Town up the hill. Jude and Lyn loved listening to their never-ending fund of stories about it and its large spreading oak in the middle of the road. Village wise men, under patronage of the Master of the Manor, sat to discuss under it in years gone by.

Lastly, there was Mrs Codd, a septuagenarian and reluctant widow, whose wealth saw that life denied her nothing. Lyn's new curtains in her room were replaced by brightly coloured ones of her choice. She won her over with a tear in her remaining sighted eye, the little light left there, glinting darkly in its socket.

Jude's company was something Mrs Codd wanted as well. She followed him everywhere. In the Wedge, now a flourishing kitchen garden, her white stick waved emphatically in the air as she helped him pick the runner beans. Once, Lyn spotted them taking tea and holding hands beneath the table in a local café. Wryly she hoped the Romeo and Juliet period would be short lived, for the Rooks were now well established in the town.

After two resident staff came to work for them, things settled into a smooth routine. This released Lyn, to get part time theatre experience at a nearby hospital. A good salary helped to bring down the mortgage and pay for family outings.

On one such occasion Jude had decided to take the family for a day visit to a holiday resort and was impatient to be off as they waited for Andrew to join them.

"Where is Andrew, why isn't he here?" he snapped, turning from trying out a tune on his electronic organ.

"He will be along in a minute. He ran up to fetch a book to read in the car" Lyn replied. "Call him Nick and tell him to look sharp." Pat appeared at the doorway with a small basket of provisions.

"I'll go and fetch Andrew sir," she offered, disappearing towards the stairs. He was still idling on the keyboard when they returned,

"Why have you wasted my time?"

There was no reply. Breaking a sullen silence, he closed the instrument, and strode across the room.

"I've a good mind to leave you here if this is all the interest you have." Andrew gave him a look of defiance, conflicting with defeat. Lyn, fearing it would end in another battle of wills, stepped in.

"He didn't mean it Jude, let's be off." Hardly had the words left her mouth, before she received a stinging blow to the ear, somersaulting her on her back.

Little Pat, scarlet with anger, ran to hit out at Jude. Above her pummelling fists Jude looked, full of resentment and jealousy, towards his son. A subdued family drove to the campus, but by nightfall two happy boys returned home. They had tried out every whirling, swooping, turning contraption in sight.

Jude confessed to the family doctor that he had caused Lyn's ruptured eardrum, and promised the boys a whole week at the resort the following spring. His olive branch was accepted wholeheartedly, but his acceptance of Pat's behaviour was not forthcoming.

Jude waited and watched until he could dismiss Pat from their service on a slight forgivable fault. After she left, she met and married a middle-aged widower. He gave her a comfortable home and a few months of happiness, before she slipped away from life through ill managed diabetes.

With the business running efficiently, Jude found more time for his district patients and his personal life, leaving Lyn to chat with their guests, ensuring they felt cared about.

She looked forward to her days in the kitchen where aromas, from baking and roasting, curled up from the steamy warmth of the stove top to the jewel bright jars, filling the ceiling high cupboards. The boys sneaked in for treats and a new puppy snuggled up to the side of the oil-fired boiler. Whilst waiting for the meal to cook, Lyn would cool off by the back door to enjoy the garden, or sit under the old chestnut tree.

Jude turned over their patch of the Wedge to produce a good crop of tomatoes, beans and other vegetables, leaving plenty of space for a sizeable chicken run. The lively good laying birds were Lyn's responsibility. The quality of St Jude's Retirement Home soon spread. A waiting list sat on Jude's desk fuelling his desire to accommodate them.

Next to St Jude's was a detached house where an aged spinster lived alone.

When they glimpsed her peering through the window at the growing activity in their own house, Lyn and Jude smiled and waved to her. Eventually she ventured a wave in return, and this remained the only communication until, one late afternoon, Jude walked up the path and rang her bell. Shuffling footsteps halted behind the closed door as the old lady plucked up courage to open her life for inspection.

"I've only called to see if there is anything we can do for you Miss Grey. May I come in a moment," called Jude, using the practised charm he adopted when talking with his guests? The door opened a crack, clutched by a red veined hand on which her chin rested. Bright birdlike eyes surveyed him. Time for him to smile, head tilted slightly to one side. The little boy role usually won any woman over.

The door inched back to reveal one foot in a well-worn slipper and buckled stocking, below a nondescript food spotted garment. A voluminous knitted cardigan hung from stooped shoulders. Another smile, the long square chin sliding forward as white teeth flashed and grey eyes twinkled reassuringly.

"Come in then but only for a moment I'm very busy." Squeezing round the un-giving door, Jude entered a musty passage smelling of mice and damp decay. In the kitchen, a small gas fire waged a battle with a cold draft from an empty fireplace. A bare board kitchen table was laden with half-washed dishes and several cups of unfinished murky grey liquid.

"Well! What do you want young man?"

"My wife wondered if you would be offended if she brought a meal to save you the bother of cooking some days, and I thought you might need help with anything out of reach or too heavy for you."

She turned in a surprisingly graceful manner in the pallid warmth from the fire, drawing herself up and extending her arm to the large room.

"As you see, I manage very well, thank you. However, a meal at mid-day would be a change since I find shopping irksome, and have to rely on deliveries." She continued to return each remark he fielded until their rally reached the subject of the old tennis courts.

Sitting in the chair, she rested her head in her hand, as memories of old days flooded back to be recounted again to an attentive listener. Jude knew he had won her over. He sat until the evening shadows filled the room, throwing the glow of the small fire into spotlight prominence. He quietly waited his chance to lead the conversation into an avenue of his making. As the gloom deepened, she confessed to her terror of the long night hours, and of dying alone in the house.

"I suffer from agoraphobia, preferring to be on my own, but now I feel loneliness. It gnaws into me, so that I am losing the will to go on." The words stumbled from her lips as she acknowledged her need.

They were words Jude had heard before when stout old hearts faltered in the face of lonely years stretching ahead of them. With the persuasive words, "I think we can help you. Have you thought…....." Jude talked late into the evening.

Before he returned home they had agreed she would become their guest after he'd bought her property, provided her selling price was right. There would be no fees for her to pay except a minimum for food and necessities. The next day he visited the bank manager for a long talk, and enlisted the services of an estate agent friend in the town.

Jude left Lyn left to find ways to raise cash to pay the mortgage and builders. His wheeling and dealing to acquire another property was not questioned. She decided to work full time on the good rates of pay then offered to nurses, until their investment could take on the debt.

Jude's agreement with their lonely neighbour allowed the family to move into the second floor of her property, once the builders had finished. Using the ground floor for office and occupational therapy, and the top floor for the house-maids, the middle floor became home and left them free from the affairs of the Home. The new venture soon stabilized, and before the end of the first year they purchased the semidetached property adjoining their first purchase.

A stroke of luck opened up more time at home for Lyn. A shortage of teach-ers loosened the government purse strings to pay those selected, to take the three-year training course. Some study and thesis preparation could be done at home. Lyn applied for a scholarship and got accepted as a mature scholar.

Life had never seemed so full the day she enrolled. On the drive across the marshes, her heart felt fit to burst as she sang snatches of song to the fullness of summer, ballooning in field and orchard. Arriving at the college she joined the throng armed with lists of second hand books, on sale from the last course. Get-ting to the book table in short order, she bumped into an equally determined woman of near her own age. Together they made as many bargains as they could. Over coffee they discussed ways to make their grant go further. Jill lived on a pittance in Hastings.

"If you train the one stop to Bexhill, I can drive us from there to save your travel allowance," Lyn offered. Jill invited an ex-fighter pilot in his fifties, to join the ferry service. Living near Lyn, his angina, a legacy from fighter pilot days, made driving a hazard. After graduating, the strain of teaching hard faced, rebel-lious teenagers, contributed to Owen's premature death. Within two terms of starting his first post,he died of a heart attack. On certification a teaching post was assigned to her where her nursing qualifications were channelled to do as much as she could to make a difference to her charges' future.

The school, purpose-built for mentally disabled children under the age of fourteen, stood in parkland at the end of their road. Now, in her second year, the clinging hands of a twelve-year-old child with Downe's syndrome and the spastic clutch of a three-year infant with cerebral palsy told the same need for love and attention. Love them she did, going to great lengths to prepare teaching material the children could assimilate with much giggling and laughter. She and her fellow teachers only allowed themselves to become disheartened when they were reminded where their charges would end up when they reached fourteen.

The Breton Woods Treaty demanded the calling in of war loans, killing measures, brought in by post war socialist principles, to educate and nurture the nation's people. The children, lovingly coached to their teens, would earn a pittance, sorting screws, buttons and other minutiae for hours on end, in a purpose built shed, because the lack of funds ended further training to stimulate their minds.

Even so, many changes for the better were made, until, a change of government with conservative ideas favoured the ideas of powerful nations. Privatization was their way of dealing with rising debt and the cost of health and education. The industries built on the people's backs for the people, came on a market ready for free enterprise. Mental Health and National Health Hospitals closed wards for economy. Mentally retarded patients and the frail aged, the flotsam on a turbulent sea of economic rationalism, spilled on to the streets and into hastily opened private homes. Lyn and Jude had joined in the rush.

Life was also good to Jude. His energies were in full flow. When he hung a new sign over the front entrance naming it St Jude's Residential Home, he realized his dream of becoming a success.

Money made his pulse race. The excitement of amassing it was an addiction that satisfied his need to spend it. He took over the banking, waiting in the queue at the old-style building with its rich furnishings. When the manager strolled out of his office, he recognized one whose business paid in substantial amounts on a regular basis.

"Good morning Mr Rook. Come into my office. Your business will be concluded more quickly." When two acquaintances acknowledged the preferential treatment as he strode out of the building, Jude smiled a greeting at them. Confident of his status in the town, he instated himself general manager of the business, overseeing staff and supervising the comfort of the guests. Donning a white coat to accompany visiting doctors, enriched the character he was gradually assuming, of a middle-aged man, at the head of a thriving concern. Lyn worked with him to fill their roles.

As their standing in the town grew and spread further a-field, Jude earned a different reputation among work colleagues as he consorted secretly with other women. Butterflying into brief encounters that soon lost their attraction, he felt contempt for women yet needed them, for all their deceit and guile. His restless search for sexual satisfaction over ruled his caution. His liaisons with other men's wives, in particular, excited his power to cause a rift. One such encounter would trap him in the clinging strands of a calculating woman.

His dalliances caught the ear of some influential folk in the town, but never reached Lyn studying in her ivory tower beneath the rooftops. Her early naivety and sexual immaturity, he now regarded as a frigid insult to his manhood. He could not unlock the responses he knew lay hidden within her. For the moment, she was on a pedestal, labelled 'childlike purity.' out of reach. Part of his psyche wanted her to remain there.

Chapter 8: Moving forward

THEY ended the day working in the warm dusk of summer. Jude was hoeing a new trench for seeds. Lyn bent to lift the last of the beetroots from its red powdered bed in the rich soil. Languor slid through her limbs as she watched him cautiously straighten up. Two knee operations had not rid him of the pain in his knees and back.

"It's time to pack up Jude, you have worked without pause and I've had it anyhow," she announced. "You are very quiet, Is everything all right?"

There's something I have to tell you," Jude replied coming across, hoe in hand. He picked up the basket of vegetables then took her hand in his to walk through the gardens. He stopped at the summerhouse, under the chestnut tree, and motioned Lyn to enter. Once seated, she watched him lower himself painfully into a chair. He looked old and defeated as he glanced at her, then away.

"I've been given the sack, or as good as, if I don't resign. They suggest I apply for a disability pension, which will be granted automatically, on grounds of ill health."

Lyn guessed there was another reason for his dismissal from the finality of the options, with no grounds for appeal. 'What had he been up to? Best not to rake things over, rubbing salt in the raw wound of his pride.'

"Well we'll manage,' she said stoutly. "Our mortgages have cleared; we have the business and my job teaching. There is enough to keep afloat on Jude,"

As the garden fill with shades of night, they sat in silence, he still smarting from the blow of his dismissal that morning. The rebuffs of his early years assailed his mind in dark angry clouds as he reviewed the growing fullness of recent years, coming to nought. The joy he got from his relationship with his patients was at an end. He slumped over the table, bursting out his despair.

"I can't sit around all day now this place runs like clockwork." She felt the waves of his anger building. Unless they found a solution, he would begin to resent her success with teaching. She spoke into the darkness.

"Jude, why don't we start our own nursing home? You will have a free hand to set it up. There are enough domestics to start with. If you offer decent conditions and pay, you will get good nursing staff." Jude straightened up and leant towards her, hope and doubt mirrored in an intent gaze.

"Do you think we could do it Ducks? I'd love to show those bastards I'm not beaten." Words flowed on into the night, as ways and means were turned over to make their objective possible. They discussed the shortcomings of private nursing homes, and the opportunity to make their own establishment an honest venture. Their patients and staff would be fairly treated, and local doctors could have trust in the care their patients would receive.

Holding hands, they made their way to the house, where their residents, the old ones, slipped back in dreams, and called to long gone friends on the quiet breaths drifting around them.

She made hot drinks, to sip in the warmth of the kitchen, before they climbed to the attic bedroom at the top of the house. They stood to look at the full moon over the silver streak of sea and listen to the swifts twittering and fluttering sleepily in the eaves, then moved to the wide coolness of their bed. Sun warmed skins touched in a soft embrace. As they turned to each other she saw the bitterness shadowing his eyes. Gently she stroked his forehead. Like a child, he responded letting the taught lines of his face soften, but his body still fought for peace.

Turning out the light, she rendered the balm of love's magic art in the room under the rooftops. Her lips found his to seal the pact made in the summerhouse. The full generous curves feathered down the lines of his throat where awakened desire fluttered in the small hollow. Smooth fingertips ran the length of the tight muscles in his back. Soft palms curved into his sides and over his belly, down over the length of thigh, moulding the rigid muscles behind his knees into compliant arcs.

He followed the arched curve of her neck, outlined against the moonlit window. His manhood swelled as his hand clasped her nape and guided her down. She enclosed him until the eternally sweet sensation rippled through his loins. His eyelids closed on the velvet darkness of oblivion. He was free of daylight's searching probe into his life. When the sound of his breathing fell deep and regular by her side, she lay back to reflect on the day's ending. This communion of their souls in an act of love fulfilled her in the quenching of his pain.

For her, making love was a soothing balm. release from the animal instinct for peace of mind and body. Youth was not to be denied its passion and the beautiful discovery of sexuality. Her mind wandered back to Clive and Roy, in Essex. If their love was kind and caring, how could they be called degenerate? Whilst loveless matches for wealth were praised, homosexual unions were censured.

She woke early to find Jude had gone. She found him in the dining room, staring at the wall abutting the fireplace on the shared wall of the last purchase.

"We shall have to break into the next house through here I reckon," he said turning with a question in his raised eyebrow.

"There are a few doors to open first Jude, and one is to get permission from somebody or other," she replied.

"I'll be taking care of that this afternoon Ducks. I know a builder in the town. I'll get him up here, to come over the place with me." Pleased to see him out of the dumps and thankful school holidays would allow her to be around, to have her say in matters, Lyn called the boys and set about the day.

Events moved swiftly to the completion of the new premises for the nursing home, and the admittance of their first patients. Lyn took over accounts and administration, with weekend spells in the ki0tchen, after school.

She was struggling with her new teaching role. Her obstinate drive to change things, challenged the retiring headmistress. She disagreed with cornering hyper-active children in a close circle for endless storytelling.

Miss Wright questioned her responsibility after she took her charges out to the never used play area, begging for use since it was installed.

Watched by her colleagues from behind sealed classroom windows, the children hung from climbing frames and bars, then the little monkeys rebelled when she tried to return to the classroom.

"You can come again tomorrow," she cajoled, when Miss Wright's steely voice jerked Lyn round to face a very angry woman.

"Do you know the terrible danger you have placed these children in?"

Lyn stuck to her rights. "Do you really think the authorities would have given us something we should not use Miss Wright" she countered?

The children, cunning in the ways of their elders and betters, knew she was being reprimanded, hence, she spent the rest of the day re-instating her authority, before going home dispirited and ready to pack it all in.

Needing to share her disappointment, she was met by Jude coming from the kitchen with more immediate problems. The cook had downed tools and walked out, after a difference of opinion with him.

"Can you fix the evening meal, and we'll talk later" Jude asked? By nightfall all was quiet and emergency meals prepared, to tide over the next day or so.

"Hopefully cook will return tomorrow," said Lyn.

"I can manage the cooking Madam. I never liked cook anyway." Gertrude piped up, putting the last breakfast tray on its shelf.

Taken on soon after Pat Wellbright's dismissal, the tall raw-boned country-woman, in her twenties, was joined by Ruby, a true Irish beauty a year or so her junior, to be resident housemaids.

Gertrude, despite the faint suggestion of a hare lip, was country ripe. At the slightest provocation, her dark lashes would flutter and full lips part. Ruby just had to pout to get her way. The natural instincts, which controlled the course of their lives and prompted a ready response to amorous overtures, produced un-wanted babies for adoption.

"We'll see Gertie. It's no surprise you didn't see eye to eye with Mrs Gage. She's told me, where she took ten minutes to take a tray of afternoon tea across to Mr Rook, it seems you and Ruby were away an hour or more. What kept you?"

Arms crossed over full breasts, eyelashes fluttering, came the cool reply.

"Well there was sometimes a bit of dusting or something to be done Madam, you being busy at school."

"There then, I'm not sure you could run the kitchen as I'd like Gertie. I'm going to make a few changes, but I'll bear your offer in mind. Tell Ruby to be down early in the morning to help me with the breakfasts. Off you go now and thank you."

On a thoughtful return to the family quarters, Lyn decided it was high time she gave up her teaching ambitions to keep an eye on priorities closer to home. She resigned and slipped back into the old partnership, managing the accounts and the kitchen, whilst Jude oversaw the rest. With a solid staff base they could turn their hands to any task and were free from the whims of the labour market.

True to her offer, Gertrude became a good cook. As Lyn identified with her staff, she took her turn to scrub the floors, in the old-fashioned way, to show her democratic approach. She ran the kitchen with the efficiency of an operating theatre.

Fortune smiled on the growth of many things. In the years ahead, fine houses would welcome patients with comfortable furnishings, and five gardens blend into a setting of colour and beauty. The Wedge would be lined with paved paths as each former owner's plot was annexed to the deeds of the business properties. St Jude's became well thought of in the area. True to their intentions, the Rooks 'did as they would be done by' for client and staff alike. Jude's pride grew with his possessions. As the cracks widened in the National Health system, corporate enterprise hurried to invest in care for the elderly. The National Exchequer subsidised pensions to pay their high fees. As the flow of patients increased the standard of care diminished. On modest wages, the minimum number of trained staff supervised untrained auxiliaries, nursing a maximum number of patients. Serving the sick, as a vocation, became service for profit when nurses bargained with employers for higher wages, raided from the nest eggs of the old.

Those golden eggs needed strong characters to withstand the over familiar approach, when they and their world were up-ended in the stifling atmosphere of long-term nursing care. Rich or poor found a common bond in the lack of family love and their lost freedom. Like others in custody, they communicated by eye contact.

Roused at five in the dark of pre-dawn, the system ruthlessly toileted and dressed them. They sat as stiff as sentries, restrained with safety straps, on commode chairs by seven thirty every day of every year spent incarcerated in The Laurels, Eventide or other such institution.

Visiting churchmen smiled benediction when they offered communion along with an appeal envelope. Doctors smiled wisely as they stood for the few moments needed to justify a private visit fee. The social services assessor smiled briefly at a safe distance, next to one of the staff.

"Is everything satisfactory? No change in circumstances to report?" she piped.

"No, no change, thank you Miss," was the soft sighing reply.

"Good, well you are in the right place. I'll see you in six months dear. Six months, six years, all that mattered was when dear would be released from the sentry box for the regulation march between window and chair. Then the searing pain in the paper-thin flesh over the sacrum would move down into stiff knee joints moving 'one more step love'.

The highlights of chair confinement were coffee, lunch or high tea, swiftly served, swiftly spoon fed and swiftly swept away. A slow attempt to speak was an invitation to push more food into an open mouth. The untrained workforce tested the limits of nurses trained in a vocation to work with the most vulnerable. Compassionate women who worked overtime without noting it on their time-sheets, whose loyalty kept the homes they worked in, up and running until stricter regulations protected patients.

Jude had re-established evening lessons in self-defence at a school for young ladies. He practiced a gentler art when opportunity arose, returning secretly in the late hours.

Always alone after watching the evening news with the family, who drifted off to their own lives, Lyn's true identity was a dancing shadow she never caught. A reflected image she chased, questioning how, why and where she was in time. It was always so until one evening Jude came to her.

"The night sister won't be coming in, and I cannot get a replacement Ducks. It needs to be a woman on at night. Could you fill the gap?"

Lyn changed and went across to fill the night duty spell. Left alone, Jude made a brief telephone call. Locking the door to their bedroom, he looked in on the boys to say good night then trod softly downstairs. and left by the side entrance, linking the houses together.

Under the green glow of street lights, he walked towards a nearby intersection where the red tail lights of a car signalled him. He slid into the passenger seat next to a driver with long dark hair. She let in the clutch with a triumphant smile and drove down to the town with her trophy. Her web was closing. Sydney had waited a long time for this night. From then on Lyn would be asked to cover for night duty more frequently.

On one such busy night the old rector had insisted he was constipated. Weighing fourteen stone, even with one leg missing, he floated above the bed on a hoist, for his bulging buttocks to grudgingly accept the relief giving suppository.

Down in the town a woman hung a whip on the wall. An American Indian born into squalor, she intended to end her days in comfort. She drove her lover home in the dark hours. Stealthily he crept upstairs and flopped on the bed. One shoe sailed across the room.

In the duty room, a heavy eyed, Lyn yawned at two in the morning and checked her watch as Patterson, the nursing, aid sat down with a novel.

"I simply must lie down for an hour. Will you be all right if I leave the intercom open? See you later," and made her way to her bed.

Jude, ready to catch up on his night's sleep, sat poised to throw the second shoe as she walked in. Startled wide-awake with the threat of discovery, he went on the attack.

"You shouldn't be here."

"I know but why are you up?"

"I couldn't sleep, so thought I'd come across and relieve you, why don't you turn in now? Patterson and I can finish the night spell," he replied glibly, and went for a very early start to his day.

Tempted, Lyn accepted his offer, and snuggled down in sheets surprisingly cool, unslept in. Whatever he was up to, Jude was paying for it this morning. If only she knew. A ripple of fear broke from the tide of sleep overcoming her.

A bright sunny day dispelled her disquiet as she gathered herbs and raspberries, to go with the lamb roast sending tempting aromas from the oven. She collected five new laid eggs from the chicken run before stopping to admire the pansies in the raised garden, now part of the walled kitchen garden where patients enjoyed planting and weeding. How beautiful it looked after six years of care.

She paused by the open door of the day craft room, glancing in at auxiliary nurse Wynn giving a forbidden cigarette to the old colonel, before lighting up herself and settling to read the wittier bits of the day's newspaper to the craft group. Not much work came out of the day room, where a wall papered with a picture of bluebell woods merged with the scents and colours outside.

In the kitchen Ruby gave a smile, that betokened something was afoot, for she usually pouted sullenly, whereas Gertrude always smiled, as she did now, asking if Lyn would like coffee.

"Sir told me to help you move some furniture Madam. There's a bed and a chest of drawers to go to top floor, ready for two new patients. Ruby can finish the vegetables."

"Right Gertrude let's get it done and I can start the custard. We will be running short on time."

The two women manoeuvred a bed frame spring around the last bend in the sharply curved stairway and set it down to pause for breath. Pushing a hand against her side to steady her breathing, Gertrude looked down at Lyn.

"I won't be able to do this much longer Madam 'cos I'm pregnant," she panted. Looking up at her, Lyn could see this was no idle statement. Gertrude must be about six months gone. How had she missed it? Aprons! Of course!

Resting her arms on the bedframe, remembering Mrs Gages words, Lyn recalled Katie with her husband and baby, and pondered.

"Have you got a boyfriend Gertrude?" she asked quietly.

"Yes Madam, we've been going out for bit now," was the hoped-for reply.

"Will he stand by you," she asked? Gertrude considered,

"Well, we get on all right. He lives with his Mum, but he don't like it at home. He's trying for a council house you see." Lyn looked at her watch. It was gone eleven. 'Heavens, the lunch would be late.'

"Does Ruby know," she pressed, recapturing the smile on that one's face?

"Well I told 'er so's she could 'elp me out a bit with the work like," Gertrude answered. "It will be all right, won't it Madam?" She stood there with the gentle swell of her belly outlined in the open doorway, her face in shadow, her voice uncertain, as she waited for Lyn's decision. It came promptly.

"Yes, we will work something out. You must bring your young man to see us this evening. Can you do that?"

"Thank you, Madam," came out on a strangled sob.

Lyn knew her maid's history. Her first baby, the child of incest, never laid in her arms, and was bottle fed by nurses until its future was decided. Lyn remembered the hunger to nurse a child, taken away forever. She heard the hunger in Gertrude's uncertain plea for it to be all right as she took the bed frame in her hands again.

"Leave it Gertie. A good push and I shall manage it by myself. Will you go and tell Mr Rook the bed is ready to assemble."

Once the meal was served, she joined Jude to interview two more new house staff. They were coming, with their counsellor, from the mental institution they had lived in since childhood.

Authority had chosen St Jude's to provide moral responsibility for rehabilitating the mentally retarded, with work training, under the safety net of a caring environment. Housed and fed in government institutions for long years these denizens of the half-light were offered a slender chance to live in freedom.

"Their lower rates of pay will be a great advantage for you," the councillor had suggested, thereby gaining Jude's attention. Lyn's comment was dry.

"Well, we shall see about that when we know how they manage. We try to act fairly by everyone don't we Jude?"

At two o'clock Ruby ushered the three visitors into the office, leaving the door on the jar, for Lyn to close firmly against her inquisitive ears.

Formalities over, Lyn looked at the two applicants on the other side of the table. Both were about forty or so. 'How neat and normal they look, could they really have spent nearly their whole lives locked away from the world?' She ventured a smile but received an uncertain response. Beside her, Jude was talking to the councillor, Colin Preece.

"So, do I understand we are to purchase clothing and personal items for them, from their pay and keep receipts for you?"

The two referred to sat quietly listening, waiting to be hired. 'Like slaves,' Lyn thought, opening the discussion for them to have a say in their future.

"Do you think you could be happy here by the sea, Ken and Daphne? How do you feel about leaving your friends?" The mention of friends added a little spark to the vacuous look in Daphne's eyes as she spoke up for the two of them.

"Ken is my friend. We go walks together. We want to stay together."

It was a statement, not a request, made in a clear voice. Ken's quiet voice followed.

"We've always been friends." He spoke slowly and deliberately with none of the mumble to be expected from the Mongolism in his features. Lyn turned to the councillor with a question mark in her eyes, receiving in return a smile from him signalling 'that's how it is.' Jude interrupted.

"You can both come on a trial period. Ken, you will sleep over in one of the attics above the nursing home and Daphne you will sleep upstairs in this house. Is that understood?"

"Like the home," exclaimed Daphne, showing interest and delight at the turn of events in their lives.

After seeing them off Jude quipped,

"I thought the chap was going to ask us to provide a double bed for them, Well, our staff is growing and just in time. Now we need a chef to get you out of the kitchen."

"Well, the kitchen may need looking into Jude. Gertrude tells me she is in the family way." Jude's eyes narrowed.

"What else did she say," he probed?

"You mean who is responsible," Lyn teased "yes, she has told me. She is about six months into her pregnancy it seems. She must have fallen for the baby whilst I was still teaching. You were around then and more likely to know who it might be."

He sat down at his desk, his lips sucked in, his face dark and brooding under his thick eyebrows.

"Well who does she say it is," he asked, hunching his shoulders?

"A young man who I've asked her to bring along, to see us this evening. They are applying for a council house afterwards, but meantime, I'd like Gert to be with us until it is over Will you be here Jude?"

"They will have to go before the youngster starts walking. That should give time to get the Council on their side."

"Plenty," she replied, "thank you for seeing things my way."

"I'd rather do things our way than like that hard-faced bitch we met at last week's meeting."

"She needs reporting Jude. I can't forget her bragging about the old woman of seventy she used, to scrub floors. At the end of a long day she shared a tiny box room with two giggling teenagers, I don't want to go to any more of her meetings."

"She gives a medical officer free accommodation as an inpatient, so she has the doctor round her little finger. Leave well alone Ducks."

That evening a short, ferret faced man with a ginger moustache and a thick head of hair to match, waited out in the garden. He lit cigarette from the stub of the last one, the red glow lighting the grey pallor of a smoker. A jack of all trades, he wondered why he was hanging about for Gert, and what was up.

'I fancy 'er 'orl right. She's got nice big tits and good legs on 'er. Tidy backside too, come to think of it, but if she thinks I'm ready to go straight she's got another think coming. It's got nothing to do with this lot, us keeping company. I'm gonna tell 'em ter mind their own business, short and sweet.'

A last puff and he pinched the cigarette out, before putting it in his pocket, as Gertrude came to take him across to the office, where they stood inside the door waiting for Jude to speak.

"Are you married, Stan is it," Jude came straight to the point?

'Ah, so that's the game,' thought he.

"No, I live with me mother and she reckons I'm enough in the 'ouse until Council comes up with some-hin' better. Reckon I'll find a missis to share it then."

"We think we can help you get a priority on the housing list, because of the baby," said Lyn. Stan eyed her warily.

"It's a two year wait Missis because we ain't got a baby." Gertrude's hand pressed against his side.

"I'm having a baby," she faltered. "It's coming around Christmas Stan. Madam says they'll help us, and we'll get a council house after it's born."

Jude saw bewilderment steal across Stan's face as he reached in his pocket for another cigarette. Sardonically, he watched the other man's entrapment, knowing he was possibly innocent. 'This chap knows his way around for sure. Might as well be Gert who gets him, as any other.'

Stan Pike rolled the slim stick of tobacco around in his fingers and tamped it down as he looked helplessly towards Lyn for assent to light up. Lyn gestured to two chairs. He felt himself propelled to sit by Gertrude.

"Gawd 'elp me," he spluttered, "what the "ell made me go to town Easter Monday? She was 'avin a cup of tea in the café and we started to 'ave a bit of a chat. That's 'ow we got together. We fooled around, but nothing like that. I'll swear to the Almighty it's not me."

"What work do you do Stan?" Well that was safer ground, and he knew the answer.

"I'm on the dole just now guv. Odd jobs, y'know gardener, handyman. In fact, I c'n turn me 'and to just about anything, given the chance." Lyn jumped in.

"Couldn't we find a job for Stan? We can do with more help in the garden Jude. The nurses find some of the men heavy to lift and, as you know, some need help with shaving. Once they are married, Stan can share a room with Gertrude." She turned back to him.

"Stan, we know somebody on the Council who can help with a house afterwards."

Stan was sifting facts. The more he sifted, the lighter the load on his back. 'It will get me away from me mother. I need a steady job, and above all else, I need me own home. All I got to do is become a husband and father. This might be my only chance. The doctor reckoned me seed ain't much good after that dose of syphilis.'

Jude made plans. 'The big cellar needs clearing of rubble and brick to make into a good workshop. There are always plenty of repair jobs, which I can't do. If he helps with shaving that can be added to the patient's "extras" account; and it will be a godsend to get the garden off my hands. I wouldn't mind having another man around and it will put Gert back in her place.'

The two men weighed each other up. Neither knew the other's thoughts, but their eyes said, 'We'll look out for each other.' By day's end three new staff members had joined the Rook household.

As Gertrude's time drew near Colin Preece found a replacement for her. Verity, called Vera, was a solid lump of flesh, who loved her food. She went about her work methodically, at a pace suited to her girth. It was of little use to suggest she move a bit faster in face of the uncompromising stare such an idea received.

Gertrude's son arrived in late November, prematurely according to his mother. Since he weighed in at a healthy seven pounds, Lyn said little and thought more. Jude bought the parents a new pram and, the following spring, furnishings to set them up in their new council house. He decided he had done his duty.

Chapter 9: Arriving

NANNY Robin's beady eyes took note of everybody and everything passing her ever-open door across from the stairwell. Nanny still wielded her influence, over the eminent men who visited her, with soft rebuke or canny advice.

"Thank you, sister." Her brogue was as strong as the day she left her village to work for high society.

"Now, I think you might just have a word with the night nurse. Last night she…" Jill Fraser broke in, waving the post in the air.

"Must take these round Miss Robins, but I do know about the night nurses, and I will look into it."

She left the daily newspaper on a table in the lounge, then on to the brigadier, reading The Times in a large armchair close by the hall fireside.

"Any for me sister?"

"Yes, one for you," she smiled, replacing a book on its shelf. Crossing the building, she reflected on the many changes which had brought the nursing home to top luxury status with a good name in the area.

In the duty room, an assistant nurse was setting down a large basket full of freshly ironed patients clothing. Bunny Upson started to sort the garments into personal piles.

"They've been in their getaway three weeks this time, celebrating Nick's twenty-first. Well they are back to one more patient than they are registered for. I wonder what she will think about us putting her mother in an attic. I'll certainly be glad to see her doing this job again. If Jude wants to penny pinch over the laundry service, she should do it. Has he been across yet Jill? "

"No, Jude hasn't been over," was the level reply. "Bunny give that poor woman a chance. You have behaved shamefully with him. If you need a man so badly, find one outside of here. Gertrude should be here any minute now. The pair of you can finish sorting this and take the coffee round by the time I return."

Stan Pike sidled into the office ahead of his wife. Gertrude Pike wore a nursing aide's blue overall, and an expression peculiar to those who have gone up in the world, and think they know a thing or two more than those they aspire to ape.

"I've left Peter in the nursery Stan. He loves it there." Giving his cheek a peck before he could dodge back, she went to help Bunny with the sorting.

"Shaves are done Sister Fraser," Stan mumbled. "I'm in the front garden if I'm wanted," and headed off.

"Mrs Young was admitted yesterday Nurse Pike. We will be moving her today.

I'm over in the office if needed," said Jill. Passing the door of the craft room, she pulled up short. Ken and Daphne were moving the furniture around.

"What's going on here?"

"Matron wants us to get this room ready her mother so's she can keep an eye on her."

With Daphne in charge, the two were moving about in a business-like fashion, cleaning the floor and boxing craft material. Ken took his skinny little friend's hectoring in good part. His brown eyes twinkled behind steel spectacle frames and the hint of a smile played around a firm well shaped mouth in his round open face, as she darted round him. The pair worked well together, as they found their place outside of locked gates. Jill moved to an unframed painting propped against a box.

"Aren't you going to leave your picture up for Mrs Young Ken? I know she will like it, because she is a Londoner. This is the first one you've painted freehand, isn't it?"

She was looking at a watercolour of a river, carrying a barge and a small steamer. There was brightness and freshness only a child's eyes would discover, overlaid with the questioning of an old mind. It had a beginner's perspectives but was pleasing to the eye.

"Goodness, those tall red funnels are well out of proportion, she chipped, thinking, 'Freud might make something of those.' Her nurse's eye cast a speculative look over Daphne's stick thin figure. Ken flushed with pleasure

"I haven't got the funnels right have I? It's harder than doing it with numbers, but Matron suggested I try, after we came back from the day in London." When Lyn had introduced him to colour with simple numbered pictures, she opened new vistas for him. After painting a print of Tower Bridge, he was eager to go and see the Thames River and London's bridges.

Eventually, Lyn took them down to the Greenline coach station, and had a word with the driver, before waving them off. Although their hands clutched written instructions in for all eventualities she could think of, she had fussed and worried all day, until they walked in tired and triumphant after their first big adventure. Daphne joined them to look at the painting.

"We managed it on our own didn't we Ken. We had tea and cakes on the boat, just like the other couples. We can go anywhere now." Jill smiled encouragement.

"Yes, you can, and I must get a move on. Is anybody in the office yet?" Daphne giggled as she went back to her task.

"Oh yes Sister, and they've been 'avin words. I saw 'im sneak out through the garden last night to see 'is tart in the town." Jill frowned.

"Better mind your business and your aitches Daphne," she said with some asperity leaving the room to collide into Jude, listening within earshot.

"Ah, good morning Sister" he said smoothly "We shall move Mrs Young this afternoon, but for now come and give me your report. Have you had coffee? Matron and I have sent to the kitchen for ours."

They settled to make the hand over. Jill looked at Jude looking darkly handsome and knew it, Lyn, brick red and peeling. 'Things are not yet smooth sailing with them. He sees the nursing home as an extension of himself and she is in conflict with his standards. It's just as well she does the accounting. I bet he doesn't know we get a bonus in cash for overtime, and she doesn't know he keeps two sets of books for patients' extras, which only I know about. They both itch with worms of discontent.' She plunged in, casting aside formalities.

"There's only one change, and you already to know about it. I'm sorry Matron, but when your mother was admitted after supper, with very little notice, it was the only room I had." Lyn shook her head in sympathy.

"I understand Jill. Thank you for what you have done. She was sleeping when I went in. Perhaps you would help me assess her after doctor has visited."

Jill nodded assent, before continuing with her report finishing with, "and thank goodness house and kitchen staff have run like clockwork."

The office overlooked the main road and the front entrance from a large bay window. It was filled with a large impressive desk where Jude's telephone and call system were arranged to one side. Behind him, tucked in behind two large filing cabinets, Lyn worked from a small trolley table loaded with ledgers and a pile of invoices. A neat stack of envelopes splayed across the lower shelf. The rest of the furniture provided a family dining area with the obligatory television set taking dominance in a wall unit.

Jude sucked in his lips, planted his elbows on the table and hunched his shoulders confidingly.

"Our patients or their relatives might be a little touchy in the next few days Jill. We are putting up the fees. Send anybody with complaints over here for us to deal with. Isn't that so Matron?" He looked directly at Lyn who turned and picked up an envelope. She folded over the flap.

"Well Jude I'm sending out invoices with the new fee increase from next month. We cannot apply them directly. Frankly, I don't think we need to, we are managing very well as we are. Things are beginning to get tight for people again and so…" She pressed the flap down firmly as she looked at them both and Jill saw the tension in her face.

"I'm sure it will be all right. We've always got a waiting list. People know where they are well looked after," she murmured, going to the door.

"I'll walk across with you Jill. Better make myself known again," Jude said opening the door for her. "By the way, does Daphne come across to the nursing home after she finishes work?"

"Why no," she replied.

"Are you sure," Jude persisted?

"If you mean does she come to help out, no Jude, but as you know, staff use the side door to the duty room after six o'clock. All other doors are locked then so it's easier for them to knock on that door, rather than disturb the house, ringing the front door bell. Ken and Daphne often go for a walk in the evening then come in that way."

"Does anyone check where she goes, after she comes in," he questioned?"

"Good gracious no, I thought that kind of oppression was all behind them," Jill chivvied as she went to see how far Upson and Pike had progressed.

Jude went to inspect his source of revenue, his holding in the new commodity on the market, the old and infirm. He genuinely cared for the old ones, and they liked him. They enjoyed telling their stories to him for he found time to sit and talk. He could be gentler than a woman when a patient's thin red skin threatened to break down. He was at home in the maze of rooms he moved through, worming his way past cleaning tools, around wheelchairs, through doors, along corridors, by staff, and into the confidence of patients sharing his warren.

Today the buildings oppressed him. He felt trapped like an insect in an alien body, scuttling from cell to cell in a monstrous hive of bricks and mortar. His obsequious and grimacing attendance, during flying visits from those who provided the grist for his mill, was rewarded. He needed more, he needed respect. His dark side spoke to him.

"That little bitch needs a lesson."

He strode back to the duty room and dialled a number to have a short conversation. 'You have only done your duty. You pay and they must dance to your tune.' He felt his bile rise within him and longed to be rid of it. Drawing in raw breaths of air, he went into the garden, where Brigadier Dicks was strolling in the shrubbery. Jude joined him.

"Good morning Brigadier, the leaves are falling fast now. Take care you don't slip, here's my arm," he said, making a little bow. "I'll get Ken to sweep the paths." J.D. declined Jude's proffered arm, and turned on his heel to retrace his steps, giving a non-committal grunt.

Rebuffed, and angry with Lyn for her outburst, Jude turned into kitchen.

"Put my lunch by chef and tell matron I may be late back." In the car park, he switched on the ignition of the sleek new Japanese car and swung out of the drive, heading for town. Reason spoke up.

'Be fair, she works hard to please. Look how far you have come with her. You've got a faithful woman, a family and a bit on the side, both sides of your bread buttered.'

'It's that carping teacher's yap,' Darkside replied, 'and the sly way she changes routines, and everyone thinks she's doing a marvellous job.' The jealous edge of hate slid into him. 'Well, She's no bloody good in bed.'

Lyn went to the kitchen wondering if she would ever get to understand Jude's greed. Chef Brilson had two young children. His eyes lit up when she suggested sharing duties over the coming Christmas.

"That's fine by me Matron. it's not often the wife and I get Christmas time together. I'll prepare ahead as much as I can to help you."

"Good I'm going on my round of the patients before their afternoon nap. It will save long chats, because there just is not time today."

She began at the top of the building, where a romantic couple, in their eighties, occupied the Rook's old rooms under the eaves. He, a man of wealth, had fallen in love with one of Cochran's young ladies. Denied marriage by his family he remained faithful to her into the twilight years, when family guardianship parted them by sending him down to St Jude's.

Love found a way when the room next to his became vacant. His sweetheart became a patient on the other side of a connecting door. They found happiness in their Pied a Terre under the rooftops. A hostile reception met Lyn's entry.

"I'm sorry if I disturbed you, but I thought …Something is wrong, isn't it? Can I help?"

A flood of words poured from the elegant woman, sitting on a small sofa with her lover. He took her hand, stemming the cultured tumble of distress, and explained their dilemma.

"As you know Matron my family have legal guardianship but, irksome as I find the situation, it is nothing to the anxiety your husband has caused us.

I was honest with him, when I arranged for Vivienne to join me, so that we could know some happiness at last. Now he has colluded with the family and our connecting door is locked every night. I cannot put into words how we feel about what's been done to us."

Lyn stood shocked and silent. 'How could Jude be such a hypocrite to these two gentle lovers?' She knew he would not brook a change to his decision.

"I'm so sorry. You will have your own key by the end of this week. I know you will be discrete and keep this between ourselves, for my position is difficult, you understand. Will this help?"

They clasped her hands, faces wreathed in smiles. She left, sickened by the widening gap between her and Jude.

Autumn laid aside summer's glory and the seeds of next spring lay quiet in earth's womb. Jude withdrew into longer silences enclosing him ever tighter in his self-made prison. Only his eyes lit with sudden shafts of hate to release dark energies massing in his soul.

Chapter 10: Perks on the way

NICHOLAS sorted the last of his engineering thesis into a file. Just the Autumn term left, and he would be job hunting. He looked across the landing to the lounge, then went there to join his mother, sitting in a large rattan chair with a guitar on her lap.

"Everything all right Mum? How's Nana? I'll go and see her before I leave tomorrow."

Lyn laid aside her guitar, with a warm smile for her eldest son. Suntanned, he looked so like Jude at twenty-one.

"Nana will be well enough to enjoy your visit. She is making some recovery, thank God." He sat in the other cane chair with a confiding smile.

"Andrew and I both owe her some. She topped up our spending money last year, which meant I could buy a pint with my mates on Saturday night. How's the guitar coming along?"

I'm looking forward to playing it, a lovely instrument."

"Yes, there's a deep sound to it. You could accompany Dad at the organ, when you get the hang of it. It might please him."

"Maybe Nick, maybe. He doesn't play much these days. Let's talk about you. Have you straightened out your problem?"

He ran a hand through his dark mass of hair. How like Jude he looked, with a thick straight brow line, straight nose and well-set eyes. Those eyes were quizzical and warm, as he answered her.

"You mean the High Street incident? That was an encounter from grammar school days. Those men in the high street used an elderly chap to wait around near the school to sell Purple Hearts to youngsters who didn't pay up They mistook me for one of them, said I owed them money.

Most of us were taking something then, to concentrate and get through the exams to please our parents. You know how it was. University places if you were top of the pack. Those bastards moved in and really started pushing drugs to boys they later pressed into peddling for them.

They hauled me up to that room above the shop, where you found me, remember?" Lyn remembered a frightened Becky coming into the office, breathless from running.

"Nicholas has been taken by some Hell's Angels from London. They have him in a room. Please come Lyn." Unquestioning, Lyn had reached for the car keys to drive down to the High street.

Outside a scratched wooden door with no bell or knocker she rapped sharply and urgently on it, fear knotting her stomach.

Footsteps fell on bare stairs, then a tall bushy bearded man in black leather trousers and jacket opened it and barred entrance. His eyes were button bright and cold. They glittered between gold earrings threading short lobed ears, bunched on either side of his thick features. His muscled forearms were heavily tattooed and decorated with heavy metal bracelets. Looking into the shuttered face before her, Lyn took the bull by the horns.

"I believe my son is here and I need to see him. May I come in," she said and put her foot firmly across the doorstep?

The fellow didn't budge but Lyn held her ground, glaring back at him until he gave way. She wobbled up the stairs to a room where a group of men, dressed in the same outfit as the doorman, sat on an assortment of wooden chairs, looking towards Nick, standing in the far corner. The doorman kicked the door shut, with a heavily booted leg, barring exit without his leave. The windows, layered with years of dust, were latched. The air was heavy and stale with smoke fumes, and coldness pervaded every corner. Nick's eyes flickered to Lyn.

"It's all right Mum. I know these chaps." She saw fear behind his smile and broke an ugly silence.

"I need you at home Nick. We have a problem and I need your help, so, if you will excuse us gentlemen." Her tone brooked no argument. At a sign from one of the ugly mob, the doorman opened the door a fraction, his booted foot still blocking their way. Furious with the lout, Lyn's eyes sparked her anger at him until he got up and let them go

Back in the bustle of High Street, they listened to a chain rattle as he locked the door. Breathing out the tension locking their chests, they had walked towards Becky guarding Nick's parked motorbike.

Lyn came back to the present as Nick put a reassuring hand on her shoulder, her memory of the incident fading. Her fingertips plucked deep, single notes from the guitar strings

"So that is what it was all about, nothing else to tell me Nick?" She spoke softly, fearing he would clamp down at any sign of urgency. Stimulating drugs in her family and she had not noticed.

"Not really Mum, I smoke the odd bit of pot with the boys, but it's just a social thing, not a habit you know. College will finish this term and number one son will be a hard-working citizen. By the way, Becky and I are sharing the cost of the cottage with her brother and his girl. You will be able to come out and have a meal with us soon, right."

"Right then," she said. It all sounded so normal, just as they imagined his life would work out, a job, his own place and a steady girl. He came across to give her a hug and a kiss.

"Thanks for everything Mum." Two of his schoolmates were heavily addicted and a third had killed himself at seventeen. Lyn decided to have a talk about things in general with young Andrew. She must protect him from going down the sinister paths she had glimpsed. She laid aside the guitar.

"I'm going downstairs. See you later Nick. Love you." In the office Jude was tapping some lists together.

"You will have to manage without Ruby for a bit today. I need help when I go for stores," Jude announced.

"Nick is leaving tomorrow. At the end of term, he and Becky are sharing a cottage with her brother. We are losing him, and it hurts."

"I'd have kicked him out soon anyway," he replied. "It's time he got off his ass and made something of himself. I'll take the new car."

Through the window, she watched Ruby smile up at Jude, as she got in the blue station wagon. Dressed to kill in a new green coat, her face was framed in its dark fur collar setting off her beauty.

'I feel a jealous, foolish old woman in her fifties and looking older,' thought Lyn, as Jill knocked at the door.

"We shall be short of linen for the night staff. Ruby hasn't done the ironing. What do you want me to do," Jill asked? Lyn heard the reproach in her voice and wondered why the blank face on her trusted ally.

"What you always do Jill, ask me to help out. I'm feeling cross tempered so working off my paddy might be a good idea."

The house staff's sitting room was large and warm. Light bled into it from two small windows. A sturdy kitchen table and chairs left plenty of room for a couple of worn settees and an armchair. Brutus now grown old and smelling of cancer, lay inert against the comfort of the boiler. His scent overlaid the rank odour of bodies that assailed Louse's nostrils as she entered the room, with an apology for invading their privacy.

Jude had turned the staff scullery into a laundry. It produced a monstrous invasion of damp sheets hanging from two long drying racks, swinging from the sitting room ceiling. Various limp garments, strong smelling of ammonia, hung between them. Dirty plates lay about one end of the table. Vera flopped stolidly on a settee, chewing through a bag of sweets. Daphne sat possessively next to Ken, who was colouring in a small sketch under the light of the window. Stan smoked, defiantly flicking ash on to a nearby plate, as he looked through a household goods catalogue with Gertrude.

Lyn set up the ironing board near the boiler as the least intrusive area, receiving a welcome nuzzle from Brutus, long banned from their own apartment.

"You got the short straw today Matron," joked Stan.

On their own ground they were familiar, in line with Lyn's approach that every role was important to a good outcome, but contra to Jude's insistence on them and us.

"Yes, but there are only a few sheets, and some smalls, so I won't be here long," she replied. They relaxed, making desultory small talk as Lyn settled down to ironing and folding the sheets. Jill came in to the room.

"Daphne, Mr Preece has come for you. No only Daphne, Ken," as he half rose with her.

"You're not important Ken, it's me he's come to see," the skinny little creature teased, tripping out of the room.

Minutes later an animal scream of anguish pierced their ears. Ken started up but Lyn stayed him with a lifted hand and went to see the cause.

In the office Daphne was backed into a corner facing Colin Preece and Jill. Lyn crossed the gap to comfort Daphne who turned into her arms with sobs and repeated "No, No, Nos." Colin Preece came to take hold of the distraught bundle, but Lyn held fast. Jill joined him and together they prised Daphne away from Lyn. He picked up a suitcase near the door as they moved out with a struggling Daphne.

"Jill, what's going on," demanded Lyn.

"I only learnt moments before Jude left with Ruby. She packed this bag. I understood you knew."

"I knew what," Lyn turned to Colin Preece? He looked hostile and his voice was cold.

"There's no need for pretence. I think we understand what's going on when I say Daphne is leaving today. However, I'd prefer you to have rung me with your concerns for moral standards, rather than ask your husband to do so."

Jill and the councillor walked a defeated Daphne to a waiting car. She went as she was, with no goodbyes to the new-found friends who had taught her to taste freedom. Through the window Lyn saw Ken, Daphne's cherished childhood friend, running after the car.

Stunned at the deceit played upon all of them, Lyn dragged herself back to the staff room. They already knew. Vera still sat stuffing her bag of sweets. Stan spat at the dog and went out into the garden. Gertrude followed without a glance at Lyn. Ken returned and sat painting in his sketch. He well knew the futility of complaining. Lyn banged the iron down on the last sheet, pressing into the board until her arm ached. The smell of bodies, the dog, stale food, undissolved ammonia, intensified until she choked to retching point. She smoothed the last folded sheet on top of the pile, and then went to Ken.

"I didn't know, really Ken, but I will find a way as soon as I learn where Daphne's been taken." He looked up with a sideways glance full of a cunning newly lodged in his soul but said nothing.

Going to the duty room, Lyn looked at the boxes of free padding and cotton wool, recalling an item on an extras invoice Jude had pushed out of her sight. She must find out what was going on. She helped an unresponsive Jill check over the dispensary. Many of the brightly coloured pills were not necessary but pharmaceutical firms gave handsome gifts to promote their products.

Drugs lulled the patients' fighting instinct and increased time's immobilising power as they met with invisible companions. If one, secreted pills away and clear perception returned beneath withered skin, their resistance was deemed difficult to manage.

"You must swallow them all down dear. Here's your bell," bright peals of words insisted. Oh yes, the bell gave free will to summon the nurse with another pill. Their promise of honest conditions, when she and Jude began, was being compromised.

"If I didn't love working with the elderly," Jill said, "I would…" as Lyn finished, "Oh to be back on the district again," as Jude's voice carried down the corridor ahead of him coming in with Ruby, carrying two baskets.

"Do you like chestnuts Jill? We picked some in the woods on the way home. Ruby found the sweetest nuts." The girl giggled.

"So long as there are no rotten ones," said Jill, giving Jude a level look.

"Colin Preece came, did he? Everything go off all right?"

"No" Lyn burst out; "I didn't have an inkling." His eyes narrowed.

"I think I did tell you Matron. Chef wants to see you, I'll finish checking with Jill." Lyn turned on her heel angry that two people were flirting and two others hurting.

His offer of help refused, Jude went to the summerhouse. He sat disturbed by his urge to hurt Lyn. She was no more stubborn or annoying than any other woman. Their patients now arrived in large luxury cars, driven by wealthy children who visited on the wing and seldom. Their opulent homes could have provided care within the family. He jested with them, boasting how many steps he took to walk from one end of his properties to the other. He shared his plan to buy the remaining house to increase an estate he intended to wrest from his partner, to satisfy an inner drive.

Outside the summer house, he watched a hen running mindlessly hither and thither, and felt he knew the hen. Leaves lay thick around the foot of a tree, leaving the limbs bare and exposed. He felt he knew the tree. Tendrils of sea mist drifted across the garden changing the landscape. He felt he knew the landscape, an inner state he was losing control of, along paths where he was powerless to resist Lady Pleasure. A soft paw rested on his knee, Brutus stood looking up.

"Yes, I've little time for you these days old fellow. Come on, I'll give you a walk. It might clear my mind." He rose, patting the dog's head, and set off to walk aimlessly along the broad roads, heedless of direction until he came to his senses outside his mistress's door. Her face smiled impishly around its edge. He went in with his dog.

The next day was sunny and the nursing home fully staffed. Lyn checked with an amiable Jude, then rang Becky who was not free until the afternoon. The morning was hers to give Brutus a run and a sniff of rabbit on the Downs.

Clear of the town, she drove through tree lined lanes. A glory of gold and red arched over her, a vaulted ceiling above a never-ending nave. The car wrapped comfortably around her as she recited the old familiar prayer of school days in this, her private chapel, where her personal space expanded. She travelled effortlessly to the edge of the downs, walked at an easy pace up the familiar track towards the cliff edge and stepped into creation.

Soft turf cushioned her feet, spreading before her lay the magnificent green curves of a primeval goddess beneath the high altar of the heavens. A hawk circled, silently suspended in time, arrowed down, rose high and continued its search. Truant skylarks, soared in the deep blue eddies above, trilling their love song. Far below, across wild waves, the lighthouse blazed warning of the treachery hidden in the rocks beneath it. She was a dust mite on the carpet of the universe, looking into the infinity beyond a dust mite world, and yet she knew she mattered.

Brutus gave a low growl, from where he sniffed among the gorse bushes bordering the cliff top. He suddenly backed away to lay, ears cocked, nose on paws pointing to the spotted skin of an adder hanging from a gold-flecked branch. It gleamed, newly shed, in the sunlight as she watched the snake slither from beneath the bush to disappear down the cliff. She patted her thanks for his warning and later shared her sandwiches, sitting on a rustic bench along the Pilgrim's Way. Continuing their measured pace along the track, the air, water, fire and earth, surrounding her soothed and loosened up her body and a light sea breeze cleared her head. She shed her skin of yesterday's anxiety before bidding farewell to the breaking surf.

On her way back to the car, she offered up a little prayer of thanks. Under the sunlit feathered clouds, a shaft of sunlight slid through the trees to cross her shoulders. It was enough.

Becky stood at the farm gate as Lyn drove up. A trim and confident equestrian, she greeted Lyn with a wide smile. Moving past an area stabling dainty Arab horses, whinnying their pleasure, Becky led her to a field where a tall stallion turned expectantly towards them.

"He's a bit big, isn't he Becky" faltered Lyn?

"Eighteen hands, but he's a softie aren't you old fellow, and he really does need regular exercise," Becky gentled him. "This is a stud for Arabs and they need the stable space Lyn. They will keep him until Christmas when I can get him agistment in a nearby field and I can keep an eye on him." The big brown cob nuzzled Becky's shoulder then withdrew, to look down at Lyn with lofty distain.

"Perhaps I have made a mistake Becky. Do you really think the boys want a horse? What's his name?"

"His owner calls him Oscar. Look Lyn, I have one more horse to exercise. Come to the stables and we'll find you somewhere to sit have a think about it."

In the saddlery Becky moved some tack from the back of a large wooden chair then, taking Brutus with her, went off promising not to be long.

The rich smell of leather and harness soap hung in the air. The sweetness of new hay spiced with a horse dropping drifted around her. Lyn ran her hands over some tack hanging nearby, the soft strapping sliding through her fingers. She felt drowsy after the day in the open air; maybe a catnap until Becky returned. She drifted into a light sleep to dream.

She was in the saddlery, but it looked bigger. Looking across a garden to where a sparkle of flowing water beckoned, she stood up feeling oddly encumbered with clothing. She brushed her hands down over a smooth woollen fabric. Looking down, her eyes met an expanse of blue skirt falling to her feet.

Voices were calling. She was running towards the river. Two minds shared the form she moved in, and one was taking the initiative. She had slipped back in time and felt mortally afraid.

Chapter 11: Out with the old in with the new

———————— ✦ ————————

BECKY'S hand cupped Lyn's shoulder.

"Wake up, I'm back. Are you ready?" Lyn floated back to her senses, feeling she had been on the brink of discovering something that was important to her.

"Have you decided to take him Lyn?"

"Can I see him again Becky? From the look he gave a while back, I'm not sure he's taken to me. He's a bit tall for me if the boys don't exercise him regularly and are we the right ones to supply that need?"

Standing in front of the bay, Lyn raised her hand slowly to stroke his muzzle. Gently she encouraged him to lower his head until she could blow softly into his nostrils and look into the long lashed velvety eyes.

"You want to be owned and loved, well we'll give it a try old fellow," she murmured softly. Oscar rubbed his muzzle for a brief instant against the side of her head, then as if hiding his loneliness, tossed his head and looked aloofly into the distance.

"I cannot bear him to be lonely. We will have him Becky," Lyn decided. "Will you make all the necessary arrangements?" With her reassurance, Lyn kissed Becky goodbye and set off for home, the car speeding beneath a sky flaring red before the shades of night closed in.

It had been a wonderful day, beginning with the country drive, then the Downs and at its end, Oscar, a dark horse if ever there was one. 'I'm a fool to get uptight over Jude's funny ways. Whatever happens we will always be together,' she summed up.

The days leading up to Christmas found every bed occupied. Lights burned late in the office as they cleared arrears of paperwork and prepared to cope with staff shortfalls. In the evenings Jude joined the family by the welcome warmth of the fire to watch a television sit-com.

One morning he breezed into the office with a smiling request.

"Come on Ducks get changed and come to Brighton to help me choose staff gifts and something for the patients' breakfast trays. Look sharp, I'll see you in the car in five minutes."

Humming a tune, Lyn chose a long tartan skirt with a pale green twin set. She fastened an amber necklace round her neck and slipped matching studs in her ears, Jude sat in the passenger seat of a new red Rover.

"This is yours. It picks up speed very fast so go easy on it Ducks, but you can let it out over the marshes," he said. Taken by surprise with the generosity of the gift, she was lost for words but took the driver's seat and eased out into the road. From an audio cassette his favourite tango, Jealousy, beat its slow rhythm around them. He took up the melody in his deep full-throated voice. The moment swelled in tune with the joy filling her heart as she burst out her thanks and delight in the errand they were on.

"I love buying presents, it's a happiness thing. We are happier too, aren't we?" Jude hesitated, then he put an arm across her shoulders.

"Yes, we will be happier. Thank you for working so hard over the years, Ducks. Watch your speed, you're doing over forty."

"I love you," she said.

"A teenage love, a first love. You need to experience more," he qualified slowly.

After wandering around tiny boutiques, discussing the merits of handmade soap against tins of homemade biscuits, they tucked into succulent steaks at a favourite café in the Lanes. By late afternoon Jude took the wheel when they made their way home with a box full of gaily-wrapped packages. A peaceful quiet rested between them as they listened to the early evening news.

"I'm thinking of going to see my family before Christmas Ducks," Jude confided as they approached home. Lyn's eyes lit up in anticipation.

"Lovely, its ages since we visited them."

"No, just me, I'll only be away for a couple of days. I'm getting myself a present. I know a chap I might make a deal with for a top-class bike. One of us must stay while staff will be short. How about it, can you hold the fort?"

Disappointed, but seeing the sense of his reason, she agreed as he turned into the drive.

"Hop out Ducks, I've got to nip down town. Go and get a cuppa." Worries were fretting inside him. The past few days had been so good as they had sent out the invitations to patients' relatives to join them for a Christmas supper of the finest foods.

Tomorrow he would be off to the alleyways of his childhood and family reunions. 'Seeing them will give me a chance to make sense of things. If I find the right bike, I'll try it out at Devil's Point. No worries.'

That evening, Alan had time off shopping with his family after he and Lyn had filled cupboards with tins of heavens knows what. Patients were coming in to the dining room as Jude opened the twenty-first window of the Advent calendar hanging over the serving hatch. He could hear Lyn singing, as she took chef's place in the kitchen.

He slid back the panel on his side of the kitchen hatch. Lyn's smiling face looked back as she handed him two plates before turning away still singing to herself. Jude's conscience burst defensively into recrimination.

"Less noise in the kitchen and send my meal over to the duty room."

Scared, Lyn shrank back from the baleful, thin lipped jackal's face, its heavy black brows scowling above angry eyes. She was still subdued when they met later, He laughed away her mood.

"Come for a walk with me and Brutus"

That night his arms were protective as she lay against him in the warmth of their down quilted bed. She was touched by his consideration when he said they were both too tired for lovemaking.

When he came to say goodbye next morning, she was listening to selections of music to relay to the patients' lounge. Sitting on the carpet, eyes closed, her head rested against a cabinet, her full lips relaxed in a half smile. Jude saw beauty in the sunlight shafting her face, as she uncoiled her legs and came to him for his kiss

"I wonder whether I should go?" he muttered She looked him up and down.

"Aren't you over dressed in those heavy boots and jacket?"

"They will keep out the cold, riding back, if I find the bike I want."

"So, what about the car," she puzzled?

"I'm taking a mate of mine, Syd, who knows how to use a bike."

"Off you go then," she murmured from a muffled hug. "We will be fine, see you in a couple of days." He kissed her and left.

On Christmas Eve, she set the table carefully, placing candles in the centre of the red tablecloth and sweetmeats in coloured bowls to finish their leisurely meal later on. 'Maybe some brandy in tonight's hot drink might…

The rain beat a remorseless tattoo on the window as she looked out yet again for a sign of Jude. A glow of comfortable achievement warmed her as she glanced at the completed accounts on the desk, alongside the off-duty roster and the menu for the coming week. She watched a group of carol singers depart. Topped up with ginger wine, they passed a tall thin figure, coming up the steps.

'Five o'clock is a funny time to come visiting, I'd better go and see who it is,' she decided making her way to the front door.

In the front conservatory, a man dropped the hooded wet jacket, he was huddled in, on to a chair and came through into the half light of the hall. Lyn saw a finely chiselled face where keen eyes questioned, before he spoke in a mid-European accent.

"You are Mrs Rook I believe?" To her quick nod, he continued, "I'm sorry to bother you, but I'm worried about my wife. She should be back from Cheltenham by now but there's no news from her. Have you heard anything?"

Shaken to discover that Jude's co-driver was a woman, she rallied to reply.

"Why no, Mr…?"

"Pater, Paul Pater." Leading the way, she invited him into the office.

"Please sit-down Mr Pater. He sat in silence until she offered some tea and called the kitchen at his nod. He sipped the hot drink as she stared at him thoughtfully.

"Have we met before Mr Pater? "He brushed his hand over thinning hair

The Looters
— 149 —

falling across a face she vaguely remembered.

"Yes, briefly, at the Summer festival in1962." Her mind flew back to the queue leaving the recreation grounds, a young woman, with a pony tail, laughing up at Jude. "Why yes, your niece took part."

"That was my wife, but we were living apart because I was still working in London and visited at weekends. I came down after I retired, although we still do not share a home. I have lodgings on the other side of town. My wife found a job with an employer who also became protective of her. She visits me at my landlords because I still maintain her. She is still a child in many ways. It is why I am here."

Paul Pater stopped in distress. She waited for him collect himself.

"Why did you agree to her going off like that?"

"Belle's always had her own way since she walked into my shop just down the road from Holloway prison. She purchased frugal necessities such as for those just released from custody.

She arrived in England, an orphaned American Indian whilst I came across as a refugee, literally clinging to the side of a small craft. I offered to protect her by legal marriage.

Paul Pater stopped his rambling and they sat in silence until a strident ring propelled her to the phone. Jude's voice connected with her scrambled thoughts.

"Is that you Ducks? Had trouble with the car and roads are slippery. I'm getting it checked and should be home in an hour or so. Don't worry. Everything all right your end?"

"Mr Pater is here. He is worried over his wife."

"Tell him she will be back soon," came the unruffled reply. Paul Pater got to his feet, apologising for disturbing her, as she reassured him all was in keeping.

"I know society's ways are very different now Mr Pater, and I feel so very sorry for your situation, but my husband loves his family and we trust him," she insisted. With a sigh of relief, he made his way out. She watched the old refugee stride off, clinging to the thin strand of his marriage knot as tightly as he had clung to the side of a storm-tossed boat years ago.

Andrew and Nicholas came in.

"Any news of Dad?"

"He'll be here soon. Do you like the table? How is cottage life Nick?" She babbled her tension to shreds as the room filled with chat of new year plans. Then Jude was there, smiling. The meal was happy, with food disappearing fast, as they basked in the warmth that comes when a family breaks bread together. They exchanged their gifts and trooped out to admire the big new bike. Lyn told the boys of Oscar, surprising them by her extravagance, then, before she knew it, Christmas was over, and the days ticked off to the end of the year.

Jude's decision to return to Cheltenham the day before New Year's Eve, because his new bike had a fault and needed to be returned to the shop, had created a staffing problem. After an uneventful day, with skeleton staff, came to a close, Lyn handed over to night Sister Wright.

She picked up the covered tray of cold food chef had left in the kitchen for Jude's return. The phone rang and she left it for the duty room to answer. As she entered the office, the intercom light flickered.

"The call is for you Matron, Jude is on the line."

"I'm not coming back…" Lyn interrupted him.

"I know, I heard the six o'clock news. For safety Jude, wait until the weather improves. We are managing fine."

"I'm not coming back," Jude repeated. "I'm going north. Syd's with me, she'll come too." Lyn collapsed onto a chair. He had promised to return for New Year's Eve. She heard the sound of her voice begging him to come back to them and asking where he was.

"At my sister's," he said then the line went dead. A great silence swelled in her head, spilled into the room and birthed the first sob. Her crying woke her to the noise of the world for life does not tarry for joy or pain. She sought advice from their family doctor.

"You must go to him at once."

"I cannot, there is no cover and the agencies are closed."

"Send one of the boys."

"Yes, yes I shall do. Thank you. Goodbye." She called Andrew to find Nick, urgently, saying she would explain later. The night sister was told there would be some staff changes for a while. From the look on her face, she already knew. Nick hurried in with Andrew. They listened with disbelief. Nick drove off into a stormy night. Next morning, he returned alone.

"He wouldn't listen to me Mum. They are living together." His words dropped like lead in her heart. Trust betrayed, she fought helplessly with her newly created singularity as a worthless reject. Pride fell in the ancient battle of love. Between its prowling on the loot and lust of war, a discarnate satyr sated its maw on the fruit of human conflict.

The boys stayed with her until she bade them go up to the flat.

"Be strong, a sword and buckler to each other. Just love us both, until he comes to his senses." Later, she found them lying in each other's arms on the floor, unsure of the next step, in their grief,

"Nick will you take Andrew when you met your mates for a drink tonight? Tomorrow we will sort out something."

Summoning the efficiency Jude regarded as a threat, Lyn deployed it to win back order and calm for her family. In the afternoon she gave them a list of shopping from the warehouse, whilst she held meetings with the bank manager and family solicitor. Their advice set the clock ticking again, and time started anew.

The challenge to keep going, stimulated her during the daytime. Crying was for the night. She let it be known that St Jude's contribution to recent hard times was a small rise in the hourly rate of pay for staff, knowing their profits could well afford it. She cancelled most of the items on the patients' extras accounts. Among the visiting doctors she sensed unease over Jude's absence, albeit they said nothing.

When the funds to his now supervised account became low, Jude demanded the bank let him reap the fruits of past years, but the woman he had deserted stood in his way. He tried to get work. Having no success, he queued for the dole and was turned away. Towards the end of winter, he called on an eminent London barrister and listened intently to his advice. Next day, armed with new knowledge, he picked up the phone in his sister's home.

January had given way to February's sleet and snowdrops heralded March winds when Lyn, wrapped in her bath robe, answered an early morning phone call.

"I'll be back tonight," Jude's voice crossed the wires. Relief spilled into her response.

"Welcome back. We will be waiting for you."

The day opened out into the single goal of being ready for his return. She instructed the staff to refrain from snide remarks and behave as if nothing had happened. Warm feelings generated healing for all, she advised.

Once again, the table in the office was laid with care for his welcome home meal. A single candlestick stood ready to light up a message of peace. She took pains with her makeup and arranging her hair then, in the protecting folds of a soft green silk gown, sat to await his coming in the early evening.

Later, in the dark hours, a cold draught of air blew in from the side entrance. Caught nodding, Lyn jumped to her feet as Jude appeared in the doorway. Garbed in black leather, grotesque heavy gauntleted hands hung to his knees. A large black helmet with visor covered his face. He raised the visor to eyes shooting venom through gleaming silver slits. She clutched her chair arm to rally strength.

"You must be worn out. Come, there's a meal ready. The boys are upstairs waiting for you."

"I'm not staying," came the grim refusal.

"Can I pour you a glass of water," she appealed?

"It's poisoned," he accused her, and clumped out of the room to follow his mistress, in her new car. They roared off, she with the spoils of her campaign, he to plan his next move. Lyn retreated, miserable and confused, to a sleepless night.

Chapter 12: The bargain

RISING early to face events, she looked from the bedroom window. Jude was in the garden, opening up Sea Dream, their first caravan home. It stood beneath the walnut tree near the summerhouse. He came to the bedroom to fetch clothing and sundry items, including all her photos of him. In silence, she watched the insanity of his coming and going until he spoke.

"I'm living in the caravan. Don't come near me or I shall go." She agreed to his terms.

From his outpost he watched his old domain, now under her command. A dark-haired beauty slipped out to the summerhouse with news of a resident auxiliary's notice to leave. Prewarned, he took over her quarters. Once inside the walls he reaped the benefits of house service and edged his way into some duties.

He watched and waited. He laid siege to Lyn's reason by cutting off communication, starving her of sight and sound of his presence. He bribed vassals, bonded by venal ties, to cause unrest. A retinue of his family called to confer and listen to his persuasive brief. Standing on the pavement, they looked from a disapproving distance at her anxious face, peering from the office window.

Woodenly, she moved about her routine. Fed on coarse gleanings of gossip, the housemaids' eyes showed pitying insolence, pricking the skin along her spine. For shame, she hid her state from her family. Her mother was old and sick with a fading memory. Nick rang occasionally from college. Andrew was away on an arts course. He now had a girl, whose parents welcomed him into their home at weekends. She felt it better that they were left out of the pantomime.

Thwarted by her determination to manage the business, an impotent Jude craved to have full control back. Until then he waited, knowing it would be on his terms when her hope was at its lowest.

One morning Jude listened to Ruby's whisperings, then crossed to the office where Lyn sat working at his desk. Her coffee tray waited on the table.

"Morning. Do you mind if I join you," he asked? She spun round at the sound of his voice. He fetched another cup, poured the coffee then went to the wall cupboard.

"I'm leaving these strong sedatives here until they can be returned to the chemist," he told her.

Leaving the cupboard open, he joined her at the table. She looked old and drawn. Her eyes, beneath the slightly hooded lids, sent apprehensive signals behind the smile, trying to fit her face. They sipped their coffee in silence until she rose to close the cupboard.

"I want to completely come back into the business, but I don't know how," he said softly. Relief surged through her tired mind.

"Just come back, there is no problem," she answered reaching for the bottles to read their labels.

"There has to be a good reason," he hedged. She could feel his eyes boring into the back of her neck.

"Well, I can go off and rest for a while," she made offer. He refused it.

"That won't do, it has to be more drastic." He joined her and picked up the bottle. "I'll see you are all right." He returned to the table to finish his coffee.

She turned and looked into his eyes. She longed to work with him again, yearned to settle into the old routine. She would do anything for things to be as they were. Bereft of reason, spellbound, she picked up a carafe of water and turned to the cupboard.

When she came to stand by him, she held a glass of milky fluid in her hand. He watched as she drank it down.

"I have taken enough opiates to make me very incapable. I've put my trust and my life in your hands, and now I need urgent help please Jude." The sun shone on the red velvet settee she rested on in the afternoons, when on call.

She moved to its warmth and sat down, watching and wondering, in fear at her madness

He stood by the desk staring out of the window.

Temptation whispered, It's the answer to all your problems.'

Caution counselled, assisted suicide won't look good.

From far away, his soul cried, don't do this. He decided to call for an ambulance, that and no more.

Panic assailed Lyn, as the drug began to creep across her senses. 'Why doesn't he fetch an emetic, call a nurse to walk me, pick up the telephone. Oh God make him pick up the phone. What have I done? My boys still need me.'

She watched him slowly dial a number. Sister Jill passed the door, glanced in and seeing Lyn, came in and pulled her to her feet to walk her until the ambulance arrived. To the sound of sirens, she sped to emergency then felt herself fading away.

She slipped through a gap in time to a land, forming without parameters, as she walked a pathway through it.

A hill emerged in the distance, a copse of trees swayed into shape nearby. Water glistened at the foot of a sudden rise ahead. She moved at an easy pace, until the sight of a figure breasting the rise hastened her steps to enquire her whereabouts.

The stranger loomed near on the narrow path. Lyn stepped aside into thorns, looked and beheld a frightening apparition. A shadowy outline of one weighed down and bent with age. Large bundles hung about it. Hands grew, holding out one of the bundles to Lyn; its label, Arrogance, caught her eye. Bundles tagged

Deceit, Lies, Envy, Fear, Ambition, Scorn, and more, piled into her arms. When the assault stopped, she stumbled forward with contrition, to confess her title to them.

As her plea fell before the figure now hidden from her view. the bundles dissipated into thin air and their keeper stepped aside for Lyn to press on. Ahead, a manor house rose phantom like from the mist. She felt possessed of an urgency to reach someone, to find secret knowledge. Desire intensified to a single point of consciousness as she felt herself within a body running over grass. She must hasten to reach the river. Green sward sprang beneath the soles of hurrying feet. The hands flashing by her side were smooth skinned. The weight of cloth swirling around her hampered her. Now she stood on a ledge of the river bank, by a willow tree on, its trailing stems sipping the fast flow. She rested her hand on the trunk as she paused to catch her breath.

She looked down to steady her feet on the steep, slippery bank, and saw a body floating beneath the overhanging ledge. She heard the sound of water pouring over a nearby weir, then she was pulled back through time.

Chapter 13: Facing facts

SHE resurfaced to a pounding in her eardrums. Water gushed from her mouth as the stomach pump did its work. Voices called, "Wake up, wake up."

Misty figures moved around. Hands sat her upright, then guided her into a restraining chair in a long, narrow room. A shapeless gown hid her identity until someone spoke.

"You are all right now Mrs Rook, you can go home tomorrow." There was reproach in the clipped tones. Lyn's mind filled with self-disgust for wasting their valuable time. There was self-loathing for some hidden past and guilt for her rejection of the present. Her burden increased.

Next morning, Jude drove his wife home. No sympathy given and no words spoken. In the short interval of her absence, he had fully re-instated himself. His coat hung from the chair behind the desk in the window. She went back to the small table behind the filing cabinet. The events of yesterday swirled on the edge of an eddy of small talk over the day's tasks, whilst each considered the outcome.

I must be patient. The two-year wait is binding decided Jude.

A long-gone discarnate soul, sailing an endless sea, took harbour in his mortal frame, unloading cold rage.

You fool, your chance was yesterday, it whispered.

I couldn't do it after all we've been through over the years, he countered.

Two long years to wait unless she is unfaithful to you, came the insinuating voice.

Damn you, that will never happen. She is out of reach on her pedestal. I love that about her. I love her still, yet I must send her on her way. I can't help myself.

Well," came the retort, "there's unfinished business to settle. You know what you must do.

Lyn sorted through bills, signed cheques and wrote up ledgers at a superficial level as she sifted the thoughts filling her mind.

Were there two Lyn's, living simultaneous lives in parallel worlds, or was she the reincarnation of one, whose karma encroached on her present? Had yesterday's impulse cancelled a past debt? Reality was shifting, eroding her stability. Characters whirled on the carousel of her mind. The running figure, the body in the water; who was it? What stories would the familiars, circling in time, tell when boundaries between dimensions opened.

She needed to feel clean and clear headed, so left to take a bath. Stripping, she pushed her clothes, tainted with the voiding of yesterday, into a basket. Hot water gushed, sending lavender scented steam around her body. Her eyes travelled over small breasts, a nice rounded Mons Venus, a compact trunk but short waisted, good legs with fine ankles and small feet, arms slender and firm with elegantly expressive hands. She sank below the water letting her hair float free and tension disperse in the enclosing warmth.

Towelled dry, she turned to the wall mirror to follow the straight path of her spine from nape to sacrum. Firm skin curved down and over round hips.

I'm no Venus, for sure, but I haven't got two heads and I try to please, she reassured herself.

She chose a light robe, then strolled into the sitting room thinking a small glass of sherry would settle her. Swinging down the serving shelf to reach for a decanter she caught sight of her reflection in the cabinet's wall mirror.

Heavens I look old and worn, I've let myself go, maybe a new hair style, she thought, running her fingers through her hair. Her hands stopped, suspended in mid-air as the mirrored fingers beckoned her. She stared with disbelief, when the image in the mirror began to change.

An ageless woman looked out with unwrinkled skin in a rounded face and softer jaw line. Lips, curved in a gentle smile, reposed still and peaceful. The light reflected in the deeper blue eyes came from great depths as their gaze slid past the excited sparks shooting towards them. Sounds echoed in Lyn's mind like cadences taking shape in words.

You waste time indulging in guilt, bred of the fear and hostile feelings rebounding and breeding around you. What are your fears and insecurities?

I'm afraid I've lost the love of a husband who I've always loved, honoured and obeyed. She remembered leaning on the arm of her new husband at the church door, where their destinies beckoned. Saw herself throwing her bouquet to her girlfriend and catching a knowing smile pass between the two. The voice took up her thoughts.

Neither of you has learned that possession denies the gift of freedom. True love does not fetter the loved. Could you let Jude go

We belong to one another, Lyn prevaricated. I couldn't live without him. There are so many things tied up in our lives now, the children, property, money.

You belong to no one. You are free spirit, a consciousness furling to its centre, seeking simple truth. Your children are the seeds of creation, falling where they will. Water them with the dew of your love and they will grow into your dreaming.

Losing ground, she hedged. If I let him have what he wants, what will happen to our sons, to me?

Your actions are but an expression of your personas on the earth plane, came the response, Come with me.

The eyes in the mirror drew her. Caught in the spell of deep blue pools of colour spreading and enveloping her in a dark blue void, she diminished to a point.

She heard a tolling of bells, chanting of deep sadness accompanied by melodies rich in joyous praise, the fluting notes of bird song. The rustle of wings, abreast of her, became the sound of surf breaking, carrying her onwards, until she plummeted deep into a landscape of grey shapes and silence.

A tiny dark brick hovel took shape, where Jude crouched under the crushing pressure of the converging roof and walls. Large tears rolled from sad eyes as he cupped his manhood, his mouth making a soundless chant, "Freedom."

Nearby, a woman caught in the mass of fine strands of a spider's web, where tiny fragments of certificates, testimonials, awards, money and deeds lay trapped. A lock of hair, from a babe's first shearing, lay snarled with the imprint of a kiss, along with keepsakes and trophies. All eluded her grasp as, hands outstretched, she continually drew the web towards her belly to feed a hungry void.

Poor wretch thought Lyn, if she stopped grasping that web, she could be free. The woman lifted her head and Lyn looked into her own face, bereft of make-up's artifice, eyelids closed behind a tracery of fine wrinkles. The throat and chin line trembled with ripples of anxiety as a new worry birthed in the death of its forerunner.

A treacly substance began to drip down from the hands of the woman in the web, to form a pool where two young boys stood naked in its glutinous hold. They strained to reach a stream of sunlit water, spurting from bright clouds around them. A voice hammered in her head. Do not bind them. The eyes of her double wide pleading, Lyn shouted back. I don't bind them. I love them.

Deep tones answered. They are bound slaves to your desires and your creed. Tears tasting of salt and iron dripped on to Lyn's lips. Sickened with remorse, she knew with an unutterable sadness, the results of all her pride and stubborn demands over the years.

Everywhere she looked, above, around, below there were forms of human frailty. Wisps of luminous mist floated in the space between the shapes, arching over some and cradling others. They could not penetrate until one opened in surrender to let the wispy tendrils reach down pouring in light. A long-denied spark at the centre, quickened into a free-flowing form of grace and beauty.

On a quick intake of breath, she begged for mercy. God forgive me. I will try to let go and stop controlling the world around me. I will learn to control only my own actions from now on, heaven help me, she cried.

As the words crystallized, the tears flowing into her lips became a sweet cooling draught. The scene changed. The pool filled with clear sparkling water. The roof over Jude's house burst asunder and he stood tall. The web and its fragments disintegrated, allowing the woman at the centre to float towards Lyn and merge with her, bringing peace and warmth. A sense of wholeness filled her, she was at one with herself, then she was drawn back through a tunnel to her own image in the cabinet mirror.

She replaced the stopper in the decanter, no longer needing the amber liquid's solace, and walked towards the window musing It is amazing how much one can daydream in a few seconds. All I can recall now is that I'm the cause of mine and my family's unhappiness.

She looked out on the new housing estate covering the fields where sheep and cattle had excited young Nicholas eighteen years ago. It was a short way down the road from their first home, but a long distance away from the family they were then. Jude and the boys had adapted to change, but she obstinately clung to the past, the mother managing the family behind the persona of the working parent. Was it too late to alter course? All she wanted was to be needed again in Jude's life. The symbolism of her dream pointed to her owing Jude restitution. For now, she must be content with an empty bed and a partner in business only. His voice floated from the intercom.

"I'm going over with Syd to feed the horse to save you going. She can exercise him for you. You'd better take it quietly for today.". Next morning, Lyn enquired how Oscar responded to Jude's handling, for It was the first time he had taken a share of caring for the horse's needs.

"We managed him all right, I will come out with you this afternoon and give you a hand saddling up," Jude offered, raising her hopes that he was holding out an olive branch.

She went to sit with her mother in the large airy room, overlooking new rooftops to the sea beyond.

"Everything's going to be fine Mum. Jude is coming up to help with Oscar this afternoon. I believe he might even ride him, given a little time." Raising her mother, she re-positioned her for comfort, adjusting the pillows to let her look out.

Her mother's speech had gone, but wisdom still shone behind the blue eyes of this sick woman she loved so deeply. Her eyes spoke and the hand Lyn sat stroking fluttered a brief moment, acknowledging unspoken thoughts and the spoken words. They sat in comfortable silence until Mercy drifted off to sleep.

Jude brought the car round early in the afternoon. He had loaded a saddle and a bag of oats and was impatient to be away. Lyn hopped into the car and relaxed during the short drive to the field. A fresh green mantle of spring leaves sprinkled the bare branches of winter.

"Oscar is a gentle horse notwithstanding his height and has a nice broad back. Would you like to get up on him today," She asked him?

"Not today Ducks. I'll take the bridle for a bit, before you trot off, so as to get him used to me," he replied. Oscar came across the field at his usual leisured pace. Most of his winter coat had fallen and he was soon saddled up with Lyn astride. She tapped her heel to turn him toward a bridle path, running below the hillside across the road, but Jude was pulling him in another direction.

"We can't go there," she protested, "I don't know who that field belongs to," then seeing he was determined to go ahead, gave in to him.

In a dense hedge of bushes and trees, Jude made for a narrow gap which she judged might just let Oscar through. She felt a spurt of apprehension for the horse's fetlocks if there was a ditch running through the tree roots, then trusted Jude to lead the way, whilst she looked down for potholes, which could trap Oscar's hooves.

Suddenly, her mount surged forward over the hidden ditch she had feared, diverting all her attention and leaving her totally unprepared for the heavy branch she crashed into. She lost her balance and control of the reins. A weight crushed her throat, cutting off her breath and knocked her backwards.

Spikes tore her face, leaves blinded her. A stirrup came free allowing her to roll over on Oscar's back and clutch the branch, kicking out of the remaining stirrup. It was all over in seconds. She fell to the ground, ending up in the ditch, looking through a tangle of leaf-filled branches at the sky. Frightened, and mad with Jude for not warning her of the branch, she lay fighting to get her wind back, before moving.

"Why the devil didn't you tell me about the branch," she stormed when Jude's face appeared.

"You should have seen it. It's thick enough woman." He lent a hand to right her, his face expressionless. He and Syd had discovered the dangerous branch the day before. When she stood eye to eye with him, she met frustration and resentment. Stunned by the implication, she turned away.

"Come on," he summoned, "I think you have had enough for today. I'll give him his oats while you wait in the car. Can you manage?" Unsaddling the horse, he took the bag of oats to a nearby trough. Moist warm flesh nuzzled his neck before Oscar dipped his head. Jude rested a hand on the flanks, sensing its male strength and calmness. He envied the animal's assurance and height.

He watched her walk across the field and was sickened with the thoughts that inflamed his mind as he struggled with the rage in his gut. The oath that bound him to her, increased the attacks of bondage he suffered. His freedom threatened, anger surged, unchecked. Without his anger, he was a hollow man, all other feeling locked deep within the puppet he paraded around his domain.

He recalled the brute force of his stepfather, heard the strident voice of his schoolteacher and craved to satisfy the demands of his mistress.

I won't have it all taken away, I must have the means to make money. The business is mine and I need it to buy my women. They understand me and bring out my manhood. She must be the one to leave and soon, before I lose all control of the violence, she breeds in me. I'm suffocating under her dominance and cringe at the sound of her voice. She must go, or else God knows. For her safety they must part. That was when he heard the voice again.

There is an answer. Charm her the right way and you could get her to provide you with the means to separate your paths, it insinuated. Gathering up the tack,

Jude strode back to the car. Stowing it in the boot, he swung into the driving seat and tuned in to soft music on the radio, then set off at a gentle speed,

"Not a very successful afternoon was it ducks?" Jude was smiling at her, but Lyn remained silent, dabbing a handkerchief to the scratches across her nose and face. He pursued his wife.

"Perhaps I'd come back to you if you made me jealous," he suggested. "You've got what it takes." She sat forward, eyes full of scorn.

"I thought you did care for me. I love you and would give anything to have you back. I don't know any men so how could I do what you suggest," she demanded? He drove home whistling snatches from the old refrain 'Jealousy'.

A few nights later Lyn lay in the deep soundness of first sleep when a hand on her shoulder shook her awake.

"Get up," ordered Jude. She sprang out to face him.

"What's wrong, what's happened," she stammered? He spun her round and suddenly his hand was in her back pressing her down to muffle her face in the quilt. He tore at her nightgown and entered her. Dry with shame, the act tore and bruised her. Its brevity and brutality raped every sense in her body. Then she was a bundle of nothing flung across the bed. The shock of his body contact, after denial, left her to crawl under the bedclothes in living torment. Curled by her side, in tight foetal retreat, his last insult cut the air.

"She wouldn't have me." He did not add, Unless I marry her.

Spring went out in a burst of howling winds, chasing scudding black clouds across the sky, until summer stumbled in. Sometimes Jude was around but spent most of the time touring with Syd on his new BMW.

Lyn remained isolated, to run the home. She resumed her old study of yoga philosophy. Its source, ancient among the great faiths, taught how to accept deceit and rejection. Buoyed up to mix with the outside world, she joined a local repertory group.

One evening she sat plucking at a small zither harp's chords, one of many she had tried to master with little success for she was tone deaf. She wore a rich red velvet housecoat parted at the knees to balance the instrument. On the road outside a stream of cars, reconnoitred a heavy sea mist, rising from the heat of the day. She struck a chord, blending with their low hum and the insistent dirge of the local lighthouse siren.

Absorbed, she did not notice Jude watching her from the door. His heavy white jowl hung in a crease over the coat collar hunched beneath. His narrowed eyes took in the silver areola of her hair, the lamplight falling on a white thigh beneath the ruby sheen of the open gown. Colour and sound fevered a sickness within him.

He closed the door to announce his presence and walked to a chair on the other side of the wide bay window. Tight lipped, words locked behind the harp of his soul, he sat, sadness flowing from him. He reminded Lyn of a crestfallen child coming with a broken toy. Sensing he would leave if she asked what was amiss, she offered refreshment instead.

"How nice to have you here, I miss you," she began then came to a halt, unsure of the next words.

"Do you," he asked? "Then see what you can do with this." Rising from his chair, he rolled on to the soft green carpet and lay at her feet, looking up at her. Small and white, his manhood lay in the open vent of his trousers,

A surge of feeling rushed to meet his need. Compassion filled her limbs to coax passion from his loins. Inhibition gave way to the primal act of arching over to cover him. The silver slits of his eyes grew large and luminous and the thin lips relaxed into sensual curves in a face suddenly young. He pulled her down.

"That's more like it," he panted then shuddered into a supine slumber. Awake to her animal crouching, her own unrequited needs, she rose and put a cushion beneath his head, then left the room to shower and dress, before driving down to the woman in the town.

Darkened shop windows lined a road, empty and cold in the night mist. The yellow green flare of street lamps lit it here and there. Lyn knocked on the door leading to the flat above the hardware shop. In answer, footsteps padded down some stairs behind it. The door was opened by someone hidden from view. Lyn waited. A face, wreathed in a cheeky smile of welcome, appeared around the edge of the door, then vanished on seeing her. The door began to close.

"May I come in a moment," Lyn requested quickly. The tall bulky outline of a woman appeared, backlit from a light at the top of the stairs.

"Yes, come up," she replied turning to lead the way. Lyn followed a pair of working man's jeans, spread across a broad beam, up the narrow stairwell. Motioning Lyn into a room at the top of the stairs, the woman closed and bolted the door before facing Lyn whilst tucking a checked flannel shirt into the top of her jeans. With a broad forehead and flattened cheekbones rising above a strong jaw line she looked between thirty and forty years of age. Straight brows lifted above the assured gaze of large black eyes under the long pony tail of dark hair supporting her claim to American Indian lineage. Jude's woman in the town was an older version of the laughing pony tailed girl laughing up at him at the festival in 1962.

Shadow flames, from an electric log fire in the small grate, flickered over the room's damp stained walls. A miniature Christmas tree, holding a chain of sparkling fairy lights, stood on the floor between two narrow windows. Among an odd assortment of furniture Lyn noted a double bed settee. To avoid looking at it she walked to the fire to warm her hands.

"What's this about then?" When she spoke, a decayed black tooth hung below the centre of the Indian's top lip which was dusted with a fine black down.

"I know very little about you except your name and role in Jude's life, but if you are lonely please join us, don't divide us. Please do not break up our family,"

Lyn pleaded. The low-pitched answer was warm and reassuring.

"There's nothing to worry about, we are just friends. Can I get you a drink?" Lyn straightened and turned to look into eyes belying the words, and knew she listened to a crafty tongue.

"I'd better go now," she said, and waited for the door to be unbolted and unlocked before following the woman down the stairway. As she closed the door Syd suggested slyly.

"Have you tried making him jealous? Go home and sleep on the idea. Good night."

In the subdued bedside light Lyn undressed and slipped into her side of the wide bed where, after a quiet "good night," they lay with backs to one another. Sleepless, she fretted on a present so different from the times she grew up in. Now, in the seventies, along with the adverts for beer and cigarettes, television offered wife swapping, indulging in sexual fantasies and having a divorce at the flip of a coin. Her gorge rose in disgust with her thoughts

When daybreak woke her, Jude had gone. He never sought her company again that summer, except to bring his mistress to join the family one Sunday lunch time. He seated Syd by his side, remarking in general.

"I believe you asked my friend to join us, so here we are." The boys stayed at table to give Lyn support. Andrew glowered through the meal. Nicholas kept an easy-going conversation to cover uncomfortable silences. Lyn made ineffectual remarks to nobody in particular.

"In our nursing home, Jude supervises women and has to allow for their needs. I worked with men and had to know the screw sizes and tools used for bone surgery. You work in a man's world, selling hardware Syd. Do you have to know all the tools you sell?"

"Oh, I'm very good with men's tools," Syd grinned, making a whispered aside to Jude. He sat, grimly eying everyone, whilst he cleared his plate. With the meal over, the boys shot off after Jude left.

Standing at the window, watching Jude and his girlfriend walk, hand in hand, to a rendezvous in his flat, she heard foul curses pouring out of her lips, their heat staining the glass with a grey mist. Jealous of their pleasure, envy flooded her soul and turned to desire.

Chapter 14: Jo

———— ❦ ————

LYN tapped together the weekly lists of their patients' pharmacy requirements, picked up her keys and headed out to the garage. There were only three surgeries to visit. Afterwards, she would call on her mother's friend, living in the flat above Mercy's, with news of her progress and check if Nan needed picking up for her weekly treatment at the hospital on Monday. She left the last list at Kinsley surgery in the road behind Syd's flat. The two had gone touring around Devon

Swinging her keys, she started back to her car along the road full of parked vehicles among them Syd's new Toyota, a gift from Jude. Streetlights began to flicker on as dusk dimmed to night along the empty pavements. Passing Syd's car, a spurt of anger vented. Slowly the key scratched along the length of shining new paint. She released a little pant of triumph, then a voice spoke behind her.

"What do you think you are doing Madam?"

A young police officer stepped out of the shadows, shining a torch into Lyn's guilt-stricken face. Her tale fell on a compassionate ear and, taking Lyn's details, she cautioned her with a smile.

"Unless I am asked, I shall say nothing about this incident, but it probably will be reported I'm afraid."

Badly shaken, and stinging from her spite's exposure to objective law, Lyn walked over to Nan's flat. From her window, on the opposite corner, Nan had a good view of the comings and goings to Syd's apartment. and she usually rang Lyn to warn her of Jude's return. She pressed the bell and waited for the balm of Nan's warm smile.

John Thomas Willey, alias Gerald Mann, was alone in the house. He had been on the run for a week. Up in the attic, when the doorbell ring, he sprang from the bed he was lying on and ran to the front attic. A dormer window gave a view on to the street to check he was not cornered.

John Willey spent most of his time as a guest of the state. This stretch, a High Court judge had sent him down, as a plausible rogue, for conning a high official in the Bank of England.

He had served time in Broadmoor Prison for the criminally insane, charged with savagely battering his 'doxy' for aborting their child. Diagnosed as a paranoid schizophrenic and manic depressive, he needed permanent medication. Released from open prison to attend his father's funeral, he baulked at returning to finish a three-year term.

Satisfied it was not the police, he moved away from the wall and went down to the door. He scanned past Lyn, checking the street behind her.

She saw alert blue eyes surveying her. They were eyes that weighed and measured everything within their range for an agile mind to process. He was about five feet ten, very thin and wiry. His short cut ginger hair, well peppered with silver grey strands, topped a freckled face of unusual pallor.

"Nan's out, I'm afraid," he said, "Can I give her a message?" Under his precise diction, his voice had an appealing trace of warm Liverpool Irish.

Still rattled and ashamed of her vandalism, she felt acutely aware of the man's scrutiny, so mumbled her excuse.

"I just called to tell Nan that I can run her up to the hospital for her physio on Monday. Perhaps you would ask her to phone me later."

When Nan rang back on Sunday, Lyn had closed the office, it being a quiet day, to be on duty in the flat. Sitting in a sunny corner of the room with an Agatha Christie novel on her lap, she lifted the handset.

"No, they aren't back dear," Nan's chirpy East End voice informed her. "Is that why you called?" After hearing of Lyn's misadventure, her voice dropped in tone to conspiracy.

"I do believe I have somebody who can help you. I've got a private investigator, staying here a few days. He said you looked distraught last night, so I told him a little bit about you. He might be able to advise you."

"Oh no, I don't really want to investigate what they are up to, but I like to know when they get back," Lyn prevaricated.

"Well it can't hurt to have a chat with this gentleman. It's his line of work you see," reasoned Nan.

"Well I suppose we could talk, if he would come up here," Lyn agreed.

Ruby's nice round bottom tripped up the stairs. He was right behind it as she tapped the door. That is how John Thomas Willey, alias Gerald Mann came on the scene.

Ruby popped her head round the side of the door

"There's a gentleman to see you Matron," then stood aside to let John Willey in. She lingered to watch him walk lightly across the room to shake hands before Lyn motioned him to a chair. Ruby hovered to gather more information to pass on to Jude until Lyn nodded her out of the room. He spoke before the silence became awkward.

"It's Mrs Rook, isn't it? My name is Gerald Mann. Most people call me Manny. I believe you have a problem I can help you with." Sitting back in his chair, he took a notebook and pen from the pocket of his blue battledress jacket and waited for her to begin. Turning to put her book on a side table, Lyn gathered together a scanty store of facts relating to her visitor, before entrusting him with her secrets.

Under lowered lids, she noted his well-manicured hands, big enough to look after their owner. His general appearance was neat, clean and ordered as if he and his affairs were well managed, albeit the raw look of a gangling boy lay under the surface. When he spoke, his muted tones were reminiscent of cloisters and old buildings, where discipline imposed silence, obedience and subservience to life's lessons. Was the slight stoop of the shoulders, with the small hump on the left side, the mark of a scholar? The spoken and written word meant much to Lyn, who valued intelligent conversation.

Nan's judgement was sound and cockney wise, and she had recommended this man, telling Lyn that he had just buried his father. He was lodging with her to recuperate a few days after an unsuccessful attempt to mend a strained relationship with his mother.

"I see you are a Christie fan," his voice broke in on her thoughts. "Do you like poetry? Browning is a favourite of mine. 'Oh, how I love thee. If I could count the ways,' he quoted. She heard the love poem to its end, by when she had made up her mind to trust this man.

Whilst Lyn recounted her fears and unhappiness, regarding her husband, Manny took stock of the lovely room. Cabinets of Delft, Copenhagen and English porcelain lined the walls. Rich carpeting and curtains furnished a room surrounded with some exquisite period furniture. Nodding his concern for her tale he continued his stock taking, noting some prints of gypsy dancers looked out of place in that setting.

The woman opposite him also looked out of place in her drab grey dress of fine wool with matching sensible grey shoes. She looked tired and defeated yet was holding herself together by will. He had met others like her, lonely and starved of affection, and had been of service to them in his own fashion. So long as she paid up, he would take the challenge. He was in schnook and needed money fast.

"I just need my marriage to be safe and my family protected. You understand, don't you," Lyn questioned across his thoughts?

The intercom sparked to life. A nurse's voice requested some advice and she rose hastily to curtail the interview. Manny Wily spoke persuasively.

"How would it be if I went down to the West to see if I can find out how things are? Maybe they are not as bad as they seem after all. This kind of friendship is becoming common now. Ah, there's a small detail, I wonder if you could manage a retainer for my fare. I can sleep on the train…"

She crossed to a bureau where same spare cash lay in a wallet and taking out ten pounds gave it to him as she walked him to the door.

"I must go now. Thank you for coming. I shall expect to hear from you then." Andrew passed them on the stairs before she saw Manny out by the side door.

"I'll explain in a minute Andrew. I'm just going across to the other side," she called out. He waited for her to return, feeling uneasy about his mother entertaining a strange man, alone, in the family apartment. The fellow looked sharp. When Lyn explained, Andrew was non-committal. He drifted away to his room, where he spent most of his time.

A few hours later Jude strode in, looked around, then left. The spying game was still being played. It must have been Ruby. She rang to tell Nan, who reassured her.

"No, Manny hasn't left yet. I'll tell him to cancel the journey, shall I?" This left her wondering why he hadn't started off. Later that evening she opened Agatha Christie where investigators lived in books and moved fast.

The following day, at the start of a new week, Lyn left the cooling draft from the ceiling fans in the bank and stepped into a blast of mid- summer's heat. She screwed her eyes against the sun's glitter on shop windows, anticipating the cool green of the pastures she and Brutus would soon be sharing with Oscar.

A figure detached itself from the languid flow of shoppers across the street and came over to Lyn. It was Manny, smiling, as he briefly saluted her with a touch to the hat brim, pulled low over his face.

"Good day Mrs Rook, it's a really hot one, today isn't it? Can I buy you a cool drink?" Nonplussed by his familiar overture, and aware that this man knew more than she cared about her, Lyn blocked the offer.

"Thank you, but I'm on an errand into the country, where I shall soon cool down." Keeping in step with her, as she made her way back to the car, he bent to open the door when she unlocked it. She settled in her seat and prepared to drive, but he kept his hold. She reached for the door only to find it firmly resist her pull.

"Look I know it's a cheek," he said with a disarming grin, "but I would love to get away from the heat of the town. May I come with you?" Feeling she owed civility to one who had listened to her problems, and fain to act churlish, Lyn hesitated a moment.

"I don't see why not? I'm only going out to give our horse some fodder and see he is managing in this heat. Hop in." Brutus, lying across the back seat, lifted his head and sniffed him, then rested down on his front paws again.

Reaching the paddock, she watched Manny fetch bucket after bucket of water to fill the trough for the horses as he stroked and talked to them. He called Brutus to follow him when he ran to the top of a hill across the lane, then urged him to race back to her when she called. She was amused at some of the strange northern sayings he came out with and laughed at his dry wit expressed in strong Liverpool Irish accent. When she dropped him off at Nan's, he brought up the subject of the retainer.

"I'm afraid I gave it to an old fellow who was down on his luck. I didn't think you would mind somehow Lyn." She accepted his excuse and use of her first name. Glad the money had served a good purpose, his suggestion that they meet for a walk, since he was a ready to listen if it helped her, was refused uncertainly.

"Well I'm not sure. I don't go out any more except for the horse and shopping,"

"Come on lass, nought's as bad as it seems. You're lonely so there's nowt wrong in meeting for a walk. Perhaps I could help with Oscar again. We got on a treat. May I come tomorrow?" The homely voice was reassuring, as was his smile.

"All right then, I'll pick you up tomorrow," she agreed.

Later that night Lyn reflected on the afternoon with Manny. What a friendly name. So sad to have just buried his father and then left his mother with bad words between them.

Brushing her hair, she angled one of three long cheval mirrors framing the walnut wood dressing table, to inspect herself sideways. Her chin line was still firm, but perhaps she should get one of those shampoo hair tints. She smiled at herself in the mirror. It felt good to have a friend, an admirer maybe. She would tell Jude she had found a friend and leave untold the circumstances of their meeting. In the morning Jude listened intently as Lyn sketched her appraisal of Manny.

"I'm glad you have found a friend, but be careful," he remarked. He set aside the roster he was preparing and left to visit Nan's lodger.

Manny lay on his bed smoking a cigarette. An empty bottle of barley wine stood on the bedside table. He wondered how long he could hold out, before they dragged him back to Norfolk and its cold wet marshes; back to the struggle to crawl up the pile of inmates festering there.

It's time to move on. I'll keep to the South coast where more opportunities are on offer. I won't get anywhere with the Rook woman. She's too timid and unready to experiment.

He swung round to sit up and straighten his tie, before going down to offer Nan a game of cards. A tap on the door brought him smartly to his feet, fists lightly bunched as he went to open it a crack.

A hand thrust the door wide open, catching him off guard. He stepped back, Jude following as he closed the door behind him and stood inside.

"I understand you've been seeing my wife. Is that so?"

"It's all right mate." Manny raised placating hands. "There's no harm done. Nan here thought she could do with a hand seeing to your horse." He turned to the wash basin.

"Do you mind, the john's two flights down." Opening his flies, he relieved himself, making sure Jude saw he was well furnished. Catching his glance, Manny sensed his opportunity. He tucked himself in.

"I understand how things are mate. If there's anything I can do to help, just say the word."

Jude sat down heavily on a rickety cane chair and looked the man over. Sharp as a razor, but it might work.

When Gerald Mann saw Jude out, they had come to a clear understanding of exactly how he was expected to help. On their next visit to Oscar, Manny mentioned the Thames Valley to Lyn.

"Have you ever been to Henley? It is a favourite haunt of mine because I love water and anything to do with it." They stood at the top of the hill watching Brutus chasing the scent of rabbit. A breeze ruffled her hair, blowing new ideas into her mind, as she imagined herself sailing a boat on the freeway of the river.

"No Manny, I've passed through there and been fascinated by the boats because I always wanted one."

"You should try boating girl. Why don't you take a weekend off for once?" She called the dog to her side and started downhill. By the time they returned to the lane she had decided. She turned to him.

"Manny, how would you feel about coming with me? You see, I don't know about boats. I would pay all the expenses of course. That is if I can get some time away from things. I'm not really sure yet."

In all his years of conning, Manny had never hooked a victim so quickly. He could hardly believe his luck. Step one in the plan, and she'll also give me cover to move around. The fuzz won't be looking for two.

"There's nothing I should like better. What about your husband though, will you tell him?"

"Yes, of course I will tell him, and the boys. The weekends are usually his so I'm not sure yet."

The enormity of the step she would be taking, frightened her. If she told them she intended to spend a weekend with a male companion, it might take her outside the approval and safety of the family. Perhaps she need not tell.

The routine of the week set in. She stayed at home, hiding behind bills and receipts, and preparing for the annual fruit picking on Friday. When she asked, Jude was most agreeable to her having the next weekend.

"You need a break Ducks. How about Friday afternoon until Monday midday?" he suggested. She replied easily.

"Well yes, I could go to my brother's if you will cover the time." The deceit fell easily from her lips, for she still could not make up her mind.

Friday morning, Ken was stolidly sweeping the front garden paths at his usual careful pace and well settled into his routine. He met Daphne in secret and was content in his quiet way. Jude arrived, full of a restless anger which Ken got the brunt of.

"If you don't smarten yourself up Ken, I'm sending you on your way. Get that job finished and see if chef wants you." Lyn heard the threat and when he entered the office, sprang to Ken's defence.

"It is none of your business," was the cold retort.

Chaffing against his control of everyone, Lyn made a snap choice to go boating, to share laughter, hold a warm hand, rest in the curve of a man's arm. She rang Nan and left a message for Manny, then turned her attention to last minute details for fruit picking.

It looked like a family outing as the family piled into the car and set off for the farm. An assortment of containers and a basket of provisions for their lunch filled the boot. They began picking at the top of the hill, working their way down into the shadows as the sun rose higher. Towards noon, the baskets were nearly full of sweet juicy berries. Under the sun's heat thin rivulets of moisture ran between the fine powdering of earth on Lyn's back. Preoccupied, she worked her way along her row. The vicar had said he and his wife had friends of both sex and that it was healthy.

Jude was working in the next row. As they came abreast, he peered through a thicket of canes at his wife. Her face was rosy from the sun, her brown arms streaked with fruit juice. She looked young and pensive. Sensing his nearness, she looked up and met his gaze, then lowered her lids in guilt.

"All ready to move off when we get back then," he asked?

"Yes, my bag is packed," she murmured. "Jude!" He bent to lower a full basket.

"Well, what's up?"

"I'm not going to my brother's. I think I'm going boating with Mr Manning." He straightened up to part the hedge of leaves. His arm snaked through and gripped her shoulder.

"That's good, I've told him to look after you. Fresh fields have a lot to offer, and you need to learn more Ducks. If you play ball with someone else, it will be better for both of us in the end. Trust me."

"Are you sure?"

"Look Ducks, we've had years of being told what to do, and for why? To suit society's ends we do what they tell us at school, at work, at play, that's why. We never have a chance to find out who the hell we really are."

"I know who I am Jude, and it doesn't feel right to me. I'd much rather we were all going as a family."

"Well we're not doing that," he insisted. "We need to put some space between us and do our own thing for a bit. Marriage is a con to gratify our animal instincts respectably and get on the treadmill of providing for a family. Go with this chap and have some time for yourself. Get some experience and grow up." Listening to Jude's persuasive tongue, Lyn decided the vicar could do no wrong, and Jude's hand still felt warm on her shoulder.

"All right I'll go," she said. He whistled to the boys.

"Right, let's get going. Mum's got to be to be off. She's away for a couple of days."

Back at St Jude's, Lyn and the boys bundled the baskets into the kitchen. She returned to the car for the picnic bag to find Jude had packed her weekend case in the boot.

"Right, off with you," he said and blocked her move into the house, despite her protests that she needed to freshen up and change. "I'll come and see you off."

Out beaten, Lyn drove down to Nan's where Manny was pacing anxiously up and down the pavement. He stopped by Jude's car for a few words, before coming to slip into the passenger seat by Lyn.

"I was afraid you wouldn't come. Thanks." She let in the clutch and they started off.

Chapter 15: River Interlude

THEY drove in silence until they came to a small country inn with a tea garden at the front. She slowed down.

"I don't know the way, do you?"

"How about a cup of tea, I could do with a drink," he replied. They sat in the cool of the garden, she with her tea and Manny with a barley wine, as they traced a route to Henley with an A.A. map,

As they drove on, he pointed out places of interest, including the prisons on route. She thought he seemed to know a lot of prisons but assumed they were connected with his work.

The Thames Valley was in full swing by the time they arrived. Hotels bustled with guests and it soon became apparent that there was little room at the inns. Bright lights and music spilled into the darkness outside the car. Bedazzled, a sleepy Lyn insisted on searching.

"There must be single rooms somewhere. Let's try one more." Finally, Manny came back with the offer of two rooms, with a connecting door. She accepted from sheer tiredness.

"You look all in girl. I will fill in the room bookings if you like. I'll meet you for a meal after you have rested," offered Manny.

"I just want to sleep for now," she demurred. "Tomorrow I have to meet Andrew in London for his interview with a marine biologist. If you don't mind, I will see you when I return." She barely remembered the luxury of hot water and tumbling into bed.

She set off in the early hours the following morning. Waiting in a side street as arranged, Lyn watched Andrew emerge from the crowd and walk toward the car to sit in the passenger seat. A sudden shyness robbed her of the familiar ease in her son's company. He put his hand on her shoulder.

"Everything all right Mum," he asked quietly? Wordless she turned to hug him, nodding assent. This whole stupid exercise was Jude's idea that it would be better for the family, but she did not feel it so. Diverted to finding the scientist's house in one of London's cool leafy squares, Lyn watched the door close behind Andrew, then sat to wait and send up urgent little prayers for his success.

His application to join the R.A.F had failed because he wore glasses. Then, as today, she had waited for him to join her after his interview. She had watched him mask disappointment, and the sibling's challenge to match his brother's success. This son would travel a hard road, hampered by deafness consequent on his stormy passage into life and a twisted bowel from neo-natal surgery. The support of both parents and the guidance of a bright angel were needed to bring balance to his journey.

She was beginning to nod off when he slipped into the car. His expression held the tight control of one used to setback.

"Well Andrew," she asked?

"It could have been worse Mum. He wants to see me in six months when I have studied more biology," he told her. "My diving qualifications are OK." They were back in the side street behind the station. Lyn wished she could drive home with him.

"Will you be all right," she asked?

"Sure, take care Mum," he smiled.

"See you Monday then Andrew," and he was lost in the crowd. She put the car into gear and set off for Henley.

It was late afternoon by the time she coasted into view of the hotel. A lone figure stood in silhouette by the entrance, rounding out to become Manny. He ran to the car as she slowed to turn in.

"I didn't think you were coming back, I've waited here for hours," he said, relief flooding his pinched face.

"I don't make a habit of breaking promises Manny," she said. "Tomorrow it's the river for us."

Manny breakfasted well on kippers and toast. They purchased a few rations for a mid-day snack on the way to the river.

Groups of weekenders milled around the towpath, idling to watch the lock gates open for the bright painted craft plying the river. The water sparkled between green banks. The lawns outside the riverside inns were dotted with tables under gay umbrellas. The throng was on holiday and Lyn was part of it in a pair of old jeans and a floppy cotton shirt over her swimsuit.

She stood waiting to board the boat they had hired for the day, as Manny finished taking instructions from the boatman, and then turned to help her into the craft.

"That's some arse you've got on you girl," he admired as she steadied herself against the gentle rock of the boat. Her pursed lips primly hid a quiet amusement and a flicker of satisfaction.

Immersed in following the lore of river craft and negotiating locks, they exchanged rueful glances with fellow boatmen, as they watched others break the rules. It was a world of shared laughter where sunlight, wind and water conspired to bring magic to the river's depths.

Along the riverbank a new woman stepped ashore to dance to a herd of cows shielding the head of a bewildered bull between their flanks. A laughing Manny used his jacket to play matador. His joy in the waterways was infectious, etching impressions of him in her mind. She watched him playing some private game with himself, as the captain of a super craft. He exchanged cheery greetings with passing boatmen, and sang snatches of song in a true, sweet tone.

Whilst they ate their sandwiches and drank cool beer at a riverside pub, he filled in more of his background. Born into a family of Protestant Irish, it pleased his mother to deck him out in their finery, to march with the zeal of the Irish protester. He recalled her as a lazy woman, never satisfied with her son, or her lot, and usually clutching a bag of sweets. He provoked jeers at school when she made him wear clogs to save foot ware.

"My father worked at the local tannery and the whole house smelt of hides. He had a second job at night, repairing watches for a local jeweller. He worked in a cupboard under the stairs, where he kept his tools," he continued grim faced.

"My father's temper was always on a short fuse. I'll never forget or forgive him for the day I saw him beating my mother, who was eating for two then." Lyn, who was no stranger to seamy circumstances, listened with horror as he told of the child standing in a congealing pool of his mother's blood, staring at two glistening shapes, lying by his feet.

"I held her up until a midwife arrived and bundled me off. There never were brothers or sisters in our family."

He told of the callow youth, with a tubercular curve to his spine, who drifted on the outskirts of working-class life, ripe with lust from ill channelled energy.

"I sang for my supper three nights a week in a pub. There was a brothel upstairs, and I had the choice of a whore, thrown in by the black who owned the pub. Then I got the chance to train as a baggage handler at a small airport nearby. The pilots were decent to me when I showed an interest in the planes. They sometimes took me up "to make weight" they said. It was wonderful. I'd loved to have been a pilot. Don't you think I piloted the boat well this morning?"

In the afternoon he began to show off his skill at steering. Several locks down he entered a one at speed and, despite loud protests, he continued to skim towards some waiting vessels, pulling up just short of the last in line. Derisory catcalls and a stern rebuff from the lockkeeper resulted in a red faced, resentful, tirade against his accusers. Lyn spoke up to end the flow.

"It's time we went back anyway." By the time the boat returned to its berth it was late afternoon.

"Look could we go for a walk along the towpath? I've found a take-away Chinese in the village Lyn. I don't much care for eating in the restaurant."

At the tail of the weekend the towpath was quiet and cool, and the river flowed at its own pace again. Their leisured walking smoothed away the events of the day. Words did not seek response. Noticing he was still in the same shirt he was wearing at Nan's house, and recalling he had no baggage, Lyn said

"I'm sorry you have suffered so. I'm wondering if you are going through a bad patch just now and how you are fixed for clothing." He laughed.

"I've got the clothes I stand up in, which is why I don't want to eat in style girl."

"Then it's a take-a-way," she acquiesced. "However, tomorrow on the way home, we will stop and buy you a few things, if you will accept my help." A nod was the only response, as he turned into the path leading down to the village shops. Lyn sat on a bench outside the Chinese take away, waiting for Manny to collect their meal. Nearby, a little group of young people eyed her. She smiled her recognition of a passing boat crew from earlier in the day. One came across to her.

"Do you want us to get rid of that man," he asked? "He is trouble."

"It's all right. My husband has sent me on a weekend with someone because he wants me to make him jealous." They turned from her naivety, as Manny returned in time to hear her last sentence. He raised his fist to the boy walking past.

"Why did you say that," he accused her?

"Because it was the truth," she defended herself, wondering what trouble he had caused during her absence the day before.

"I had a few words with that mob yesterday," he said. "Forget those louts. Let's get back to the hotel and eat this." They ate in her room. She could feel his dark anger mounting in a menacing silence. It was a relief when he suggested they go down for a drink. Manny's good humour returned with a bottle of barley wine and some small talk with the manageress.

"Are you enjoying your stay Mrs...?" she began when Manny cut in.

"No formalities please, its Lyn isn't it m'dear?" After a few words, the hotelier moved on, suggesting they might like to listen to a small group of musicians in the lounge. Lyn excused herself on the pretext of starting back early next morning. She left Manny chatting to a woman sitting alone. Cigarette in hand and a barley wine on the table, he looked ready to sit and talk into the late hours.

Whilst packing she discovered a heavy gold bangle was missing and evaded the question it raised, sidestepping it in the oblivion of sleep.

At two in the morning a pounding on the door whipped her wide awake. She tumbled out of bed stumbling into strange furnishings on the way to the door. Manny stood in the corridor clad in vest and trousers.

"I shouldn't be mixing with the likes of you, decent woman that you are," He blurted before she could ask what the matter was. His voice rose as his face contorted to one of self-loathing.

"I've not long been released from prison, but I need to talk to you." Fearing to disturb sleeping guests, she pulled him inside the room leaving the door ajar.

Jo Willey gave a fine performance of repentance as he walked back and forth in the room. For good measure, he turned the screw with an account of the misfortunes which had landed him where he was.

He picked up his tale of a young baggage handler who conned friends that his dream of training as a pilot was true and chose to back up his fantasies with stolen money. Conning became second nature, with break in and entry where opportunity arose. On occasion, he boasted of a clever con which took him into

The Looters

high places that Lyn knew little of. Before long he knew the inside of Borstal, then tougher schools of correction. Most of his life until now was spent behind bars.

Once assured of his audience, Manny told his story in a matter of fact manner, though his face sometimes betrayed his true feelings. He knew what he was well enough, but whether he liked what he knew, was hard for her to fathom beneath the flow of words.

"I was protected by one of the Barons, after a prison gang abused me," he continued. "He at least kept the bullies off my back, and I paid for protection in the usual way, when you're inside. They can see to it, that you get roughed up, if you don't fall in with their demands and it earned me extra fags. The Barons never wanted for anything I can tell you, including women." He sat down by the coffee table and covered his face in his hands.

"Now I just want to go straight. I don't want to end up in the gutter again. You've probably guessed I'm out of a job." He stood in a resolute pose as he watched thoughts flit across her expressive face.

Her vivid imagination built up brick-by-brick and scene by scene a hell on earth she would never know. She reined in her scattered thoughts to make a controlled enquiry.

"Have you given thought to how you can do that? You make my worries seem futile. I have so much, and you've never had anything Manny."

"If you could help me find some work Lyn. I'm pretty good at shadowing people and hiding from the cops behind a lamppost, but I mean kosher work," he ended with a cunning grin

She sat and weighed him up. Behind the shiftiness and cunning in his angry twisted mind she thought she saw in front of her not a criminal, but a fellow soul bowed down with crushed hopes. Had fate chosen her to help this man, ten years or so her junior. Perhaps she could be his mentor compassion quickened her old fault of managing people's lives.

"Well Manny the threads of our lives have crossed at a very bare patch in Life's tapestry. I cannot weave a spell for my own happiness but maybe I can do something for you," she reflected.

"I think I can get some sleep now I have told you. It's been a wonderful help. Do you think I could have some tea," he asked, timing his next line to her offer? When she queried asking for service at that hour, he assured her with a rueful smile.

"Room Service will bring it up if you don't mind adding it to the bill. I can ring the porter. Is it all right if I use the connecting door to go back to my room? Good Night." Manny popped his head back round the door with an afterthought.

"Oh, would you like a cup? I can use a tooth mug. I'll knock on this door after the porter's gone. Better observe the proprieties eh?" She shook her head, thinking over his tale until a light tap on her door summoned her to redirect the porter to the next room.

Before she closed the door, Manny re-appeared, dressed, with a cigarette in his hand, to direct the porter to place the tray on the table. The pot of tea looked inviting and since there were two cups and saucers, she poured for both. Manny took his cup to stand by the window.

"You're sure you still want to be my friend, now you know I'm a felon?" She sipped her tea, considering.

"Jude and I may be able to find you work. You have paid your price and now you have to make a go of it in society."

"I never thought of your sort helping the likes of me. Thanks girl." He put his empty cup on the tray which she took out to a trolley in the corridor.

When she returned, Manny lay on her bed minus his trousers. His eyes were blank, his face withdrawn as he cradled the soft skin of his testicles, cushioning a big erection.

""This has given quite a few women satisfaction," he boasted, prostituting his wares. Do you want me to make love to you? You can check I'm free from infection." His huge member repulsed her. Cool nurse's eyes surveyed him.

"I thought you understood Manny that I need a friend, not a lover. All I really want is to have my husband back. He tells me if I make him jealous, it might happen," she stated bluntly. She stood gingerly near the foot of the bed ready to make for the door.

Quick anger lit his face, as of a child whose gift has not found favour. He sprang up, hand rising to strike her. She recoiled with fright, watching him control the movement, to stretch his arm and yawn then turn and drew on his pants.

"I won't hurt you lass, and its fine with me because I'm homosexual by nature as well as by past circumstance. See you at breakfast then."

With a friendly grin, he disappeared into the next room satisfied that he had played his part and well aware that he had not told her the whole story by a long shot.

I need to keep her on side, or I'm done for, he muttered throwing himself on his bed.

Lyn bolted both doors before sitting hunched up in bed. She knew her role in this strange friendship. She was going to reform and save the incorrigible rogue sent down for three years by a judge. If I help this weak man, then surely God will help me. She remembered an elderly patient saying, 'Never bargain with the Lord.' Well she didn't intend to, but since it looked as if He was using her, her conscience was clear. She hoped Manny would co-operate. She shook the pillow and slept soundly.

Over breakfast they heard a nearby couple discussing road blocks on the route back. Fearful of arriving home late, Lyn jumped up.

"We must start straight away. I had better pay my bill before the clerk gets busy." Manny followed her to the desk and waited until Lyn reached into her bag for some notes.

"Why don't you go to the phone booth, whilst it is empty, and let Jude know of the delay. I will collect your receipt." She handed him the money and ran to the phone. Whilst she was explaining the problem to Jude, Manny came and took the handset.

"I have found another route we can take. Let me talk to him." He closed the door on her with an apologetic smile. She watched him talk briefly and urgently, then the smile on his face showed all was well. He fingered the few notes of change and the receipt in his pocket until a flicker of conscience bid him return the change to Lyn.

"Did you get a receipt," she asked?

"I didn't think you would want it. It's in one of the trash bins," he said smoothly.

"No matter, it is of no importance," she smiled.

They made their way back via Croydon, stopping at a bank in the High Street to replenish her purse. Manny was quick to seize the sheaf of notes pushed through the grill. She waited a long moment for him to hand them to her.

In an outfitter's shop, she watched him move up and down the long counters, critically examining every garment, leaving a trail of unfolded shirts, pants, socks behind him. When they finally emerged from the store, a large carrier bag enclosed a battle dress top and trousers, similar to those he wore, and fresh shirts and underclothes.

Eager to get home, she had let the car pick up speed, when he conjured a new vest from inside his jacket.

"Well I got this one myself anyway," he claimed.

"Why on earth did you do that? Now we'll have to turn back and pay for it somehow," she snapped. Unable to turn in the heavy traffic flow, and pressed for time, she let herself be over-ruled by his persuasive retort.

"They expect loss and can well afford it. I could be in deep trouble if you go back." Her ill-judged acceptance made her an accomplice to theft. She drove in troubled silence, thinking of Jude's response to her return.

Manny sat thinking of the life he'd squandered. Between prison spells, he made out by conning and pilfering. Homosexuals looked after him, enjoying his wit and willingness. He made sure the women paid well for what they demanded of him, suffering the cloying odour of their fluids, sensual reminders of bad times. His mother's sweat stained armpits as she pushed him from their doorstep, after his second spell in Borstal.

This bitch, driving the car so efficiently, was different. She's generous with dosh and so is her old man. Manny intended to manipulate the pair to his advantage to get the break he needed. Christ! What a day out in the boat, that was. She talked like a mate about anything and everything. She looked a bit of all right when she was animated. No ogling or simpering. Quite a few blokes had looked their way.

On the outskirts of town Lyn stopped to make a phone call. Jude's tense voice answered her breathless, "Is that you Jude?"

"Yes. You're late. Where are you ducks. I've missed you?"

Her heart skipped a beat. She could barely believe her ears. He sounded like the young Jude who had walked her up the hill overlooking Newcastle, years ago.

"I'm five minutes away. Just have to drop Manny off at Nan's and I'll be home. I have missed you all so much," she confided.

"Wait there for me" he said, "I will meet you down there. I have to see him. I need to talk with him." When she told Manny, he smiled

"I thought he might. That's it then girl. Unless you both can help me, I have to move on. I'm going to miss your company. It's a strange thing to say but I think I'm in love with you."

"I cannot say the same to you, as you must know. so please don't embarrass me Manny." A strange excitement welled, as she realized she had spent a weekend with this funny man. She marshalled her thoughts, as she started the car and drove on. She envied his rootless life for its freedom from possessions, pleasure in small things and acceptance of his lot. She felt she was abandoning a stray to feed on scraps. She dug into her bag to find very little money left.

"Unless we can find some work for you Manny, it seems I won't see you again, though I would dearly like to help you get on your feet," she said.

"If you and your husband can see your way to giving me a job, I will work hard to pull myself out of this way of life," he pleaded. His bid to survive taxed her resolve and humanity. She felt pulled in two directions. One moment her mind was set on helping a stranger with whom she had shared some fleeting happiness, and the next minute, she couldn't wait to see her husband. Jude has missed me. I cannot believe things are coming right after so long. She turned at the crossroads and pulled up outside Nan's house.

I want to give you a gift of thanks for discovering I could laugh again, but I shall have to use a messenger. I suppose in a way it is to let you know that you are cared about by someone. The money is not given as a cold indulgence you see. Can you come to the corner of the road near the nursing home around seven this evening? There will be somebody waiting with a parcel, it is a small volume about the four loves. Some money will be in the chapter on love expressed as charity. It will tide you over until, maybe, we can sort something out." She had no idea who she would trust

"I'll be there," he said, his eyes expressing his gratitude. "You won't let me down, will you? I'm in desperate need woman."

Jude drew up behind them as Manny jumped out then walked to his car. Folded notes changed hands as Jude got out. He strode to Lyn and took her arm to walk her away.

"Goodbye and good luck Manny," she called. "He needs some luck Jude, we have used him for our own ends."

"Oh, I don't know Ducks, he knew what he was doing. It's done the trick anyway, I can't wait to get you home. The weekend's been a nightmare. I've worked like hell and so has every other bastard."

"Are you sure? It's not a case of wanting an old toy back, is it." Her reply threw him off track. He turned her round.

"You've no worries about that. This weekend has brought me to my senses, but there's a small problem." They had walked to the end of the road and stood looking down to the sea.

"A while back I fixed to take Syd, the boys and their friends to the Malta villa for a week. The flight's booked for day after tomorrow and I can't change things now. It's why I wanted you to have a few days off, but when I come back things will be different, I promise.

Another week was of small account if there truly was change ahead, and she could do with time to get used to her old role.

"I understand. You must go. When you come back, we'll make sure things will change," she murmured.

Jude's ears pricked. Underlying the soft tone, he scented her past attempts to change him. Coaxing or goading, she had left her mark on him in their early years. For now, bedevilled with jealousy of an imagined cuckolding, he wanted his bond mate in his bed to claim the rites of old lore. They turned homewards.

That late afternoon, he ordered Gertrude and Ruby to bring laden trays to their bedroom. They served tea to their mistress with sly looks. Lyn slipped on a happy smile for their benefit. He summoned their sons to welcome her home. They stood unsure at the foot of the bed, young fishers trawling Life's ocean. They sighed thoughtfully over their elders' meagre catch and departed. The double backed creature danced another jig before sleep closed the curtains on the masque.

In earl evening, they rose, and Jude went across to the nursing station. Lyn, true to her promise, looked for the Lewis book and slipped money between the pages before going in search of a messenger.

Ken was alone in the staff room. He bore no grudge for Daphne's dismissal, but he knew whose word was law, Jude Rook's.

"Ken would you mind taking this parcel to the telephone box at the end of the road, after you've had supper," requested Lyn. "Just give it to the man waiting there, that's all, thank you." He took the package with a nod, passed it to Ruby who passed it to Jude.

Chapter 16: In deep waters

THE early morning sun roused Lyn. She wriggled her toes and stretched luxuriously as a corner of her mind opened on a nectar of joys waiting to be
sipped. A new day dawning and for the first time in a long while, she looked
forward to it. Beside her, no longer curled away, Jude slept peacefully on his
back. He opened his eyes and gave her a sleepy smile, then reached for her just
as the phone pealed. Rolling over, her took the handset and listened.

"What's this all about," he asked, passing it to her?

As she lifted it to her ear the message continued '…. you betrayed me'. Ken
hadn't gone to the corner

"It is a message from Manny.".

"I know that. I thought we'd finished with him." She explained about the
parcel.

"You mean this," reaching into his bedside drawer to bring out the book. "I
think we've given him enough, don't you?"

Things were turning sour, her stomach churned. The risk of losing her happiness broke her resolve to keep Manny's background private.

"Jude the man's recently come out of prison. He's penniless and needs to
find work. I put some money in the book for him to start afresh. We've used him
and I feel we should help him." Pity moistened her eyes.

"Right, let's go and see him." He swung out of bed. "Get dressed, I'll get the
car out." During the drive down, her goodwill to Manny hardened into a silent
protest against his intrusive sabotage of her hopes.

She knocked quietly at Nan's front door and listened for the sound of her
shuffle, along the passage. The door opened a crack and her head, festooned with
pipe cleaners, peered round the edge.

"It's seven o'clock. What's the matter," Nan demanded in a grumpy tone?
Manny appeared, eyes red and puffy from crying, his grey face had a tired defeated look.

"I'm so sorry Nan. We came to see you Manny," said Lyn.

"Get in the car," Jude ordered him. They drove up to a bluff overlooking the
sea.

"Lyn wants you to have this." handing him the package.

"Thank you, I'm sorry about the message," Manny mumbled, turning to
Jude.

"It was the best time I ever remember, bliss, sheer bliss." Lyn felt Jude stiffen.
She avoided further emotive issues by saying,

"I hope things turn out…"

"Well, that's settled. We'll drop you back," Jude interrupted. They left him in the road outside Nan's house.

"So, you had a blissful weekend. Is that what the tears are about," Jude quizzed, watching her pull out a handkerchief?

"Blissful is a bit strong Jude. The day on the river was lovely. You know I've always wanted a boat for the family. No, the tears are a mix of things, I think. Relief we are back together, tension over this morning and you finding out my deceit, and just sadness that so many people have such bitter, lonely lives." She sighed and dabbed at the moisture around her eyes.

"You're crying for that bastard. Don't tell me you're not," he snarled, accelerating up to the house. He got out, slamming the car door to, and strode ahead with Lyn hurrying upstairs after him.

"No, no Jude, but we did discard him like an oily rag after greasing the nuts and bolts of our marriage. I know how it feels to be cast aside. There are hundreds like him and they all have a place never mind their shade or shape. A little help could sort one of them out."

"I don't want to hear any more of this rubbish," he sneered and walked out.

She straightened her dress and clasped her belt when there was a crash in the sitting room, followed by a loud snap. Running through, she found Jude with her music stand twisted and bent in his hands, his face tight and dark with anger. On the floor, her guitar lay broken in two.

He left her to sit in his car, fighting his jealous rage. His feelings had overwhelmed his push for freedom and restitution but for now go softly, softly. He must keep to his plan until he had sole ownership of their properties. She had to go, and she would in the end for betraying him.

He coasted downhill into the town, until he came to the railway station where a man hailed him, it was Manny. Jude slowed down and waited for him to catch up and lean in the window.

"I'm off now, to try my luck in London. I did the best I could for you, but free love's not her style. If you ask me, you don't know when you're well off mate. Shall I keep in touch?"

"Maybe," Jude muttered, "You have our phone number?" A nod, a tattoo on the car panel and Jo Wiley, alias Manny, was gone.

Back in the house, Lyn picked up her guitar, a fine old instrument bought in happier days in Malta.

So much for jealousy Jude she thought You'd better stick to harem mode, I think. It gets things out of your system, and I know where I am. The intercom buzzed and Alan Brilson called through from the kitchen.

"We're short of carrots Matron. Is there a chance of someone getting some for me?"

"I'll go Alan, quarter of an hour all right?" The walk up to the Old Town gave her breathing space before starting the day. The sun warmed her back on the way home and a breeze smoothed the worry lines from her forehead.

A week later Jude and Syd returned from Malta, leaving the boys there to spend a few more days on their own. Sun tanned and fit, after plenty of swimming, Jude looked handsome as left the office to parade through his domain.

It had been a lonely week for Lyn with the boys away. Her imagination fed on events in Malta but so long as the family stayed together, she would go along with Jude's strange ways. He returned, surfeited with praise.

"Ducks, how about coming down to the town with me. We'll call and have coffee with Syd. Poor bitch will be feeling down today."

"Yes, I'll come with you." When they walked into the hardware shop, Syd was sitting at a table, writing up some sales. Dressed in jeans and a man's checked shirt, she offered no greeting.

"How about a cuppa Syd," prompted Jude? He followed her into the back of the shop. When they came back, with three mugs of coffee, she was smiling. Lyn noted that the black tooth had been replaced with a false white one. She took her coffee.

"Thank you. This smells good. Did you enjoy Malta, the swimming is wonderful, isn't it?"

"I am afraid of water, but I loved the island and the sunshine." Lyn stirred her cup, Afraid of water eh? They say the devil doesn't like water.

"Oh, what a pity, the water's crystal clear. Thank you for my coffee Syd. I need to walk down to the chemist now, with some scripts. Can you pick me up there Jude?"

Her trust in Jude's promise to reform was strictly exercised during the following weeks, but she never questioned his comings and goings with the staff, knowing they and some patients were well aware of their personal drama.

For his part, he spent more evenings at home, watching television with the boys, before wandering off to chat with a patient. Both worked hard to settle the unrest in everyone's minds. After arranging for a major remodelling of the kitchen, when the workmen arrived, Jude decided to go Plymouth for a few days. Lyn was left to work with chef in the evenings, helping to prepare the next day's meals under the drapes of a small dust free area,

When Jude rang to say he was bringing Gillie back for a short stay Lyn brought out her best linen and softest pillows to repay the kind-hearted friend from twenty years ago. Showing Gillie into a room where the sun shone on a bedspread patterned with daffodils, whilst real blooms filled a vase on the side table, Lyn waited, looking forward to her hug.

"Yes, very nice," Gillie made the pleasantry and Lyn knew the gap between them was more than a span of years. She was being judged and found wanting.

There had been the same feeling when Jude's sisters visited recently.

The following afternoon, Jude arranged to take the family out to dine at a cliff head restaurant, forestalling Lyn's assumed inclusion with a request.

"Will you keep an eye on things here, Ducks, in case of an emergency?" They were in the kitchen, standing in front of two large baskets full of fresh scarlet runners picked by him with Gillie earlier in the day.

"Isn't someone going to help me with preparing all this lot for the freezer? I've got meals to plate up for tomorrow's lunch as well," she began, but he had gone. When they returned, lights were burning in the office where she was carrying out a few of next day's chores to fill in time. Gillie handed her a paper wrapped offering of cold fish and chips.

"Sorry we left you in the lurch," she said smoothly, "but Syd had made plans for us." Gillie's eyes watched Lyn swallow back a retort. Both knew there was more to her attitude, than sadness for what might have been for her daughter. It involved Jude. Were Jude's black humours still stirring trouble under a sham pose of reconciliation? Lyn bit her lip and turned her attention to mending bridges for the remainder of the visit.

Jude exerted further control through the staff. If Lyn made a request in the course of her duties, it was politely acknowledged but never carried out. To reinforce the pressure, he would often countermand her instructions. They struggled through the ensuing weeks, keeping open argument at bay, but tension simmered around the pact between them. Christmas came and went, with Jude sharing his time between Syd in the town and those of his family who were disposed to stay around their unsettled home.

Early in the New Year night sister summoned Lyn.

"Come quickly. Your mother has taken a turn for the worse."

Lyn sat by her mother's bed, enfolding her hand. Fear of the unknown was mirrored in Mercy Young's deep blue eyes, A phone call, made to the doctor, allowed a gentle sedative to sooth her terrors. Lyn recalled her words from years ago, "She will stay and look after me." Soul entwined soul as eyes held long union, until Mercy's closed.

At her funeral. Jude sat apart from family, alone with his thoughts. In the atmosphere of disunity, the gathering shuffled uneasily in the silence. Afterwards, they thanked Lyn for taking care of Mercy then went their ways, back to the warmth of homely dwellings.

The following Autumn Lyn was invited to join a small group representing British Yoga, in Switzerland.

"I should like to go, it's only for a week Jude," she hinted one morning over lunch. "It's short notice because someone has dropped out." He didn't look up from the midday news bulletin he watched at mealtimes.

"Fine by me, when is it?"

"Saturday, that's six days away. I will leave all the paper work done in advance to cover pay day etc." Assured all would be well, she booked her plane ticket to leave from London airport.

On the Friday morning Jude came in with the family deed box under his arm and left it unlocked on the table. Before she could ask why the deed box was out, he quit the office.

Humming a happy little tune, she stretched before resuming work. Wonder what he needs this out, for she mused, resting her hand on the box before opening it. On the top of a pile of documents lay an envelope addressed to her in a strange hand. The postmark was two weeks old and the letter had been opened. The single sheet inside was from Manny. His message was stark.

"I have been ill with pneumonia and am in financial distress. Can you help me please?" She stood staring at the letter with a sense of guilt for reading it. Impulsively she wrote down the address before replacing it in the envelope and returning it to the box. Why didn't Jude give it to me and talk things over? Why didn't he destroy it? I wish to God he had. The longer she fretted, the more responsible she felt towards solving a problem for someone she knew, in trouble.

She went to the bank to cash up the week's wages, stood a moment in thought, then turned her steps towards the Post Office. A brief telegram informed Manny that she would see him in the check-in area at the airport before take-off the next day.

Waiting at the check-in desk, with the small group travelling to Zinal, Lyn spotted Manny slide out from behind a column and look towards her. She finished her business and left the line saying to the others,

"I will catch up with you in a few minutes in the departure lounge." She walked across to him and conscious her deception, she gabbled,

"Hallo Manny, you look dreadfully thin, what does your doctor say? Is somebody looking after you?"

"It's a long tale Lyn, and this is not the time to tell it to you. If you could let me have a fiver for now, I'd like to meet you when you come back and tell you the whole story. Will you do that for me please? It is very important."

"You are welcome to some cash Manny, but I need to go straight home when we get back."

"Just a few minutes of your time would help. I really am in deep trouble," he pleaded. "I could meet you at the platform gate in the station. What's your return flight number?" Drawn in to his drama, she opened her purse and read out the figures on her ticket thinking, 'it will only be an hour before the next train back if I miss the arranged one.' Somewhere "devious" was added to "accomplice to theft of a vest" as Lyn slid another step down the slope.

The week in Switzerland was refreshing. Buddhist philosophy flowed through lectures and discussion groups. They were all sorry to leave. During the flight back, Lyn concluded it was no good reading and talking, when action was more important. Imbued with fresh ideas of compassion she felt that helping others called on more than the pocket.

At the London rail terminal, she said goodbye to her friends, and waited until

Manny surfaced from the crowd to join her. She was shocked by his appearance. His clothes looked as if he had slept in them. He wore a near threadbare jacket over a frayed shirt and old jeans. His cap was pulled low over the stubble on his cheeks, and large boots anchored his thin frame. A dry rasping cough shook him. Lyn decided to see his situation resolved, before going home.

"Here I am then, but I must catch the next train back," she stated bluntly. "How about getting you something to eat whilst we talk?"

"Can we get out of here, we might need a cab?" He had taken her suitcase and began steering her towards the exit with his other hand. She pulled back.

"Look here Manny, what is going on? I'm not going anywhere except this station," she protested. He eyed her warm fur coat and the lamb skin lined boots.

"Had a good time did you, with all your rich friends? You should meet some of my friends before you leave."

"There isn't time. I must catch the next train."

"Oh! So, my friends aren't good enough for you." His voice resonated causing passers-by to turn their heads.

"I thought you wanted to discuss your problem."

"My problems are the same as those of the hundreds out there tonight, but you rich are all alike, no time for anybody but yourselves."

"I do care about others," she snapped, nettled as people looked their way.

"Then prove it. I've managed to find digs," he wheezed, "but I need to collect my things first. They're with some friends I'd like you to meet. I will explain on the way. It isn't far. I won't let you miss your train I promise. Please." She let him walk her towards an exit deciding she would stay a short while. In for a penny, she thought as she let him hail a cab.

The cabbie dropped them off on the river side of the embankment opposite a railway station. They crossed the road, now empty except for spasmodic evening traffic, and entered the forecourt. On a wall, at the far end of the square, a green shade released a tiny fan of light on a strange scene. She stubbed her toe into something which crackled and moved beneath her foot. The ground was full of mounds of paper.

"How did it get like this, it's disgusting?"

"Look again rich woman," said Manny touching a mound with his foot.

"Sod off," a voice muttered the obscenity from somewhere below her. Other voices joined in. Among them she heard women's voices.

"Bleedin' cops is it?"

"Nah, a couple of fancy ones. Get the shite out of 'ere and give us some quiet. G'arn, bugger off."

"Is there something going on tonight Manny. Where are those people going with the cardboard boxes," she asked, staring at shadowy figures moving around the perimeters and alcoves of the square?

"There's something going on all right woman. These people are getting ready for bed. See that pile of newspapers over there?" She nodded assent, a light dawning in her eyes, as crackles of newspaper rippled round the square.

"Rosie, a lovely old woman, is already asleep under those. This square is where I've been sleeping for weeks."

Manny walked across to a man sitting in an alcove. Lyn could see he was very tall, but he was wrapped in so many ragged blankets his frame was hidden.

"Come to fetch your things old chap?" The man looked up, intelligence smiling out of clear blue eyes, free from the bloodshot veins of a drinker. Lyn was startled by his cultured accent. How had he come to this?

"Thanks for looking after 'em mate. I hope things turn out right for you. This is the friend I told you of. Come on Lyn, hurry if you want to catch that train. We can catch a bus from here." He took his bundle from elegant hands, explaining as they walked across the square.

"I've kipped in that alcove with him, for the last week. A lovely bloke to talk to. Says he was a professor of old languages, but they only want science these days. That and other problems landed him here."

Across the road the waters of the Thames flowed dark and deep, unreflecting the pale street lights lining the Embankment. A police launch slid quietly along the flow keeping a weather eye open for human flotsam.

He hailed a passing bus which barely paused to let him swing her on to the platform. Lyn was losing track of time. Everything was moving so fast, she could barely catch up with events.

"What landed you there?"

"Maggie closed all the spikes, and the Sally Army's hostel is brim full. Where are we going to go, eh?"

"I thought the money I gave you would pay for lodgings, and with an address, you could sign on Social Security while you find work."

"Not that easy. I'll explain when I get to the new digs." They rode to a darkened area, in the London outskirts, before alighting at the corner of a square. The tall terraced houses hid behind the few broken street lights. She kept close as he hurried down the street, skipping in and out of deep shadows, until he came to a stop at one of the houses.

"Here we are. Will you come up with me?"

"Well I'm petrified of stopping out here." They passed the landlord, a Sikh she guessed. The two men exchanged a few words.

"It is all right for you to come up for a bit." They climbed endless narrow stairs to a landing with three doors. He opened a door and stood aside for her. In the otherwise empty room, there were two triple bunked, iron frame beds and four small wooden chairs.

"This is for six people," she said, a question in her tone as she looked around.

"It's a doss house room I'll share with five other men. We only have a few minutes before one of them comes up." She sat on one of the four wooden chairs, the odour of used blankets hitting her nostrils. He stood by the door, blocking her exit.

"I hardly know how to tell you this but I'm on the run from prison. It was all true about the old man's funeral. I didn't tell you I had compassionate release to go. Well I didn't report back, and that was fourteen months ago when I lied to you." He looked warily towards her, ready to block her move if she upped and ran.

Lyn stared back at him, frozen in disbelief. A few hours ago, she had bid farewell to the purity of sparkling snow on a mountain side, to deep chants and silent meditations, giving her strength and peace. Now she sat in a foetid attic with an escaped convict. She shivered from the damp cold in the room.

"Well, you'll have to report back, that's for sure. How long have you left to serve?"

"Seven or eight months from a three-year stretch. I want to give myself up, but I can't do it girl. I was arraigned at the Old Bailey. Got friendly, you know what I mean, with a chap well up the ladder in the Bank of England. Well, I put a bit of pressure on him to let me go down to see the gold vaults during lunch hour. I only did it for a lark, but he got cold feet.

I was nicked when I went up the steps to meet him. I just avoided conspiracy to rob a bank. The judge said I was an incorrigible rogue and deserved a tough sentence."

"What happened to the man," Lyn wanted to know?

"He got the push. He would have done anyway when they found out he was a queer. They've no time for people like us, and he was a damn nice bloke." She stood up and picked up her case, moving to the door. Manny didn't budge.

"Look Manny I must go. Don't you see all I want to do now is get back to Sussex please. When I get home, I'll be able to think straight, and maybe sort something out. Is this room paid for?"

"No, the room isn't paid for, so I'd better go back to my friends in the square. They're not good enough for the likes of you, neither am I. I was hoping you would see your way," His eyes held her gaze.

"Yes, yes, I will settle that, and no, I don't think I'm better than them. It's unbearable how they suffer in the hell you have shewn me." In her intensity, she matched the power of the bright blue eyes looking into hers until he glanced away then swung back with desperate pleading.

"I will give myself up, when the last of the autumn leaves fall. I love the autumn, but I'll need help and support for a time. I suppose I couldn't come back to Sussex to turn myself in. I won't bother you, honest. Apart from rent for a room, I can get by on a couple of quid a week. You can see me walk through the prison gates to prove I mean it woman." She nodded slowly. He took her case, moving away from the door and opened it for her to pass through.

When they returned to the ground floor, the Sikh stood waiting. Lyn handed some notes to Manny. Two or three men stood about the ill lit hallway. A door opened and someone in a dressing gown looked out. Lyn gave a half-smile. There was no response from the sixteen-year-old, looking back from under a heavy layer of aging make up. Lyn nudged Manny's arm.

"I don't think that child should be staying here, do you. She may not be safe."

"She's as safe as any other prostitute is in London. Don't worry about her, and don't say anything, or she'll give you a mouthful. Look, could I take you up on that offer of a bite to eat? I am hungry as hell. There's a café still open near here."

They walked back through the patches of shadow, into the main road where a cheap café served the inhabitants of the area. Lyn had tea and a bun as she watched Manny wolf down a plate of liver and bacon with piles of mashed potato.

"Tell me how you got my telegram Manny," she pressed. "you weren't living at that address."

"There's a little shop behind the square, where the shopkeeper takes our mail. Some of the down and outs have relatives who think they are living there. If they send money, the shopkeeper gets a cut. It works." She looked at her watch and saw with dismay that it was nearly eleven. No bus had trundled by whilst they ate.

"I'll leave you to finish your meal. Where do I get the bus? I haven't seen one since we came here," she asked him urgently. Replete with food and looking forward to a night in a bed, Manny looked surprisingly fit again.

"We may have missed the last bus, but I'll ask the owner if you can phone for a cab. I'll see you to the station."

"Yes, do that, please, and no, I don't want any one coming to the station. Just get me a taxi, and see me safely inside, then go and get yourself settled, thanks Manny." He phoned. They waited and waited. Theatre goers had first claim over taxis, whereas in questionable areas a driver could get a beating instead of his money.

When she entered the cab, Manny put a hand on her arm.

"I've confided in you Lyn, and that makes you an accessory, because you know." Jo Wiley made a second phone call. It was to East Sussex.

In the cab her mind homed in on the word accessory. Oh, why did I listen to him? The week in Switzerland crystallized into one word, charity.

When the cab finally drew into the station forecourt, she settled her fare and rushed to the platform, only to see the tail light of the last train disappearing round the curve of the line.

She stood disconsolate and frightened in the big empty station, its space pervaded with the scurrying sounds of the night creatures. Tomorrow's newspapers, stacked for the mail train, stood next a large crate. The crack between them sucked in the tip of a large rat's tail. She shivered. Why did I do it? What a fool

I've been to put the happiness of the family at risk. What about Jude and me? So many questions, no decisions. She berated her massaging of some imagined vein of goodness and charity, for an outcast of society.

Finding a phone booth where the instrument was still attached to the wall, Lyn dialled and waited, Jude's voice answered.

"Jude the plane came in late. I've missed the last train." How easy it was becoming to lie.

"Just have to wait until the mail train around four thirty," Jude's voice was impersonal. A man leered through the booth window. Home felt so far away. She clung frantically to the fragile connection with Jude.

"Couldn't you come for me please, it is only an hour's drive," she implored.

"No! Listen! Keep near the lights, and don't go near the toilets. Look out for the station police and ask them to keep an eye out for you. They come around every so often. Do you understand?" then the phone went dead.

Jude rolled back on his pillow. She met that bastard after all. Let her get on with it, then his mind filled with images of the station at night. He reached for the phone.

As Lyn came out of the booth, two women confronted her eye to eye. Theirs was not a friendly look, but she took courage to ask the best place to sit and wait. Their suspicion gave way to sympathy.

"Go and sit over there luv. We'll keep an eye on you if we're around. Anyone comes up to you, say your friend's gone to the loo and tell 'em to skive off." They lit cigarettes and strolled on their beat.

Around two in the morning, a man approached her as she sat head drooped, eyes heavy with fatigue. He put a hand on her shoulder. She sprang away but he caught her.

"It's Mrs Rook, isn't it? Your husband sent me to fetch you. My car's just outside." Her eyes focused on the mechanic from the garage where they had the cars serviced. By three o'clock she crept into bed and curled up, sick with shame at the lying. Jude turned his back.

Chapter 17: The bad penny

NEITHER of them referred to that night again. Their deceit stifled words until Jude took a phone call at the beginning of December. He passed the handset to Lyn before walking out of the room.

"I believe this is for you. Don't say you weren't expecting it." A frisson of fear shot up her spine when she heard Manny speak. So, Jude did know she had lied and opened the door to her nemesis.

"Hello, Is that you Lyn? I'm in Hastings, in a room on the seafront. I am ready to turn myself in, but I can't do it on my own. I need some moral support woman. Will you come with me?" How could she not help, if he was going to do the right thing.

"Are you there, will you help," the voice persisted?

"I'm glad you decided to finish your sentence. Afterwards you can start afresh. Yes, I will be across after I finish work tomorrow evening. I don't know what time. What is your address?" She noted the address and put down the receiver with an unsteady hand. Jude returned with his supper.

She made two failed attempts to get Manny to knock on the door of a prison in Maidstone. On the next occasion, a few days before Christmas, Lyn walked him across the cobbled entrance leading to the massive old gates of the prison fortress in Lewes. After ringing the bell of the small door, inset in one of them, they stood waiting and listening. A tiny window slid back.

"Yes?" The monosyllable was discouraging.

"I'm John Thomas Willey. Sir. Prisoner number 556643, absconded from prison sixteen months ago, whilst on compassionate leave, Sir. I've come to give myself up, Sir." A short silence, then the voice replied.

"Just a minute please." They waited, Lyn scared that Manny would run for it again. A rattling behind the door and it was opened on to a prison yard. They stepped through. A uniformed officer inspected them, motioning them to follow him, until he stopped outside the open door to a small room.

"I've sent for the Governor. In here please." He shut them in, and she felt the impotency of being behind a locked door, the pressure of walls closing in, and she sprang up ready for flight. The Governor, a pleasant middle-aged man, arrived and left the door open, before coming across to shake hands with her. He turned to Manny.

"Good man. You've managed for quite a while, haven't you?" He cocked an eye at Lyn.

"This lady knew nothing until yesterday Sir. She brought me in, Sir." The

Governor gave a thoughtful nod.

"An officer will escort you out ma'am." He pressed a wall button. "Thank you for what you have done. Willey since you have reported yourself back, you will not be under tight security. Right, get moving and we'll book you in."

"Yes Sir." The rigid shadow, that was John Thomas Willey, moved out from the wall to begin its role of repentant sinner for the warders.

A wooden faced officer appeared at the door, beckoning to Lyn to follow him. She obeyed his summons. A nebulous fear of her surroundings restrained her from giving Manny more than a timid smile of good luck. Once she was outside the gates, the warder's expressionless face creased into a warm smile.

"Thanks for your help Ma'am. He'll be alright now." She unlocked her car and stopped to look back before stepping into its warm interior. A leaden sky spread overhead, pressing down on the massive grey stones of the prison.

Night clouds raced before the car's headlights, their beams channelling a path between the dark hedgerows. A prism of rainbows lit her tears as she prayed to God to make things come aright in her own troubled life and reunite the family. When she reached town, its lights welcomed her, and home was around the next corner.

Later that night, lying on her side of the matrimonial bed, she confessed to her part in Manny's history, now that he was behind bars again.

"You don't think I didn't know what you were up to," Jude asked, steel eyed? He had raised himself on his elbow, looking down on her.

"Why didn't you speak out if you knew? The compulsion to do what's right has felt like a giant web closing in on me. I couldn't think clearly. I needed your help with the outcome, but it seems we still go separate ways most of the time." He levelled his gaze.

"I wanted to see how you dealt with it. I didn't know he was on the run though, or I'd have seen him inside, sooner. Now you're free of that bastard, how about a few days in Malta? Could you be ready by tomorrow?" She closed her eyes around her thoughts.

Will things be the way they were when we first opened up the villa with such excitement over our Shangri La? Can we go back? I'm not the same, and neither is he. Why do I feel sadness for an incarcerated man, and an unrequited love for another? It must work for the family. She opened her eyes and smiled.

"That would be good. I can be ready for an evening flight. There are one or two things in the office to clear up."

At Gatwick airport, muted echoes eddied around Departures and Arrivals, floating above a constant flow of movement. Finally, they fastened into their seat belts as the clarion voice of the hostess told them they were on their way. Opening her book, she remembered her promise to write a letter to Manny.

"The others chi'ike if you don't get any mail, will you write," Manny had asked? A passing hostess supplied some writing paper. She had never written to an inmate of Her Majesty's penitentiaries. What do you write about, for heaven's sake, that does not touch on your freedom, and their lack of it? Why do I always feel the guilty one? A deep sigh escaped, and a tear of tiredness and self-pity fell on the notepaper. Jude noticed. She crumpled up the paper and put it in her empty glass.

Outside the airport at Malta, Lyn looked for the familiar face of their gardener.

"Is Miguel bringing the car for us?" Jude steered the luggage trolley whilst signalling for a taxi.

"It's not worth opening the villa for a few days. We can call in to pick up the car if we need it. I hope to get our old room at The Corinthian." he explained. The gracious old hotel was where they had all stayed at intervals, during the building stages of the villa.

When they entered the vestibule, a porter recognized them. Taking their luggage to the desk, he joined in the welcoming smiles from the manager and staff then took them to their old room overlooking the pool. Lyn looked round the well-appointed room. High ceilings and beautiful curtains enclosed many memories. Opening the doors to the balcony, Jude stepped through to lean over the balustrade.

"There are quite a few guests from the number of lounge chairs in use. Care for a swim before turning in?"

"If you like, and you might order some ham sandwiches and coffee for us to come back to," she replied. "I wonder if the sea will be warm enough for swimming. It would be heaven to swim in the open, in winter."

The large twin beds were refreshingly cool for the sultry nights on the little Catholic island. They slept late into the morning, before taking a light breakfast on the veranda. Lyn's mind niggled over her promise to write to Manny.

"Jude, do you mind if I make a phone call to the prison, and leave a message for him? It's really only a keep your pecker up message at Christmas time." She knew she was on thin ice, but her commitment stood firm.

"Do so if you must. Syd will need cheering up, I'll call her as well," he agreed.

After their calls to home he demanded that she let Jo Wiley fend for his self from there on. She, all unaware of the double-dealing between the two, obstinately defended her crusade for a repentant sinner. They were still at an impasse.

They visited Valletta, entering the city through the beautiful gated arch that was locked every night. The shopkeepers, who had furnished the villa, came to their doors to bid them well.

Wily priests gave them searching glances as they passed by. Were they Catholic and would they get the message from the loudspeakers, installed in the village squares, to ensure recalcitrant Catholics returned to the church and paid their dues?

The gardener and his wife, their housemaid, welcomed them into their home.

The wife slipped a little card with a prayer for marital happiness into Lyn's hand as she assured her the villa would be well kept.

Their busying left very little time to talk and kept them together and yet apart. By afternoon they had reached the far end of the island. Small beaches rolled from the waves to petal the grottoes, laticing the rocks.

"Are you still game for a swim," asked Jude? She nodded. They changed on a secluded beach, leaving their clothes on a rock ledge.

He led the way into a grotto and she followed him. They left behind a world of bright sunlight and colour for eerie, age old tunnels reverberating below the ground. They came to a dark labyrinth of water swirling through the chain of caves and in the dim light they slipped into the race. Deep channels of water twisted and turned between the rocks, dividing off here and there in different directions. Sunlight torched down, through small openings in the low ceiling, dappling the moving stream with rippling patches of light. Jude moved surely ahead, with Lyn fast on his tail. Afraid of being lost in the maze, she shivered with the drop in temperature

"Are you sure you know the way back Jude, because I don't," she called out?

"Yes, I've been here before with Sid, using a small inflatable. These hidden waterways are seldom used now. It's said you could drown here, and not be found for years." Her memory opened on Becky and the river scene in the stables. She shivered again.

Of a sudden, their channel flowed into a wide circular expanse of water. A rock ceiling belled above with a central funnel opening up the outside world and the sun. Light flooded down. The jade green water became warm and sparkling. Her fear subsided and she relaxed, floating on her back, laughing with the joy of discovery. Jude swam round the perimeter, making smaller and smaller circles until he was by her side. His trunks were in his hand.

"Take your costume off. I'm going to make love to you." He unclipped the clasp at her back and the green silken scrap of material floated away. The back of his hand slid down her thigh, drawing with it her remaining garment. He swam to the rock side and draped them on an outcrop, then came to her.

He let his body float below the surface looking, through the meniscus, at the green lichen covering the ceiling. She floated above him, curving to cradle his head and kiss him. As his face rippled below her, his eyes changed from hazel to dark black orbs full of anger. She was staring into the face of the boy in the river... The pool churned. Wild willow branches lashed her back.

Mesmerised by the scene mirrored in her eyes, Jude watched an image of a riverside grow until it filled the cave. She was bending over from a grassy bank, looking down at him. Her hand, with the stain of the vine in the palm, came towards him. He knew her again, as his annihilator. The cave pressed in and down upon him as he shot upwards, collapsing the scene back to the present,

He shot high out of the water. She blinked spray from her eyes and looked into wary hazel eyes bursting with an urgent need to escape. He headed for the tunnel opening in frantic haste and disappeared. Panicked at being lost, she followed his trail.

He exploded into the outer grotto, to look out on a little bay. He saw the bright sails of small boats bobbing up and down. He was back at the sandy beach where they had left their clothes.

What the hell happened back there? I felt different. She looked different. I could have sworn she was going to kill me. How much does she know of my plans? That was our last time. Lyn caught up with him, breathless and questioning.

"What on earth happened to us, we've left our costumes back in the cave?"

"Sorry, I suddenly remembered the tide comes in fast down there," he lied. "I heard you following. We'll buy new costumes tomorrow." He brooked further pursuit of the nightmare experience.

Back in the hotel, a seasonal dinner and dance had been arranged. For all their wealth, Lyn had a very small wardrobe. She unpacked the only long evening gown she possessed. The pale lemon chiffon skirt, filming a soft tangerine underslip, was pleated into the low waist of a silk top, beaded with seed pearls. The shawl collar of layered chiffon, in shades of deeper lemon and tangerine, was highlighted with pearls.

She had worn the gown, for the first time, to accompany her father to see Emlyn Williams in Night Must Fall. She was a young woman, seeing her first adult drama in psychological suspense. Now, in her fifties the dress still fitted, and she knew more about the drama of mind games.

"I don't look like mutton dressed as lamb in this dress, do I Jude?" He turned from setting his tie.

"It's all right because you have a young face when you aren't fussing, you look nice. Come on, let's get a move on and go and see what the food is like." He straightened the well-cut jacket of the lightweight grey suit he wore, checking the white pocket handkerchief was neatly in place, and moved to the door.

Candelabras sparkled in the old-fashioned settings of the dining room. They shared a succulent meal with four other diners, to the strains Que Serra, Serra, on the grand piano. Wine flowed sufficiently to encourage witty conversation with the Jewish family of husband and wife and their two sons. Later, in the small ballroom, Jude sat moodily watching the dancers whilst she sat hoping Jude would offer to take her in his arms as he used to. One of the sons approached Lyn. It was a relief to be asked for a dance. Tall and slender, the son was a good partner leading her into intricate steps with ease. She was flushed and happy as she thanked him for the shared pleasure when he returned her to Jude. A quickstep struck up.

"Shall we Jude, it's a nice floor," Lyn invited him. He'd watched her happy smiling face as she danced and felt jealousy. He stood up and lead her on to the floor. She curved into him as of old, but he danced away. Her steps faltered as they lost the rhythm.

"It isn't working is it Jude. We are out of step, and in more ways than one." Forlorn, she looked to him for answer. He led her to the side and guided her back to their table. The fear, fired by the vision in the grotto, still quivered in his body and senses. He wanted the safety of St Rooks, away from the life-threatening scene he had seen in the eyes looking down at him in the pool.

"That's it I've had enough. We are going back tomorrow."

"Please let us not argue Jude. I dearly want things to be right again, and I'm struggling to get used to the way things have changed. Why don't you see that I want help someone to get back on their feet? I don't want to keep my commitment on my own but keep it I will. It is my promise to God for bringing you back."

"Have it your own way, I know that swine better," he snapped. "I'm going to bed. Are you coming?"

They took the early morning flight to Gatwick, and were back in their familiar routines by early afternoon of yet another Christmas Eve.

The next day the boys joined them for Christmas lunch. After their presents were exchanged, they drifted away to meet with friends. Jude spent the remainder of the day with Syd, leaving Lyn on her own to visit the wards with small gifts for everyone. Visitors came to share an early evening meal, and she garnered warmth from the smiles and thanks for the generous plates of fine food.

Later in the evening, relaxing with a glass of wine, her thoughts travelled back to one Christmas that had birthed a man who told of a great spiritual source within all life. How, governed by the law of attraction, a common bond of love and compassion was gifted to man.

In the beginning of the human story, only the means to survive were sought and shared in community. Man turned that gifted love to a desire controlling our actions.

Now minds, emotions, bodies were looted and plundered to satisfy man's sensual greed, and his hunger for power and dominance. Earlier times had been simple and free of the unwanted material junk that surrounded her now.

She remembered being five years old on one Christmas Eve. Lying still with lowered lashes, she had stayed awake to watch the pillow slip, with its exciting bulges and bumps, placed at the foot of the bed. Her hands explored the curves and shapes, until they froze on hearing her mother's voice in the darkness, from their room next to hers.

"Don't do that." Her father's voice pleading, then silence before, "Leave me alone Bertie. I'm sorry dear. We can't afford to feed another mouth." Bewildered, Lyn had huddled down beneath her sheets, with restless dreams of searching for food. Looking back to those hard times, she knew compassion for her mother, whose conscience had bidden continence from the love feast. Now birth control beckoned abandon.

When she was nine, a family friend came for Christmas. The elderly widower had called her to his room. She confided her hopes for a bicycle as her gift. Smiling, he promised she would have her gift as he lifted the hem of her dress above her waist and bade her sit still. His hand fell soft on her bare knee, above the long, knitted sock.

"It's all right dear, uncle's a friend of the family." A flush mantled her brow, swept hot through her body as his eyes held her fascinated gaze. Suddenly her mother's voice calling, made her bound swiftly away. She told nobody, but she felt threatened.

During the Second World War, on route to a new posting, she had stopped over in London to see her father. He was spending a lonely Christmas far from her mother and the two younger children, evacuated to southern counties.

The house, her mother used to keep so bright and welcome, was blackout dark and cold. The kitchen was filled with a cumbersome table shelter, where the meagre weekly rations for one dotted a large plate.

Dad had been so pleased to see her. News of the scattered family was pieced together, as they shared some of his food for a simple meal.

"You know Joy's serving with an Ack Ack Battery down in Hell Fire Corner."

"No! Really! We don't keep in touch much. It's difficult moving around so much."

"I'm in the Home Guard now, posted to the Tower of London," The old World War One sniper spoke with quiet pride. "Get good rations on duty, and I'm doing my bit."

"Well, with Mum running a W.V.S. hostel, and me in nursing, nobody can say our family hasn't pitched in Dad, can they? I'm surprised you got into any service with a history of mustard gas last time, and your health being so poor."

"They'll take anyone now things don't look good for us. Your mother wrote in her last letter that Joy's got a young man in the same Ack Ack unit as her. Of course, she is worrying they'll behave themselves, but you've all been brought up right I told her. What about you, any boyfriends come along?"

Next morning, he brought her a cup of tea. She was dressing. The last time he had seen her so, she was still a school girl. Then her thank you kiss, and a hug were responded to by a playful pat and an admonishment to, "Get a move on, or you will be late for school."

Sitting in her petticoat, she sipped the hot sweet liquid, its warmth coursing down her throat, driving out the December chill in the room. Setting down her cup, she gave him a hug and a good morning kiss, and then started for the stairs to go down to the scullery, to wash. He stepped in front of her. The strained pleading in his face and the hunger of a lonely man lying deep in his eyes, disturbed her.

Folding her to him he slid his hand to her waist and held her fiercely. Inarticulate words stumbled from his lips as he kissed her neck. Lyn stiffened against the hardening of his body, pushing him away. The shock in his face matched hers.

"Sorry dear, I'm so sorry," he said and ran from the room.

The incident was archived away with old history in their minds. Over breakfast, small talk covered the sadness of another parting in the family. They discussed bus routes to the main line station, then made a few sandwiches for the journey.

He waved goodbye, a thin lonely figure on the platform. She sat small in her corner of the carriage and worried that she had been disloyal to her mother.

Now, sipping her wine, she recalled her father's deathbed and the communion she had witnessed between them, as he sang love songs in farewell to his Mercy.

There were the Christmases in the early years of her marriage. After attending Midnight Mass, the following morning had seen them cycling, together, through near deserted streets to visit the daily insulin patients, the very ill and the lonely. They had taken small gifts of food to those impoverished in health and in pocket, then returned home to simple fare by a warm fire.

How royally rich they had felt opening small gifts of thanks from some of their patients. Finally, they exchanged a gift that had been made in secret or saved for from a modest wage. In later years came the joy of watching the children coo and laugh over their single present

Each succeeding year the gifts grew larger in number and value and seemed to give less pleasure. The gift of love's healing power usually lay unopened at the bottom of a pile of useless, tinsel wrapped boxes. She had never felt so bankrupt of Christmas joy.

"Is there one in the bottle left for me?" Jude's voice startled her from her reverie. Turning she saw him standing in the doorway. He wore a casual blue shirt and a darker blue crew neck jersey. His dark hair crested from his broad forehead below which his grey green eyes caught the light from one of the lamps. A tentative smile hovered around his lips.

She caught her breath, for the sight of him took her back over the years to their first meeting. She stood and started towards him.

"I didn't expect you. He turned to the cabinet and lifted a bottle.

"Will you have another before we turn in?"

"Yes, please but just a small one for me." They took their glasses and sat in the wingback chairs in front of the fire.

"Shall I turn on the telly, there's not much on except repeats," she suggested.

"No leave it, I would like to talk. Have we got any chocolates?" She rose and fetched a box to offer him one, then sat waiting for him to speak.

"I think we should find a property nearby, to get us away from the business now and then. There were times in Malta when you looked young and happy.

Perhaps that is what we need; somewhere without this background colouring the way we see each other. I always put you on a pedestal Lyn, and you let me down. Every time I go into the bedroom, I think of that damned phone ringing after you returned from Henley.

"I didn't do anything wrong except…," she began, but he cut in.

"Come on, don't give me that. I sent you away to learn a thing or two, but you chose to go the whole hog," She bit her tongue on a sharp retort, unsure where he was leading her. Jude, recalling his main objective, reached for her hand, holding it in a warm clasp.

"A local get away will be for the best, trust me. You have had a rough patch over this past couple of years. We both need to give ourselves a break from here. What about Eastbourne, you like that area, don't you. We can furnish with some of the clutter from this place to start with."

"What about the boys Jude? I like to be here when they come home, especially if I'm free."

"If we find somewhere, it could be useful for Nick later on, now he is going steady with Becky. We could lend it to them to set up home until they save for their own."

"What a good idea. Yes, Jude, I will start to look in the local papers until something reasonable comes up. How much shall we go to?"

"I've got another idea Ducks. Look for something small and consider buying it for yourself. You have enough to buy outright if you go for the lower price range. I need to keep money back in case the business won't stand the asking price for the house at the end of the row. I want it to accommodate more staff and then we shall own the whole block. What do you say?"

"I haven't really got so much money you know. My savings, from the nominal amount we pay ourselves, will hardly let me buy a house on my own. You make extra cash in quite a few ways." Jude pursued his ideas until, weary of discussion she agreed to look into them.

"I'll make enquiries in the new year, now let's see what is on the box shall we," she said at last. They enjoyed a perennial farce about a butler, chuckling at his antics, before going to bed. The year drew to a close.

Chapter 18: Plots and plans

LYN gathered the late delivery of newspapers from the vestibule and went through to the office, where the morning post waited on the table.

Today was her brother's February birthday, on the same date as her mother's passing last year. Jude had returned from celebrating his own birthday down south.

Outside the open window a thin stream of traffic flowed silently over a fresh blanket of snow. Ken was clearing the path of the soggy grey remains of yesterday's fall. Sunlight bedecked the trees with a million sparkling diamonds. Jude looked up from where he was supervising Ken and waved, signalling coffee was a good idea. Lyn called through to the kitchen to order some and closed the window.

Rubbing some warmth back into his hands, Jude met Gertrude at the door with the coffee tray. He made for his chair as Lyn finished sorting post and papers to send round to the patients. The last newspaper in the pile was yesterday's edition of the Eastbourne Gazette, with no delivery name scribbled on the top.

"Do you know who ordered this Gazette Jude, it isn't marked up," Lyn asked handing papers and mail to Gertrude?"

"No one so far as I know. Maybe a visitor left it on the table in the vestibule. How about we look at the property section over our coffee. Bring the biscuits with you."

She had no interest in house hunting and had done nothing about looking for a getaway.

"I must ring Frank later to wish him a happy birthday. We both still miss Mum." She warmed her hands around her hot cup, coming across to Jude to look over his shoulder as he sat riffling through the gazette.

"Here we are, look at this Ducks. A two-bedroom cottage for sale by executors. Now they usually go cheaply. Why don't you give them a ring and find out the details?"

"Perhaps I will Jude, perhaps. It's too wintery to look for houses now," but from habit she obeyed him and saved the page.

"It could be a winner, like the one you bought for your mother, but it's up to you. What a coincidence, that the first time we get this newspaper, it has a possible bargain for sale."

Lyn always liked a good bargain, and the idea of renovating lit a creative spark in her. He had pressed her curiosity button. After he left the office, she picked up the phone.

"What price are you asking for the cottage please," she requested? The reply jolted her into making a provisional offer to lay claim to the place. After a few more details she arranged to go across the following week.

She drove through the narrow entrance of an unprepossessing little road, hidden behind the railway station. At its end it was blocked by the doors of a furniture repository stretching from pavement to pavement. In days gone by it housed the boats and nets of fisher folk, living there. The hoot of a departing train reminded her of the cherry tree in her grandparent's garden.

Twenty cottages, ten on either side, hugged each other wall to wall in the short stretch ahead of her. The narrow twittern she had noticed before turning in to the lane, must run behind the dwellings for the old-time night soil man no doubt.

She cruised to a stop behind a car parked outside a cottage towards the end. Must be the executor, she thought.

An elderly gentleman got out to meet her. His parchment coloured skin creased into interrogative folds, lifting his drooping grey moustache a fraction, in step with his eyebrows. His grey pin stripped suit wafted puffs of camphor as he moved towards her.

"Ah, Mrs Rook I presume." He raised his black bowler just the right amount, before setting it back firmly on the thin grey tonsure crowning his head.

"Yes, that's me," smiled Lyn, holding out her hand and wondering if he would bow over it or kiss it.

He gathered himself together to wave his hand in the direction of the cottage they stood outside. The uniform greyness of its low structured wall was broken by a door and small sash windows one up, one down. This was not what she had imagined.

From a pocket, he took out a heavy old-fashioned key. Intrigued by a sense of bygone times, she followed him through the door into a small low-ceilinged room, stifling a little gasp of pleasure. Where was she to look first in this time capsule? She walked through to a back room.

"I love the low ceilings, but the rooms are very small, aren't they? Oh, this leads to the bedrooms, does it?" She peered up a steep narrow stairway built behind one wall, then turned to front a wooden slatted door leading to a tiny scullery, cum kitchen. This opened on to a backyard smelling of cats and an out-door lavatory.

"Where is the bathroom, is it upstairs," she called, diving back into the house and running up the stairway? Behind her the bowler hat waited at the foot whilst she stood on a two-foot square of landing, looking from one small bedroom in to the other.

"Is this it," she queried, hoping by a miracle he would open a secret door to more? She came down the stairway thinking of winter and middle of the night trips into an icy yard. Lord, they must use a jerry at night, she thought as she met the eyes in the parchment skin.

"Well it needs a great deal done to it, which is going to add to the cost Mr Greystone," she observed with sufficient disinterest to start bargaining.

"That is precisely why it is modestly priced Madam," he countered.

"Adding a bathroom alone means main drain work you must agree. It could be too costly for me I afraid." In her mind's eye, the wall dividing the two small rooms downstairs was already pulled down, a bathroom added, and a small conservatory filled the bleak back yard to hide the neighbouring fence. She decided to take the challenge and turn this doll's house into a quaint Pied a Terre.

"You may have noticed that there are several items of furniture which are good pieces and of use in furnishing," Mr Greystone smiled proprietarily. She had noticed and liked what she saw.

"Oh, I don't think so, but you can leave them here and I will deal with that matter for you," she offered graciously. "That is if we can agree on a price. Two thousand is really too much don't you think, without an indoor toilet. I'm not in a hurry to purchase. I'm just looking around for an interest, as it were."

"What are you prepared to offer?" His parchment skin felt as if it would crack in the cold damp air. This near empty hovel on his hands must be disposed of. He had done his best. It wasn't his, and he needed his afternoon tea. Lyn knocked four hundred and fifty off, keeping her satisfaction concealed when he accepted her offer. Settlement was swift, and the big key of 18, Strait Street soon hung with the others behind the office door of the nursing home.

Jude looked pleased when he heard of her bargain. He sat with elbows spread on the table, sucking at his lower lip whilst his eyes searched hers for answers.

"When will you start alterations?"

"Maybe in late spring. What's the hurry, it's too cold for messing around with major works now. This is our home." Getting up, she pushed back the cuffs of her nurse's dress.

"I'm going across to help with baths. There is only one nurse on this morning since everyone seems to have a cold. Can you help me with getting the stores in this afternoon? It is a big order and the roads are still slippery."

"Take one of the girls with you," he replied, annoyed that she was delaying the building project

Eventually, after a bad start losing money to a bankrupt builder, Lyn found one to put her plans into effect. Well satisfied with the result, she recommended him to a new neighbour who wished to follow her lead. A few years later a row of expensive Chelsea style town houses graced Strait Street.

Meanwhile, life became an empty monotony. Nicholas lived with a group of friends, while learning to be a programmer for the mysterious machines invading the business scene. Andrew spent his weekends with his girlfriend's family. Jude was correctly polite when they met in the office. Social events came to a halt, but the nursing home continued its pace, until Lyn's nerves screamed at confinement within its walls.

One morning in June, when she was ripe to respond to any stimulus, she opened a letter addressed to her, postmarked Norwich, and withdrew a single sheet of paper and a small card. Jo Willey had written to say she could visit him. She turned the card over. It was a visitor permit for one person once every two months.

Why is he in Norwich, she wondered. She had written a couple of brief letters with desultory news of the outside and hoping all was well for him, addressing them to Lewes Jail. The letter she held in her hand pricked her conscience. Impulsively, she reached for the phone.

"May I speak with the Prison Governor or the Welfare Officer about a visitor's permit," she asked cautiously. With memories of the grim Lewes goal, her impulse weakened as she waited. A pleasant voice asked what she wanted.

"I have received a visitor's permit for a John Thomas Willey who is an inmate. I was wondering how many visitors he is allowed. I mean does he get any visitors, because it is a fair way for me to travel. I am not a relative just a friend."

"Permits are usually only issued for family madam or close friends. Will you wait a moment?" The line went silent for a short time then the voice resumed, "We think it would be helpful if you could make a visit. This man has not had any contacts since he arrived on Christmas day. He is in a depressed state but cooperative otherwise. You must understand I am not in a position to discuss this with you. I'm sorry, good bye."

"Wait a bit. When are visiting days please?" Lyn cut in quickly.

"On Sundays" was the patient response.

"Where do I come to, and what time shall I come please?"

"You will probably be better catching the ten o'clock prison bus at Victoria for your first visit. It arrives in good time and leaves punctually," he suggested. She put the phone down still unsure over the step she was about to take, but she meant to continue her supportive role.

On Sunday morning, she raised her head from a pillow still damp from the night's well of loneliness and fought off her fears. She left the emptiness of the night hours and went across to the busyness of the nursing home where Jill Fraser was sorting out the day ahead with her staff.

"Jill, can you manage if I am away for several hours today? The kitchen is fine, and Alan will be in shortly. I should be back by five o'clock."

"Yes Lyn. We'll be fine. Juce rang through to say he was travelling back from Plymouth later today," Jill reassured her.

The near empty roads made the drive up to London swift and parking simple after she was directed to a safe back street by a policeman. The big bus terminal had a relaxed air to it with excursion coaches inviting travellers. A porter gave her a sympathetic smile as he directed to the prison visitor's stand, where an ill-assorted group of women waited.

Some wore smart outfits, whilst others wore shabby, well-worn clothes. They seemed to know each other, talking across one another's shoulders and smiling companionably. They eyed Lyn as a stranger in their midst when she joined them. A little twinge of shame at being a traveller on the bus, eroded her confidence until a woman smiled, and made way for her to take a seat after they boarded.

"I haven't seen you before, your first time is it dear," she lightly probed, taking in the pleated floral skirt and matching top? It had been a tossup between that and a neat grey tailored outfit, Lyn having no idea what to wear.

"Well yes, it is my first visit to a friend and I don't quite know what to do when I get there," confided Lyn. Heads turned as soon as they heard her clear concise tones, then bent low as questions buzzed between them.

"You follow me dear. There's nothing to it and the boys look forward to today no end. Are you taking anything in because the rozzers can be sharp if you've got anything iffy?"

"Oh dear, I didn't think. It's a bit like visiting hospital isn't it when you always take a bag of grapes."

"If you haven't got anything for him at all, we'll soon set that right. My Ronnie won't mind going short of ten fags. Hey, any of you girls got some tenners to spare for this lady? It's her first time." Two or three packets of ten cigarettes were passed along and when Lyn opened her bag to pay, a chorus of, "That's all right girl," met her ears. She was one of the girls.

The soft chatter of womenfolk surrounded her as the bus made its way out of London and towards Norfolk's flatlands. Her companion confided in short sentences with long gaps in between.

"He's been a very naughty boy, my man." Lyn smiled acquiescence.

"He was always good to me. They don't know him like I do." The road unwound with their tensions as they reached the prison and climbed out of the bus.

Several buildings and a large grassed over area, marked out with lines for sport, were surrounded by high steel fencing. By the time she had taken this much in, she found herself being pushed through a door. Once inside the olive-green walls, she was confined by a turnstile in front of an inspection window. Here her visitor's permit was quizzed and handed back as she herself was scanned by a pair of well-informed eyes.

"Go and sit at a table dear and wait for your friend to be sent up," Ronnie's wife said as she moved confidently across the room they entered.

It was a bright room with plenty of windows lighting the rows of bare tables lining the floor. The chairs placed either side of each table quickly filled with couples holding hands and talking animatedly. It looked like a social event. Cups of tea were fetched by the men, who lit a cigarette for their partners, before their eager questioning about family affairs. This open prison was different from the dark grey stone walls of Lewes. Lyn appreciated the difference as she looked around for sight of Jo.

There was a small door in the corner of the far end of the room. It opened, and Jo shot into the room, staring around like a rabbit stupefied by a bright light, until he fixed on her whereabouts. He hurried across. He looked well fed and fitter than when Lyn last saw him.

"Thank you for coming woman. Shall I fetch you some tea and biscuits?" Without waiting for an answer, he went off to a small hatch at the side of the room, returning with two cups and a small packet of biscuits.

"You're my first visitor. It's good to see someone. They moved me from Lewes on Christmas Day. It seems your old man made a phone call and asked to have me moved." After the first rush he sat silent, at a loss for words, for once, as was Lyn.

What on earth am I doing here, she asked herself, struggling to get a footing in the strange environment. 'We have no family history to fall back on for small talk. It is as if a stranger sits across the table. Then she remembered her supportive role and opened her bag to produce the cigarette packs and hand them across to him. He restrained her from withdrawing her hand. His hand felt warm and comforting. The contact reminded her of how much she ached for affection, for a human touch.

"I'm sorry that I came unprepared. A nice woman collected these for me, and they wouldn't take any money. She's visiting her husband, Ronnie."

"Ronnie, which woman was it?" Lyn pointed across to where the two sat. Jo gave a laugh.

"My goodness woman, he's a baron in here," and mentioned an infamous name that even she had read of in The News of The World.

"Do you know him?"

"I don't mix any more than I have to. I keep myself to myself, apart from being banged up with three others each night. They let me work in the library where I spend as much time as I can."

Looking around at the men in identical battle dress suits, she noted how ordinary they all looked. She wondered how many Ronnies there were sitting with hair neatly brushed, clean shirted and smiling into their wife's eyes. Could a modern prison, such as this, reform these monsters and re-align the warp which separated them from society. Was she being naïve and foolish to believe she could change the habits of a clever con man, where a long history of incarceration had failed.

"Speak to me Lyn. The others will wonder what's up if you sit silent. How are things with Jude, does he know you are here?"

"I'm sorry Jo, it's hard to know what to say. There is a fragile truce at home, but things will get better I feel sure. Oh yes, Jude suggested I buy a small place to get away from the business. I got a wonderful bargain." She felt on safer ground talking of the new property. Jo was stumped by her manner.

What is this woman on about? She's giving me hope by visiting me. She must have a soft spot for me. Is she saying the house is for us? Is she leaving that bastard? She's a bit long in the tooth for me, I'd need some fresh meat from time to time, but I'd be in clover. She was still running on.

"...and I'm having it done up with a bathroom added on and bits and pieces."

"That's nice. Perhaps you can find me a bargain when I get out of here," he said. She didn't notice the irony in his tone.

"Of course, I will help you to settle. Have you thought where you will go? What about being near to your mother now she is on her own" He gave her a sharp look then a bell rang.

"It's time to go Lyn, will you come again," he appealed? She stood up, relieved yet feeling she had given little comfort.

"Yes, of course I will come again." another quick clasp of hands.

"Thanks again." The women departed, leaving hungry eyed men sitting at little tables.

On the return journey, the women sat quietly with their thoughts. The same travelling companion proudly showed Lyn a model made of hundreds of spent matches. It was exquisitely made with a delicate touch. Lyn thought of newspaper articles citing smashed kneecaps the craftsman had inflicted on those who crossed his path.

"It is beautiful. I'm sure he will keep it somewhere special when he comes home," she said.

"Oh, he'll never come home dear. He's in for life," Ronnie's wife replied.

Back in the prison the Ronnies and Joes were banged up for another night. The men sat and waited for the signal to begin, as they did every night.

It came like the soft thud of a winged pheasant striking the earth, then another and another until it was as though the sky voided. An angry murmur of men's voices swelled from the tiered cells that caged them.

Jo and Ronnie went to their separate barred windows and hurled their parcels into the courtyard below. Somebody would be detailed to collect their body waste in the morning. In the long months or years ahead, they would only breathe in the rank sweat of their cell mate during the heat of the enclosing night.

Arriving home, Lyn slipped quietly through the side entrance and went up to change before taking the report from Jill Fraser.

Over breakfast next morning Jude said he intended to raise the fees again. Some damaged ligaments in his knees were sending exquisite darts of pain and he was in no mood for her query.

"Don't you think it is too soon to…?"

"Where did you go yesterday? One of us must always be near at hand. You were away most of the day and left no contact number. Where were you?" He held her eyes across the table. She returned a steady gaze and managed a smile. Had Ruby or Gertrude told tales? She collected the crockery in a pile and brushed a few crumbs off the table.

"The weather was fine, so I visited my sister. I haven't seen her for a while." The tell-tale colour rose in her cheeks and they both knew she was lying and that was the way it was now. She was accessory to stealing, aiding an escaped criminal, and now lied with ease. How much lower must she sink?

In the ensuing weeks there were problems with some of their more experienced staff handing in notice to leave. Relatives came to the office and, if they found her alone, complained bitterly of Jude's rudeness to them. It took time and persuasive reassurance to change decisions to remove loved ones to another nursing home. Even so there were empty beds for the first time. The reduced pressure of work enabled Jude to have some knee surgery he needed.

He was in the care of an old nursing colleague of Lyn, a wiry, wise cracking spinster. She had known love for a brief time. During a dying man's last months as her partner, he had made her whole. When reduced circumstances forced her back to nursing, she was unperturbed by the carping authority of a jealous matron. Bronwyn gave Lyn a quizzical smile as she took her to Jude's bedside where he lay relaxed and semi-conscious after surgery.

"He's had another visitor today. She's coming back."

His thick dark eyebrows lay straight and smooth above heavy eyelids. All mistrust had gone from his face. The mouth curved full and sensual in some sweet dream as he lay there, defenceless. He is too beautiful for a man Lyn thought, as she bent to steal a kiss long denied her. When she straightened up, dark eyes regarded her from across the bed. Jude woke and turned towards Syd. Lyn nodded acceptance and left.

The Exit corridor stretched endlessly ahead of her. A flutter behind her eyes became a swishing movement enveloping her, filling her head with pulsing darkness. Weightless, she became a point of pain borne upwards into a void, expanding into a kaleidoscope of sunlight and shadow where two butterflies flirted and danced in display, their chameleon iridescence a courting lure. Flame and gold shot through rising spirals of blue, green and purple then burst into a thousand coloured droplets falling, falling. A wall light pierced the prism of a tear, floating across her lashes, trickling down her nose and salting her lips. The Exit sign lit up. She left the hospital building.

Earlier in the day she had received a request to meet prisoner Wiley on discharge. It filled her with a sense of foreboding, but she knew she would honour her promise to meet Manny once more.

Chapter 19: The old lag

JUDE was convalescing at home when she told him of her decision to consent to the prison pastor's request to meet Manny on his discharge. She had suggested to him that she would try and reunite Manny with his mother. who might be persuaded to give him shelter for a time. It was thought a good idea and she felt happier about her part in Manny's rehabilitation. She asked Jude to accompany her. He refused and accused her of playing him false.

"If you go, you go on your own." In the early hours of a summer morning, having made sure all Jude's needs would be cared for, she set off at five in the morning, to reach Norwich at the appointed time. The soft purr of the engine, cruised away the miles between St Jude's and Norwich, quieting her anxieties and sense of guilt, until the car reached the prison gates.

Three men stood in the playing field behind the high wire fence, the pastor and a prison warder on either side of Manny. The sleek red machine streaked quietly through the opening gate and came to a halt. She got out then stood in awkward silence until they reached her and waited for her to say,

"Hallo Manny." He stepped across to her and whispered,

"Please give me a kiss as if you were pleased to see me." Hot with embarrassment, she pecked him on the cheek, before turning to say goodbye to his escorts. The pastor smiled his approval. He was a tall strongly built man with the weathered, rugged face of a farmer who understood his animals. John Murray cared about the social rejects that he steered into freedom from their pens.

"I'll see you at home then, Wiley," he said as the two drove away.

"John wants to meet you Lyn, so he's invited us to lunch. I've been to his home before. I'll show you the way." Over a pleasant meal in the stone flagged kitchen of a converted farmhouse, Lyn listened to the two men talking about Manny's future. All the time she was aware that she was under scrutiny and when the time came to leave, knew she had been enlisted to help Jo.

"This man thinks a great deal of you Mrs Rook. With your help, he may make something of himself. Thank you for coming to his discharge today." With a waved goodbye they walked towards the car

"What does he mean by that Manny? How does he expect me to influence what you make of yourself? You already know we cannot give you work. I made a promise to take you to meet your mother today, and then I must go back to Sussex and my family." Startled, he stopped in his tracks, suspicion filled the narrowed eyes, following the angry flush suffusing his face.

"What's this about my mother? That cow turned me out. Does she know we are coming?" She shook her head. He stood in the lane looking helpless.

"I thought you would spend some time with me. I don't honestly know what I expected, but you can't dump me in my mother's suburban hell and clear off. I've got nowhere to go woman, you said you'd help me."

She struggled to meet the accusing eyes judging her. She had not thought past her stubborn intent to honour the promise to meet him on discharge. A net of commitment fell over her, dragging her in the wrong direction.

"I need a drink more than anything, to think things out. Will you buy me one and then take me to Richmond? I might be able to find a room there." Wordlessly she nodded, hoping this would be the end of trying to do good. She had taken a wrong turn in the maze of life. I am out of step with thee oh my soul.

Richmond was full of visitors. They eventually found rooms in a large hotel at the top of Richmond Hill. The spectacular view was the only good thing Lyn could see ahead of her, as she took a lonely walk along the ridge, before turning in. She was tempted to jump in the car and run for the safety of home, but the likeable part of Manny's personality loomed up to prompt charity. She went to bed.

Around midnight her slumber was rudely broken by a woman's scream in the dark, followed, a few minutes later, by a second cry which sent her running to the window. On the ridge down below, two figures stood beneath the light of a lamp post, to be joined by a third, running up to them. Confident that somebody was going to the woman's aid, she slipped back into bed and lay thinking of the strange circumstances she was in, until a tap at her door, and Jo's voice. brought her up on her feet.

"Lyn, can you take this young woman in, she is in danger?" That night she shared her room with a girl who never gave her name, and who slipped away in the early hours, before Lyn awoke. That was the good side of Jo. He acted for the waifs and strays crossing his path.

After persuading Jo to see his mother, they made an early start to a London suburb near the Thames, arriving mid-morning outside a three-storey house, divided into flats. Jo left Lyn in the car to go up a wide flight of steps to the first floor and knock on the door. It opened partially to allow room for a face to peer out. Its fat flabby features stretched in a soundless "oh" and the door began to close on Jo's foot until his hand pushed it back. A brief exchange of words before he turned to run down the steps to Lyn. He looked excited like a child promised a treat.

"It's all right, come in. I've told her you are a friend so don't worry if she makes something of it." Inside the airy flat, furniture skirted the walls with middle class comforts. Coming south had improved the Wiley family's life.

From where she spread her ample form on a settee, Bridie Wiley appraised Lyn, keeping a weather eye open on her son. She had reason to fear his mercurial temperament, but if the woman in front of her was daft enough to...Well, she would button her lips for now.

Manny moved from room to room, calling to Lyn to come and see his old bedroom, the kitchen cum scullery where he used to eat his meals alone, and the cupboard space where his father used to repair watches. He moved like a panther, staking out its territory, whilst his mother's eyes followed him, ever ready to defend her ground. Her silence made Lyn tense, and resentful of the effort made to visit this woman.

Manny brought in a tray of coffee and biscuits and waited for his mother to break her silence until she spoke to Lyn.

"The bathroom's behind the kitchen if you want to use the toilet." When Lyn returned to the sitting room, Jo asked a favour.

"Lyn, could we take my mother and her friend down to the river for an hour? She doesn't get around much these days."

When Bridie Wiley struggled up to inch her way to the front door, Lyn's resentment subsided. The poor wretch was crippled with rheumatism. She ran to her aid, supporting her weight down the front steps and into the car. A tall well-built woman appeared saying she was Bridie's friend and would come with them to the nearby tourist spot on the river bank.

Whilst Jo installed the two older women in comfortable chairs, Lyn was dispatched to buy ice creams. It was the first of many trips to the ice cream vendor, in between watching a marathon cornet eating contest which left no room for conversation. Lyn listened in vain for one word of warmth or enquiry regarding Jo's situation and his future prospects. All she saw were looks of apprehension passing over the cornet tips until Jo's next offer of "another cornet Mum" was refused with a final lick of the lips and a request to be taken home. The three of them battled their way up the steps with Bridie and waited whilst the key turned in the lock and her foot was over the threshold.

"We can manage now. Goodbye," and the two friends shut the door firmly between them, leaving Jo staring at the closed door. Lyn's disbelief at this lack of affection spilled out.

"What's wrong here Jo, she doesn't want anything to do with you and she is your mother?"

"Leave it girl. It's a long story. I didn't want to go there anyhow. Will you take me back?" They drove in silence until they reached a small park in Richmond.

"Will you stay over tonight again, please? I don't want to be on my own. Will you do that? Let's walk a bit. I need to stretch my legs." Once they were out of the car and away from the tension that had built up, she felt safer to speak her mind.

"Jo, I cannot help you anymore, except with money to find a bed-sit or some accommodation whilst you sort your life out. I must go home and try to make my family life whole again." She reached into the car for her purse, then handed him his bag, before jumping into the driver's seat and closing the door. He grabbed for the handle, but she clicked the lock and started the engine, turning away from the pain on his face and his contorted features as he smashed his fist against the window and her rejection of him.

The car eased forward, increasing speed as she took control and drove away from a mess she could not cope with. Deep down she knew this was not the end of it. Jo Wiley was out of prison and hovering on the perimeter of her broken family circle. Rather than fight, she must go with the flow until she found a way out of her dilemma.

Jo turned into the park and made for a bench screened by bushes. He was used to kipping in the open and he needed her money elsewhere. He still had business with the Rooks, they hadn't seen the last of him. A foxy grin lifted his lip from pointed canine teeth.

When Lyn arrived home, Jude came to meet her in the car park. His mood was surprisingly pleasant.

"I hope that's the last we hear from that bastard. I used the time you were away to get a few pieces of furniture across to your new place. You will be better off spending some free time over there. I might use it as well if that's all right with you."

"Oh, did you? I should like that Jude," she smiled, feeling relieved and hopeful of spending time together again.

Chapter 20: Downsizing

AUTUMN was around the corner. Summer's heat littered the grass with scorched leaves and the last fruits were ripe for picking. Lyn settled to work for the day with Jude standing over her as she sat balancing some figures in her ledger.

"I don't think you need to enter so much detail in the credits. From now on, I'd like you to take over writing up the patients' extras invoices. To simplify things, I'll give you a hand with them and tell you what to enter."

"Why alter things now Jude, my accounting is simple? We agreed you should check my nursing services invoices and then add your extras invoices before you send them out."

"Because I say so! Let's get on with it, shall we." He sat at his desk, writing invoices into a duplicate book, which she copied to his dictation, sitting at her table behind the filing cabinet. Suddenly she put down her pen and ran a finger down the list on an extras bill.

"We get some of these items on the National Health subsidy and they are not entered in my debits ledger. In fact, there aren't any chemist purchases. Did you forget to give me the receipts?"

"Never mind the receipts. Write what I dictate, or I'll give someone else your job," he threatened as he stared her down. She backed away from an argument, leading to another silence only he would choose to break.

Whatever he says I know this is fraud, Lyn decided, her mind busy seeking a solution to keep her book-keeping honest that he would not detect. Her recent suggestion to raise staff wages and keep fees static had ended in being called a fool and not fit to run a business. Jude tapped her sheaf of invoices together.

"This should help pick up on our losses until we get more patients. Have these addressed and ready for the morning post please." The tangled web of deceit he was involving her in, was common practice to shady business. The spin was that personal nursing needs were reimbursed by the patient, for items hidden in payments for supplies for the business, which boosted running costs. The cash payments were taken from pensions collected weekly and should have been invoiced as such. She remembered managers boast of illicit practice but had no time for such measures. she once again poured over her ledgers.

She solved her problem. In the event Jude consulted her books, which was rare, he would find it hard to detect where true credits were accounted for and she could live honestly her accounting. Her eyes stung with the strain of close work, and her head buzzed with the checking and re-checking of figures,

I must lock these scrap notes away. It's best he doesn't see them, she muttered to herself. She closed the ledgers and put them away, unlocked her table drawer to tidy away pens and working notes to be re-checked tomorrow. As she closed the drawer, the bottom slat fell into her palm, stopping it from closing. Emptying the contents, she bent to inspect the cause, finding some small tacks were missing.

Stuffing the scrap paper into her pocket she went down to Stan's cellar workroom. In the musty dark a spider's web clung to her face. The rank smell of Stan's genital signature hit her nostrils. She flicked the light on his tools, scattered in tidy disarray on the bench top and found a small hammer and some tacks. Her hand rested, absent mindedly, on a heavy mallet. The hammer was laid aside. Night had fallen when she went to find Jude.

Passing the dark alcove outside the kitchen, she heard voices. In the lighted vestibule, beyond the front door, Bunny Upson was smiling intimately up at Jude. Seeing them, Lyn stopped at the foot of the hall stairs. She felt like a soiled rag left to be picked up or tossed aside, inviting his women's contempt. Her anger mounted. Bunny Upson watched Lyn move.

"There is no one in the duty room. The nurses are on the first floor," she called out, her tone dismissive, then winked at her boss and bum wiggled across the floor with, "See you later Jude."

Jude eyed Lyn's image in the window. A nimbus of hair shone bright in the light at the foot of the stairs, His dark cap of hair curled into the nape of his neck. She stood with her memories, her hands enfolded in the full sides of her long skirt.

It looked like that when I walked up the aisle all those years ago, Nick's hair grows like his father's. I miss the boys' chi-eking. Now they are growing away from me, yet still come for advice with hesitant words spoken in trust.

"Mum, what shall we do, the condom came off and she is worried.?"

"There's this girl I've met, and I think I'm in love Mum."

'The department has put me in charge of the college exhibition. What do you think Mum," Andrew had confided?

It is all so empty now, because of him. We're broken into little pieces, separated, lost.

Jude watched her image. Her hair shone like that when she stood at the altar. Now what's she up to.

He saw the reflection jerk forward, flow forwards in the dark pooled glass, eyes flared above a gaping mouth, spewing soundless words. She was tumbling down the abyss of the mad, clawing on space filled with vengeance. The mallet raised high as she sprang the last step.

Spinning, he flung her to the floor breaking the fury into a huddled heap pinned beneath his foot.

"Let me up Jude. What's wrong?" she cried.

"Jude, are you coming to hear the handover?" Bunny Upson came into the scene.

"Call the police," he ordered grinding his heel into Lyn's shoulder.

A local officer who knew the family, managed the incident with calm authority. He cautioned them both to hold their peace and departed. Shaken by the violence, they took refuge in their quarters.

"I'll sleep in Nick's room tonight. Get some rest and we'll talk in the morning," he decided. "Stan will mend the drawer tomorrow."

"I didn't mean to hurt you," she whispered, huddled over the warmth of the fireside. She flinched from the pox festered face of evil, leering at her. You wanted to kill. She shivered. Turning on his heel he left.

In Nick's room, Jude gave in to the dominance of another migraine. Lying in the night's cool, tensed against a head-splitting throb, he contended with pain until a sedative took over. Words breached the barriers of his drowsy mind.

Use her to get you off the hook if you're found out.

She deserves it after playing around with scum.

So, what are you doing?

That's different I was one of the boys, but you expect your wife to behave decently.

Avenge yourself you fool, said his old friend. She tried to kill you again. Don't trust her. Claim what's yours before she succeeds. You have evidence so use your wits.

She's never looked at anyone before this bastard.

Don't kid yourself man. Did any of those drama group sissies fuck her? You can bet she's had more affairs off stage than on it, the voice pressed on.

He remembered her coming back excited and happy from a rehearsal.

She made a fool of you. Conscience edged in.

That's not true. She was excited she got the best role, but she was always around for us.

Yes, fussing and bossing over every move you made. You've had enough. One of you must move on. Make sure she pays in full, the voice wormed in. Jude buried his head in the pillows.

Once I'm rid of her these voices will go. He drifted into sleep with a plan. Next day workmen were called in to hang a new door. He came up to where she sat by the window.

"I'm having a partition built across the landing leading to our flat. It's time we had some privacy. Have you pulled yourself together now?" She nodded.

"Good! Then go across to the cottage tomorrow and sort things out a bit. The sooner we get some time apart and space from the business, the quicker things will fall into place." She nodded again, waiting for further reproof.

"Let's have a drink to the future then," pouring both a glass of wine. "Don't forget to take some linen when you go."

Carrying a bundle of linen, she opened the door of the fisherman's cottage. Sunlight flickered over the assortment of furniture standing in the centre of the living room. Upstairs, the bed she had bought with the house filled most of the small room at the top of the narrow stairway, leaving a corner alcove for hanging garments. Soon the bed was freshly made, and the downstairs room took shape as furniture was pushed this way and that until she was satisfied. Ready for a cup of coffee, she reached into a cupboard to find no crockery or cooking ware.

Fired up with her task, she dashed down to the shops where she spent a pleasurable time choosing some pretty china and the newest cookware. Adding a few provisions to start the first visit, whenever that should be. The cottage was dark when she returned, until connected to electricity. Leaving her purchases on the table, she closed up and left.

Well pleased with her efforts she drove home, looking forward to a hot bath and a quiet evening to try and reconcile with Jude after her strange behaviour the night before. Eager to see him, she turned the handle on the new door, but it resisted her efforts. The light on the landing above came on and Stan Pike's head hovered over the banister.

"You won't get in Matron. It's locked and he's gone off to Malta with his lady friend."

"Well Stan can you fetch me the key. Somebody must have one and I need to get in."

"Well I ain't got one Matron and "e said you wasn't to go in again." Stan sounded defensive and sympathetic at the same time. It was easier to enlist his aid than plead her cause with the Bunny Upsons on the other side of the building.

"Fetch me a ladder Stan and put it against the wall below our bathroom." He nodded and reluctantly the ladder was pitched steeply against the high wall in the narrow alleyway.

Obstinately determined to have her way, Lyn climbed up toward a pale patch of light, from a nearby a street lamp. The window was locked. Clinging fast to a rung, she took off a shoe and struck with all her force, found the hasp and pushed it open. Panting with success she clambered inside.

Down below Stan Pike heard her gasp of disappointment and watched her edge her way out. Beaten, she looked down at him.

"The door is locked on the outside Stan," but Stan knew that. The ground looked so far away. She made a slow descent into the darkness knowing a new siege had begun.

"Thank you, Stan. I will see you in the morning. I suppose the office is open?" He nodded assent.

"Good night Matron. We will have coffee ready when you come." He hitched up the ladder and disappeared into the house.

Her eyes craned for comfort from every door and lighted window beyond the long drive across the marshes. Coming to the end of these homely dwellings she drove through the social end of town to spend her first night in the unlit cottage.

Next day, she found two large suitcases, packed with all her possessions, in the office. She set about arranging the services for her future home, each task doggedly attacked with a singular lack of feeling. Every morning she drove across the marshes to start work at eight, returning in time to watch the seven o'clock news, before retiring to sleep in the bed at the top of the narrow stairway.

Towards the end of the first week the personal phone pealed on Jude's desk. Lyn reached across to take the call, half expecting him to be on the other end.

"Hello, Lyn Rook speaking," she said, pencil poised over the duty roster.

"It's Manny, I need to see you. Could you come over to Eastbourne?" The pencil clattered to the floor.

"I've found a good bed-sit, but the landlady wants a month's rent in advance. I was coming to the nursing home but…." She interrupted violently.

"No, don't ever do that, and your name is Jo Wiley. What are you doing down here?"

"I thought you might need a bit of company lass." Information from the usual source had brought Jo hot foot to his next con. He waited on the other end of the line, for the fish to bite.

"No, I'm fine and just now very busy because, because," she stumbled back from an admission of her plight.

"Look Jo, I will help you but not today. I will come and see the landlady tomorrow. I'll be there at two o'clock, where is it?" He gave her an address and rang off.

Later that evening she eased the car into the curb outside the cottage and got out, fishing in her bag for the door key. The street light didn't reach to her end of the alley causing the usual fumble to find the lock. She was turning the key when a hand closed on her shoulder and a body blocked her from fleeing. A hand stifled the scream of fear in her throat.

"Let me do that for you. You shouldn't be coming home in the dark. Where's the light switch?" Light sprang out of the door. "I'm sorry I startled you."

Jo gave the ingenious smile of his trade and stood with just the right amount of expectant hesitation, waiting for an invite into her life again.

"How did you know about this place?" Frustration that her refuge had been discovered, followed shock.

She was beginning to love the little house whose closed door screened her from the ugliness on the other side of the marshes. Soft lamplight on drawn curtains, and familiar faces smiling out from the new television screen, cushioned the illusion that she was managing her life.

"I can find out anything I want woman, I know my way around," laying a finger to the side of his nose, he winked at her.

"I'm skint, I suppose you couldn't manage a cup of tea, or what say we go to the little pub on the corner and you buy me a barley wine. I need some fags too if you could manage it."

It was news to her that there was a public house on the corner of Strait Street but relief that it offered an avenue of escape. The door firmly shut, they walked to a little old-fashioned inn, plying its trade to its regulars.

Cramped it was inside, and spartan to boot. A high-backed wooden bench, hard, shiny, and more suited to a church, pressed the length of a wall three feet away from the single bar counter. Four aged men sat there, resting their beer on their bellies for want of a table. For all that, there was a comfortable air of companionship as of men below decks at sea, where women were bad luck.

Jo fronted up to the inn keeper as if he knew the old sailor, whilst Lyn sheltered in the shadows behind the door.

"Barley wine landlord and a Baby Cham for the lady please," adding softly, "and a double measure of vodka in the lady's. Oh yes, a packet of crisps and twenty Marlborough." Yellow light from the ship's lantern over the bar counter followed the landlord's silent search for the Baby Cham. Jo returned, the courteous cavalier.

"Here we are m'dear, sit down here." He looked meaningly at four expressionless faces. They heaved a few inches along the bench.

The landlord had unearthed a miniature parasol which bobbled in Lyn's glass until she saved it from capsizing, then, not knowing where to put it, followed custom and dropped it on her lap.

Jo knew the pub and had set the scene to his liking. He lit a cigarette and drew in hungrily. Lifting the barley wine to his lips he looked at his future meal ticket, fantasizing he might even get her to marry him, then he could claim a wife's pension. Bit long in the tooth but she'll soon knock into shape and move over for a fresh bit of meat when I fancy.

"So, you see m'dear I've nowhere to go until the flat's vacated tomorrow. It's frightfully good of you to you to help me out," he said in the Southern Counties accent he had groomed to perfection. Four pairs of ears beside them waited to hear more.

"Yes, but I don't think…" she started, when her ego stalled at being thought mean by their audience and finished, "it will be a problem," having no idea how she would solve it. Thinking was becoming confused in the warm room with its dim lighting and maybe the Baby Cham was stronger than she expected.

"I think I should leave now."

"I will escort you home m'dear," and Jo led her out into the cool air. The spiked wine had brought her guard down. She felt protected as she walked home a mite unsteadily. It was good to have a man's arm to lean on and she felt so tired.

Jo was telling one of his funny stories in a droll Liverpool Irish brogue, breaking off to tell her she was an angel of a woman, too good for Jude's ilk. He knew she would help him for she had a place waiting for her in heaven, all of which she soaked up into her mazy mind.

"So, could you put me up for the night, just one night, m'dear?"

"Yes Jo, if you don't mind sleeping in a chair, and tomorrow we will get your lodgings sorted out," said the angel in waiting.

Next morning, she waved her wand and Jo became a bedsit resident of Eastbourne, and the angel's friendly confidante, over their nightly meetings in various hostelries, after her workday ended.

Jude eventually returned to his desk and their routine might have been established for years, for the quantum wave it made in the flow of St Jude's. He was distant but courteous in exchanges and left the office for his own quarters soon after she arrived each morning.

Jo, euphoric with his reinstatement in society, applied for work and landed a kitchen hand's job in a boys' school, where he worked hard at the kitchen sink. When he collected their empty plates, his tongue made malicious inroads to the gullible minds of the young masters he served. He was soon sent packing to re-join the ranks of the unemployed, dependant on the angel to supplement his dole.

Another Christmas came and Jude asked her to man the kitchen with him on Christmas Day. to allow Alan Brilson time off with family.

"I'll take you out to lunch with the boys afterwards," he said. When she asked Jo what his plans were, it was a relief to hear his answer.

"I'm helping the local vicar cook a meal for homeless vagrants like I was a few months ago. They turn up from miles around for an eleven o'clock feed. That gives them time to get to their lay-byes before dark and settle down. I'll get a free meal anyway and my landlady might offer me a mince pie for supper unless you invite me round."

"I'm sorry Jo but I'll be working and having my meal over there. It's lovely of you to help others. See you Boxing Day perhaps."

"If there's any chance of you coming by The Drum before it closes at three will you look in and have a drink with me?"

"It's unlikely Jo but maybe," She smiled picturing herself wearing the blue velvet dress Jude liked, drinking wine with the boys in a favourite seafront hotel.

On Christmas day she dressed with care, fastening a pair of sapphire and diamond earrings with pearl lacquered studs in her ears and slipping on her opal and diamond engagement ring, then set off for St Jude's.

Alan had prepared ahead as much as he could, but there was still opportunity to handle favourite saucepans and worn knives. The morning was busy preparing for guests, expected for afternoon tea. She made tiny sandwiches of salmon and cucumber, a special batch of tiny mince pies, and miniature sausage rolls to go with the bought Petit Fours and finally small glasses of freshly cooked Zabaglione, stirring the Marsala into the custard with great care. The main meal was served at twelve thirty to avoid disrupting the patients' routine rest. By one thirty she was sitting in the office with the boys waiting for Jude to take them to the family celebration. He appeared in the doorway.

"Right, ready to go then," he said, jangling the heavy bunch of keys hanging from his belt. They filed obediently past him. Their route took a turn away from the seafront, to go through a seedy area of town, strangely quiet and free of the usual heavy traffic.

"Have you found somewhere else for a meal today," Lyn asked brightly?

"Yes, we're there," he replied turning into the loading alley behind the tag end of a row of closed shops. "Hop out all of you, it's around the corner."

Silently the boys escorted their mother back to the main road. They knew better than to tangle with the old man but looked sick with embarrassment when they saw a billboard standing in the middle of the empty pavement in front of Truckee's Café. It advertised Christmas Dinner.

They sat on forms, either side of a bare linoleum covered table, with plates of greasy potato and tinned meat in front of them and picked at the contents. It was more a duty to the café owner than their host, who masticated his way through a couple of forkfuls before rising to pay the bill. The meal had lasted twenty minutes.

"Nick, you can drive and drop me off at Sam's, and then see your mother back to her car." Words stuck in their throats as they trudged back to the sleek green Toyota and Nick slid behind the wheel.

For once she could not mend bridges with well-worn platitudes but thanked them quietly when they reached St Jude's car park. She was half way across the marshes before her mind registered that she had not even asked them what they would do that night. Tears spattered the blue velvet dress as her crying filled the car. Through the windscreen, grey skies were etched with wild swans on their way to mates in deep grassy nests. She needed mateship, so sought The Drum when she entered the town.

She found the pub flattened into the wall between a kebab shop and a derelict patch of ground where Boon's Hotel once stood. Before she took the key from ignition Jo, ever on the lookout, stood outside, by the curb. She lowered the window a crack.

"Thank God you're here woman. We need some help."

It wasn't fair she needed help for a change. Somebody to listen, before she lit the fire in the cottage and slept in front of it, like lonely old women world over.

"I'm tired Jo and I feel ninety. I thought you asked me to have a drink with you I go home."

"Forget about yourself, there are half a dozen souls, poor sods, who have nowhere to go tonight and no hope of a meal this side of Christmas. You've got to help them. You can afford it, if anybody can. You can't prate on about God and His love and forget them sleeping rough without warmth in their bellies, when you draw your curtains tonight."

Intense blue eyes stared accusingly from under the woolly beanie, askew on his head. His face, sharp featured and red veined from the cold, pressed against the window.

Lyn stared back into eyes that mirrored his changing moods, in their depths an ever-present fear behind the glint of a smile which did not reach his lips.

"Spare an hour to sit and talk with them. Buy them some sandwiches and a drink won't you."

She joined him to walk inside the inn where six men and a woman sat along a faded, red plush covered window seat in the corner of the bar. Three empty glasses stood on the round table in front of them. None were in rags, but their garments were ill fitting handouts from the Salvation Army quarters nearby.

Jo introduced Lyn, saying she might help. All eyes turned to them with the instinctive response of a group of stray animals to a sound. There was no hope in them, not even curiosity. Jo went for a word with the two bartenders and eventually returned with the only fare on offer, a large plate of cheese and meat sandwiches. A tray of drinks followed with a request to go and pay the bill. She bought a ginger wine for herself and returned to sit in nervous silence whilst they ate, until one of the men and his woman and came across and sat by Lyn.

"Is it true you will help us," they asked? She judged they were nearing sixty and had led regular lives from their wholesome looks and tidy mien.

"What's your problem," she replied acutely aware of their intense interest in her response.

"The hotel, where we worked as resident staff for most of our lives, was taken over by new owners last week. They brought their own staff and we were given two days' notice and a week's pay," the woman answered then relapsed into silence after so much effort. Lyn's eyes signalled, "Well."

"We can't get a room anywhere because the place is full for Christmas. Social Security's closed. We've no accommodation address anyhow because we haven't got a new job, everyone's fully staffed." her husband tumbled out in a quick burst of words.

"What about the others, are you all in the same boat?"

"Old Stan left with us," answered the woman. "He won't even look for lodgings. Says he worked there for twenty years and he'd rather sleep rough. We've been sleeping in the Italian Gardens near the lavatories. The other three are from Boon's. It's nigh a month since that happened, and they've been on the toby since. They walked in this morning hoping for the Sally Ann to give them a meal."

"Since what happened a month ago," persisted Lyn?

"The fire burnt it out," took up the husband. "Boons was at least a shelter from the cold, though that old Shylock charged every penny he could for his bug infested, mice ridden cubicles, sleeping four apiece. The corridors stank of stale pis and burning fat. A cat could get stuck in them, because of the mattresses stacked along the walls." He dipped his head to Lyn and retired into gloomy silence.

"Why go there then," asked Lyn?

One of the three men joined in the tale, his eyes peering out from the gap between a full beard and the lowered hood of his top windcheater. Rule number one of the road, don't take anything off.

"You don't find out until he's got your pension book Miss. Y'see, he takes the books while the Salvos pay the first week's rent until you've got through dipping and cringing to Social Security for your vouchers. Your book and one week's rent for service, Boon style, are his terms or else it's eviction Miss."

"They are all to blame, they know he holds the books. Sanitary man knows there's only two toilets and they're usually blocked. Fire Service knows there's no fire extinguishers, but none of 'em want to know because there's too many of us on the streets." Another voice chipped in.

"That old buzzard sits in his cubbyhole of filing shelves, hidden behind piles of paperwork on his desk. When he shifts his big belly forward to take your book back, you can hear his chair creak and a bit more horse hair drops on the floor."

"What's more you don't argue about being charged for use of a kettle or saucepan in the communal kitchen," added a third voice. "It's all there is to make a warm drink, to keep out the cold at night. We're just no hopers to him and he grows rich and fat on us, because we can never save enough to get away."

Lyn pictured a steady stream of life's flotsam swirling through the scum behind Boon's walls, waiting for a break to shoot them out through the spittle stained doors again. When the devouring flames destroyed their one port in a sea of misery, dismay mixed with a faint hope somebody would help them.

She could feel the nervous trembling of the woman beside her, and sensed the raging hurt, caged behind her man's blank gaze. fighting for release.

"So, you haven't found a room," persisted Lyn?

"Yes Ma'am, there was one, down towards the east end," he replied in the soft tone of one long used to service.

"How much will you need," she wanted to know.

"Twenty-one pounds would do it Ma'am. They want three weeks in advance. We will pay you back as soon as we get on our feet, if you could see your way to help us."

"I don't lend as a rule so take this as a gift for Christmas," she smiled back. "We had better go together because I'll have to settle with a cheque." Another plate of sandwiches and small beers were paid for and handed round to the accompaniment of, "Thanks Missus'. Nell's shaky hand pressed Lyn's and Tom's eyes filled with unbelieving relief. With Jo's help two suitcases, holding all their belongings, were heaped in the car and the four set off along the esplanade.

Passing the bandstand, a scarlet coated military band played the annual ritual Viennese waltzes. Wealthy stragglers, in fur coats and Harris tweeds, from the homes circling the affluent side of the promenade, danced round about. The posh hotels and three storey guest houses gave way to modest two storey dwellings. Here fisher folk supplemented meagre pickings with rent from their top front bedsit.

Nell and Tom's transfer to a top front heaven was smooth, after the landlord took quiet stock of the car they arrived in and of Lyn's demeanour. She bade them "Goodbye and God Bless," then returned to the inn with Jo.

The three gentlemen of the road had cut off to find a sheltered spot in a nearby churchyard where, with luck, if the door was open, they would take a nap in the pews until the verger ousted them. Under centuries old cedar trees cigarette ends would be shared out for a last smoke to relax stiff limbs, before they slept with the dead, on Napkin's gravestone. Baby Napkin was so clothed when found and sent to the church orphanage, before serving the church until his death,

Old Stan was left, snoozing in a corner. He had a full head of white curly hair and fresh pink cheeks. A clean white shirt collar peeped above the heavy grey topcoat reaching down to his ankles. Bright periwinkle blue eyes opened as Jo approached to have a few quiet words with him. After much head shaking, Stan shot a speculative look towards Lyn. He had found a measure of satisfaction in his freedom from service. The small fund of savings in the sole of his sock ensured urban security should he choose. For the present he had finished with living in other folk's homes.

"Lyn why don't you invite Stan home," said Jo. "He needs warmth and a good bowl of soup, but I suppose you think you're too good for the likes of him milady." His mocking gaze and the challenge stung an impulsive reply.

"Certainly, you can come home Stan, if you wish." Before she could condition the invite, Jo accepted for the old fellow.

After setting a chicken to braise with spices and vegetables in a large saucepan, Lyn busied herself making tea whilst Jo lit the fire to dispel the late afternoon gloom. She slipped upstairs to change into some warm slacks and a jumper then sat quietly during Jo's playing the host as he regaled their guest with funny anecdotes. Sam was silent apart from "Thank you" when his cup was replenished, and the biscuits handed round.

Later, as they sat watching television, Sam, divested of his greatcoat, rewarded her efforts by accepting a second bowl of the thick chicken broth. She watched him relax as they shared food and entertainment, then settled back in her chair only to start forward at Jo's next words.

"Why don't you stay the night Sam? We can put you up." Her startled gaze was met with a hard stare from Jo as her ears caught a half-hearted demur from Sam. His cheeks were rosy red in the firelight as he rested, replete and comfortable in his armchair.

She was stirred to offer the tiny conservatory built at the back of the cottage.

"Thank you, Ma'am, just for the night," he accepted. The conservatory hid confining neighbouring' walls. She had made it cosy with a daybed and a radiator, against which two kittens snuggled in their basket. Colourful pot plants hung from three white washed walls, enclosed by a glass wall with a door, opening on to the tiny backyard. A twittern ran behind cottage backyards.

Soon after the late-night news Sam was settled down, warm and snug under three blankets, falling fast asleep before she closed the kitchen door on him.

"You did a fine job. It might make him change his mind about staying on the road," Jo praised her, restoring her self image after Jude's treatment earlier in the day. Jo had a knack of restoring the confidence she needed when they met for an evening drink. A Baby Cham chased away the dark corners in her mind and softened the ebon shadows lurking by the furniture repository's large doors. The barley wine also resurrected a respectable self-image for Jo each night.

This dependence on his company, weakened her resolve to shun his influence and the inferences that she was not safe, living on her own. It ruffled her long-term plans for family reunion to hear she would be better with him taking care of her.

Now she sensed he expected to stay this night and had probably used Stan to gain entry to her home.

"You did most of the good work Jo. you must be tired after your long day and ready to get to your own bed. How about a lift home," she suggested?

"You can't turn me out and have a stranger in the house," he countered, finishing off the third bottle of barley wine.

Her silence shot an epithet from clenched lips as he stood near the fireplace, clenching and unclenching big fists at the end of long reaching arms. Flight was uppermost in her mind as his drink bright eyes flared sudden hatred at her. Before her second quick step to the door, he stood in the centre of the room, brandishing the sharp wood axe from the log basket.

"No, you don't. Move and I'll strike you." He stumbled to a chair and sat with the chopper across his knees, staring grimly at a terrified Lyn. Five minutes crept by and his head fell forward. She made a dash for the door and the next minute was flung to the floor, the axe swinging menacingly over her head. He resumed his seat, mumbling threats.

Rigid, she sat on the floor, listening to old Stan snore fitfully into the silence. In the cold hours before dawn moonlight revealed new falling snow and Jo asleep by the dark hearth.

Step by step she inched her way up the stairs, missing the third tread's creak. As she reached the top a low growl sounded from below and footsteps padded towards the stairwell.

Mindlessly she ran into the back bedroom, flung up the window casement and scrambled out onto the conservatory roof, her fingers searching for the eaves of the main frame. The cold numbed her mind and body as she sidled along the

The Looters

guttering and clawed her way up slippery tiles, to clutch a chimney and rein in her senses. They flew to the winds again when she saw Jo framed in the window. A black cat sitting on a nearby roof watched the comedy, arched its back and made its way to a quieter spot,

Deaf to his words of apology, she shot spread eagled down the tiles to fall across the wood box. She regained her footing, and ran through the shadows in the alley, in search of refuge. The Grand hotel came to mind as she remembered afternoon tea by the huge log fire which never went out. A twenty-minute trot brought it in view and daylight closer.

"Could you manage some coffee whilst I wait for assistance," she asked the night porter, after her white lie, of a car breakdown.

"Most certainly madam, would you wish for some buttered toast with the coffee," was the imperturbable reply as he led her towards a rosy fire and made room at the inn. Bathed in the fire's warmth, she reviewed yesterday evening. For all her purse dipping, she was short of enough charity of heart, to keep alive Jo's pretence of home ownership to Stan. It would have been kinder to let him share her roof in the spare room on a Christmas night. Killing his illusion caused the insane response of a man robbed of a fantasy.

Was Jude's behaviour his response to crushing his illusions? How many other lives had she blundered into, challenging another's idea of reality? How many realities were there? Was this reality, or a dream she would wake from, to find Jude smiling by her side? Was her vision of the heavily gowned woman, running towards a river, a warp to some other space time? Was she herself, some nebulous continuum stretching from an emergent past to an endless future? Nothing made sense.

She left the Grand, and retraced her steps along the twittern, entering the gate to the tiny yard, and conservatory. Old Stan had neatly folded his blankets in with a note saying thank you. Inside the house the fire had been re-laid and the room tidied up. Both guests had gone.

A busy Boxing Day at St Jude's blocked all thoughts of revisiting yesterday's events until she got home. Shutting fast the door, she plumped her bag down and sat looking round the room feeling safe, until the chill in the cottage tore open her loneliness. She sought the sight and sound of familiar faces on the television screen. Tired of their company, she made her way upstairs for an early night and for sleep to block out her need for someone to share her bed, her body, her life.

On her bed lay Jo Wiley, boots and all, a cigarette between his fingers and a single barley wine bottle on the bedside table beside him. He drew on the weed, blew out a smoke ring and grinned.

"You see m'dear, I could have broken in anytime. Your window is right next to a drainpipe. It's all right, I mean you no harm, I'm going now." He swung on to his feet moving lightly round the bed, empty bottle in his hand.

The Looters

"I'm sorry I spoilt yesterday girl. It was this," waving the bottle. "I suppose you haven't got the price of another. No? Well I'll be going. Get that window seen to," and he was gone. She heard the front door close and let loose a shaky breath. If only Jo had been the knight errant, he'd conned her he was. She took his advice, ringing a security firm who advised her to connect the system to the local police station.

This entailed a visit to request their permission and give her details. The sergeant at the desk was a countryman, the sharp tones of city colleagues rounded down in the soft inflexion of his Sussex drawl,

"I take it this is to do with a John Thomas Wiley. We lost track of him until he went on to social security down here. It is a very dangerous man that you are helping Mrs Rook. Do you want to make a charge against him?" He tapped a file taken from the shelves behind him.

"I should not be telling you this, but you have had a good influence on him. He is a paranoid schizophrenic and manic depressive who has been confined to maximum security for grievous bodily harm. Get some bars up to your windows as well as a security system." She nodded her head, appalled that her life was laid so bare to authority.

"A patrol will check your place each night and you will be safe. If he continues to cause trouble you must report it for his sake as well as your own. He needs supervised medication." He replaced the file to indicate their business was over. A kindly look returned her thanks as he pondered on the ways of the world.

In January Lyn got Jo a job through a friend's brother. The alcoholic ex-fighter pilot manned the call centre for a TV rental firm. He had been dry for months and holding his own. Jo soon became the social drinker offering a couple of barley wines to his work mate and together they drank themselves out of their jobs. Jo boasted he could make do with a single beer and a book of poetry to fill the day. The fighter pilot, in a lucid moment, committed suicide. Jo had dreamed of becoming a pilot so what hidden envy prompted his actions, he never conceded.

He told her of the tragedy as they walked over the downs next weekend. She was sickened that Jo's actions had caused the death of a worthier man. She could not change him. His mental instability plus his refusal to take medication, left her hopes of his redemption as far away as the sky they walked beneath. His claims on her time and money had stopped whilst he was earning, but she must break free of the cocoon of words Jo spun. She would sort herself out and learn to stand on her own.

Jo began reciting from Omar Khayyam,
"Oh Love! Could thou and I with Fate conspire,
To grasp this sorry Scheme of Things entire,'
"Well we cannot Jo. I can't grasp my situation right now, but I do intend to change it. I've let you depend on me, to satisfy my need to give. The sooner you

manage without me, the better because when Jude takes me back you will suffer. I'm thinking of finding a post further afield." He stopped in his tracks searching apprehensively for the right words.

"Don't go away, I'll join Alcoholics Anonymous and get another job. We could make it work if you would give me a chance."

"Jo, we both know a relationship has to progress or end. I cannot offer you that hope but I will keep in touch I promise." He was silent for the rest of the walk.

That night a brick was hurled through her window and shouted threats added emphasis to the heavy banging on the door. In panic she pressed the emergency button. The police took him away and charged him with disturbing the peace, calling Lyn as a witness.

In the oak panelled courtroom, Jo took the stand and made an urbanely respectful bow to the magistrate. Immaculately dressed in a light grey suit. When asked questions, there was not a trace of the Irish brogue to fleck the quiet Southern counties accent in his responses, He assumed the role of a wronged hero, pleading guilty to the charges, for to do otherwise would involve the lady in question and he had no wish to do so.

She flinched from the knowing glances in the visitors' gallery when she responded to the magistrate's questions.

"Yes, I do know Mr Wiley."

As she passed him on the way back to her seat, his downcast eyes opened for a millisecond to signal, that's nailed you my high and mighty lady. It did, for her conscience hammered until she paid his large fine to avoid the alternative of his imprisonment.

At the first opportunity she told Jude of her plans to move to another location.

"I suppose it will work," he surmised cautiously, "I'm advertising for a resident qualified Sister. The good accommodation offered, should draw some replies." She offered to work at weekends to keep the books in order, for as long as needed.

"Now I've told you Jude, I will start job searching. Will I see you at the weekends?"

"I don't know, maybe. You know where the keys are."

She sat the cottage table, where several newspapers were spread out. Perusing the nursing columns revealed there was nothing of use, now that the days when a nurse had to be resident were long past. She smoothed out the page to scan once more, and found her hand resting above a church notice for a Resident Assistant in a Women's Refuge. It sounded safe and there was little else. She applied for the post.

An Anglican priest had left himself nearly penniless to provide the means for two nuns to start a hostel for women alcoholics only. In a wealthy outer suburb, laid waste during the London bombing, the large derelict property was bought for a song.

Two intrepid nuns endured a bitterly cold winter with candle light and wooden box furnishings until charity, in many guises, rewired the house, and poured in furnishings from ashtrays to a zinc sink for the vandalized wash house.

Within a year the nuns transformed the place into a comfortable refuge for eight women. They supported them through three steps from detoxification, in a nearby mental hospital, to holding a job and independent living. The effort took its toll of one young nun's health, creating the vacancy for Lyn.

During the interview she was asked to provide an atmosphere of homeliness and calm for women who had turned to drink through broken lives. When Lyn drove to London to take up her new job, March winds buffeted the car. They heralded the fresh air of change.

Chapter 21: The derelicts

GUSTS of wind blew into the car from the green heath of the common, bordering an area where nannies once pushed Rolls Royce bassinettes, and below stairs life was rich with gossip. The servants were now above stairs, living in countless bedsit conversions to the stately mansions of yesteryear. The wealth was now in the variety of nationalities, coming and going along the broad tree lined avenues. Dark eyed, sari clad beauties, tiny Malay men, dancing Irishmen and drably neat mid-European mothers and their children rubbed shoulders with each other, passing the defiant native teenager, estranged from his English family circle. These wayfarers had raided and salvaged from empty houses, to improve their own impoverished dwellings, leaving the shell of a house the nuns took over.

That evening, drinking coffee with her new charges appraising her from the comfort of assorted settees and chairs, Lyn knew she was in the right place. She felt an affinity with their sense of rejection, and their hopeless attachment to the unattainable. Her mentor, the remaining nun, retired to her room with a firm injunction in rounded Yorkshire vowels.

"Be careful, they will tell you all kinds of tales. Maggie isn't in yet. Check that she hasn't got a bottle on her when she comes home." Blue eyes twinkled in a large rosy face, before her tall, big boned body swung out of the room. The others drifted off, leaving a plump, comely, dark-haired beauty in her twenties, sharing the settee with a ready listener.

Bridget came from a family across the Irish Sea, to seek her fortune in London, then found herself pregnant and alone, after the birthing. Her soft Irish voice told her story.

"I sold myself to any man for the price of a tin of baby's milk for my babe. The men got me drunk more often than not, you see, and Social Service took my bairn away for fostering. I'm clean now and want her back more than anything so, I'm wondering if I might have my daughter come to lunch on Sunday."

Bridget settled back to see how her tale was received when the front door bell rang,

"Ah that'll be Maggie, I'll come with you. Maggie might be temperamental, not knowing you. She is supposed to have gone to an A.A meeting," rising with a wink in Lyn's direction.

Under the porch light, a scraggy little Welsh woman glared at them.

"Who's she," she asked of Bridget?

"The new Sister," she replied, patting Maggie's pockets and relieving her of a bottle of cider.

"You Irish bitch. Where's my buddy, is she still here?" They watched her battle her way upstairs.

"Well they'll comfort one another I suppose. If ever you feel lonely Sister, I can take care of your needs," offered Bridget.

"Oh, I'm fine thank you," smiled Lyn, wondering if she looked as sex starved as she felt sometimes.

"Sex oils the wheels of the chariot but if I'm going to be fucked it will be a celebration of life, not a panacea." She felt mildly shocked at her use of old English but not ashamed. Bridget bade her a respectful good-night.

Over the following months Lyn heard many more stories from nurses, successful sportswomen, wealthy wives and jilted lovers. No sector of the community was immune from the gene dancing in their blood, inviting them to sip up and be merry. All were sad at heart and unable to tolerate their suffering.

She went shopping for a wedding dress with a big Jamaican girl whose sweetheart was giving her another chance.

A nurse rang her in the small hours, to rescue her from a nursing assignment she could not cope with. Lyn drove for miles in the dark, to a bottle strewn room and a paralytic woman.

One night she closed the door against Bridget, standing drink sodden in drenching rain, and wept for her although she knew she wore a body belt full of money.

There was always a ripple of suspense disturbing the pool of tranquillity she aimed to create with the senior nun, who insisted on calling her buddy.

Maggie got into serious trouble, brawling, and landed back in the detox unit where she drunkenly betrayed her buddy. Lyn's North Country colleague left suddenly, leaving her to tidy up the pieces and a wardrobe full of empty cider bottles. She wished she had found time to befriend the woman from Yorkshire.

The night Maggie returned she stood at the foot of the stairway, threatening Lyn with a broken bottle. Behind Lyn, Bridget's reassuring voice encouraged her down the stairs to face Maggie in her misery and enfold her back into the watching group of women.

She set about making a warm and happy home for them all, their highs were her highs and she knew their lows. Who was she to judge when not so long ago her feelings of loneliness and worthlessness fuelled a murderous anger.

Her efforts were closely observed by a woman of noble birth who took the veil at the end of world war one. She was very tiny and delicate looking, eating less than a sparrow when she joined them for a meal. Her habit floated lightly through the house and Lyn wondered if a gust of wind caught it, would there be a body beneath.

Mary Trudeaux relieved Lyn for her two days off duty every weekend. Now, nearing the end of her life, schooled by years of obedience and experience, there was no frailty of the nun's spirit. Light streamed out from her, comforting all who sought her wisdom and the sober truth of her words. She knew some of Lyn's story and approved her dedication to the church charity, despite the pull to be with her family.

One Sunday evening Sister Mary sat waiting for the rattle of the garage doors, heralding Lyn's return. Shortly after, her footsteps on the stairs told their own story. The door opened and Mary Trudeaux gathered herself to listen.

"Hello Sister Mary, I'm back. I'm sorry to have kept you up, the traffic was so heavy. Is everything all right. It's good to be back. Can I make you a warm drink to take up with you?" Short sentences tumbled out with a stretched smile jellying out of control, as Lyn stood by the chair nearest the door, ready to flee to the sanctuary of her room. The nun read it all.

"We've missed you. You look tired, would you like to talk?" Lyn's smile faded, leaving dejection and defeat in her eyes.

"He is divorcing me Sister and there is nothing I can do. He says he will prove I committed adultery," she swallowed. "I didn't but I have agreed to sell him all the property because he threatens to sell the business and our home, leaving the boys with nowhere to go."

At Mary Trudeaux's calm invitation to continue, Lyn recounted the scene in the office, when she arrived on Friday evening, to find an official letter addressed to her. It stated that, now two years had elapsed, divorce would be granted on incompatible grounds, unless she made a plea. She pleaded with Jude.

"Jude don't do this to us please. I can't agree to it." He laid a hotel receipt before her on the desk. She saw it was a booking for a Mr and Mrs and everything fell into place. She remembered Jo saying, I will book us in, and I threw it away.

"It's not the end of the world for heaven's sake. You are living on your own anyway. I told you we should give it time and maybe we can start afresh. If you make a fuss, I will make this public," Jude threatened.

On Saturday came his demand to buy the properties and take over her share in the business. He would pay the deferred sum in five years. Under repeated threats of selling up their home, she gave in, to end the surreal performance, Tomorrow, he might think differently, but on Sunday he was gone, and work engaged all her time before returning to Sister Mary and a full confession.

Mary Trudeaux listened, as she had done countless times, to one more out-pouring of the eternal human need to have love's offering accepted. The never-ending pain of a rejection which stifled the heartbeat and crushed the will.

She recalled the boy she was going to marry, returning from the trenches in 1918, a broken man who took to the bottle. His incurable addiction ended in a padded cell where he took his own life and changed hers for ever.

Strong church ties and loving hands reached out to show her the way to turn her loss to advantage by working with such afflicted souls. She entered a seminary as a novice with her youthful desires unappeased. One of Nature's initiates, seeking the mystery behind the rapture of union, impaled on the cross of a man's body.

Revelation came that all love flowed from Eternity. If love was pure it manifested in the human act, as an offering to the Source. She offered her love to God in caring deeply for the men and women she met in her work and never regretted the pain she shared as she walked the path with a fallen traveller. Mary Trudeaux lived to fight with them against their dependence on alcohol, to appease their craving for love, success and acceptance.

She watched Lyn fold her hands in her lap as she finished her tale, then lean towards her with concern in her eyes.

"Sister Mary I've wearied you. You don't look well today. Is there anything I can do?"

According to her doctor's recent diagnosis this might be the nun's last visit to the hostel. Terminal care was advised. Mary Trudeaux knew she would need all of her patience to accept the rigid routine of the convent infirmary under Sister Clarence's strict surveillance.

"Yes, please if you will, I need help to remove my veil. My arms won't lift so easily these days Lyn. If you will come to my room with me, that will be all the help I need."

Lyn laid the black veil and white coif on the small white chest by the bed. She marvelled at the dark brown cap of hair revealed, for it was known that Sister Mary was ninety if a day. Soft brown eyes smiled a thank you as the little woman sank to her knees for a quiet moment, then lifted in mute appeal for assistance to rise. Her head fell back on the pillow as she lay on the narrow bed and took Lyn's hand in hers.

"Thank you. God sometimes needs us to be on our own Lyn, to find ourselves. He gives us all the strength we need to walk alone. Think about this. We will talk again in the morning if you wish and perhaps find a solution to help Jo," Her eyes closed as she breathed out on a soft sigh, wondering what might have been in her own life.

The next time they met was at the convent infirmary a few days before Mary Trudeaux died. The visitor's room was behind the convent doors. A cold, dark bare cellar, it reminded Lyn of a prison. A door opened and a nun wheeled in an old invalid chair. The hard wheel rims were thin, catching every bump in the uneven stone floor. The unpadded seat sagged from use, not the weight it carried, which was feather light. The nun left Mary by the table and departed as silently as she came, leaving Mary Trudeaux covered only by her well-worn black habit, where her hands sought the shelter of a fold in her skirt. The veil of death hovered above the head dress surrounding a face beautiful and serene. Her smile of welcome lit the space between them and warmed the air around them. How Lyn loved this tiny mortal who never wasted time in banalities.

"Sister Mary, I've come to say goodbye and to thank you for the lessons learnt from you. I've found my path and I truly believe my feet are on firm ground."

At Mary's invitation, she sketched in the details briefly for fear of tiring the dying woman. The nun's hand reached out to the one curled against hers to give her blessing as the door re-opened. Mary's escort signalled that the visit was at an end. Lyn stood to watch her depart into the mysteries of the convent. She made arrangements for Jo to be offered rehabilitation before she died, leaving a legacy of great strength and honesty,

Jo agreed to his rehabilitation programme because it was in his old stamping ground, London. He had been through it all before but as far as Lyn knew this was the big breakthrough, and others would lift responsibility from her shoulders. It was arranged he should come to the hostel for Lyn to take him for three months of isolation in the Rehabilitation Unit.

He arrived one Sunday morning smartly dressed and very affable. A roast was on the table with all the trimmings. The women invited him to join them and asked him to carve the meat for plates, well heaped with vegetables and Yorkshire pudding.

After the prayer of thanksgiving, he cast anxiety and resentment into the contented silence, with the bottle of Barley wine he dumped by his plate. Bridget caught Lyn's eye and gave a tiny shake of her head as Lyn made to remove the bottle. Inwardly wincing from the soured atmosphere, she faced her cowardice and longing to be rid of the burden of Jo's behaviour.

Her mood lasted until they reached the hospital, where she watched his thin figure follow a nurse down a corridor. She remembered her spell in Greystones and ran after them to reassure him she would keep in touch during the three months of his rehabilitation. Afterwards, she would seek her freedom from the mesh of errors she was caught up in. For now, she must return to the cottage and nearness to family, as soon as she could be replaced in the hostel.

Father Frank listened to her request to leave as soon as possible. Mary Trudeaux had spoken well of this woman and hinted at the problems in her life. It was a pity that her urgency to leave left no option but to ask the convent for help. The grey-haired priest reached for the phone, giving a silent prayer that his need would be answered, before going down to join the weekly men's A.A meeting.

A week or so later, Lyn nosed her car back home like a hound at the end of a hunt. Some trails had been found, scents missed, but the fox was holed up. Humans were a funny lot, struggling against the double bind of social rules and their own desires, like puppies chasing their tails before running back to the pack.

Back in the cottage, she put the kettle on then rang Jude to say she would be in to work next day. He sounded pleased and greeted her amiably with a bright smile, when she walked into the office

"Can you make time to drive out to Brighton? I need a new commercial dishwasher and I'd like your opinion."

"Of course, I'd love to. I haven't been there for ages."

They wandered round the old Smugglers Lanes, stopping for lunch in a little Italian Restaurant. The lemon sole was lingered over, as Jude talked of his plans for St Jude's. It was a promising start to her return. One evening, seeing her off after work, he gave her a red rose growing near the car park. She wondered, but cautious of expecting too much, too soon, sought ways to fill her free time.

She went to seminars on colour healing where a mixed bunch of gentle people wanted to add to the quality of other's lives and, maybe, fill a gap in their own. Life became an easy routine, outcomes not hungered for.

One evening whilst she heated some milk for a nightcap, the doorbell of Fisherman's Cottage chimed. Slipping the safety chain on, she opened it hesitantly to confront Jo, standing with one foot on the step.

"I've left the AA lot, I don't need their bullshit to lay off drink. They were glad to see the back of me anyway. Fancy a drink with me?" She shook her head.

"Sorry Jo but I'm off to bed. You can tell me about it some other time eh?" She made to close the door, but his foot stayed put.

"Will you give me the price of a barley wine?"

"Yes, if you let me shut the door." He complied and was still muttering under his breath when she returned, to hand him some coins, but had the grace to thank her before swinging off down the road.

Snuggled in the warmth of bed, sipping her hot milk, she congratulated herself for resisting Jo's demands on her. She had walked the mile with him but would no longer carry his burden. If it dragged him down to the gutter again, so be it. He must find out how to be responsible the hard way.

To keep distance between them, she rented the fisherman's cottage to an elderly couple, after finding work as a resident part time warden in a retirement village. She kept her whereabouts secret from all but the family, secure from his threats and invasion. To soften the blow, she arranged to meet Jo for a meal at a country inn once a week.

He ate his counter meal grumbling about her secrecy, until a barley wine restored his humour. Eventually, reassured that he was coping and keeping out of trouble, she stopped meeting the lonely man.

Nick and Andrew often called in, bringing their girlfriends and treating the place like home when they came. It was good to have their confidences again. Life took on a routine that smoothed out any wrinkles, leaving room for anything to happen out of the blue.

On her first Christmas Day in the village, Jude found half an hour for an unannounced visit. Thrown into confusion, she rustled up a tray of tea with Arrowroot biscuits and apologies. Jude stirred sugar into his cup.

"Stan and family are moving out to their new council house in a couple of days and I need a new resident girl. Have you any ideas? Resident domestics are difficult to come by."

Lyn checked the jobs wanted section in her local paper, finding there a single advert. A mother, with a child, was willing to consider anything offered for a resident post. A telephone number made contact possible then and there.

"Why do you need residency," Lyn asked the woman at the end of the line?

"Because of my husband, he is being unfaithful." It seemed women everywhere were in flight.

"I understand. Can you come to see us after Christmas, say Monday?"

"That was lucky, you've done me a good turn. Thanks for the tea," Jude said as he stood to depart. "See you both on Monday then."

The festive holiday over, Jude waited impatiently for the woman's arrival. He appraised her through the office window whilst she stood scenting the air like a wary fox, before going up steps to the door of the nursing home.

Face to face, her sharp pointed features and dark fringed green irises excited him. He led the way to the office and introduced her to Lyn.

Roxy Rustle told them she was a wayfarer who lived in a caravan with her husband and child. They earned a living working for farmers, but mainly from gathering watercress from dykes of running water. Her husband was often unfaithful, and she wanted to make a new life for herself.

"Where do you hail from Mrs Rustle? You have a familiar accent."

"Gloucestershire is where my family live, and please call me Roxy. That's my name," she confided.

"Can you and your son manage in a large bed sit?"

"Yes, we will come tomorrow, and I can start work the next day if that is all right." She gave Jude a searching look when they shook hands at the front entrance.

"I hope you will find me satisfactory Mr Rook."

Hot on the heels of Roxy and son settling in, her husband arrived the same afternoon, bringing a skinny waif of a daughter and the family mongrel. He left both of them in the office with Lyn, who fed them milk and biscuits but could not fill the longing in their eyes. She sat with them, until Jude arrived to sort things out. He bundled both in with Roxy and somehow the three settled in to one room.

Roxy was a good worker and soon found her way to taking care of Jude's apartment and the office. It was she who brought the coffee tray to the office in the mornings, stopping to advise Jude about the other maids' cleaning routine in the nursing home. She was always within call to take his messages and was helpful to Lyn.

"Roxy's doing well, how are the children settling," Lyn remarked some weeks later? Jude's perfunctory reply came with a smile and a cheeky wink before he went to the stairwell and called up.

"Roxy be ready in five minutes to go to the wholesalers." Lyn sipped her coffee thoughtfully, recalling that Ruby had been favoured for such outings in the past. She would put out a feeler.

"Jude, I have to attend the villa owners' yearly meeting at the end of this month. Is there any chance of you coming to Spain with me? It's a long drive on my own."

"Sorry but I have rather a lot on my plate just now. Why don't you fly out?" He locked his desk. "I'm still not sure how things will turn out for us."

Lyn tucked his response away with other unanswered questions and turned for a warmer response to her new friends in the healing group. After one meeting, two widowers came up with the same idea of inviting Lyn for a country walk. Both had come prepared with picnic baskets, which the three of them ended by sharing and enjoying the countryside together. One of the widowers, a quiet, lonely man who had nursed his wife during her terminal days, offered to accompany Lyn to Spain.

Their journey abroad was a happy experience. They shared the driving, and a day or so enjoying the life of her mountain retreat in Spain. When they returned, long walks over the downs became a shared pleasure to look forward to. Her life became easy and relaxed for the first time in many months.

The seasons came and went whilst the world went about its business as, here and there, its creatures found their place in the scheme of things. Two were whisked into new pathways.

Chapter 22: Goodbyes

IN THE quiet following a torrent of summer rain, Jude's eyes followed Lyn's towards the window. Pearly clouds obscured the sun's warmth and stole the morning sunbeams from her desk.

"Damn rain!" His joints seized up in cold moist weather, as did his speech which had been noticeably abrupt since her return from Spain, curtailing his earlier warmth and interest. He had found new pastures.

"It will pass," she placated. "Weather changes, just as we change. I've altered, I've less fear of men now. I'm free of male dominance and their fear of imagined rivals or loss of power. They pull the corset strings of convention to constrain us with jealousy tightening every rein"

"That's how women expect us to be," he chivvied her. "You're a fine one to talk. Women are deceitful and meddlesome, always putting us down. It's a fight to keep our credibility as men. Anyhow I'm off," and he made to escape.

"No Jude, please wait a moment. Changes in our lives call for new paths. We have to break free from all that gave us security and happiness at one time. I want to have a measure of what you have now." He retraced his steps to sit across the table.

"So, you've heard." They talked earnestly for some time before he stood again saying, "Well let's hope it works out. A month it is then."

A month later Lyn arrived very early, on a late autumn morning. She parked the car quietly and walked towards the kitchen garden for a stroll.

A shadow land of trees and bushes danced on the high garden walls. Her outline danced a duet with her, light of foot, hand holding skirt gently aflutter. Black menace hovered in a cloud creeping over the ground. She shivered at the threat of rain, taking shelter in a corner of the wall. Hidden fears stormed her mind, bringing it all back. The hand that lifted the mallet against Jude, uncurled from the port wine mark in its palm. She rubbed it savagely across her body to wipe out the stain, wipe away the knowing of the river bank. Echoes of the dream girl's desire for the boy in the river still pulsed soft between her thighs. Could she be a reincarnation of a woman with a debt to pay? Had a quantum of the universal pattern strayed from its loom to weave a warp of time anew?

No, her fears and dreams were symbolic of events happening now. Her failure to abandon herself to the sacred rite of love was the cause of the rift sending Jude downstream of her. She had dammed the flow of his love behind the barricade of a prude's ambition.

The Rubies and Gertrude's of this world gave with bovine content. Innocent of shame, they opened their bodies unconditionally, and yet, one and all they were deceivers, and she not the least.

Deceit was their shield against aggression and anger. Fuelled by guilt for supping honey from too many flowers, male jealousy stifled open honesty. Fear that their women might sip the same nectar was to blame for this silent vendetta between the takers in God's Eden.

The potter moulded Eve in Nature's kiln for His Adam, who enslaved her to his ideal. Eve fought her bondage behind a fan of deception with a submissive Yes when she meant,

No, I will not dance for you. Together, we will weave an endless dance of love, our offering to the rhythm of life.

She sat on the garden tool chest until her whirlpool of thoughts centred into union with a sense of belonging to a vast creation. A peaceful silence filled the garden until the church bell chimed for Matins. She rose, brushed her skirt and began to walk slowly towards the house. Thought fired anew.

Mine and Jude's story is closing. It tells only of deceit, shielding me from pain. It hides witness to the truth of the whore which writhes within me, the broker counting his profits, the falsifier praising my servile effort to please and the controlling tyrant. The distant past is history, a karmic jigsaw of lives. When the final piece is in place the picture will make sense. Until then all lies in confusion, without hope for a future still clouded in mystery. To begin with I must be honest with myself. The present is a gift to be used with wisdom.

She walked back through the kitchen garden to where the big bay tree and the flower covered arbour had given way for the new car park behind the last two houses. The old glory was gone along with many other things. Cars parked sentinel around an over large fountain at the centre of a pebbled square.

On the lawn, Jill Fraser paused in the pegging of night wear on the line. She came across to where her former employer looked back at the changed scenery.

"Hallo Lyn, everything all right for today," Jill enquired solicitously, adding, "They are in the office."

"Yes, everything's fine Jill."

She took the side path behind the kitchen. Chef was busy on the far side at his new work bench, below a recently installed window. He waved at her and she waved back, her mind going back to other days, when a single oven and hob had provided good fare to put on the plates. Under the window she next peered through, the wooden deal table used to be covered with waiting plates. Now she looked on new equipment, gleaming from shelves and walls. Some good always comes out of upheavals to make life easier for all the staff, she thought, hoping some goodwill would come out of the morning's future events.

On she went, past the side door of Jude's many furtive night exits, and down to the roadside. The front doors were open for the morning airing, inviting her to enter. The purple and ruby leaded windows of the inner door no longer caught the eye. Heavy gold damask wall paper covered every wall from floor to ceiling, demanding admiration. The lovely old mirror was gone from the bend of the dark stairwell. So too, the fireplace with the imitation fire where the brigadier warmed his hands, from his chair beside the small shelf for his books.

Opening the door of a nearby ward she saw the beds were the same, but the cosy armchairs were replaced by metal furniture with restraining trays. They would cause many a sore elbow as a weary head rested on a frail hand. Well, that is as far as I dare intrude, she decided, and turned into the passage leading to the office.

The office door was locked. She tapped lightly. Roxy opened it a crack, then seeing Lyn, gave a tight smile and swung it a fraction wider, allowing her to edge round the door.

The woman, recruited to the staff a few months earlier as a maid, now sported a trim navy-blue skirt and cream silk shirt. A tailored navy jacket hung over the back of a chair. She had worked her way up to supervisor by the time-honoured manner. Roxy went to stand close to Jude, where he was checking some lists at his desk.

His attire was impressive, from the hand-made fine woollen suiting tailored to fit, the blue silk shirt and navy tie, to the soft leather hand crafted shoes on his feet. A gold pen displayed against the white handkerchief in his top pocket, and a gold Rolex watch encircled his wrist. He looked across to Lyn, through the gold rimmed spectacles he now needed to wear and nodded a good morning before continuing his work with Roxy.

"What time is she expected," asked Lyn, slipping out of her cardigan before settling to work at her table behind the filing cabinets.

"Any minute now, you've only just got here first, what kept you," Jude said curtly?

"Will you lay out the books on the table. We're going upstairs, call me when she arrives." Roxy gave her a triumphant glance as she left to accompany Jude to Lyn's old apartments.

A dog was barking in the house staff's rest room. Lyn went across, memories of Brutus flooding back, to find Stan Pike brushing a young long-haired collie bitch. She patted the dog.

"Morning Stan," Lyn greeted him, "does she spend the whole day on that running lead in the garden?" He nodded assent as she looked round the room. Despite all the money spent on improvements to the main building, nothing had been done to brighten these quarters.

Sheets still hung from the ceiling runners, the central heating boiler rattled, the chairs in a dark corner still sagged and the damp smell of urine wafted in from the laundry room, where washing swirled behind the glass door of a big new commercial machine.

She returned to the office to scan the road outside the window, until she saw a car stop by the curb and a neat little woman step out. The visitor looked around before walking up to the front door where a maid directed her to the car park. Lyn patted her hair nervously, re-arranged the books, then waited for the sound of steps coming along the passage. Jude had also seen her arrival and ushered her in.

"This is where you will work. My clerk is all ready for you," motioning towards Lyn. "Would you like some coffee? No, well I'll let you get on. We will see you upstairs in my private quarters before you go."

"Where would you like to start" asked Lyn after they exchanged names?

"I think it best to check the ready cash and cash to be banked first," Mary Lake suggested.

"I'm afraid I don't hold the key any more, but Mrs Rustle usually has one." Of course, Roxy Rustle had one and would shortly have a lot more.

"No matter then. We can start on the books," said Mary. They were opened and Lyn sat by her side, waiting to answer any queries, until Mary Lake finished her inspection.

"Would you show me where to find Mr Rook please," she said, closing the last of the big ledgers?

"Yes, I will let them know you are going up," pressing the intercom button, before guiding Mary to the door. She left her at the foot of the stairs as Jude came to meet her, calling down to Lyn.

"Will you wait a bit, we won't be long?" She nodded and went back to wait as she had so often in the past. When he returned, he brought others with him, filling the room with all the staff on duty that day.

Uncertainly, Lyn stared around, not believing this was happening. Jude stood by his desk with Roxy at his side, opening a cardboard gift box. Jude cleared his throat and began for his curious audience.

"We all want to wish you a happy retirement," and he took a small silver-plated lamp, powered by a nightlight, from Roxy.

"This is to commemorate your years of service," as he handed her the lamp. Jude had used a cheap fairground prize to suit his purpose. She took the gift searching for words. If I say thank you for a lovely gift it's dishonest, surely the staff had donated enough… then she saw the puzzled surprise on their faces. They had not been told.

"Well this is a surprise. It certainly has a Florence Nightingale touch to finish my happy association with old friends among our staff," she said wryly.

"The extravagance of your gift Jude overshadows the thirty years or more of the partnership of Rook and Rook working together. I thank you, one and all, for the lamp and for your good wishes." She caught Jill Frazer give an encouraging wink and finished in a rush, "Now I must be going."

"Get back to work all of you," Jude instructed, "except for Ruby and Stan." Lyn followed the file through the door.

Back in the office Jude turned to Ruby standing against the wall.

"You are still going down to the taxi rank to associate with the men down there when you are supposed to be walking the dog. What have you got to say?" The girl looked up defiantly, black curls framing the Irish beauty of her face.

"I take the dog out in my time off sir, and I go down the town." Her hands fumbled anxiously, for all her nerve. "One of them sometimes gives me a lift home."

"And you pay the usual way. Am I right?" She bobbed her head.

"You know what to expect. Stan!" The handyman nodded and grabbed Ruby by the neck, bending her over towards the floor. Unprotesting, she waited. Jude's hand crashed down again and again until he was satisfied.

"Now get out the pair of you. Shut the door." He waited for them to leave, then slumped down at his desk. It's done. I've played my role and sent her on her journey, yet I still love that naïve innocent on a pedestal. Tears ran down his cheeks as his head sank into his hands. His sobs were those of the child sitting in the cold alley of Spreadeagle Terrace, his back afire with welts from the buckle end of his stepfather's belt. Roxy's voice called softly through the door.

Chapter 23: New beginnings

LYN settled into her car seat, then reached for the glove compartment. Good, there were a couple of squares left. The rich dark chocolate melted on her tongue, covering the bitter taste of the last hour, until its sweetness soothed her pique at letting Jude still rattle her. Would women ever free themselves from their instinctive need for equality, she pondered. Now that she was free to start afresh, would Jude always have freehold to a corner of her mind?

The car cruised through Old Town, past the lane leading to the boys' infant school. She paused near the church gate for a woman to cross over to the Post Office, where she used to cash the children's benefits. She picked up speed and drove on down the hill to the traffic lights and the open stretch across countryside. Verdant fields rose on either side. The skyline etched with a bold rabbit here and there, popping up like a rebel from the new feminist movement, daring the next shot of irony from a chauvinist press.

Maybe I am a feminist. I'm finally foot loose and fancy free of the need to do routine work. Marx had it right, creative work is our real birthright. There is so much I want to do, explore my world, my thoughts and voice them creatively. What freedom there will be in such a private world.

Her thoughts wandered on until she reached her destination and parked the car. A month ago, she had voiced the changes about to happen in her life, and her plans for a new life style, with the executive of the retirement village where she worked part time. They offered her a similar post, with a beautiful new unit in the grounds she now stood in.

The walled kitchen garden and many of the lovely trees still remained. The old manor had been carefully replaced with a building to suitably grace the site. Spacious lounges and public rooms on the ground floor supported second floor roomy apartments beneath red tiled rooves and attractive eaves.

"I am so happy here," she said out loud, running up the stairway to turn the key to flat twelve. Softly she closed the door, tiptoed into the lounge, and ran into the arms of Daniel, he who had driven to Spain with her. He had taken her for country walks after their group meetings, where the eternal questions of why and where were discussed in philosophic and spiritual explorations with others.

Married for just a month, both sought a meaning to life beyond the material benefits and losses. Daniel began Lyn's education into Nature's laws for he knew much about wild flowers, herbs, the birds and small creatures of the countryside. Their sharing was balm to the loneliness and hurt of their recent pasts. Feeling that they could support each other through their declining years, it seemed natural they should ask God's Grace to bless their marriage. Dan looked down at the woman by his side for she was a bare five feet tall.

"Everything alright sweetheart? I'm glad you are finished with that place. Now we can begin our new life. Are you ready for a walk before dinner?" She smiled agreement.

They went down to the river where the haze of high summer lay heavy upon all the countryside. Grain drooped full pursed on each golden stem. The juice of wild berries scented the warm air with rich invitation to the birds' parched throats. A trillion insect wings flashed and flew over nectar-filled flowers, their brilliant dancing colours bejewelling the earth and sky as they sated their thirst for living. Meadow flowers spread their petals wide in abandon to the sun.

Among the animals, the urgency of spring mating had given way to bovine contentment. Sheep lay in nudging intimacy by the river, winding through their pastureland. An old bull, drowsy with heat and surrounded by earlier conquests, had surrendered his vigour to the cows, now vigilant for their young calves playing in a corner of the field. They herded back the more adventurous youngsters, seeking sweet relief from the swarming insects patching their hides, in the cool stream,

A hawk pulsed in a rising spiral of warm air until fresh prey brought it to hang motionless on a thread of eternity. Of a sudden it swooped, with the gift of eternal silence, to its quarry. The trees belled out, leaves lifted on currents of soft air. Fruit swelled along the full arms of apple orchards. All Nature was in touch in a continual caress before autumn withered their embrace to let earth drift into the sleep of renewal.

Walking on Daniel's arm through meadows where narrow deep running streams plip-plovered their course, they came to rest on a bridge. Dark damsels skimmed the surface below in a frenzy of delight, one moment lying motionless, like dead blossoms, floating on the skin of the water, the next glancing up with quivering wings. Above them, Meadow Blues and large white cabbage butterflies drifted in slow motion. Below, tall grasses lolled elegantly across ribbons of water threading through massed banks of amethyst and white balsam, cushioning peacock blue butterfly wings, and the dainty feet of slender green grasshoppers.

In the depth of the dark water below the bridge, starry twinkles refracted the sunlight in surface currents and eddies. A large trout swam from the shadows to lie motionless, then flip to expose a silver flank to the warmth as sunlit water flowed over its speckled outline. A smaller shape slid alongside, and they circled before swimming downstream together.

Lyn looked at their image mirrored below. Daniel's gentle aquiline face with silver hair growing high off the brow and her rounded countenance, framed with silver, smiled up at them. Her thoughts wandered to an incident he had shared with her.

A down to earth man, who held a government post all his working life, he had sought out a clairvoyant of good repute after his wife died. The seer had told him things about the manner of his wife's final moments that only he knew. Before he left, the seer told him he would meet someone from his past, giving him a name. She foretold that the woman would help him to rebuild his life, in karmic return that he once helped her become a famous gypsy dancer.

As Lyn turned to him, his bright blue eyes twinkled at her from a brown, clear-skinned face. Etched there, a blend of stable citizenship and the mysterious wisdom of the roaming gypsy hinted his parentage. Stooped now, he had been tall. When he walked his leisured strides belied the soldierly swing of his arms.

"You've been dreaming again my dear. You missed the swallows gathering to roost," he said.

"Yes, my darling, and that's where you and your gypsy dancer are going," she replied.

Guiding Lyn over the furrows in a patch of uneven ground, Daniel mused over the past months. Life had changed from a lonely stretch of empty years to moments filled with joy, walking by the side of this woman, her head poised and confident and full of ideas which often turned out for the best. To be sure she was not the easiest of mortals to live with. A quick temper and over sensitive reaction to an ill-judged comment from him, had needed a firm hand and patience, whilst they adjusted to each other's temperaments.

"We'll make our plans this evening. Where shall we go to first dear, my cousins will want to meet you?"

"I leave it to you to decide. I know I'm still a bit of a bossy boots, but I have improved, haven't I, and I'm so excited about the holiday."

"All it takes dear is for truth between us and we will succeed. We are making a new start, a big leap away from all we know, so, we must trust one another. No more conniving to get your ideas put into practice."

He took her hands. They showed early signs of arthritis, but they were still beautiful. He loved the way she walked by his side with the grace of a dancer. Above all he knew he loved her dearly for herself and the open honesty they now shared as man and wife.

"You know," Lyn confided softly, "We may be a bit old for high passion, but I never knew heart love until you taught me. Truth and Love are so entwined aren't they Dan? Love becomes selfless when you are true to someone. It has led us to really know each other in so short a time. I guess we'll make out."

During the following year they travelled widely, visiting America to meet a branch of his family, and driving around Europe encountering the small dramas of foreign travel. They frequently visited the small studio in the Spanish mountains of Andalusia. Their last trip was to see Andrew who had immigrated to Australia with his new bride. This visit ended in the biggest leap of all, buying property and successfully applying to live in Australia on their return home.

The Looters

One afternoon, a few days before they were due to emigrate, Daniel answered the doorbell. Jo Wily stood on the step, dressed in a smart grey suit that hung from his painfully thin frame. He looked so ill that Daniel had not the heart to send him on his way. He invited him in, after appraising Lyn of the identity their visitor, who stood in the room with an air of finality until Daniel beckoned him to sit down.

"What's your business here then," he questioned?"

"I heard you were going abroad and wanted to say good bye to you and Lyn. I don't suppose we shall be seeing each other again."

Lyn broke a pregnant silence.

"How are things with you Jo? You don't look well. Are you getting enough to eat?"

"Not too good Lyn, thank you," he murmured. "The doctors say I've got AIDS. As a matter of fact, I was wondering if you could see your way to help me one last time. I want to go and see my mother and take her out, maybe down to the river again, where It's quiet and we can talk. I need to make my peace with her."

"Are you sure, Jo, you can't con about a serious thing like AIDS," Lyn pressed.

"Oh yes, I'm sure," he answered grimly, "I've managed to keep straight and I sure as hell do not intend to die in prison for a con, and with God's help I won't. The rent gets deducted from my assistance money and that leaves enough to get by, with the odd barley wine now and then." With a half-smile as he went on," If it hadn't been for you Lyn, I would have been back inside long before now. There's a place reserved for you in heaven."

"Come on now Jo" she joked, "Save those lines for the vicar. I am so very sorry it will end like this. Would you like a cup of tea?"

"No thanks, but could I use your toilet?"

Whilst he was gone, they took some of their cash, set aside to start up in Australia, and placed it in an envelope. He took it with a sincere "Thank you," and after a few more words, Dan accompanied him to the door.

"Take it easy old chap. Goodbye." Lyn joined them.

"Good bye and God Bless Jo."

They watched him go on his way. He walked slowly with stooped deliberation as he moved into his bleak future. 'Good bye Jo' was the key note of his life.

Dan and Lyn would soon dance to a new note in their life melody, stepping across the other side of their world. In a new country, they would test their resources and depend on each other's loyalty.

END

THE THREE LOVES TRILOGY

LOVERS & LOSERS

JO MARTINEZ

Lovers & Losers

a novella

Jo Martinez

Book 3 of the Three Loves Trilogy

Chapter 1: Arrival

THE tiny air craft skimmed above the treetops. A never-ending carpet of green, spread out between Perth and Denmark in the far south of Western Australia.

The pilot called back to the two lone occupants holding hands behind him. "You will find some gear at the rear to make a drink. Help yourselves."

Dan raised an eyebrow and Lyn shook her head. After the long international flight from England with all needs catered for, she felt safer sitting tight until the plane landed in Albany.

Albert was waiting for them as they came through the single exit gate in the small country airport.

"You got here safe then. Give us your bag, love," he greeted them taking Lyn's luggage from her.

"Yes, and we're here to stay this time," said Dan with a wide smile on his face as he helped Albert stack their luggage at the back of his ute.

"You sure made a quick turnaround. It's only three months or so since you caused a stir by buying the house on the hill after you stayed with us. That was the first we knew you were coming back." They had stayed with him and his wife during a visit to Lyn's son and daughter-in-law the previous year. The young ones had emigrated three years earlier and were the first of their families they called on during a round the world holiday, to feel reassured all was well.

"We both always wanted to live out here and after seeing Ty a y Cerrig, that's what we're calling our house on the rock, we knew it was where we wanted to live. Things went amazingly smoothly with immigration and all the paperwork and health checks. We wondered if being in our sixties would block us, but Lyn offered to nurse in a time of emergency so maybe it tipped the scales."

They settled down for the thirty-minute run to Denmark catching up on local news from Albert's monosyllabic asides as they pointed out places they remembered from their earlier visit.

Dusk was falling as they drove up the steep drive to the house, built on the incline of a hill. Peppermint trees wafted their cool scent round about. Smoke spiralled from the wood fired burner on an outside wall.

"Water should be hot for a shower. We've put up two camp beds and there's all you'll need until your shipping container gets here. Here's the key. See you in the morning," said Albert unloading their bags.

"Thanks for everything, we won't forget it," called Dan as the ute backed down to the road and disappeared. The evening chill hustled them inside to the warmth from another wood burning stove.

They stood in a large circular room overlooking the peppermint tree tops.

On the far perimeter of the circle, a balustrade bordered a small sitting room at a higher level on the hill Bubbling with excitement Dan ran up the three steps leading to it and leaned over the balustrade.

"Friends romans and countrymen lend me your ears," he recited. "C'mon darling, bed." They slept like tops until the morning sun woke them to the reality of what they had done. Now sitting on the side of their camp beds they looked out of the windows circling one wall. Tree tops surrounded them filling the hillside down to the valley.

Yesterday, they had left England, leaving behind the pain of a broken marriage and the death of a loved one, to find liberation from emotional ties, and healing within the bond of a second marriage to a new friend and lover for they had been married for two years.

Fit and full of enthusiasm for life and adventure neither had been daunted by the move from west to east. Familiar faces were thousands of miles away and friendly voices an echo in their minds.

She turned to Dan with a question mark in her eyes.

"It's going to be fine dear. We're going to need transport straight away so that's today's agenda. First let's see what we've bought. Who would have thought accepting an invite to run a workshop on crystal healing could end up buying a property we only viewed for half an hour on our way back to Perth? Small wonder the family thought us mad especially Frank your brother."

The designer-built home was a small gem, the dream of a dying woman who filled her days living amidst beauty in this patch of forest and her nights in the care of nursing colleagues at the local hospital. Curved walls enclosed two bedrooms, a bathroom with sunken bath, the two sitting rooms and a generous kitchen. The apex of the huge rock the house was built on, thrust through the cellar beneath as if to anchor the tiny building to its side. In the shade of the forest, every window looked over ancient rocks standing like sentinels guarding the domain.

During a brief inspection with the sales agent, each had stored an image of a corner that appealed. Now the pieces could be put together in the slow walk from room to room with sighs of satisfaction sealing the end of a big decision and a long journey. Dan made tea before, mugs in hand, they stepped into the glory of nature on the veranda running around three sides of the house.

Brilliantly coloured Rosellas called from the low branches, a kookaburra looked at them from a nearby rock and startled parrots flew across the hill in flashes of green and purple. The early dawn air, still damp on the peppermint leaves, swept a wave of perfume before the sunbeams slipping down through the trees to warm them. Dan leaned over the veranda.

"We can extend this area to make a patio extension which will give us a carport below and somewhere to stack our logs. Let's look around the hill."

The large corner block followed the rise of a vertical wall of rocks bursting through a lane running to the summit, further uphill. The lower road curved through a tree lined cutting, on the hillside leading down to the valley. They made their way through the tall grasses and flowering shrubs along tiny paths snaking downhill to the corner where lane met road. Leaf litter, piled high, hid many paths and the treacherous little rocks they stumbled upon. The roadside entrance drive gave way to a large patch of empty ground filling the space between their house and a rugged line of rocks dividing them from their nearest neighbour.

"We can plant an orchard here with fruit we've never heard of probably. I'm so happy Lyn, how about you," he queried still concerned for her morning's doubts. He looked so young, so eager to live to the full again, it caught at her heart strings.

"I can't wait to get started on making this even more beautiful if that's possible. I'm going to get some breakfast, come on."

By the door they found a box of vegetables and fruit and a plastic bag full of the wriggling movements of fresh caught herrings. Albert had visited.

A few days later, as owners of a good, second-hand campervan, they made the forty-kilometre journey to Albany. After the breath-taking view of the harbour where the early settlers landed, they loaded up with stores. Negotiating the twists and curves of the narrow lanes taking them home they felt they had lived there for years. Now was an ever-present wonder in the dream line of past and future.

An invite, from an unknown couple, to a small party given to introduce them to the village, enlarged their group of friends. They moved through a room full of people during a lazy evening of small talk making future contacts among some of the five hundred or so villagers of Denmark. They left the tall A-frame shaped house with its apex pointing to a night sky studied with brilliant stars. Walking through the bush Lyn and Dan felt their radiance foretell nothing but joy. The following morning the container arrived with the furniture from England.

The days filled with endless activity setting the house to rights. Dan engaged contractors to carry out his idea of carport and patio deck with a small summerhouse adjoining the kitchen corner. A mountain of dried leaves grew near the drive ready for burning later. On the highest point of the property, he built a three-stage compost frame behind another deck. There they would sit and look out over a panorama of forest and distant hills. By the end of a month he was satisfied enough to agree to taking some time off to reconnoitre the area in the campervan.

They made no plans as to destination. On the night before leaving, he lay back against his pillow contentment in every line of his face when suddenly it contorted, and a violent tremble shook his body. Lyn leaped out of bed and ran to his side to check his pulse. It was racing and he was struggling to breathe. She got him up on all the pillows to hand and raced to the phone for help.

The ambulance crew was quick to arrive and manoeuvre the stretcher down the ramp after giving a prescribed injection of morphine to stabilise his condition. At the local cottage hospital, the doctor made a diagnosis of cardiac failure needing further investigation.

Lyn went home, to lay sleepless in the room overlooking the treetops, praying to God for his safe return. England seemed so very far away.

Dan rallied and came home subdued and thoughtful about their future. Arrangements were in place for tests to be done in a Perth city hospital and until then he was advised to rest and live as quietly as possible. A near neighbour popped in for a chat to cheer him up and allay his fretting over his inability to share the load of jobs they had still to do.

"My Dorothy has a heart condition Dan. She's had it for years, but she gets around it and still manages the stairs and a good roast on Sundays," he confided. "You'll be right as rain once you get up to Perth."

Getting to the city was easier said than done. In the past, public transport had connected to Albany by a train. It ambled through bush and scrub so slowly passengers would jump off at the front to pick flowers then scramble back on to the rear carriage of the old locomotive they called 'I'll walk beside you'. Things hadn't changed much except for the vehicle. They boarded a long bus stopping at Albany for refreshment before continuing the five-hour trip to Perth.

Dan was told he needed three by-passes to survive. The specialist offered to perform the new surgery for arterial occlusions the following week. He fervently accepted the major surgery. Before returning home, they booked Lyn into a nearby hotel for the duration of his stay.

The days before admittance were lost to memory before the long walk in the early hours of the morning beside the trolley taking Dan to theatre. As she held his hand beneath the coverings, he gave a reassuring squeeze then continued the meditation he had begun earlier in the morning. He opened a sleepy eyelid to wink, then he was gone beyond swinging doors to deep anaesthesia and the surgeon's saw to his sternum.

He made a good recovery on the strength of his strong willing to conquer pain, and his determination to see their adventure through for a few more years. The line of metal staples laddering his chest was the only visible sign of his ordeal.

Spring was around the corner by the time they were settled back in Ty a y Cerrig. The wood burning stove indoors supplied twenty-four-hour comfort for Dan with very little effort from Lyn. The water heater was replaced by a modern gas heater and the village stores provided sufficient produce to get by on. There was plenty of time to look around their own neck of the woods and leave travel for later.

They did not have to look far to quicken their interest. The folk who lived on the hill were a bunch of characters with the same zest for life that had brought the latest newcomers there. Italian prisoners of war had sparked to life, the sleepy little village on the southern tip of the continent, followed by the talents of migrants in postwar years and a colonial exodus from around the world. A big hippy colony lived up in the hills north of Denmark.

Albert's wife, Olive had placed the notice for somebody to run a workshop on an occult science subject, that Lyn answered on their first visit. She had chosen Magnetic Crystal Therapy, studied under Harry Oldfield of good repute in England. The two-day visit was taken up with lectures and activities, leaving little time to get to know Olive. This reticent woman had begun a small group of friends to seek spiritual knowledge.

Albert the good neighbour who left the vegies and fish on the doorstep took them round his garden. The small parch was bright with flowers and cram full of vegetables. Lyn was surprised to hear Olive's group had grown larger and she soon to be confirmed as a spiritualist preacher.

"The Missis has got mixed up with the spiritualists. More fool her I say. I won't give a bar of it. Come and see my chooks."

Despite Albert's suspicions he dressed up in a dark suit and took round the collection bag at the well-attended services in the village some months later. By then, it was the local vicar who took a dim view of the movement. On Sundays Dan and Lyn joined the congregation filling his small church built for the needs of early settlers. Their circle of friends grew.

Taking a gentle morning walk down the hill and stopping to admire a garden full of large coloured poppies, they were greeted by a wiry little man leaning on his garden fence. Dobrik left his native Poland many years ago to find work in the local saw mill. A big source of jobs, it provided fine grained woods from the old forests which local craftsmen turned into beautiful furniture. With the depletion of the forests and growing awareness of the damage to the earth, sawmills were closing under pressure from public opinion. Dobrik, nearing retirement, was first to be laid off. The settlement the mills gave him allowed for the purchase of his plot of land and the modest dwelling which were his pride and joy.

"I'm Dobrik and I will make you a special cup of coffee if you step inside my home," he offered.

"Thanks, Dobrik, that sounds good. Your poppies are fantastic. I've never seen such a variety of colour and large blossoms," Dan said.

"They will be gone soon," was the rueful response. "The police think I am up to no good growing them and have ordered me to destroy them. Aren't they the most beautiful sight?" Puzzled that their new-found paradise harboured such draconian authorities they went in to the tiny kitchen where Dobrik busied himself with the coffee. He popped large pieces of chocolate into the steaming mugs and when Lyn asked for some honey produced a large dustbin full of raw honey.

This became the topic of conversation about bees and trees and certain wild flowers whose nectar was gold dust to the honey man.

"We need a table for our kitchen," said Lyn. "Where can we find a craftsman?"

"Go and see Michael, he's Glenville's son-in-law. He's reckoned one of the best with a plane and chisel. The old man owns the top of the hill and property roundabouts. Michael's house is below Glenville's."

With Dan quickly gaining strength they set out a few days later to climb the steepest part of the hill to find Michael. Small properties hid in the trees on both sides of the track but none had Glenville or Michael's names. Most were retreats from the summer heat in the city and lay empty except for one tiny A-frame puffing a spiral of wood smoke into the peppermint trees.

"Let's knock and see if they know where Michael lives," said Lyn trotting down the path to a door festooned with spiders' webs and their occupants. A tiny woman with an elfin face smiled an enquiry from her open door.

"You're the newcomers down the hill. Come in and I'll show you how to get there," she answered their request. Once inside Lyn looked around, then whipped round to make a quick exit bumping into Dan who looked as if about to do the same thing. There had been many warnings of the danger these creatures threatened and now they stood in a room full of spider's webs hanging from ceiling to furnishings, veiling pictures, daisy chaining table and chair legs together. All had large round bodies in their centres.

"Sit down, they won't hurt you. I love them and cannot bring myself to break their webs," Jill reassured them.

"What about the poisonous ones," asked Dan?

"I don't encourage them and usually put them on a bush with some of their web. Now let me show you how to find Michael's place. You must go well into the forest near the top and you will see the roof of Glen's house to guide you. Call there first."

Thanking her they left with relief to cross the lane and plunge into dense trees to continue the climb to the top until Lyn pointed and panted,

"Look there it is, that's glass reflecting the sun, it must be a window." The window turned out to be a massive glass dome supported by glass walls encircling the crown of the hill. Within, a house stood in a large clearing and, like Ty a y Cerrig, sloped downhill. They had come upon it from behind. Moving round to find an entrance, they passed a brick-built alcove jutting out at an angle. It housed a lavatory open to wind and rain and the most beautiful view one could imagine.

"Well that's not it. Go down further," suggested Dan when a voice behind them spoke up.

"Follow me, I'm Glen. What brings you up here?"

"We're looking for Michael to talk about a table," Dan offered following Glen into his home. Close behind Lyn gave a little gasp of pleasure as she turned full circle within the spacious ring enclosed by the glass walls.

She focused on the distant Darling Range sliding endlessly along the skyline. Switched to the glitter of rivers twisting through forest, and the nearby sea shore and finally withdrew to the beautiful coloured slate floor beneath her feet. In a marble topped circular base the kitchen hotplate, oven and storage cupboards drew the hungry for its comforts. Empty space invited as much as the comfortable armchairs arranged in one curve of the circle. It was a veritable palace, designed by the clever architect offering them a glass of fruit juice as he waited for their comment.

"It's beautiful beyond words," breathed out Lyn. "What a perfect place to meditate."

"You can do that on Thursdays after yoga with Lyndall my girlfriend."

"Would that be the Lyndall we met in Perth on our first visit? She is a friend of Henny the home birthing advocate." It was so, leaving Lyn to send a silent prayer of thanks to God for guiding them to this blessed part of the world. Maybe they could continue their work started in England offering healing and peace to any who had need.

A tractor engine cut out nearby and the figure of a tall young man with flowing black hair strode by the window.

"My son-in-law," said Glen when he entered the room.

"Paths are cleared of leaf litter, Dad. That should take care of the snakes for a bit," he said looking enquiringly at Dan.

"These folks have come to see you about some furniture, tea or juice?"

Sitting in the comfort of the armchairs, they liked Michael's idea to carve a circular table with a central support stem in one piece. He would use the trunk of a tree which fell some years ago in a nearby forest. As they left Glenville invited them to call anytime. One more friend made.

A visit to Dan's GP for a check-up opened further fields

"You've made remarkable progress Dan," said Dr Rob, "How can you account for it?" He listened with interest to their work with The Bristol Clinic regimes and Harry Oldfield's Magnetic Resonance therapy, then sat for a space reflecting.

"How would you like to take a few of my inoperable cancer patients? They need some supplementary help to see them through a rough patch. We haven't anything in the village like your alternative."

"We'd be only too pleased to on a voluntary basis of course and if you are not happy with how we work you will tell us," beamed Dan. It was arranged for patients to contact them to avoid coercion because alternative medicine was still regarded with mistrust.

"It's happening love. We committed ourselves to healing and once you commit your service there will always be a way opened. My hands have been itching to do some work," confided Dan as arm in arm they made their way along the village high street stopping for a few words with friends here and there.

A few days later he answered the phone to a soft feminine voice asking if she could call to see them as a patient. On the day he opened the door to a young couple. A good-looking man stood protectively by a pretty woman.

"I'm Jim and this is my wife Rosaline," he initiated the meeting when Lyn joined them to listen to the rush of words from his heart's spring.

"It started in Ro's breast and now it has spread everywhere. We haven't got long and there are the children, three of them two, six and eight. It is hanging over us all the time; we're cooped up in the house and the kids know something is up. How do we cope"? He dropped his head in his hands and the woman by his side laid her hand softly on his knee. Pale skinned and slender with dark curly hair she looked with calm and resignation towards Dan her green eyes holding a spark of hope.

"Can you help us"?

"Yes, if you really want to be helped, I think we can work together for a peaceful outcome which can include your children. Can you stay for an hour now so we can begin right away? What do you think Lyn?"

"Yes of course. How long does your doctor give you Ros?"

"A few weeks at most and we want to make the best of our time."

"We can work with the essentials then. They are meditation, strong visualisation, and some discussion of beliefs and your view of life which is far simpler than it sounds. I don't think you need change your diet or make changes to the family routine because that could stress the children at this stage."

"Do you feel strong enough to give healing Dan while I show Jim and Ros how to visualise and drop their anxiety for short periods during the day?"

"We can allow some time to discuss how they feel before they go home to the family. That should start a healing that we can build on in the coming days".

"I'm ready dear," he said with the sincerity they shared when working together.

Forty-five minutes or so later Lyn made tea before they sat to chat about Jim and Rosalyn's view of life.

Like many others, they were uncertain of life's continuity as religion sermonised the mystical truths of the Book under the restriction of the church. The scientist struggled to vindicate his math when he hesitated to listen to his heart. Multitudes of sects and occult societies seductively offered the answer to the universal question of Why.

"It's the thought of losing forever the one person I know and love that hurts so. There must be something, a God I suppose but the preachers and teachers don't get around to talk together about this god. It's all about what it's done, or I've got to do. Between science and religion, I'm left with empty air to hold on to," Jim fumed.

"Empty air sounds interesting, how about empty consciousness," suggested

Dan.

"There you go you see. What do you mean by that," snapped Jim?

"All the great religions tell about it but as you say only in half truths. Buddhism, Judaism, Islam and the Hindu, all refer to the Father God of Christianity, in a more direct way Jehovah, Allah of Islam and Shiva of the Hindu but there are subtleties in them that need clarifying for the ordinary seeker, you and me," responded Dan.

"Why not go to the library and choose any book on those topics you feel comfortable with and next time we meet we can pick up on this conversation."

"In the meantime," said Lyn "I should like you to find time to make good memories for the kids and yourselves. Have you thought of taking half an hour to go down to the beach at sunset? Just you two on your own with the beauty of the evening is one idea."

"Sounds good shall we try Ro," he whispered helping her up to leave?

"Look thanks, I think you have helped us so we will be by again."

While Dan went to see their visitors off Lyn made fresh tea and joined him on the veranda where they sipped in silence reflecting on the beauty surrounding them and the horror confronting Ros.

""Three children two, six and eight, oh! Dan how heart breaking. It is they who will matter in the future with all the other children who will shape this world. We feed them worthless values and expect them to balance the false account we shall leave."

"We won't be having any children to teach so let's go down to the beach to watch the sunset," he replied.

"There's many a word spoken in jest. I could do a Sarah my dear Abraham," she giggled taking his cup.

Chapter 2: Settling

MICHAEL delivered the table. The unvarnished honey coloured circle fitted the round alcove at the end of the kitchen perfectly.

"Wonderful work Michael I don't suppose you could…"

"Sorry I'm off up north tomorrow but you could try Robin out on the Walpole road. I'd recommend him any day," was their cue to drive a few kilometres west into another wooded area.

Outside a small dwelling a saw was busy at work in the hands of a suntanned man, shirtless, with his woman by his side. They were working on a tiny chair and table in a clearing filled with similar sized furniture, cupboards and shelving, all crafted to child size perfection.

"I can make what you want in a month," he offered when they explained, "but right now Mab and I have a deadline. We open school next Tuesday in the old hall opposite the church. It's to be a pre-primary Steiner School."

"We had some connection with the East Grinstead School in England. I never imagined… will you have enough pupils? Do you need any help I teach," stammered Lyn wide-eyed with excitement?

"I have one teacher who is trained but he could do with some help. How about coming next Monday to look round when we've set it up. We've been wondering about staff and you turn up," said Robin giving a cheeky grin.

"The opening day is important. Will you come? I have my heart set on providing good education in places isolated from the city."

They left after a friendly cup of tea. Lyn took her turn to drive while Dan scanned a map of the area to find a small farm on the way back. The farmer's wife had phoned for help with her sick husband and could not leave the farm to visit Ty a y Cerrig.

A kilometre before Denmark village centre, they saw the sign Hills Farm and turned in to a welcome from two bounding red kelpies. The dogs followed the car up to the farmhouse their barking alerted the woman standing in the open doorway.

"You must be Dan and Lyn from Dr Rob," she greeted them. "I'm so glad you've come. My husband won't accept that he is dying and won't hand over running the farm to take more rest. Maybe if you talked to him about your therapy he would listen." Finishing her confidence, she made way for them to enter the cosy sitting room cum kitchen where she had been preparing a quiche in a pastry case.

"Len these are the two people we were expecting," she introduced them and went across to finish her cooking still within earshot.

He sat as straight as the chair back he leaned against in an old rocking chair. The handsome fifty-six-year-old looked at them from piercing blue eyes set in the translucent skin of the dying.

"I don't know why you have come, I don't need anybody, I've got her," he announced. "You might as well sit down now you're here."

"Thanks," smiled Dan. "We don't have to stay if..."

"No, no we can chat a bit. The doctor reckons I've got prostate cancer. I've had a bit of trouble with the water works but what can you expect around my age. I will prove him wrong because I don't intend to die as he thinks I should."

"Nothing wrong with dying when your time comes," observed Dan. "It's a matter of how you meet death. How do you think you will meet it?"

"Well I've dealt with animals since I left school and took over the farm from Dad. We've always run cattle and a dairy with a bit of breeding stock. Death comes with the stun gun and the knife. The seasons come and go, and you feel them in your blood like the weather changes and the animals' behaviour before bad weather or dying. Yes, I reckon there is something there but I'm not ready to go and find it."

"Lyn and I and many other people believe that there is something we cannot see but nevertheless is real enough for us to trust we will journey into after we finish our journey here on earth. Many faiths tell the same thing so that adds up to a lot of belief don't you agree."

Len sat forward staring at Dan then turned abruptly to Lyn.

"I want to talk to you alone privately in my room. Will you come please?" She turned to Dan who nodded as Len slowly got to his feet then followed him in to his bedroom. He eased onto the bed taking a moment to get his breath.

"I don't want to go and leave her for another man. It's wrenching my gut." He closed his eyes to avoid meeting Lyn gaze. His honesty cut through his possessive love chaining him to his pain ridden body and his adored wife. There was no point or time for ethics for Lyn felt his man might die at any minute.

"Len how deep is your love for Lisa?"

"I love her with my life, she's always come first before my needs," he fisted away some moisture on his cheek and looked for her help.

"Then let's put her first now. She is going to miss you and need you at times. I believe you can help her. Have you a favourite place on the farm?"

"Top of the hill behind the house overlooks the river. There's a fallen tree we sit on."

"May I call Lisa in with Dan to share an idea?" He nodded and she crossed to the door to call them. Lisa sat against Len's pillows, holding hands. He motioned Dan and Lyn to sit on the other side of the bed and waited expectantly.

"Whatever you believe in, I can see you trust in your abiding love. If you cannot believe in this other dimension Dan and I believe we go to when we pass over, let your deep love be a channel of feeling and memory. Lisa will you go to the top of the hill at eventide and talk to him about your problems and your loneliness? Talk as if Len stood behind you. Imagine the wisp of air caressing your cheek is his response. Sit silently for a while then come home."

Len cradled Lisa to his breast where she looked up into his eyes.

"I will dear, every evening," she promised softly.

Dan and Lyn moved out of earshot after catching his reply.

"Good I can go now," he told her with a kiss. He left that night.

Lisa managed the farm with the help of his cousin from a nearby farm. They married eventually and walked to the top of the hill every sundown.

The following Monday Dan and Lyn arrived at the old quarters of the local Returned Service League to find Robin and Mab putting the final touches to their new Steiner School project. A bearded man nearer their own age was arranging sea shells and an assortment of flowers and leaves on trays. Robin introduced him as David a Steiner teacher who was to become a close friend sharing in their lives. His origin in the highlands of Scotland coloured the soft brogue he welcomed them with, thanking Lyn for her offer of help.

"There are only five bairns at present, and I can manage easily, but later perhaps," he smiled.

"I wonder if you could take a sixth bairn," asked Lyn and explained about Jim and Rosaline's two-year-old. The toddler was welcomed, with Mab offering to pick her up on her way in from home, if the parents accepted a place in the school.

"They will feel safe leaving the little one here. Once they see how much thought you've put into furniture their child cannot help feeling at home. We will call on them today. This will allow them get a few hours together while all the children are at school."

In the village they found Ros and Jim's place, an old house with the original lace portico around the porch. Hollyhocks and roses sheltered pansies and fragrant wallflowers in profusion bordered the neat lawn they crossed to the open door.

"We saw you coming, come in," called Jim.

A comfortable litter of personal possessions overlaid a tidy room where Rosalind rested on a large couch piled with cushions. A smile lit her eyes as she raised a hand in welcome. There was little change in her appearance which radiated the calm acceptance that had impressed them on first meeting her.

Dan was explaining the purpose of their visit when a little head popped up from behind the couch. Dark lashed blue eyes took a solemn stocktaking before the rest of Sally came by the side of the couch. The tiny fair-haired flirt made straight for Dan and snuggled her hand in his.

"My mummy's going away soon. Want Mummy to come to school with me," she lisped through a gap in her teeth.

Dan's raised eyebrow semaphored to Ros whose nod had him squatting down to Sally's level.

"It is a special day tomorrow. Suppose you bring Mummy, then, on some days another Mummy will fetch you. Would you like that?" She dipped her head and returned to her hiding place behind the couch.

Jim walked to the gate with them reassuring them about fees. Jim suddenly cut in.

"Ros is holding on and I'm getting the hang of things she used to do for the kids. We go down to the beach and it's special. Somehow, we feel filled up with peace down there. Ro's has been reading some stuff about consciousness and the different levels which seem to separate beings. I'm afraid I don't get any time for that and it's a bit beyond me but so long as it helps her, I go along with it."

"Um, I recall you weren't too happy about it when you called on us. Could I suggest you look at it this way Jim? We are standing in your lovely garden and we are conscious of it. You remember planting it, you may even dream about it or a garden similar to it. You saw the garden in your dream state so you must have had a consciousness of it at that time. The idea that consciousness is something we are surrounded by in waking life isn't new. It also seems to be tucked up inside and you're in it when you dream."

Jim's eyes took on a distant look; he wasn't listening so Dan spoke a bit louder.

"What if I told you we know people who have been helped by this consciousness, to feel in touch once they are parted, whatever the reason," he asked a suddenly ready listener?

"The love you share with Rosalind is very much part of this consciousness. I like to think of love as an elixir poured into a chalice for all to sip from."

"There you go again with airy fairy ideas."

"Ah! So, love is airy fairy."

"Don't you suggest our love is not real mate," was the heated reply.

"We have great admiration for the real unconditional love uniting your family. We have never heard you selfishly begging Ros to stay longer. Your steady acceptance of her journey allows her to take this new road peacefully. We cannot see your love but it's real as consciousness is real Jim. They fill the world like the sun's light, shared by all it shines on."

Dan laid his arm across Jim's shoulders, a comrade finishing a quiet conversation.

"I don't wish to confuse you Jim, I can see you have enough to do taking care of everything. Nobody really understands the core of this mystery. Thousands have faith in some continuity, and some have experienced amazing proof of life after death. Give the idea time to settle without fighting it.

"I mean no offence so please keep in touch."

Jim bade them a quiet farewell and made his way back to his family.

The school opening was a big success with more children signing up for the morning sessions. Sally made friends with young Tom as they sorted seashells into half coconuts and hardly noticed Jim and Ros drift away to talk with Robin and his wife. Mab was true to her promise allowing Rosalind time to settle her affairs.

Three weeks after the opening she slipped away after bidding the children goodbye before they left for school one morning.

Dan and Lyn were invited to the commemoration and celebration of her life. In the garden where hollyhocks bowed over wallflowers wafting incense into the heavens, children played on the lawn their laughter innocent.

Chapter 3: Pantomime Time

DAN looked up from the local newspaper spread on his knees.

"They want people to audition for a pantomime, love. You've done a lot with drama groups. Why don't you try for a part?"

"There won't be many roles for white haired old ladies unless it is the witch and I'm not sure I want to get tied down with rehearsals. I tell you what, let's go along and see what they are doing, and we can offer to fill in the odd jobs for fun."

Lyn's long silver hair landed her the part of fairy Moonlight in Babes in the Wood, and her agility prompted the producer to add a dance routine for the fairy's entrance. Twice a week they romped through missed lines, false entrances and new friendships leading to the final week when rehearsal went on stage. The creative world of theatre revived hidden skills bringing back the old thrill of entertaining after hours of hard work, minor disputes and shared laughter.

On stage meant down on the banks of the river running through the village. Nightly rehearsals hid behind canvas screening which served to build a makeshift theatre for the week-long production and create an air of mystery in the days leading up to opening night.

The church organist was roped in, a fine ivory tickler from classical to blues. Carpenters, painters, electricians and humpers of all manner of furniture went about the task of bringing magic to children from local family groups.

They picnicked on blankets patching the steep grassy bank sloping down to the gentle river. Behind them the upper diamond lit windows dropped glow-worm lights to the sleeping fish in its depths.

Over six moonlit nights numbers burgeoned as news of the event spread to Perth and Mt Barker. Audience and cast shared common ground, caught in the same spell through an invisible proscenium arch, the door to fairyland for the entranced children.

"I never thought I would do this again and Mari has asked me to audition for a play to be put on in the Civic Hall next year. Would you mind," Lyn asked Dan as they drove away after a wild closing performance. The audience had thronged the banks weaving among the performers to thank them for their show.

"I've not felt so young and happy for years sweetheart. I enjoy watching you, filling in for prompt and chatting to the others. Why should I mind?"

The spontaneity of life shawled their hearts and minds. The wide horizons swallowed up the calculating thoughts of cities on other shores in this southern tip of a faraway land, where generous souls lived simple lives full of hope.

Throughout the long summer days of Christmas, house gatherings introduced new groups and budding producers who sought Lyn and Dan's interest sufficiently to fill the autumn and winter months ahead.

In the lazy warmth of summer, they rolled from their hammocks to cool in emerald green pools, sparkling n curves of granite rocks standing sentinel along the small bays on the coastline. They searched the horizon for an albatross from the high dunes or lay back and watch the seabirds circle overhead. The magic never ceased for them and their joy in one another increased.

One summer the camper van finally found its way up North to let them dance with the dolphins, before Shark Bay became a commercial tourist trap. They watched old movies in the outdoor theatre in Broome and tip toed over a beach full of minute crabs scuttling down to the sea. In Darwin crocodiles grinned at snakes looped on the trees lining the banks of rivers filled with lotus blooms. Small wonders filled the days until one morning Dan woke feeling very sick. He had pneumonia. The doctor gave him antibiotics and advised them to make for home.

Lyn drove for three days taking short stops to rest then took on water for the desert stretch of the journey. It was the desert which kept their spirits up.

Colours of ethereal beauty crowned the Spinifex cushions covering the desert floor. Glorious sunsets lit the skies before the peace of dark night followed the quiet solitude of day. Never had they felt the spirit of the earth so near, so comforting as it encouraged her to keep driving until late one evening, they drove up the hill to Ty a y Cerrig.

During Dan's lengthy convalescence the village telegraph informed them of plans to build small retirement units in Busselton a small township nearer Perth. Time was passing. Eight years had flown by since their emigration. and his recent scare alerted Dan to suggest they go down to meet the visiting investor in the project to see what he had to offer.

The meeting was in a room above the butcher's shop used for protest groups. Where strategies were planned to overcome the village council's latest intrusion on villagers' rights, the room filled with the elderly seeking protection in their declining years.

They listened attentively to the glowing description of life as it would be once they handed over their savings to him to build a village that had no plans to substantiate his claims. The smiling shark telling this tale glowered at any who asked why or how. He met his match in Annie the eldest and well-seasoned in the smell of a bad fish.

"Some of us will come and see the site next week. Then you can show us the plans and building permission before we divvy up our money Sir," all four foot five of her announced. She closed the meeting by walking out.

Asked if he and Lyn would reconnoitre fitted in with Dan's plans. New fields to discover and maybe the chance to choose a prime site for their home set them off in the direction of Busselton a few days later.

The building site was a wire fenced area squeezed into a corner between an industrial estate and an unofficial dump full of disused cars and household goods. Mr Shark never turned up, which was no surprise, after a journey ending in disappointment

A tree lined entrance had beckoned them into a seaside town with esplanades and attractions built around a long sandy seafront with a pier. It was the longest in the south and the main attraction at the time, stretching like a centipede on a mile of strong sturdy piles.

"Let's have a mosey around before we find a place to stay tonight," suggested Lyn.

"I noticed a scenic drive sign on the way in. Shall we try that?"

The drive across marshes bordering the seashore has that lonely eerie feel that attracts a melancholic mood bordering on mystical. The silent rise and fall of winged shapes etch darkly on the limpid skyline and the narrow lane stretches out forever.

They drove in comfortable silence until they came upon the first sign of habitation on rounding a bend revealing an inlet. At the head stood a handsome old property of some worth and in fine condition thanks to a Heritage Trust. It was the original farmstead of the first settlers in Western Australia and had many a story to tell.

Further along they passed the town flood gates bridging a river that sprang from nowhere. A couple of miles on Dan stopped the car between two proper-ties facing each other their fences at a friendly tilt towards its neighbour

The sea sang in the background of one house and through a grove of pep-permint trees they glimpsed the river flowing towards the town behind the other.

"It's so peaceful," breathed Lyn.

"See there is another house on the other side of the river and look at the all the white birds sitting in the trees along the bank. I could live here, never mind Sharkey's set-up."

"You might just do that darling," said Dan, getting out to walk a few paces up the lane where a board was nailed to the fence.

"I thought so, it's for sale. How about having a look?" She scrambled out joining him to peer over the fence.

"We couldn't manage, look at all that grass to cut. There must be two acres here and the house seems pretty old," she pointed out walking towards the gate and along a path to the front door. A son-in-law said he was renting from the original owners while he and his wife built in the town.

"But if you'd like to be shown around. My mother-in-law and her sister couldn't bear to be parted. They persuaded their husbands to build the neigh-bouring houses until age moved them nearer town last year," he explained as they walked along the bank of a river flowing through the marshlands.

Two old barns and an outside loo hiding behind an ornate veranda were part of the deal. In the house, the cooking was done on a wood burning oven top from the original build. Peering round a dark corner of the draughty shower Lyn thought she saw a little shadow disappear along the dusty window ledge. The remaining rooms with a wood burning fireplace in the bedroom, were graceful lace curtained reminders of days gone by.

"It's in good condition although it's old and we are willing to talk about the price," said their guide gesturing them to join his wife in a corner of the veranda running all round the house. "Our agent is in the high street and may still be open."

"Who cuts all the grass," asked Lyn?

"We will throw in the drive on mower in the barn. It does a good job in no time." After being told the price Dan shook hands on a possible deal.

"We will call on the agent and he'll let you know."

"Well what do you think," he asked starting the car? "Shall we go and find this agent?"

"Didn't we have this conversation before and end up in Ty a y Cerrig," she teased ending with an enthusiastic, "let's go." Banes and Co.'s agent was ready for them.

"Sorry, someone else is interested and will view tomorrow. We can take you round after them if you wish." They knew it was a spoof, but it had the desired effect of pricking their desire which Dan hid behind a casual reply.

"Quite, we are only passing through and looking around at present. It depends on what is being asked and maybe a builder's check-up if we decide," Having bounced the ball back in their net, there it stayed until next day when a young couple needed to come up with a mortgage for a sponsored family refuge project. Banes asked Dan for an offer if they were unsuccessful and surprise, surprise they were.

Flushed with success and now thoroughly in love with the place they agreed to buy without more ado. The move to Busselton was not as dramatic as their last one and the train of events culminating in packing up and bidding goodbye to friends went smoothly, leaving some funds from the Denmark sale to boost their bank balance.

The different environment made the most impact. From forest to flatland and seascape; from designer-built to the nineteen twenties challenged their flexibility to adapt. Dan cleared their private pathway to the beach for daily swims while Lyn got the better of a grumpy old drive on mower and tore around an acre of grassed area. The kitchen stove repaid their extra attention by welcoming them to a warm kitchen for breakfast, but the not so warm shower room sent Lyn shrieking from the toilet.

"Dan, Dan there's a big rat. Come quickly."

The constant 'Aaah' of the ravens decided the name 'Ravens Rest' for their patch. So many little creatures became part of their daily life. The bob tailed lizard living in an old drainage pipe in the barn came under Dan's protection from tiger snakes. The magpies singing on the front porch for bread crumbs, the flat mullets cruising along the river bed below the water rats' holes in the bank were as familiar as their neighbours across the river. Ducks waddled and black and white fantail fairy wrens flitted about the verandas. One veranda became the site of a dispute with a possum some weeks later when Dan noticed a wet patch on the bedroom ceiling. He took to star gazing on one side of the veranda until one evening he came in triumphant with discovery.

"I saw the possum tonight and I know where it comes and goes. Tomorrow I'll get some wire to seal the gap, leaving room for it to come out, then bingo a couple of nails and our squatter is gone." All went according to plan except for the resulting fury of a possum that spat and chattered anger outside its old home before camping out on a nearby rafter.

They enlisted the help of the ranger who brought a possum box and high ladder to install a new home in one of the trees. When netted, the possum turned out to be a very pregnant she who turned her back on the new home after a chase around the tree tops. After the fourth time, the ranger left her on a nearby branch. They turned their backs and walked off. No longer the centre of attraction, she nipped into the box and had her family in due time.

Once the euphoria of living in their two-acre heaven settled, memories of Ty a y Cerrig rose to question the comfort Ravens Rest afforded. A builder came to discuss renovating and informed them that the place was riddled with white ant and needed to be bulldozed down. It was devastating news and their years and funds were diminishing.

"There is enough money to buy one of the packaged homes on the market now, I will look into it tomorrow. A new build will add value and we can be comfortable," reasoned Dan clearing the anxious cloud of doubts assailing them both.

"We were a bit mad, but I don't regret buying this place do you. I know we are in our seventies, but I never feel any different. Your heart doesn't give you any problems or don't you tell me dear," asked Lyn?

"I'm fine my love. Cheer up we can take this step in our stride. We can get on main water supply instead of depending on rain water tanks."

True to his promise the following weeks he sought planning permission and took the necessary steps for the day to come when the builder arrived to put up the house on its prepared foundation.

The comfortable sound of hammering interspersed the homely sounds they loved. When they heard the soft tapping of the tiler laying an Indian slate floor in the living area, they knew the opalescent sheen on the honey brown tiles would soon glow in in the light of the all-night wood fired burner in the corner of the room.

The magpies and fairy wrens moved with them and all was well. Well enough to go down to the Old Ship tavern in the town after a wind blow walk along the pier. Warmed by huge three-foot logs on an open fire, they lunched in royal style.

The old pier stretched out for a mile into crystal clear green waters. Twice a day the toy town sized train took passengers to its terminal. Those who preferred, walked past the line of fishermen casting a rod before sitting to dream with a wary finger on the line. The walkers' reward was to sit on the stout bollards at the end of the train line and imagine being on a liner surrounded by ocean before hopping back over rail tracks, smugly satisfied you were the better for the effort.

"We had better call on the RSL and tell them where we are," said Dan. The Veterans looked after financial concerns for the two, but the Returned Services League was a social outlet and a source of voluntary help. A pert seventy-year-old ginger head greeted them while they were checking out the notice board.

"Can I help you? I am the secretary of the War Widows group," said Betty. When they left the club, she had persuaded them to agree to use their home for a group of ex-servicemen with prostate cancer. After the usual recommendation and the organisation's approval, they were to offer alternative therapy.

"It looks as if we are in business again. Let's see how many turn up before we plan a course. It's a good setting for a relaxed start and we've done this before," mused Dan starting the car.

"Do you want to go along to the meditation group she offered to introduce us to?"

"Yes," Lyn said looking with interest at a small theatre where the local repertory company performed. They were settling in.

A group of six men turned up for the first therapy session, all ex-servicemen from the allied forces working in Asia and Europe under UN directives since the end of World War Two.

They carried themselves well and sat hands on knees, feet planted defensively apart with a question mark in the eye as they faced Lyn in the living room. Used to the first meeting atmosphere, Dan handed round some cookies and Lyn poured tea. He sat close to her to allow questions to come to both although she answered from her greater knowledge of the illness.

Her service association with men as well as women fitted Lyn to talk candidly and with ease about a very private matter to these men. Some had gone into civilian jobs until retirement; others were not employable through age or health. What mattered to them now was what was going on inside them, their manhood and their relationship with their partners.

Tension eased as physiological matters were explained to their satisfaction, filling in the gaps left during specialist consultations because they hesitated to ask questions. The men shared the after effects of treatment in jocular fashion, but all hedged around what they most feared; impotency in their marriage if the prostate was removed or the cancer returned unchecked.

She chose one man who had been generous in sharing his side of his marriage, trusting her judgement was sound.

"How has your wife taken this? Do you talk about the future and your sex life? It is quite a shock for both of you but one that can be absorbed as you discover the real depth of love,"

"She's been fine, and she's used to managing, with me being away quite a bit but we don't talk about it really." There was a general murmur of assent until a thin sandy haired man spoke up. He was the youngest in the group looking about fifty years old.

"I wish I could say the same. My wife left me a week after I told her the news and I haven't seen her since." An uneasy shifting in chairs, as the others looked at him askance, settled when Dan got up to take the tea tray to the kitchen. He gave the confidant's shoulder a firm clasp.

"You aren't the first man we've heard this story from. I'm sorry it's happened to you. Why don't you all bring your wives to the next meeting to talk matters over? Stan you bring a friend with you because that is the way we usually work. Lyn will start you off today while I wash the dishes."

Before the next meeting there was time for Lyn to get involved with the local drama group enriching their growing circle of friends.

Betty's meditation group was run by a spirited old Canadian whose wife occasionally slipped outside to smoke one more cigarette. The couple's early years were at the whim of dockyard gaffers picking one man from the long queue turning up daily for back breaking work. They decided to move on and see what the world had to offer two loyal companions whose friendship Dan and Lyn valued until his heart gave out with his wife at his side.

Life was simple and easy going, enlivened with small incidents like Lyn going down to their landing stage on the river with tea for some local fishermen netting mullet. Unaware they were poachers she was aiding and abetting, she returned to the house with a dish of fresh caught fish as the rangers turned up by the landing stage. A small boat, tied to the same landing stage, sent Dan to reprimand a cheeky boater.

It was a surprise birthday present from Lyn tor exploring the Vasse River. An outboard motor was supplemented with oars and muscle as they bumped over limestone deposits in the shallow places. When he relinquished the rowing to her, after ever shorter periods, concern flickered away in the laughter of the next moment.

Visits from family were occasions to explore further afield, take river cruises and make a fuss of the visitors. Lyn's remaining younger sister came unexpectedly one summer.

An excited wait outside the arrivals gate ended with them barely recognising her languid entry in the stream of passengers. Lyn recalled the nubile young acrobatic dancer she made a forbidden journey along the autobahn to visit during the war. When Joy's Ack Ack unit released her to Stars in Battledress, she danced her way into many a heart. Now her changed appearance reminded Lyn that time was passing.

"Hello darling, long time no see," she greeted them in the soft drawl men loved. Her curls, cut into a short cap of touched up chestnut, enhanced her profile and the laughter lines crinkling her eyes.

Dainty food was prepared which she took a long time to swallow. Chaperoned sea bathes were taken to bolster her frailty, but she assured them she was well and even managed a lone encounter with a large tiger snake with calm aplomb.

In the departure lounge at the airport her goodbye kiss was brief, her smile enigmatic.

"'Bye darling, lovely seeing you here's a little keepsake," and she floated through the departure door.

On Joy's return to England her state declined quickly. After her brave effort to make the long journey she had kept it secret that she was dying.

So were some of the RSL group of cancer sufferers. Dan had taken to sitting with the men listening to Lyn give visualisations and meditation techniques. He joined them in carrying out her instructions.

"That was clever of you darling to engage with the boys, it breaks down barriers and gives me their trust." Dan gave a non-committal lift of his shoulders.

"What luck Stan had a recently widowed cousin to come with him. With the right support he might make it and so should the bus driver, their PSA counts are down."

Both men did beat their cancer and were still working a year later. The remaining four met the approach of death calmly. As man and wife gave of their hearts unconditionally from the ever-full cup of compassion, the new love discovered opened hidden strengths. The wives became close friends and were a comfort to one another at parting time.

The property took more time to manage than expected. Dan tired soon after any exertion he attempted, leaving Lyn to fill in the gap and finish the job in hand. He took more and more to his armchair by the window, his apologetic smile saying it all, until finally he spoke out over morning coffee. She was waiting for his words.

"I'm wondering if it's time to move to something smaller love. I feel uncomfortable watching you on the mower all morning. Maybe I made a mistake and ought not to have…"

"No don't think like that," she cut in. "Look at the fun we would have missed but you are right. It's time to move on but where, and will we have enough to buy another home?"

"I think we can sub-divide our plot. The council has been trying for years to jump in and get rights to the river bank which is ours at present. We have a chance of selling to two buyers or one who wants an investment if they will let us sub-divide in return for river rights." As always, Dan had planned ahead.

The council meeting ended in their favour with a satisfied town planner giving permission. They left his office with their own plans to spruce up their wares for a settled property market.

"The barns will need something done to hide the rust on their roofs," Lyn commented as they stood in the high street.

"Dan can we buy some green paint while we are here?"

For the next two weeks visitors held conversations with a pair of shapely legs as she made muffled replies behind the leafy branches above them.

Resigned rebukes to husbands unwise enough to remark "fine shape for their age," as they turned from an overlong look at the treetops, were met with "I meant the trees my dear. They are in fine shape eh?" Above them Lyn smiled to herself.

Interest in Ravens Rest was sufficient to encourage them to start looking for themselves in nearby Bunbury City. Lured by an old steam train link many commuters, working in the capital, had settled there.

Late one afternoon a fruitless search ended the day. They stood just outside of town, under a bridge spanning a wide river, at the foot of a hill.

"That's it then," sighed Dan "this is a beautiful stretch of river, shall we drive up the hill and enjoy the view before we go home?"

"Must we, I'm tired dear and there's the long drive back?"

"Up the hill and then back home, promise," he cajoled so up they went.

At the crest the hinterland stretched out for miles to a hazy blue never never-land and the river all but ran past the doorsteps of the few houses on the far side of the road. They sat and revelled in the sight.

"There must be something further along the coast. We'll have to keep looking," she reckoned. "Let's go now."

He made a slow turn of the wheel to bring them alongside the row of houses and there was the sign. A neat little bungalow on the peak was for sale.

"To tell the truth I had a feeling in my bones," he confessed taking the agent's name and details. "One more stop then we'll start back?"

They moved home two months later although the tiny bungalow turned out to be a four bedroomed house running back to a small lawn. Some fifteen feet below its fence line the vendor had planted a sunken orchard and a small vineyard with all the ardour of an Italian farmer. "

"I should be able to manage it Dan and look at the fruit we'll get," Lyn commented on their first inspection.

"It's lovely soil, I can plant a few vegetables," he offered.

The change improved his health and he abandoned ideas of checking on his health for the time being. They explored new territory socially as well as locally, often driving far into the Darling Ranges and beyond, returning at nightfall tired and happy.

Nagging doubts still dogged him about the pneumonia attack up north. Men had died of it during the war. Crackpot schemes toughened men up on manoeuvres carried out in winter when his unit slept in the lea of snow filled ditches. After embarking for Malta or north Africa's heat a few men died before they saw action. Was the past catching up on him? What seeds were sewn in the East?

His thoughts dodged the issue until he decided to have a talk with Lyn one evening. They sat on the front veranda with a glass of wine to watch the sunset over the distant hills.

"One of us has to be alone one day love. Have you thought about that?"

"Not really Dan because the volunteer work, I do with palliative care nurses has made death part and parcel of life. It's tough and I only hope it isn't me first."

"Only a man can understand the fear of leaving a woman to fend on her own with no family at hand. Children are unpredictable and less caring now it seems. Andrew means well but he has his own battle with ill health and an unstable lifestyle."

"I worry about him, about all of them in fact. Our generation seems like the last of a breed with the knowhow to survive so come on out with it. What's on your mind?"

"A retirement village perhaps," he hazarded with a rueful smile. They upped stakes once again to be near extra medical services.

When they moved in, the village was unfinished, roads unsurfaced, swimming pool empty and a small group of new residents were backing up the owners of the project. They were competing with hard faced business Investors, in a budding new industry. Deals were made with builders to plant villages in fast diminishing spaces, where vaunted services promising to care until the end soon made their own exit.

Dan and Lyn offered to answer emergency night calls as temporary volunteers for the village staff of two. At a meeting of the resident's council Dan shared his hopes.

"At least we are in the unique situation where we have a big say in how this place is run even if we missed out on being a title holder which was the original plan."

"Don't be so sure of that. There's a buzz an American group are bidding for this place'" said one wise in village law. His surmise was a reality within a year.

From then on, the hopes and savings of many shrank under the stranglehold of the sharks. In later years government leeches would ensure that seniors partly compensated for a collapsed mining boom.

For Dan and Lyn, the present moment was too precious to dwell on such concerns. They crowed with pleasure over every little triumph the residents' council group won to make life more comfortable as the village took shape and soon became a beautiful setting for their little bungalow.

Chapter 4: Trecking

NIGHT trips to the bathroom began to disrupt Dan's sleep enough to finally send him to his doctor where a group of men sat in a room. Some were with their wives and others on their own waiting. It was Dan's second visit to the big man now calling him into his consulting room. The preliminary shuffling of papers preceded portentous news for Dan waiting with his customary quiet composure.

"You've got prostate cancer Dan, but I can offer surgery in your case. I'll arrange it for the next list in a week's time. All right?"

Back in the car Dan looked at the woman who was his friend, companion and lover. She shared his love for his first wife Olive in a trio unseparated by death's borderlines.

"I will carry the baggage for this leg of the journey," he decided. Looking into a steady gaze shadowed with sorrow, he looked back on all the good times she'd opened out for them when they came across the oceans.

"It's a bit of a blow but we'll get through this love."

"Of course, we will," she smiled, "we always do."

So, it was that Dan lost his manhood but never his strength of will to continue his journey with Lyn in his role as protector. Pain was hidden, bleeds kept secret as walks gradually became a shuffle around the village gardens. One morning saw them sitting together, hands clasped waiting.

"What a gem our nurse is. I couldn't have lifted you up from the floor without her help my love." She stroked his hand as much to soothe herself as Dan.

"It will be for the best dear. I didn't reckon on the growth being in my bladder from the beginning and now my time is up. I will be going on the great adventure, but Olive and I will be waiting for you." The words came slowly as he fought off the effect of the secondary brain tumours which caused his fall in the early hours of the morning.

A paramedic came through the door to see two old lovers, their tears spotting the arm of his wheelchair and spilling down her cheeks. He shared the pain of their parting as he gently lifted Dan on to the stretcher.

"We will drive to Palliative Care slowly my dear to allow you to follow us. Mind how you drive now. Are you ready?"

Lyn drove behind the ambulance to an old country hospital set among trees where birds flew to sit upon his window sill and kind hands nursed Dan. The soft voices that gave comfort as she sat by his side, called her to come back quickly one dark night.

In the small hours, she drove home behind the hearse, dipped her lights to their parting signal and watched them drive into the distance before she turned into the village.

In the bed they had shared she curled into a tight ball with her loss. Of a sudden the coverlet quivered as if tiny feet were running across the quilt. Scared of mice she jolted up in the lamplight. Nothing! The ripple ebbed and left. Dan had come to say 'Goodbye.'

Chapter 5 :Gershon

LYN set about moving nearer to her son's family by advertising the village home for sale. An answer came one day when scones were light, chairs set to invite.

A knock sounded on the front door. The open aperture was filled with his presence. A tall man, broad shouldered and sparse, hesitantly looked towards her. She made an old friend welcome as she gestured towards Dan's usual chair by the window.

He had called some months before, after his wife Lalla's passing, only to find Dan was terminally ill. His recent brush with death moved him to shoulder his loneliness and leave them to face their own parting.

The four had been friends with decided views on old age and infirmity. There had been a tacit agreement to look out for one another but as is the way when all is well, tomorrow would do to settle final details. He eased down, guarding his back, looking about the room before his eyes followed her on her way to the kitchen.

She set down the tea tray and sitting across from him poured tea and made small talk, but it was apparent all was not well, and he desperately needed to talk to someone.

Dear reader please pause awhile for Gershon's story.

Chapter 6: Gershon's Story

WHILE passion rules my senses, I am a prisoner in my body.

My dear readers may I introduce myself. My name is Gershon, born in 1923 in a ghetto in Lodz, Poland. In my youth labelled as a Jew under German occupation, my life changed to one of many incredible experiences when I was fifteen years old. By 1939 the Nazi Occupation had become threatening and soon after the Germans occupied Lodz, they seized any males on the street to work for them. I was one of them. At fifteen I was a tall gangling boy, broad shouldered with strong hands] a shy youngster. Sensitive to my world, I was happy to be on my way to my apprenticeship with the carpet weaver that morning. I still felt the shock of witnessing violence in the home for the first time.

At the meal around the extended lid of the box table, which housed provisions, their voices broke my daydreaming. Crockery and food flew in all directions as mother whipped the tablecloth up in the air in response to my father's gently sarcastic 'Taki you'.

Crippled with scoliosis of the spine, affecting her chest and shoulder, much younger and more active than him, their union had been practical but short on love as she ruled the family. She gave me all her love as she guided me through my growing years. She was stepmother to my widowed father's two older sons, now grown men.

Morta, my father, was deeply religious and took me to the synagogue where spoken Hebrew was foreign to me. Father rarely spoke, so the ceremonies were never explained, but I loved them both.

That raw cold dawn, I was ordered to join the group aboard an open truck then hunker down from the cutting East wind as we drove to the forest. As the truck rolled under the forest canopy of tall birch, my morning tension increased to anger with what lay ahead. A rifle butt jabbed my shoulder.

"Work Juden rats." I reached for the small hand saw at my feet and went to the wide bole indicated. The work was hard and without rest or food. Slow progress quickened frequently by brutal beatings until the end of daylight.

In the gloom we stood bruised and hungry, shivering in the evening chill, watching the young soldiers eat their hearty rations. Tormenting began again as they barracked us.

"Want some Jew boy? Dance for your supper and sing us a song," they jeered, holding out scraps of bread. "Dance or else."

We formed a circle and began to dance, singing an old Polish nursery rhyme, until some bread, thrown at us, took the edge off our empty bellies.

We were tipped out of the truck in the town square. I limped home to reach my mother, a tiny hunchback who poured love into her only child. She had been waiting near crazed with fear for my safety when I did not return from the weaver.

She ran to the dirt encrusted creature standing inside our room. Her arms enfolded a bundle of volcanic fury, spitting out hate, before erupting into a storm of body shaking sobs.

Mother patted my calloused hands to sooth me.

"There were happy times when you went up to play with your two cousins or visited your uncle's family to play with his children and their friends. Those times will come again." She silently made plans to rearrange my future.

After German occupation of Lodz, her quick mind had found ways to make life bearable in the three-storey house, we shared with family and neighbours. The night baker even shared the big double bed with Morta for he rented Liba's half by day and she made a little money. She and I slept there by night.

When I reached fourth grade in school, at thirteen, she apprenticed me to a carpet weaver.

I was awed with the complexity of the Jacquard loom hanging from the ceiling, and spent extra time teaching myself how it worked, when the teacher was absent. I knew she watched through the weaver's window. Content that my future looked bright, she would go to open her stall in the market, trading goods unredeemed from small loans she had given to others. Her acumen with money provided good food for our family, cosseting me with the best of everything. She kept a sharp eye on the easy way I exchanged the fresh herrings, she had packed for my lunch, to crafty friends offering yesterday's stale fare.

Yesterday, the Nazi Occupation ended her dream, when they plucked me off the street on my way to the weaver's home. Before I openly reacted to their bullying domination, she acted quickly.

Moving across the one room we called home, she opened a small cupboard on the wall and reached for a bottle. It held the remains of the brandy bought for my father to lessen his agony when dying from untreated and unmedicated cancer.

Sitting by my side, her arm across my still heaving shoulders, she began to talk.

"Sip this and listen very attentively to what I am going to say Gershon. You are in danger of losing your temper with the forest guards and they may shoot you. Do you understand?" At my nod, she continued.

"You must go somewhere safe for a while, but you will come back to me."

"Can't we go together," I interrupted repeatedly, as she continued to expand her ideas. Finally, I agreed to her plan even though I was strongly attached to her, as my only teacher and guide.

A few days later, strangers came to the house. She talked earnestly to them, beseeching them to take care of her son. She gave them all her savings and me a small bag of clothing. Crying unashamedly, we embraced and kissed for the last time.

I now know that she closed the door knowing that a hump back was doomed. She made her final sacrifice next day, after I was missed from the labour squad. She opened the same door, to hear a barked "Cummen" She marched to the cattle trucks heading for a concentration camp and died in the gas ovens.

I began the journey to Russia, confident I would be back with my family in a short while. I travelled by train with the strangers and a few others until we were near the border then began to walk by night through a forest until we reached Russian territory. A lorry took us to a synagogue filled with refugees. Standing amidst so many displaced beings, their babble and the confusion shook me to the core,

"We are just going to find somebody. We will be back," said one of the smugglers disappearing into the moving mass. I never saw them again. They stole my bereft mother's savings when they broke their promise to introduce me to a safe home.

Moving outside away from the rank odour in the synagogue and the turmoil, I was stunned with fear and betrayal. Drops of loneliness stung my eyes. Now memory must serve in the long vigil of seeking my mother in my dreams. Her scent, a blend of the markets, our home, the bed we shared, her essence, wrung tears from the secret places of my heart.

The Rabbi's voice was comforting as he took me to a corner of the synagogue.

"Do not worry Gershon, we will feed you and take care of you. You will meet good people who will open their homes to you on the day of Shabbat. Come, get some sleep,"

I spent my first night sleeping on a crowded floor, watching armies of lice covering the floorboards. Next day smiling Jewish citizens came.

"We can give you work to help with your keep. You will sell cigarettes on the streets for a few roubles." They took me to their home on Shabbat to share a family meal and join in with the dancing and ritual observances. Saturday became a day to look forward to in my new life until, in 1939, the Russian bureaucracy needed to mobilise young workers to go to Siberia. At this period Russia had not entered into war with Germany.

Thrilled and excited because it was said the Communist ideals embraced everybody, we travelled in cattle trucks for many days. The journey finally finished, far from any city, in a Siberian village set aside for industry. The freezing cold was unlike any I had known but the warmth of welcome from the villagers during the two days of rest filled me with hope. A vast barrack room, filled with endless rows of beds, became my next home.

Our group, the new work force, was no longer hungry since only limited rationing was practiced. The villagers were very good to us and later, in the 1941 siege, starved alongside us and died like some of us, from starvation.

We were taken to a factory manufacturing heavy aluminium. The workshop was dark and separated into spaces where many different stages of the work were allocated to groups who assembled, painted and finished the products.

Along with others I was put outside to work in freezing temperatures. We had warmer clothes and boots and though the quality was poor, it gave some protection. Six days a week, through a long working day we dismantled old machinery with heavy hammers.

Come nightfall, in the light of fires, we loaded our work on to a cart drawn by two powerful Shire horses, for delivery to the factory floor for recycling. Inside, we helped unload the cart and under dim lighting helped the assembly line until the end of the shift. At the end of the day, my whole body was wracked with pain until I fell asleep from sheer exhaustion. My efforts did not go unobserved however, and one day the manager called me aside.

"You are a good worker. Would you like to work inside on the assembly line?" Soon I was supervising a group of workers, where my gift with machinery earnt approval. One day, a scuffle broke out in a far corner of the shed. Paulina returned to her table, holding a still wriggling rat by its tail. She drew her finger across her throat as she sucked some blood from a small knife. Next morning, I noticed a fresh wound on the back of Isaac's hand. I wondered whose blood stained the blade in their struggle to live.

The constant pace of work deadened my ever-present grief for my mother, and in its way was a reprieve from my emotional stress.

The invasion of Russia began in 1941 and times changed drastically for the worse. Working hours were extended to twelve-hour shifts and only one day a month was allowed for rest. The pace of work increased, while food supplies diminished to starvation point. I was hungry every waking moment. My teeth began to fall out and my hearing was lost in the din of the hammers. Dust filled my eyes until I lost the sight of my right eye. Then, near the end of the war, I spat blood as I coughed up the dust.

They sent me to hospital where they found my left lung had collapsed with a large hole, and the right lung had become black with tuberculosis. They gave me the best care in the harsh circumstances. I didn't worry about dying but centred all my thoughts on the next meal, small though it was. The wonder was having something to eat. Experiments with radiation appeared successful so that after four months or so I was discharged to the village.

Back there I was given lighter work, helping the wholesaler weigh out food supplies for everybody. When I worked well, he sometimes gave me a little extra bread.

I stayed in the Urals for another year, until a law was passed to allow the Poles to return to the Russian occupied zone of Poland. In the summer of 1947 when I was twenty-four years old, I found my way to Lodz in a cattle truck. I made every effort to contact my mother, but her name could not be found anywhere among the concentration camp survivors. The Jewish Red Cross only operated inside city borders. Movement outside its boundaries was prohibited so prevented wider searches.

With my savings in my pocket and high hope in my heart, I was ready to start life anew, still a quiet, shy fellow who found it hard to socialise.

The first thing I did was to find a Jewish community through the local synagogue. They introduced me to a tailor who gave me a shakedown in his workshop. I had a home from where I could look for work as an experienced weaver. I got employment straight away in a Jewish business under State control. I worked long hours again for low wages until I discovered that the boss was sky lighting and making a bit on the side two- or three-times state rates. He offered me extra time and I was pleased to accept at the better rate of pay. It allowed me to buy food on the black market and put on some flesh as I recovered my health.

My fascination with the intricate machinery drew me to spend unpaid hours exploring its potential. This proved an advantage for I was offered a more responsible position in the factory and better pay. In no time I had enough to negotiate with a local official through a middleman to pay for better accommodation. I was allocated an old shop in the centre of town. The shop had a small room at the back and little else, but I was allowed to renovate it into a place fit for living.

At the end of five years or so during which time I began to feel more comfortable in company and made friends among my folk, my boss took me aside.

"I know you very well now Gershon and I think, I have a woman to make a good couple with you. She is a good woman who comes from Russia and her name is Karina. She is very bright with business and the market." His description reminded me of my mother and her market.

"Yes, I'd like to meet her," I said. He brought her to my home in the renovated shop where we met for the first time. I opened the door to see in front of me a good-looking girl of medium height and sturdy build. She gave me a lovely smile.

Over a cup of tea, she told me she worked for a clothing repairer and her specialty was hand mending the ladders in the new nylon stockings coming on to the market. She also skylighted for her boss and bought and sold things in the local market as well. Like me she saved money and was arranging to have a state regulated kiosk in the market. I saw in her a powerful Russian Jewish woman with the same drive and business ability as my mother. Here was somebody who might bring me the happiness lost fourteen years ago. I had my mother back.

After telling her my history we both felt a strong attraction and desire to meet again. Before long we arranged to get married. Two days before the ceremony I expressed my delight in Karina, and all the hopes she promised by giving all I possessed to her. One Sunday we had a simple registry office wedding with a few friends present.

On Monday I returned to work and the usual banter then at night returned to honeymoon time, until two or three days into the week. Arriving home one evening after a twelve-hour shift, I found Karina dressed in her best to go off to a dance with a girlfriend. I had fallen in love with my mother's image and Katrina had made a business contract. I went to sleep dispirited and hurt beyond measure.

She took the lead as business partner and I took the subordinate role, one I would follow all my life with her. Our housekeeping was straight forward, she did the cooking and kept her job where she made very good money, twice as much as me. My father's example of forbearance and acceptance was the only way I knew of dealing with all this, so it was natural for me to follow my father's precedent and accept her decisions about our way forward. I handed all my money over to her. Her business acumen in risky areas allowed us to survive on black market produce, causing me constant worry for her safety.

Indeed, we made a good couple neither obstructing the other's path over-much, and by late 1952 we were able to move to a bigger home in a nice suburb for we expected our first child. Our baby was born in 1953 in the local hospital, a lovely daughter, Elizabeth, who brought us all the joy needed to complete our family. A Russian nun solved the problem of us both continuing to work. She moved in with us and took the most wonderful care of the family as it prospered.

During the following year a new liberal minded president was elected in Poland in 1954. A law was finally passed allowing the return of all Polish citizens including Jews. I registered for repatriation only after I was assured I could leave Warsaw, a point of immigration, to go straight on to Israel We stayed in Warsaw a month or so while official formalities were completed and finally set off for Israel in 1955.

Chapter 7: Israel

WHEN we landed in Israel, government officials were waiting to welcome us and arrange escort to Hulon which was about half an hour's drive outside Tel Aviv. There were temporary two and three-bedroom houses ready for immigrants. We got a two bedroom one which soon became home after the container with our possessions arrived from Poland.

It was a great feeling of a coming home as fellow immigrant families settled in around us. We soon made friends among neighbours from many countries. A job was hard to find at first but was no problem after I contacted the weavers in the community. They set me to work straight away and before long Karina had also found work. Neighbours looked after each other's children, as shift work allowed, and soon Elizabeth had a group of caring friends in a safe environment.

We lived in a state of euphoria. With the sea in easy reach it felt we were on holiday on our leisure days. Above all the freedom to make decisions for ourselves and to later to set up my business was as heady as drinking champagne all day. Memories of the strict controls in Russia and Poland soon began to fade although they are never forgotten.

Setting up in business for myself came about this way. My boss appeared to value my knowledge with machinery and asked me to teach a relative the ropes during working hours. Since my pay at the end of the week depended on piece work, the hours lost in teaching reduced my pay packet to some extent. Teaching was arduous. In the end I decided I would be happier with half my income if I earned it myself, so I gave my boss notice. He was not too happy and enlisted Karina's help, hoping she would change my mind.

Surprisingly, for jobs were still scarce, Karina backed me up. I knew I could always depend on her and felt very safe in the knowledge.

I managed to buy the Jacquard machinery with our savings, but I still needed a wooden frame to suspend it in. A retired carpenter, whose health was too frail for regular work, volunteered to help me and soon, the wood took shape and I was ready to make carpets. in one of the bedrooms that Karina had cleared.

I already knew the popular pattern most in demand in the local markets and used it as a base to create my own design. After I had twelve carpets ready, I went to Tel Aviv to try local shops and markets. I found sufficient interest among the marketers', keen competition for me to trust them with my wares and pay me on sale of goods.

Soon they were coming to my home to buy more merchandise. Their cheques were not honoured for three months, but I had no choice, unless I was fortunate enough to find customers who paid on demand for a cheaper price.

In a short while the volume of trade increased to the extent, I was unable to keep up without help. Karina left her job and we became totally dependent on our own resources. Thanks to her thrifty saving, for she managed all our income, we were able to buy our supplies and keep going. By the end of a year, demand outstripped the machinery's output and, I needed another loom, but where to put it.

Karina made enquiries from the Kibbutz council who found us a place where we could set-up our first factory in one vacated by a man who needed larger premises. After we negotiated a price for the renovations, he had installed we were two very happy owners. Once the new machine arrived and was ready, we took on another worker freeing Karina to finish the products.

It was the beginning of good times in the sense that as life became more stable with our own business and associates, as parents we watched our daughter grow happy and healthy.

Of course, it was not all plain sailing because we worked in conditions where the sun scorched down on the tin roof and the heat inside the workshop became unbearable. We could not afford a car and had to go to Tel Aviv on a hot crowded bus to buy raw materials which cost more to have delivered.

During all the time we were in the Kibbutz I made regular visits to the immigrant information centre for updated news of survivors from the concentration camps. On one occasion the name Fishel leaped out at me from the list on the board. My heart pounded for Fishel was my father's son by his first wife.

I had met him frequently in Poland where he had a barber's salon in one of the luxury suburbs. When my father was too ill to work and provide for us, Fishel gave money to my mother every week. I was sent to collect this at the shop and got to know him quite well as a kind of uncle. Now, by a miracle, here he was, already in Israel and living in Heifa.

We lost no time in contacting him through the centre and finally Karina and I were welcoming my stepbrother and his wife to our home. The excitement of seeing them and exchanging news charged their visit with overwhelming joy. I learned that my step sister was in Australia.

When our joy subsided, I sat eager for news of my mother. Fishel had been in the same concentration camp with her and would know her whereabouts. Quietly he told me that she had perished in the ovens after becoming sick. As she lay near death, knowing the gas chamber awaited her, she gave Fishel a family photo that she always carried close to her heart

"Fishel, if my dear son is alive and you find him, will you give him this photo for me please," she said between murmuring my name constantly. Gershon would be the last word she uttered.

Stricken anew though I was, for some time I had accepted in my heart that we two would not see each other again in this world. Tears flowed soft to heal that final goodbye for the passion of grief had burned low during the stress of surviving. She dwells forever in my heart and my one and only photo is always near me.

Our families kept in touch with occasional visits until one day, after a few more years living in Israel, Fishel came to tell us he was going to join his sister in Australia. He gave us addresses to contact before we said goodbye. It was so good to know I had a half brother and sister and was part of a family again.

Although our factory output was growing and sales increased, their shady practices and unreliability of buyers to pay their bills stretched our slender resources and our patience. Finally, I'd had enough and decided to follow Fishel to Australia. Karina was more than pleased for her business acumen had little outlet in Israel. We decided that I emigrate first to allow me to set up a comfortable place for Karina and Elizabeth. She would keep an eye on things in Israel with the help of a new partner who bought into half of our business on the understanding we would sell the other half when she came to join me in Australia.

Because we were self -sufficient with our own business, the Australian Embassy granted me a visa straight away. Having family to join strengthened our case and in 1960 I stepped off a plane to be greeted by Fishel.

Chapter 8: Australia

MY PLAN was to find work to pay for settling down in Australia and set-up a carpet factory. Fishel had successfully set-up a barber shop with living space above for his family.

To my dismay I discovered hand weaving and other labour-intensive crafts were not practiced since cheap goods were brought in from India and other third world countries.

I stayed with Fishel for a short time while I searched for accommodation, but I was afraid to go too far afield because I spoke no English and could not communicate if I got lost in the maze of streets in the city. He eventually found me a house to rent near the synagogue in a street inhabited by the Jewish people. Able to converse with ease again, I soon found out that knitwear was a product with a future I could trade in once I learned to use new machinery. Most factories only wanted skilled knitters, but I persuaded an owner to employ me for whatever unskilled work was needed in the background.

From owning my own factory, I was back to sweeping floors, carrying yarn, anything and everything he ordered. All I asked of him was his permission to stay behind, without pay, with the second shift of workers to help out here and there so that I could watch and learn about the mechanics of the new machinery.

The knitters had to constantly refer to the instruction books for this exciting new circular machinery. Moving around the large area I came across a specialist in knitwear, a Jewish worker who spoke a little Russian. He was a kind fellow and took the time to teach me the technique as I worked alongside him most shifts, while telling him some of my history.

I quickly picked up some English phrases to get by with. Yiddish is a very Germanic language which in its turn had many Saxon similarities. Maybe the need to learn Hebrew with the Rabbi my mother paid to teach me plus Polish, German, Russian and the Yiddish spoken in the ghetto quickened my ability to become familiar with English.

Finally, after two or three months like this, he told our boss that I was ready to manage a machine on my own.

I had a home and a job, and it was time to ask Karina to come and join me in our new country.

She had managed successfully on her own and set about selling the other half of the factory. Being a true business woman, she made a good deal. All our possessions followed her over, in a container.

My neighbour took me to the airport in his car to bring them home and we three were together again. So much talking, laughing and hugging made for paradise after the loneliness and toil of the past few months. It was such a comfort to have her capable presence around again.

Karina wasted no time in seeking the means to add to our income. Finding a market, she made enquiries about setting up her own stall. A Rumanian woman with the same idea made friends with her and eventually the two set-up a stall where they would sell jumpers. They made the rounds of textile factories to buy up reject garments for stock, and when they called at the factory where I worked the boss was agreeable to supply them with jumpers.

They did so well that, in a few months, their earnings plus her husband's and my wages, enabled us to rent a large house which we shared. We lived amicably together finding some leisure time to enjoy the new black and white televisions coming into the shops.

We all had the same goal, to become self- sufficient. My overriding goal was to buy a machine to produce knitwear for myself.

I knew of an agent to would order the machinery from England. Karina's knowledge of the best- selling knitwear in the market guided my choice of the right gauge circular knitting machine. It was a long wait for our ship to come home, almost a year if I recall. Somehow word got around that I was setting up in business and my boss sacked me. This was no big drama for my skill was good enough to land another job straight away. Fortune smiled on us because by the time the machinery arrived, we had a new baby. We knew where to put the baby, but the machine was another matter.

My new job was in a very big factory where a decent boss found space among store rooms and cutting rooms for me to set up my machine. He made room when I purchased an over-locker and cutting machine after doing the rounds to find a banker who would trust me with credit. He understood when I gave up working for him to set my mind to my new undertaking. I owe him so much.

Karina was no longer in the markets but helping me to make garments. After buying the yarn I produced the material and she cut and sewed the jumpers. They were sold to the many contacts she had made in the market.

My designs took off and were much in demand, so much so that in no time we needed more over-lockers and staff and more room.

Lady Luck was on my side. We came across a man, desperate to rent out a large space above several shops, in a light industrial area. It was an old wooden structure, over brick-based buildings, with access by an outside stairway. Inside was a sizeable area to set up the factory equipment and, along a corridor, living quarters of adequate but simple layout.

We parted company with the Rumanian family and moved our furnishings to set up home once again. The knitting machine caused a hitch for it was too big to go through any conventional opening. At the back of the premises we found a large window which could be taken out. My landlord offered to help with this after special transport equipped with a crane brought the knitting machine to its destination. The crane lifted the machinery up and through the opening. It was quite exciting, and we all stood in the backyard checking every move until all was safely installed, including our family.

By this time, we had settled on making a range of garments to fit children up to their teens. Anyone who has children will know how discriminating they can be. My designs had to appeal to them especially, when I started to approach wholesalers demanding I satisfy the season's fashion trends.

To begin with I tried three wholesalers, thinking that if even one gave me an order for selling on to their traders, it would give a good return for our labour. Imagine my surprise when all three sent in requests for sizeable orders. It seems a blur to my mind now, but we found a second worker to run the new over-locker who was willing to wait a bit for her wages. In the end, to pay her, I took on a night shift with my decent boss, working on a simple combination that was not too taxing.

Although the wholesalers could not order until my samples had done their rounds of the shopping outlets, once the orders came work was fast and furious entailing long hours for both of us. I was able to give up my second job. Soon we were employing more workers and I was hard put to supply the yarn for the extra over-lockers. I kept my knitting machine working twenty-four hours a day. To cover the few hours sleep I snatched each night, I rigged up a light to our bedroom to alert me when one of the spools of yarn ran out.

Money was coming in regularly from all sources but there was always something I needed to invest in. Yarn and over-lockers wages and shelving to accommodate stock ate up much of our money so that I had to know how much I was owed to invest wisely without getting into debt. In nineteen sixty-two I needed another knitting machine from England, a big item but fruitful.

I remember that year so well because it was the year Karina and I received our Australian citizenship. We had achieved much in so short a time and I was proud of my wife and young family.

Within the next four years we passed another milestone through her diligent saving for she still managed all the money. The bank gave us a sizeable mortgage and we were able to buy our own second-hand factory, brick-built and spacious in a good light industrial zone. A year or so later we were able to approach the bank again for a mortgage to look for our first house.

We knocked at a door in a lovely suburb and it was opened by a woman of great gentleness. It was after many more inspections in the area that we returned to her and bought her house.

The constant strain of setting up the new factory with our old stock, plus new machines imported from England, and setting a larger operation in smooth running gear completely depleted all my energies. I was worried about having so much debt.

When we became established enough, there was some freedom from slavery to enjoy our staff. They were a loyal group we regarded as friends we could trust. What a dream time it was.

Once I relaxed, I became aware of tension in my neck which increased to an unbearable pain at times. My freedom would come at the price of my health.

Karina's business acumen drove her to use the bank backup to buy empty factories which we rented out. Once the loans were repaid, they brought in regular income to add to our own thriving business. I trusted her intuitive ventures and she repaid my trust by succeeding handsomely. Our goal had subtly shifted. Money became our god.

For me the tender years of success with one machine melted into a head over heels affair chasing Mistress Gold. I was driven to make money riding on the back of one risk after another.

We bought a second-hand Holden for the business, prudently saving money as we continued to work long hours, six days a week.

Business also meant a new lifestyle, eating out with friends and business associates in the best restaurants. Our image needed a new wardrobe of custom-made clothes and a house with beautiful furnishings.

We were able to bring Karina's two brothers over from Russia and guarantee them. Our family was growing and visits to my half siblings and her brothers were looked forward to.

Shabbat was always welcome to rest but my pain increased.

Visits to the doctors started and pain killers were handed out with little effect. I gave a short sharp "No" to the suggestion I have a course of therapy in a specialised nursing home. I carried on working and made my life easier by taking on an apprentice, a very bright Jewish boy.

I finally was able to give in after the betrothal of my daughter, Elizabeth, to a young man interested in the factory. On their marriage my gift to them was half the factory and all my time teaching him how to manage the whole system. Karina and I could retire.

This allowed me time to seek medical assistance further afield. Karina accompanied me, to a clinic in Czechoslovakia, for a two-week treatment. It helped but the pain returned after a short while. Back home, life was unfulfilling with time on my hands.

There was the usual round of meetings with old associates over coffee or wine, but the conversation always centred on their ambitious ventures and I quickly became bored and restless. There was one chap who played chess and many a game we enjoyed while others chatted. All the while pain darted in and out on its close pursuit as I went from doctor to doctor seeking freedom from so unwelcome a friend. I did not know then that suffering is an ally but more of that later.

Karina only settled into half retirement. She enjoyed our social activity, but it was not enough to satisfy her tremendous drive. She soon found an outlet for her old skills.

An old friend from Israel had immigrated to Australia with his son, who needed help to start a garment factory, using sewing machines only. I believe the idea of fresh fields may have enticed Karina to invest and work alongside him to ensure his future. Whatever it was, she spent less and less time with me.

Each day I enjoyed a three or four-mile walk for the daily ritual of joining them for lunch at a nearby restaurant. I was surfeited with food yet empty of something I could not express. My grief for my mother, surfaced. Without blaming anyone, including myself, our marriage was no longer working for either of us. Living in security and comfort and all that money could provide, I was starving as much as during the Russian siege.

Finally, after trying to resolve our problem, we made the painful decision to separate and I filed for divorce. I can honestly say that I was lost; I didn't know where to turn.

I purchased a large plot of land outside the city, to get close to nature, and set-up a temporary home in a large second-hand caravan. Then I set about having a house built.

To break up my loneliness I sometimes went in search of societies and groups who were seeking a different meaning to life.

I visited the Jewish synagogue, the Christian Church. All religions told me belief and faith are the answer, but how could I embrace their tenets when my mother and my wife had no belief and I had spent so long in a land where God did not exist, Russia?

Among the many new friends I made, one introduced me to the words of a man called Krishnamurti. His first words caught my attention.

"You heard my message, why are you coming back and looking to me for your salvation? you are responsible for your own." This was enough to beckon me to look further into the teachings of this man.

Still limited by my English comprehension, I certainly got the message that he wanted me to be free. He wanted to share his experience of finding freedom from religion, love, death and of life itself as it is met in its different forms. I understood him to mean that to be free one must find truth in the present moment. The truth lay hidden under layer upon layer of memory. Memory conditioned my responses to the present moment. He offered no instructions, no practice, nothing. Just mirror yourself in your relationships and watch your deep-rooted habitual dependencies.

I found that I had to start looking at my relationships in a completely different way. Not just with my intimate friends but with everybody. I needed to develop an awareness of how I spoke, how I thought and how I wanted benefits for myself at the expense of others. I learned of the deep-rooted emptiness and loneliness, which we all suffer. My enthusiasm extended to joining the Theosophical Society who arranged for tapes and films of Krishnamurti to be sent to me. I hired halls to give public viewings and meetings for people to listen to this strong man's philosophy of life.

By this time my new house was built and comfortably furnished, allowing me to organise a meditation centre there. There was plenty of room to allow the various teachers and lecturers to stay in the house during their courses. Much of the organising was done by friends who shared my feelings. They set up weekly seminars and other activities based on the work of Krishnamurti.

One of these seminars was attended by a lady who made enquiries about the organiser, which was me. When we met, her gentle nature and voice, and her integrity and honesty attracted me to her. She was a senior lecturer in psychology and a teacher of nursing. I felt that I needed to interact with her to help me with my own growth. We were both around sixty years old. Lalla had never been married before and had no intention of marrying anyone until she met me.

Thus, I met the love of my life, Lalla. We married within a couple of months. She loved the beach and lived near the sea, so we decided I should move in with her and learn how to love without either of us losing our independence.

Twenty-two years later we were still growing together through the study of Krishnamuerti's teachings.

Chapter 9: Lalla

I WAS still in terrible pain with my neck, but I found that when I had a good rest with my mind quiet, the pain was less. Was it possible that all the advocates of meditation were right? It was time to seriously learn meditation. I decided to take the simple breath as the subject of my meditation.

Like all people learning meditation, I soon realised that I had almost no control over my mind which was restless and constantly active. One needed to deal with every other aspect of life, cause and effect, consequences of behaviour and thought patterns. At times I despaired over my ability to meditate in this lifetime.

Lalla's support gave me the will to continue through all the difficulties of changing a life, which was not healthy for me or for the world. Not only did the pain in my neck go, but I felt so much stronger to deal with the pain of loss and grief in my entire life. There was healing happening in my whole body and soul.

As the years passed and I began to feel more joyful. I wanted to find a way to help myself and others find a purpose and meaning to life, yet I knew that there was a lack of soul connection in the way we humans communicate with each other. At first, Lalla and I searched for ways to help others by supporting charities financially, but just giving money was not enough. I needed to be involved on a personal level.

I tried many avenues until finally, I contacted a representative of the Kibbutzim movement in Israel. He gave me some material to study. After very careful thought, we decided to go to a Kibbutzim in Israel.

I have no words to express how impressed I was with the organisation, the order, the cleanliness of this place. It was very clear that the Kibbutz movement was born out of a need to survive and for security, rather than a need for spiritual growth.

Most important was the level of love and care for the children and the elderly. Old people never retired but continued to do useful work but do less and be more cared for.

When we came home, we saw that the security and comfort Westerners enjoyed did not foster deep connections like those between souls who shared suffering The Buddhist concept of realising happiness whatever the outer conditions, and thus attaining peace also pointed to the way being through one's own inner activity. Could sharing really embrace the eastern concept of changing one's self to change the world?

We both were enchanted with Krishnamurti's lectures which said find the truth through reasoning and meditation, to change yourself. I continued to try meditation techniques. It took me twenty-five years. The written words blocked my progress until I realised that non-verbal experiencing opened the way to inner peace.

We learned that daily living required memory for material progress, but the true growth came through human relationships. We experienced the joy of unconditional love, ever-present, untouched by the events of yesterday. From Lalla I learned to become very independent in managing my life. Now that I am grown older, I value those lessons which enable me to take care of my needs without putting a strain on others.

Living, as we did, by the sea we decided to buy a small yacht and learn how to sail it. I steered the craft and Lalla kept a sharp lookout to keep us safe.

As time went by, we graduated to a bigger boat to make longer journeys along the coast. It was a good time for us with many wonderful things coming our way as we still searched for truth and the right way to live.

Out of the blue fate changed the way we lived. Lalla felt unwell enough to visit a doctor. The results of tests showed that she had a pancreatic cancer with only three per cent chance of recovery. The shock that I could lose my dearest companion and lover is indescribable.

After surgery, to excise quite a lot of her intestinal tract, she became a shadow of her former self, losing weight and not able to eat to aid recovery.

Finally, the doctors told me to take her home and do the best I could for they could do no more for her. I honestly did not know what to do for the best. My naturally volatile nature filled me with intense emotions affecting me strongly in adverse ways. In a quiet moment I realised that this was not going to help the situation. I must make our time together a hundred per cent meaningful.

To add to her frugal diet, I and racked my brains to invent dainty fare to tempt her. In fact, she became my baby needing to be washed and completely taken care of as she slowly regained a will to go on trying. Walking was the biggest hurdle to surmount for she could not walk a step. We began with one step, in the garden where I wheeled her daily, until finally she started to make a recovery. It was many months before my dear Lalla was herself again. She told me I was the best nurse she could have and later, on her birthdays, reminded me of that time of struggle together.

She dreamed of living in a house where we could look out across the ocean at all times. Our search in the East was unsuccessful so we decided to try Western Australia. In 1999 I left her to rest while I searched for our new home. I arrived in Perth and organised a coach drive stopping at places between Perth and Denmark

The first stop was in a city south of Perth. In a suburb ten minutes away from the centre there was a house, a little way back from the seashore, promising a quiet retirement for us. It was elevated on a gentle slope at the head of a one-way road. The large airy rooms tiled in gleaming porcelain smiled a welcome to me. I fell in love with the place and planned to return to buy the property but travelled on south, to take a look around.

I discovered a tiny island where land and property were privately owned. It was a paradise with the river flowing peacefully around its sandy shoreline of native bush and tall trees. Wild animals, kangaroo and small creatures peeped out trustingly at me as I strolled along the paths. I knew I must have a home there someday, but my first purchase must be the house south of Perth.

I hurried back to tell Lalla the good news, and then followed a busy time packing and saying goodbye to old friends and family.

Chapter 10: Western Australia

—— ❦ ——

WE FLEW across later that year to a life of freedom and the pleasures of swimming in the ocean, walking along the shore and quiet times at home. We drove many kilometres discovering the area and I introduced Lalla to my island. Of course, we bought a lovely corner property there which was my intention all the time. We had really retired and soon found new friends and discovered new activities.

The most exciting part of my relationship with Lalla was dialogue. Most days we sat and talked about life and the mystery of the Universe. Philosophies of various well-known writers l guided our way of living, ensuring a positive approach to life.

Because of the political circumstances when I was a child, my education was poor. A Jewish Rabbi taught me Jewish reading and writing and that was the limit. I struggled to get along with the various languages I needed to converse in, as I moved around in those traumatic years. I decided to read simple grammar in English, which allowed me to read a good selection of authors and subjects.

Life is never static and the emotional upheaval following the dissolution of my first marriage birthed a spiritual approach to understanding the twists and turns of fate.

Thus, I was a little more prepared when one day Lalla came to me and confided that breathing had become difficult for her.

It was the beginning of a round of specialists again. After various scans a growth was found in her trachea. She stayed in hospital while they tried various therapies. When morphine was commenced, allowing her some peace, she began to drift away from me, murmuring a few words between the sleeping. Two or three days later she passed away. We were together for twenty-two good years.

Now eighty-six years old, I was in a state of shock and lost without her. I began to contact old comrades, among them Dan and his wife Lyn. Our friendship was on safe ground and though we did not meet frequently, we promised to look out the surviving partner after death. Lyn and Lalla were nurses and shared a strong belief in mankind's spiritual journey as the goal of earthly experience. Like us, Dan and Lyn still practiced meditation daily.

I visited them to discuss buying a place in their village, but on finding that Lyn was nursing Dan through terminal prostate cancer, I left them in peace to live out his final months. Nearly a year later Dan also passed away.

Like me Lyn found loneliness hard and set about putting her home on the market, to go and live near her son in Perth. She was having difficulty selling and recalling my interest in village life, she rang me to enquire if I was interested.

I was not interested but it gave me an opening to reconnect with somebody who I could talk openly with. I had much on my mind. Several women had answered my adverts for a companion. They sought material gain and left my soul at loss. One companion in particular caused a costly problem

We shared the experience of losing a loved and I needed to open my heart. I was knocking at a door once more so to speak.

I went along one afternoon to find a quiet woman determined to tackle a new life. We sat over tea filling in events of recent times. Before I left, I asked if I could visit again the following week and got a smiling assent. Somehow, we both had an unspoken feeling of togetherness in our common grieving, where time had not lightened our loss.

This was the start of regular visits and little outings around the local area. Every time I returned home, my loneliness was highlighted. The house was sorely in need of a woman's touch for like most men I was inclined to leave things lying around. The pantry was overstocked from imprudent shopping and the fridge needed cleaning out.

For a change I suggested that we walk along my favourite track by the sea. Having a woman walking by my side, as Lalla had in time past, was a joy, the wind and light rain on our faces a shared pleasure. My feelings for Lyn were becoming more personal than friendship and I believe she found more than comfort in my company.

Later in the year, I tentatively asked her to come and live with me, but she was not ready. Then shortly before Christmas I suggested she stay over for the festival to make the gap in our lives less painful. We would see what path our lives would take from there.

It seemed normal for me to prepare Lalla's bedroom overlooking the front garden where palm trees nodded good morning when she woke. Knowing Lyn slept there gave me ease when I settled down that first night in my somewhat smaller quarters.

That is my part of this story dear reader.

Chapter 11: Trust

WELL that's how Gershon and Lyn came to live together because the start of the New Year saw her permanently installed in Lalla's old bedroom and the beginning of a gentle love affair with the house and its owner.

To be sure her heart had stirred on the day this handsome man walked back into her life again. As he bent to kiss her hand in greeting, she was flying through a gap in time from the other side of the universe to meet him. When he raised his head Lalla's husband smiled at Dan's wife.

That sunny afternoon they faced each other sensing a new warmth filling the cold gap, left by a soul mate joining the long gone. Tendrils on old vines spiralled across a lonely void reaching for a lifeline. Both well-seasoned in years, intimate friends were now few, a rustle of autumn leaves waiting for life's last swirl.

She looked forward his visits, each time the gap becoming shorter until one day he looked up from bending to kiss her hand, his customary greeting.

"Come dance with me sweetheart, come dance with me." Strangely she felt no guilt at changing partners while the warmth of Dan's embrace still wrapped her heart. The dance never stops, so dance or swirl helplessly in a stagnant pool of self-despair.

Two days before the Christmas festival she awoke at dawn on her first morning in his house, to walk by the seashore with Gershon. They spoke little, being content they were no longer alone.

"Can I invite my son and his family for Christmas day?" she asked.

"We will go shopping," he said.

With their trolley nearly complete she turned down an aisle for a forgotten item, leaving him on his own. His voice trumpeted through the large store again and again with the anger of a frightened child.

"Where are you Mamoushka?" Breathless she returned to his side and his adolescent anguish of being alone in the world.

On Christmas day, he sat as the head of the family ranged both sides of an elegant long table, graced a splendid meal. Andrew's wife had invited her sister and family. The Muslim sisters had married Christians, Lyn's son, and Mark an Australian geologist. The men, prevailed upon to convert to Islam for their wives' safety, chatted easily. Old religious differences forgotten in the men's joy in their wives and children.

They waved goodbye to the families as dusk fell. His arm around her shoulders felt as natural as a long-standing habit. Yet it was not so, there were memories. She spoke first.

"We still tryst with the dead, laughing and lingering in old haunts before we hide in the misty shrouds of sleep."

"We are all one, Mamoushka. I am Dan and you are Lalla."

Before nightfall, she went down to the dunes. Along a shoreline without ending, the surf crawled like a thief up the beaches. Grains of sand gravelled protest as they slid into the sea's bondage, leaving a new dune etched, a barricade against the mysteries of the deep. Horizon merged with flaming sky, the glory filling her soul.

She had come to him whole and without shame, uncertain of her role except that it was to heal. Her only baggage a purse full of memories opened generously to share with him. Now she felt useless for he still suffered. Her cuckoo heart fluttered outside another woman's shrine, with a sorrowing to know the ending.

The sea breathed quietly below. In the pregnant womb of the waters she watched a ripple become a wave, grow large and surge for release. Its long underbelly shone with evening light before it reached its peak, curled then erupted to leave a phallic imprint on the outstretched shore.

A cumulus of cloud fanned around the vault. Sunbeams, still dancing at day's end, stippled the clouds with gold before fleeing to an arctic dawn.

Light slid behind anvil heads of dark clouds, hiding its molten source, to reappear sullen red on the far reaches of a leaden sea. Darkness gathered. She turned for home.

As the bedroom door closed behind her the crying began. Unquenchable tears, sobs dying on a gasp. He came to her concerned.

"Shall I sit with you sweetheart? What is the matter?"

"Thank you, no. I have to deal with it on my own."

She felt she was at a Wake, grieving for the departed. A part of her was dying. The core of her womanhood, her reason for being, shrivelled and left her and she knew peace from the demands of her sensual nature. Tenderness would enrich this friendship as befitted their age. A tenderness that understood the fears behind the winks and the smiles they exchanged. She went to him.

"Maybe I am Lalla and you are Dan. I hope our dreams give joy to their souls, for I will dance with you to the music of our heart's strings. The far corners my mind will open to your tender touch. Hold my hand and stand with me on the shoreline of eternity to watch myriads of sunsets."

He kissed her hand.

"Thank you for everything Mamoushka. Thank you."

He came to bid her goodnight.

"We will learn of unconditional love Mamoushka," he said before his lips pressed firmly upon hers.

"Yes, my dear, God Bless." Later, curled up in bed watching shadowy palm tree sway across the curtains, she knew she could accept any condition to stay with this man. Had she not crossed the bridge of time to find him.

His room was at the heart of the house. All the general rooms radiated from it including the kitchen where he liked to watch her cook for them. From his big soft leather chair standing in the centre he had a view of everything going on through glass doors. A trolley carried his personal needs and on a chest of drawers, on the other side, a telephone and files from his office he was working on.

Everything was usually in organised disarray around him, papers fluttering in baskets, on the floor and sliding off trolley shelves but he knew where every paper was. Her manic need for order raised his ire after she tidied up his patch.

"She likes to be tidy and I like to be untidy," he told all and sundry, scattering another sheaf of papers as he stretched to ease the pain in his spine.

A huge television screen dominated the wall in front of the chair. He programmed it with documentaries and episodes from his favourite series, dealing with human frailties and broken relationships. After they watched a programme, he quizzed her about it, drawing out ideas she was unaware of, then sliding into one of their philosophical discussions.

Along the side wall was a huge wooden bookcase stocked with educational books but dominated by writings of authors to guide his quest for truth and the meaning of life. Theirs was a shared journey and a shared joy the same road travelled for many years with the answer always a step ahead.

Describing a house does not describe the owner. Lyn discovered a very complex personality, during the week leading up to the new year.

The vulnerable child who talked often of a mother so close in his memory said: "she sent you to me Mamushka. You remind me of her with your tidiness."

The orphan, surrounded by strange faces, still constantly alert and defensive calling: "I'm watching everything you do." as she accustomed herself to the house, his ways and needs.

The rejected father and husband muttering, after dutiful, brief phone calls from a family member: "They only want my money. They turned away from me and shut their doors after Lalla died. I only have you I can trust sweetheart."

The cosseted boy whose anger cried out against Nazi blows, minded his health in the smallest detail, often calling for her nursing skill to bring him comfort from pain.

The business man who ran his office in the house, meticulously and saved his accountant hours of work, with good preparation detailing income and money spent generously among his family.

He was always well dressed and, like Lyn, used the local charity shops to buy his clothes and many of the small ornaments scattered through the house.

"Somebody had to make them for little return," he said remembering old times.

The essence of his personality shone through at all times, a noble man with a great and gentle heart. The commanding voice was an open expression of his confidence in his power.

On New Year's Eve she was preparing a supper tray to share while later they would listen to the annual concert from Vienna.

He relaxed in his chair watching her tidy the kitchen

"I think I've fallen in love with you Mamushka," he said.

It was his habit to make remarks, after a silence for reflexion, but where feelings were involved never discussed them further.

"I don't want to be analysed," he would say if she made to follow up a remark, so she kept quiet and happy.

At the end of the evening that weekend, he took her hand and kissed it gently.

"Sweetheart will you stay with me permanently?"

"Yes," she whispered.

***

When she stepped through his front door carrying the bag containing her small wardrobe, her household goods remained behind until the village property was sold. Many a time, in her mind's eye, her furnishings replaced the packing cases used for tables all over the house. When her modest load of furniture arrived, she soon set-up her sitting room and bedroom using the remaining pieces to replace those packing cases in the palatial home. Gershon was considerate in making space for her and allowing her to move things around.

"Do as you wish. You look after the house now." She thought he liked the final result though he made no comment until days later.

"It is a lovely home now sweetheart. Of all the houses we lived in, Lalla and I loved this the most. Its gleaming floors, its rooms lighting up with the sun's course and the space. Above all, the space here is paradise. Who needs a holiday living in such a beautiful spot? You and I walk by the sea every day at dawn and sometimes take a swim. We are happy."

Chapter 12: Settled Times

THE New Year was warm and balmy. At dawn's light Gershon, well-known to many residents, responded to their greetings as they welcomed Lyn, walking by his side. Then watched them go down to the shoreline and he help her into the waves, his hand encircling her wrist, securing her balance, until the water lifted them clear of turbulence.

The glint of early morning sunrays flowed towards them, joining in the kiss they exchanged before swimming alone in oneness with the water. Early sunbathers shared their smiles, seeing two old ones embrace before he helped her past the surf line to walk hand in hand up the beach. No words expressed their peace and new-found power to return to life. They swam through summer and autumn into the time of warm winter rain pitting the sands then they resumed the long silent walks morning and evening.

The seasons flowed swiftly like their love for one another. One morning she paused at his open door on the way back from putting the wash on before breakfast. He lay as usual reading his treasured Krishnamurti discussions. Turning his head to her, he laid down the book, and extended his arm. She joined him on top of the bedcovers, snuggling into his shoulder while he talked. The next morning, he came in to her bed, the heat of his strong body warm about her curves.

"I'm just trying. I may not come again" but he did, lying on his back for twenty minutes or so before getting ready for his walk. She was never sure if he did so for his pleasure or to please her. She loved the opening of the day once more as a woman feeling wanted and needed to give comfort. Their simple lifestyle enriched the harmony age played on life's chords.

Family members came from across the country and overseas to find out what the old ones were up to. Some came to ensure the property would not pass to Lyn. Happy in Gershon's delight in seeing his family again, she signed legal documents to reassure them. There were moments when they felt Dan and Lalla's presence and wondered what hand they had played in their reunion when they recalled good times shared with their old loves.

"She was a wonderful woman but you're different sweetheart. You are my soul mate," giving her one of the many kisses he gave her as they prepared a meal or listened to music. Their one or two brief skirmishes, to let her know he was the decision maker, always ended in a kiss.

"We're too old to fight dear. Do it your way," she caved in during a nightmare drive to his island home. Gershon only had sight in one eye which caused him to occasionally veer off course. That was fine on the country roads but nail-biting stuff on the highways when he increased speed. For all that he was a fine driver who loved his car and the independence of driving himself. When his back played up Lyn took over, enjoying the big car and all the gadgets.

That's how it was with them for the next few years, their love refreshingly innocent amidst the conflict and deceit in the world around them.

"I want to marry you sweetheart," he said one day.

"We don't need ceremony Gershon dear. We love and trust one another, don't we?" He let it ride but got his own way during a visit to Andrew to plan a granny flat for use when one or other was alone again. When Lyn was out of earshot, he got Andrew on his side.

"Your mother is a giver, happy to give affection, time and care to others. She shares her family with me, something I miss very much. I know she's not well off, but I notice she always finds something to give to one of you in need. When she agreed to come and share my life, we talked over our feelings for each. In our eighties the old excitement stirred in us, and I've thrived on her love. Now I'm going to marry your mother When she comes in, I am going to tell her we will be married. Will you back me up?"

Well he got his way although Andrew said she reacted like a stunned mullet, neatly netted, before accepting his proposal.

"I leave you to arrange everything sweetheart but let it be soon," he told her on their way home.

Lyn prepared for their wedding in practical fashion, aiming in every detail to please Gershon. She had no misgivings, no regrets. Deep down she knew this was as it was meant to be and felt complete. Family and friends showed excitement when told, pausing on a breath then,

"Well that's wonderful news. Your love for each other shines out for all to see. We are so happy for you. When will it be?"

"It's next month. We shall have the ceremony at home with family and celebrate at a restaurant with friends like you."

On a mild winter's morning their families travelled again to see them wed. Nick had flown across for his mother. In the spacious room chosen for the ceremony, he wreathed tall columns with roses Gershon waited with him as Andrew brought her to hear his words.

"My love is deep in my heart for you, my dear."

Friends came to the candle-lit reception to share the joy of age finding love. Their smiles full of warmth as Lyn danced for Gershon, before all joined in the Jewish wedding dance. The happy chain of dancers furled in to the centre then wound out to the laden tables.

His family responded reservedly to the welcome all gave them and departed before the end of the meal. Earlier in the year Gershon had asked for an invitation to a family wedding. They arrived to meet a wall of dismissal. Neither the bride nor her mother had more than a passing moment for the generosity ensuring the bride had a house as his gift. His grief itched under his skin until the end of his days.

The day finished on a happy note, when friends waved goodbye. They were husband and wife for richer or poorer, in sickness and in health.

That evening, sitting in his chair, he called her to him.

"Come and sit by me, give me your hand." She went to him, as always, to sit in the swivel chair by his side. When they talked, he liked her to face him where his good eye could watch her responses and he could bend forward to kiss her often.

"I cannot be a proper husband to you sweetheart. My health is not so good now, but we shall know unconditional love. I will take care of you. You shall see. Tomorrow we will go to Perth to the Title Office. I want you to be safe when I'm gone. We are going to put your name with mine on the title to this house."

"Remember I signed a document for your daughter to say I would never lay claim to this house."

"We were not husband and wife then. Your love for me has given me joy again. They do not love me. It is only my money that they love, and they will be well cared for. We will do what I want you understand."

Nick returned, from a short stay with Andrew, to spend a few days before returning to England. They spent time walking the beach, his arm across Nick's shoulder as they laughed and joked. At the airport parting he hugged both boys in a warm embrace.

"I have two sons now. My heart is full," he confided.

Later that evening they sat watching television. Night's shadows gathered outside the pool of lamplight enclosing them. Pouring her some wine he lifted his glass of vodka.

"Can I invite my son and his family for Christmas day?"

"You look beautiful my dear," tracing the clear outlines of her face with a gentle finger.

"I want to tell you something," she began shyly. "You have stirred me to depths I never knew, without one single touch. Strange as it may seem I can now cup my breasts and feel their fullness for the first time in my life. I didn't mature enough to breast feed my babies and I yearned for what other women found so simple. I never knew a woman's desire to receive a man because only giving satisfied me. Now I want to know you deeply and intimately, but it is too late for us."

He lay back in his chair, lids hooded, his blue eyes veiled in thought until, bright and clear, his gaze penetrated to the depths of her soul. For an eternal moment she felt enclosed and enclosing. Warmth flowed into her.

"Our love is innocent sweetheart. We are true soulmates whose love is boundless and un-seeking. Deep in my heart is a love which will flow forever. I cannot bear you to be away from me for long. I need you and am always terrified you will cast me adrift. You remind me of her, my mother, in so many ways."

He rose up in his chair to clasp her hand and to kiss her lips again. "I will sleep in your room from now on."

They sat contentedly watching the rest of the program. That night he came to her bringing his books and arranging small paraphernalia to serve his bodily needs.

They kissed goodnight and he drew her arm around him to hold hands as they drifted into dreamland.

They took up their journey with ever lighter hearts and a growing sense of the wonder of life, sharing small adventures, and in a world whose beauty unfolded for them in their joy of living.

Visits to the Emergency Department, for midnight health issues besetting Gershon, became a romantic event shared by staff who saw their love for one another shining through the pain of the moment.

Sadness tinged the sale of his island paradise, towards the end of the year, when the journey became too arduous for him. He was aware of a dark stain seeping the edges of time and soon into the New Year acted in his own fashion.

"I want to teach you how to run my office sweetheart. Then I can sit and watch television while you keep the ship afloat. We start tomorrow."

An exacting teacher he berated her often as she struggled with the details of filing documents and entering income from investments. She spent hours with a big backlog of work, sorting papers, labelling and filing until order was restored.

He checked everything before making his reports of final income and expenditure, in private.

He rarely talked about the horrors of the past, the cruelty and savagery of brutal domination inflicted by an enemy, starving them into submission, in subzero conditions. Corrupt power over the helpless repelled him. He shut away such thoughts until his strength began to fail him and his eyesight deteriorated.

She came upon him one morning in his old bedroom surrounded by an odd assortment of gas cylinders and tubing spread around the floor. He looked tired and defeated.

"I want you to help me with this," he said in a tone which brooked no denial. A chill shot her spine. Sitting by his side on the bed, she folded back his flapping shirt sleeve to regain her calm and master the tremble in her voice when she spoke.

"I didn't know you actually had all this stuff Gershon. Where do you keep it?"

"It's kept in the garage on the top shelf. It's only for practice. it's nothing to do with you so don't worry. Now what do I do with this?" He lay back on the pillow holding a plastic bag in his hand.

Printed word became reality as she helped him go through the instructions

Lovers and Losers
— 302 —

until he was satisfied with the result then the equipment was packed away, to her great relief.

"You won't let them send me into a nursing home sweetheart. I don't want to be bullied and dependent on others. Homes aren't what they the used to be. I want to die here in the home I love," he requested.

"It will all be manageable with a little extra help," she promised

The next day she visited his doctor who knew how Gershon felt but was certain his life was not in danger.

"We keep an eye on him, my dear. Don't oppose his ideas. Run along with them and let him talk it out of his system. He's lucky you came along. You have made a lot of difference. Keep it up."

Come winter, wild gales howled across the ocean and blew the waves to excited heights. The winds shushed them home, from ever shorter walks by the shoreline, to the warmth and comfort of his beloved chair and discussion about one philosopher or another.

When spring arrived, the blue mists of the Jacaranda trees threaded avenues vibrant with rainbow hues. Nature flung carpets of colour over the dunes to vie with the brilliance of the sea.

His long legs loped further each day, leaving her behind to wait for his return downhill, the elegant swing of his hips, outlined against the setting sun. She loved him.

The languor of approaching summer overtook both of them overshadowing a deeper tiredness he took pains to hide from her. He defended his acceptance of needing her help more frequently, since he had taken to using a walking aid about the house.

"If it pleases you to wash my feet and cut my nails, you do as you wish but I can do it myself."

"Yes, it gives me pleasure to do small things for you dear," she acquiesced, knowing how much his independence meant to him.

There was a flurry of visits to banks where she waited, apart, while he talked earnestly with managers. Papers were presented for her to sign. She became aware that he was placing shared responsibility and power in her hands. When she demurred, he rebuffed her.

"You are my wife and can make things easier for me. Leave things to me please. I want to provide for you and intend to take care of you my way. Tomorrow we will go to the solicitor."

The solicitor drew up a new will for Lyn, according to Gershon's instructions. No more was spoken on the subject and any concerns she had were forgotten in caring for his comfort.

In mid-December heat she emailed the family.

"He is not well I wonder if you could come on a surprise visit. I can meet you at the airport. I will go indoors and leave you to ring the bell for him to answer. He will be so happy."

Lyn got a gentle rebuke the next morning. He pointed to her forwarded letter in his mail box.

"Don't meddle with things my dear. They are too busy." He closed his eyes on any discussion and lay quietly thinking. Next day he made a routine visit to his doctor and on returning he called across from his chair,

"I'm going on the twenty-fourth." She knew it was his dark side speaking. Plans for a quiet Christmas included a Christmas Eve Lunch with Andrew and family.

"You can't do that dear heart because the family will be here," she answered cheerfully but he was not put off so easily.

"Well! I will go on the twenty-eighth then. If I can't walk, I'm useless."

A small weight pulled on her heart strings. To dislodge it she called his surgery.

"He's been saying this for years. Now stop worrying and have a good Christmas," the doctor soothed.

He spent the following days welcoming friends who called on them over the pre-festival days.

"You both look marvellous and we can see you're happy. See you in the New Year," was the parting remark of one and all.

"She's my sweetheart," he declared, standing near her as she busied herself with preparations for family visits.

Chapter 13: Fickle Fate

ON THE twenty-fourth a cool breeze tempered the December heat. Lyn relaxed back into her chair, by Gershon's side, as they waited for Andrew and family. They had grown used to their late arrival occasioned by his little wife's demands to stop on the way for a market or coffee. Everything was ready.

"What time are they coming," he asked again, looking at the clock on the wall.

"They'll be here any minute," she assured him. Hardly were the words out of her mouth before his body stiffened and his expression changed. A sly smile pulled up one side of his face, one eye stared unseeing into hers as the other swivelled up into its corner. She shot up in shock afraid that his mind was under a devilish attack.

Instinctively she checked his reflexes then rushed to the phone to summon his doctor's aid.

"It's Gershon's wife speaking. Will you ask doctor to come to the house he's had a cerebral incident, but I don't think it is a stroke? We need help," she pleaded urgently.

"I'm afraid that's impossible. It is Christmas Eve and we have a full surgery which is closing shortly at twelve."

"He promised he would come if Gershon was in trouble, please help us," she cried out.

"Doctor is sending an ambulance team. They will be there soon."

The ambulance team surged through the door as he was regaining command of his actions and laying back, bemused at all the activity. Finding no significant signs, it was suggested he go to emergency.

"No," was his vigorous response, backed up by Lyn.

"I promise to take him to hospital if it happens again," satisfied the ambulance crew. They took off as Andrew and family arrived and helped in the kitchen.

Gershon insisted on joining them at table, holding tightly to her hand until he was back in his chair. The young ones tidied up and left at his request. The calm of evening was edged with watchfulness until they were in the safe haven of their bed. Sleep's hidden powers of the night restored and guided them to a new day when Andrew returned to stay and help out until the twenty-eighth when normality returned.

After taking Andrew to the station, the anxious fretful mood returned during the afternoon, jogging her memory of his earlier intentions for the twenty-eighth.

"I'm prejudiced against everyone sweetheart, even you," he muttered. He put down his mobile after phoning her for the third time, repeating her answers to shut out a baneful voice in his head. Lyn, unaware of the trespass, thought his repeat was a check on her response and felt reassured all was well when his gloom passed.

The following evening the return of his suspicions interrupted his pleasure in her company. Tired, he went early to bed to read until she joined him.

He closed his book, putting it by his spectacles on the bedside chest, adjusted the walking frame by the side of the bed, then lay back on his pillow. Lyn drew back the curtains to let in the cool of the night air before slipping back into bed beside him. She turned to switch off the light, but he stayed her hand.

"Talk to me, say something, keep talking," he said in a strange husky voice. He seemed stricken with a fear of silence.

"Shall I read to you or what shall we talk about," she answered hoping to settle him soon for she was eager for sleep.

"Shall I read to you or what shall we talk about," he replied rising up on his elbow. His eyes were unnaturally bright demanding her attention.

"What's wrong darling? Why are you…,"

"What's wrong darling? Why are you…," he cut in, repeating word for word whatever she said except to affirm every now and again,

"I won't hurt you." The madness continued with Lyn helpless to get any sense from him.

"We need help dear," she made to move but he restrained her in a strong grip and fear welled in her.

"We need help dear, we both need help," the crazed repetition continued. She pushed him away and scrambled out of bed to run for the front door. He followed heedless of his state of undress as she made for their neighbour's door and thudded a tattoo. With their help an ambulance arrived and took them to the local hospital.

In Emergency a bottled-up frenzy ran the gamut of filled beds and over-worked staff. His condition was urgent enough to receive immediate attention and medication to soothe him until a consultant could visit. The long wait began. She sat on a hard-wooden chair by his side holding hands as patients came and left, nurses took tests and readings, doctors conferred and dry mouthed, she answered the same questions again and again.

The day shift arrived to continue the readings. Andrew came. Eighteen hours later a stretcher trundled ahead of Louse and Andrew along the twists and turns of long corridors. Gershon was under observation for a paranoid anxiety state.

On the ward a huge mountain of a nurse sat at a desk. Blank faced and seemingly indifferent to one and all around her, until, a small commotion in a side ward sent her stalking across to stand arms akimbo in the doorway. Her height and girth blocked out the room's dim lighting as she silently stared away the chatter and hope of the poor wretch inside.

She returned to sit blank faced at the desk then point along a corridor.

"Room six."

A slave of the system led the way, the empathy in her eyes belying the routine words on her lips.

"We'll soon have you comfortable. A good night's sleep is what you need."

Confused inmates passed over the worn tracks of the slaves, stumbling by a protesting Gershon who entered a tiny dark room to share it with a dying man.

"He won't like this. I think we should take him back home Andrew," Lyn whispered. "I'm going to let family know." After a brief talk with them on her phone, she handed it to him. Rambling incoherent words poured out as he begged somebody to come and save him. She listened, stunned.

He agreed to stay overnight if he could return home next day. She was refused permission to stay and it was a further thirty-six hours before doctors agreed to his discharge strictly under her care. She had a vague feeling the delay was requested since there were no further protests from Gershon who barely answered her as she sat with him. His eyes were distant, and she knew he blamed her for abandoning him.

Family kept in frequent touch with him through the hospital and made plans to come over for a brief visit on the day of his discharge. Again, the time for departure was delayed.

"We must be there for the family," she protested.

"They are still on their way. You will have plenty of time," was the enigmatic answer.

Back in the spacious home he loved, she watched him make his way purposefully to his chair and settle in with a contented sigh. She gave him a kiss and hurried to the kitchen to prepare a light lunch, smiling happily at Andrew who came to help. Once family came to back her actions up, it would be a good day. Then her world changed.

A man and a woman strode into the house. The woman ran to Gershon and threw herself across him. He listened, as she whispered words in his ear. She moved and as if at her behest he rose and followed her.

Lyn tried to catch the words spinning in space around her then she and Andrew were alone. The house was empty.

"They have taken him for a walk Mum. They will be back." Endless minutes crawled towards an hour of unanswered fears. Three strangers returned to convene a meeting with Andrew and Lyn standing at the kitchen bench.

A chair was brought to allow the man to face the stranger in Gershon's chair. The woman stood by the man as he gripped the figure in the chair by its knee and tapped purposefully on it to command attention.

"Tell her you don't love her."

The figure in the chair repeated tonelessly: "I don't love you. I only said I loved you to make you happy."

"Tell her you want to come back with us."

"I want to go back and be with my family."

"He wants to leave you."

I don't love you. I don't love you. I don't love, you exploded in Lyn's brain, fragmented her soul and shattered the face of a dream. Rejection dismissed her with cold eyes. Nerves aquiver under the lash of cold indifference, she leaned against the bench hearing herself say,

"If it is what you want, I will help you, but can't we do this gracefully. You are not well." She felt split into two beings, one acting from an inner impulse and the other watching mesmerised and paralysed to stop the words.

Words spun in the air again "Wills, titles, investments, separation proceedings. Fetch you to the bank to sign documents." She felt herself moving about the house, nodding her head in agreement, handing over papers. Heard Andrew's voice suggesting some sense and an effort to reconcile an unknown problem then the emptiness of the house enveloped her to the marrow and her tears drenched Andrew's shirt.

"What have I done by agreeing? I love him and want his happiness whatever the cost, but will he be happy? Will he be safe? They seemed possessed about money and not one concerned word for him. The house stinks of greed." She opened a window and stood breathing deeply until the tears dried.

"I think you'd better get some advice Mum. You are tangling with cruelty and evil. Every word they said was meant to hurt you and you've done nothing to earn it," he suggested, going over to the phone.

"I can't believe Gershon knows what he's saying. He's acting so strangely, almost like a puppet. How the hell could they drag him off when he's barely out of hospital? All they talked about was money and property within minutes of coming in to the house. Why don't you ring the doctor and possibly your solicitor because he may need protection and I don't know what to think." He handed her the phone.

Surprised ears listened to the halting tale she told between sobs. Voices asked her to repeat her words, keen questions probed, and on her behalf, decisions were made for his safety.

"Leave it with us. Stay home and try to get some rest," was the well-meant but impossible advice.

The long night hours dragged on to mid-morning when the previous day's rehearsal was followed by a finished performance. Chairs set in place, cups, saucers, notepads arranged, the actors entered. A pompous man took the lead. The woman walked busily in the background.

"We are taking him back with us today. We can sort the rest later. You realise he only married you to save tax. Now he wants to be with his family, and he will sign this paper saying he wants to leave you." He thrust the paper and a pen towards the chair. A hand signed the paper.

Earlier that day, the family visit to the banks had not gone smoothly. From behind opaque glass barriers, wary bank managers watched the three in the lobby. They heard the man bullying his crying companion to get on with things and managers declined to negotiate with them.

Lyn ran to the woman and clutched at her shoulders.

"Please let me come with him. It's all I want, to be with him. Can I visit him?"

"No, there's no room for you. Take your hands off me or else." Naked hate spewed out to batter her defences. The man in the chair sat silent and immobile, listening. A scream welled up in her throat as the doorbell rang. Order flowed into the room with John, the lawyer's, voice.

"Hello Lyn. I called to see you're all right."

"We saw you at the bank this morning talking to the manager," cut in the woman accusingly.

"Yes, you did. I suggest we calm down and talk things over," John smiled inviting all to join him. He was a small wiry man who cycled wherever he could to keep fit. A country solicitor he disliked the taint of city work. Many years wise in the ways of humanity, he enjoyed working for the underprivileged.

His invitation to negotiate troubled waters was ignored and the hostility extended to him with their repeated intentions to take Gershon back with them. His patience wearing thin, he cut in, holding out a letter.

"You cannot take him anywhere while he is unfit to travel as this medical opinion states. You will be unwise to disregard my advice because steps have been taken to ensure this. I suggest you seriously try come to an agreement. I have to leave now but I will be in touch Lyn." He looked towards her, his face crinkling into an encouraging smile, then left the set and tongue-tied actors.

They consulted mobile phones for prompts off stage then changed their approach.

"This has all been a complete surprise to us," said pompous man. "I understand how you feel but we must do as he wishes. We will leave you a little more time together." He turned to the chair.

"We will return in four days to take you home to your family and your grandchildren and you will be happy with us. You must be patient, but we will return," they promised, leaving Lyn to thank them in floods of tears for small mercies. The man in the chair spoke indistinctly to an indelible recording in Andrew's mind.

As in a dream the man and the woman disappeared leaving the opening scene where three people waited, and food lay prepared.

"We've run out of Gershon's raison bread. I'll go and get some." Lyn started towards the front door where Andrew joined her.

"I'll go, do you need anything else?" She thought a moment then shook her head.

"No thank you. It is better I stay with him," turning back into the kitchen. Gershon's chair was empty.

"He's gone. Andrew he's gone." The sound of a vehicle sent them to the door to see him disappearing down the road.

"How could he have slipped past us so quickly," she panicked. Andrew calmed her down.

"Give me your keys Mum and I'll check the roads. He may have gone down to the beach to think things over." By the time Andrew eased out of the garage he was back.

"I've got some bread. See I can drive perfectly well." He slipped out again a few minutes later and returned in half an hour. Settling her fear, he promised

"We shall be all right Andrew. You can go home now. Thank you for coming." Andrew looked towards his mother. She nodded.

"We'll be fine dear. I will take you."

"No Mum the walk will be good. I'll take the bus." She walked him to the door, hugged him tightly and watched as he started down the road then turned in to look around the beautiful room, the scene of her wedding.

Slow steps past the table used to sign the wedding certificate, between the tall pillars still wreathed in roses. Pledges of unconditional love and care resounded in the dome of the ceiling. Her fingers turned his ring on her hand. Her heartbeats, still steady in age, told her their love was an eternal bonding of two spirit beings innocent of betrayal. She missed the shadow at the end of the corridor leading into the room and went back into the kitchen.

His chair was empty. She searched for him in the house. In the garage her car stood alone. Uncertain she stared down the road.

"Please be careful dear heart. Come back soon," she whispered and turned in to wait for his return. The minutes turned and, on the hour, she rang Andrew.

"He passed me at the end of the road Mum and offered me a lift to the station then sped away when I said I was OK. Leave it a while. I'll keep in touch." He remembered hearing the indistinct words, I won't stay in this house for five minutes, then called John.

By nightfall police were keeping a lookout for him, his family denied all knowledge of his whereabouts and asked to be kept informed. Lyn sat by the phone afraid to leave its summons. The family rang.

"Which one of the family will he stay with when you take him', she asked?

"We have arranged for him to go to a village with safety measures in place. A one bedroom flat he can manage himself with supervision."

"He needs space. A tiny flat will torment him." The phone went silent.

He was fleeing like a fugitive from the devils in his mind the spawn of false words whispered in his ears. Vulnerable as a child peppered with small shot and thorns from life's journey, he was crying for the warmth of his family in a world so different from the one he entered ninety-two years ago.

In the ghetto, family values did not loll upon the shifting sands of expectations and love was not paid for in gold. Now he believed she had joined the devils among the mob of looters clamouring for a share of his hard-won savings. He'd turned tail on her to join a fantasy family unaware they would deliver him to a residential safe unit for the aged behind locked gates.

"Please God bring him back to his home, to his beaches and the sea and me," she cried aloud.

Our love faced up to this future and we found enough joy in life to walk on together. Now he is…. Oh, please God bring him home, please God….

Her thoughts came to a standstill. Emptied she sat in limbo as the hours passed.

A ringing split the silence. She grabbed the phone.

"This is Constable Evans. Am I talking to Lyn …?"

"Yes, you are talking to her."

"We have found your husband. He had a slight accident and has been taken to a city hospital for a check. He appears to be all right, but we thought best to make sure. You will find him in the emergency ward. I would advise you to take a taxi because the roads are quite busy tonight. New Year partying is still going on. Take it easy now my dear. He is safe and sound. I might still be here when you come. Good night." He gave her the name of the hospital. She fell back in relief. It was nearing eleven. She rallied to phone a taxi first then Andrew. She asked him to go to the hospital and to let the others know then she went to the front steps to wait.

She looked up at the stars. Their steady radiance beamed down into the feelings and thoughts swirling in her. There was a lucky star up there looking after him. No, not luck, the world of spirit was at work, a light breath of air feathered her cheek. The headlights of the approaching taxi flooded the drive and soon she was on her way to him.

Andrew was waiting outside the ward. He guided her to a chair and sat by her, every bit as tired and anxious as Lyn.

"The staff are very suspicious of you Mum. You are being blocked from seeing him so don't expect much. He knows you are coming. You OK?"

A nurse arrived looking very determined, almost hostile.

"No, you cannot see your husband. It is too late. Go home and come any time after nine tomorrow."

Next morning, on the drive to the hospital, Andrew took a call from Mari to say Gershon was phoning repeatedly for Lyn and begging her to come and get him before they took him away again. Negotiating the frustrations of early morning rush hour and hostile traffic lights they finally hurried up the ward towards Gershon's bed. As she came around the curtain his eyes lit up. He threw his arms wide and she ran into his embrace. Tears merged as fingers gently wiped them away. Andrew watched and found a tear welling in his eye.

"So, what's the next step Gershon? What's happening?"

"I have to get out of here. They are flying back to take me, but I want to come home. When they come you will see the real me when I will tell him I'm going home with my wife, you'll see. I've been playing roles." He lay back against the pillows and closed his yes. He looked so frail, tiredness etched in the bones stretching the skin across his face. It was no time for questions, the whys and wherefores could wait until he was ready.

The ward sister came to explain that a request had been made for the chief psychiatrist to assess Gershon's ability to form his own decisions. It meant a delay, and, in any event, they must wait for the family. They settled down quietly until turmoil at the end of the ward heralded the approach of two men. Brushing Lyn out of his way one man stood over Gershon crowding him back against his pillow.

"They tell me you want to go home with her," he stormed. "You want to come with us, don't you? We've come back all this way to take you home. Why have you changed your mind?" As his relentless rattle engaged the two men in a battle of wills nearby patients became anxious.

Lyn ran down the ward for help.

"Is there a private corner we can use please," gained access to the Holding Room opposite the office. Stewarded by two nurses who Lyn asked to remain, the five sat down. She feared the man's influence as he went and stood over Gershon. Gripping his knee his two fingers began to beat a tattoo and words fired like repeater shot.

"Look at me Gershon. You want to come with us, don't you? Speak to your family on this phone. You want to come with us, don't you?"

Hidden memories of a pain clinic for incurable patients where gentle rhythmic contact and soft voiced repetitions influenced minds to accept the unacceptable surfaced in Lyn. She reached across and pulled the hand away.

"Don't harry him. Remember he is sick please and let him rest." The second man chided him to sit peaceably but the assault began again. A determined Lyn suggested that she and the persistent man wait in the corridor leaving Gershon free to make decisions.

After a while the other family member joined the man striding up and down with his mobile asking someone what she wanted him to do.

"I'm so sorry for this pantomime Lyn. He wants to return home with you."

"Thank you. Their greed has done violence to him and for why? I only want to have him home to care for until he is himself and we can be happy again."

She went across to the office where many of the staff had waited listening over the intercom.

"Can I take my husband home now?"

"Yes, you are perfectly free to go. We will send a report to his doctor for a follow up," was the smiling reply. Arm in arm Andrew, Gershon and Lyn walked past the furious man on their way to Gershon's car and knew they hadn't heard the last of the pair.

The drive back was quiet, his hand on her thigh trusting her to return him to the sweet salt air of home and the soft murmur of the sea.

Andrew arrived in the evening working unobtrusively in the background for the next few days as life took up its old rhythm. All three went for early morning walks among the dunes and sunset walks together. They spent quiet evenings listening to much loved music or favourite TV programs.

They fielded off questions from lawyers and banking officials, along with suggestions to safeguard them from further assaults.

Gershon rested reflective and undisturbed by questions but at intervals his anxiety broke loose.

"They will hate me for the rest of my days," he suddenly grieved aloud.

"I have treated you badly. I made a big mistake," he said to the space between him and Lyn in the kitchen.

"I was playing roles," said the character in the well-loved face she smiled into before a goodnight kiss blessed his sleep but left her awake holding his hand wondering why and when she would know some answers.

She knew of his unspoken fears. How long before I can't stand without help? During the day, his plans to escape from life if faced with the purgatory of a home for the aged. His hopes the end would be quick, leaving the children free to realise their dreams. They were also her fears always waiting in the closet of her mind to leap out and terrify.

Night and day, he hung on with grim independence, determined not to burden others with old age's frailties.

Six days after returning home, Gershon went to Andrew and embraced him.

"Thank you for all you have done. We will be all right now so return home to your wife. We will take you to the station." Andrew gave both a long hug when they dropped him off.

"Enjoy your evening walk I'll be in touch tomorrow."

The tranquil effect of the dunes set the mood for an evening with the Vienna State Opera and Beethoven's magic before they fell asleep lulled by the lazy dance of palm shadows on the bedroom curtains. All would be well.

Gershon rose in the night to come around to her side of the bed.

"I'm going to my room sweetheart. It's nothing to do with you so don't follow me. Go back to sleep." He bent to kiss her mouth and left. She waited until his light went out before closing her eyes to sleep. As dawn broke, she felt him sitting on the bed by her side

"I'm going for my walk are you coming?"

She scrambled to sit up facing him.

"Yes, give me five minutes dear. Can I ask you something? Why did you drive up the motorway to the airport?"

"I don't know," was the vague almost vacant reply.

"Well that makes two of us so let's forget it," she smiled and swung out of bed to dress and join him for their usual walk in the cool of the morning. He swung along the path in the long loping stride she loved, his head up sniffing the salt breeze. Their neighbour passed on his morning cycle ride.

"I haven't seen you looking like this for weeks Gershon. You're back to your old self. Good on you." Lyn left them to chat and made for home walking slowly until he caught up with her.

"I want to listen to the Vienna recording again over breakfast," he said. "Are you going to play Ma Jong with your friends today?"

"I'd love to go and spend a couple of hours with them if you are sure you won't mind being alone. I'll come home early. Is there anything you want me to do before I go," she asked?

"Yes, a letter to the solicitor."

Back in the house he suggested getting the letter typed before breakfast.

"You type it and I will print it out. You are to put the letter in this envelope along with the titles to two properties. I need him to confirm that these are the originals. Kindly deliver it to him before going to your game." He handed her a large envelope. She did as he bade then sat to enjoy a recording of Beethoven over breakfast.

"Excellent, excellent," he repeated several times as he listened, taking her hand in his to stroke it gently. He pushed aside food he had been toying with and stood up to hold her close in his arms before kissing her lips.

"It's time to go sweetheart."

"See you for lunch then. I won't be long," and she went, turning to wave before closing the main doors.

The pace of play was quick with three friends who matched her game and kept her mind fully occupied. During the setting up of the wall for the next round idle chat flowed and Lyn gathered information about coach outings to places which might interest Gershon. She left before the end of play, anxious to get back to Gershon and share some fresh ideas with him.

Running into the kitchen she called out.

"I'm home dear," then set about preparing a light lunch. The place seemed unnaturally quiet. Her thoughts sped to recent events. Had he gone again? She ran to the garage and finding his car sighed with relief. He's gone for a walk, and went back to wash up a few dishes and wait.

She crossed to his chair to straighten the rugs and cushions and tidy up his side table, glancing as she did so towards the door of his day room. Through the open door she could see one of the gas cylinders he intended for future use.

Blow, he's having a practice again. I'd better go and see.

Tubing snaked across to the inert figure lying on a blue duvet. She threw herself on him to snatch away the bag covering his face. It felt warm

Electrified with shock and disbelief she dragged herself upright to call his doctor. The soothing sound of a voice above the wailing in her head took over.

"Call a friend Lyn and leave things with me."

She dialled Val who had joked over a smart Ma Jong move earlier then let out the first scream of pain as she ran back to him.

She kissed his sleeping eyes, pressed cheek to his unsmiling cheek, moistened his lips in embrace, laid her head on his heart, soft touched the roundness of his belly and cradled a warmth now stolen away, traced thigh and firm calf and washed his feet with tears.

Holding him close his countenance wavered beneath the flood in her eyes. She clasped the hand cuddling his pillow. Fleeing from family exile, he had outrun threats and demands, never to face them again. He lay in his Father's arms waiting for mother to come and comfort him.

The ambulance crew rang.

"Turn him on his side and try to resuscitate," but she could not move him. Local police filed through the house and a policewoman's voice spoke.

"Please come to another room. You must leave him to others now."

Val arrived with soothing words to fall on deaf ears as the wait began. The policewoman's arm curled around her shoulder and a firm hand lead her to the phone to inform the family.

A woman's voice answered the call. She felt compassion when the wailing began and no fear when it stopped to demand it speak to the police.

The policewoman listened attentively to the insistent voice, turning to look with suspicion at Lyn. Special ambulance crews and forensic police were called to take over from the local team.

Lyn's finger prints were taken before she was sent to the neighbour's house away from the investigators. The policewoman brought her a letter found beneath his body. She reached eagerly but it was withheld. She read his last words across a gap before she was escorted out of her refuge.

She sat with Val watching children laughing and leaping as they splashed around at a pool party. Mothers sat clinking glasses smiling at their offspring and laughing with one another in a dream world of happiness. Hot tea was offered.

Andrew took Val's place. A doorbell rang. The police informed them they could return for the body's departure. He was wheeled on a bier through the home he loved. They let her look once more into his face then moved on and out of sight. A copy of his letter lay on a table.

He was gone. In her hand his last loving words to her. The time ahead would try her endurance. Andrew, bereft of speech, comforted her in a firm clasp.

"Why don't you go to bed early Mum? Sleep is what you need; I'll be on hand if you need anything."

She turned back the covers of and sank down to lay sleepless amidst tumbling scenes over the hours. Suddenly the entire coverlet quivered as if many tiny feet were running across it.

The same thing had happened the night Dan died. She froze to deep quiet until the patter ceased.

Gershon had come to say Au Revoir.

Would it be years or aeons before their eyes smiled a welcome again?

Her thoughts raced to a mountain scene where a group of shrouded women offered a maiden for a blessing from a statuesque figure. The love of two soulmates warmed the drifting clouds. One. clothed in the skin of a venerable sage, looked into the face of an adoring child.

She raised up laughing, flinging wide her arms in triumph.

No thief will loot my jewel casket of memories my love.

Lyn turned to pillow with the mystery of the night

Epilogue

THE village garden slumbered in summer languor. Heat had thinned the roar of passing traffic to a bumble bee's hum. Scarlet clad trees leaned across the high border wall too admire the thirty patches of colour outside the homes of the old ones.

She sat at her open door drinking in the scent of peppermint and the trill of a golden warbler. The weight of years a burden summoning a constant prompt to straighten her shoulders and the curve in her back.

After they passed, she had kept in touch with her dear ones in spirit and the loved ones around her. Gathering all in a circle each day, talked flowed from the shadow land beyond nature's leaping blue flames of energy to the warmth of embraces with family still sharing her world.

Her senses tilted towards an echo in the distant hills, then caught a sweet familiar fragrance and knew it had been following all the time.

It came along the path, to where she sat, with that enigmatic smile that encompassed the garden. The radiance in its eyes illumined each blade of grass.

"Hurry Ducks, take my hand love, come dance with me" it chorused.

Her form was gathered and carried to its shoulder like a strand of gossamer floating down to rest.

Through the trees, the outline of her church where bluebells chimed a Sunday welcome. A vivid arc capped the spire, a rainbow discharge of a promise as the sky turned gold with sun's sinking light.

As it raised her through the portal and its glory, they called to the earth bound: "Keep in touch."

A village neighbour found Lyn at rest, in her last sleep.

Thank you for reading

If you enjoyed the book and have a moment to spare please write a review and help spread the magic.

About The Author

INEZ Minc is 50yrs going on a 100yrs and blessed with a rich life. Born in 1922 in the south of England, she emigrated to Australia in 1986. Both countries have her loyalty and her love of their unique beauty and heritage. Privileged to serve in WW2 with British Overseas Forces, the Australian Vets made her and her ex-serviceman husband welcome, soon after arrival. They, and some local GPs made it possible for her to voluntarily contribute the nursing skills as a Queen's District seniors Nursing Sister, added to her English registration, in service to others in various ways She is now widowed with two fine sons in a close-knit family and leads an active life with other seniors.

Gypsies and Gentry (the first book in the Three Loves Trilogy) was her first novel.

www.ingramcontent.com/pod-product-compliance
Lightning Source LLC
Chambersburg PA
CBHW070100120726
47909CB00002B/455